MW00463134

THE CRUSADER IS BACK IN
A DUEL OF LUST AND PASSION!

Julanar the Lioness: *She was a magnificent female of striking beauty—arrogant, ruthless, and seductive—the captain-general of a band of armored women who struck a heartless bargain with the Crusader....* Luisa de Vermandois: *When the city of Tyre is threatened with siege, the Crusader is pitted against the wiles of this stunningly beautiful and notoriously vicious lady....This rousing tale of war and women storms the senses with its violent depiction of the age of chivalry; its hero, Guy Kingsaver, whose appetite for women is matched only by his thirst for heathen blood, returns in two more spellbinding installments from one of history's most terrifying pages....*

Also Published by Grove Press

THE CRUSADER

Book III:
JULANAR THE LIONESS

Book IV:
MY LADY QUEEN

by John Cleve

Grove Press, Inc., New York

Copyright © 1975 by John Cleve.

All rights reserved. No part of this book may be reproduced, stored in a retrieval system, or transmitted in any form, by any means, including mechanical, electronic, photocopying, recording, or otherwise, without the prior written permission of the publisher.

First Black Cat Edition 1981
    4 5 6 7 8 9
ISBN: 0-394-17736-3
Library of Congress Catalog Card Number: 80-1000

Manufactured in the United States of America

GROVE PRESS, INC., 196 West Houston Street, New York, N.Y. 10014

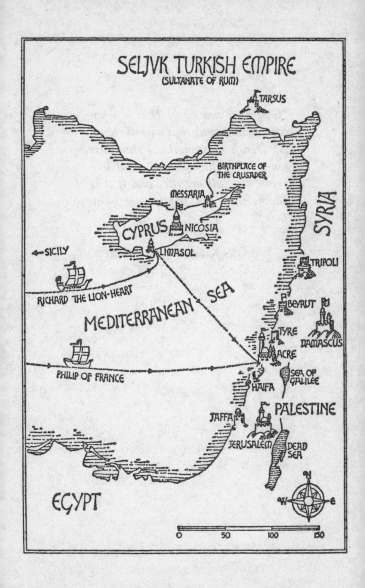

"*God does not care. That is what life means, and that's what death is. Death is something that just happens. I shall* live! *I shall live every day, all my life, and if it is short, then...I shall have* been *here!*"

—Guy Kingsaver of Messaria,
The Crusader

BOOK III:

Julanar the Lioness

ONE

The Night Slayer

Round and white as a buxom maiden's breast the moon hung over Palestine. Its silvery rays picked out the pennons and gonfalons rising above the sprawling encampment of the crusading host of Richard the Lionheart. A gentle breeze rustled among the tents and great towering pavilions, pitched to stand like sentinels over the camp.

That same brilliant moon picked out the silvery steel in the hand of a bent, skulking man.

Step by slow, gliding step he moved through the night whose silence was broken only by the occasional low whicker of a horse—or the snore of a sleeping soldier. Slowly and quietly, his feet making only the faintest whispering sounds, the night stalker moved forward.

His dark eyes were fixed on the back of a helmeted sentinel.

The sentinel was not alert; this the stalker could see even from behind, and a smile twitched his black mustache and biforked beard as it twisted his thin lips. His eyes, though, did not smile. He took another slow gliding step, foot planted carefully.

Now he was but two paces behind the yawning guard.

One hand of the skulker was empty, powerful warrior's fingers curling restlessly. The other hand was fisted, and the moon struck a quicksilver glint from the long dagger that projected from the enwrapping fingers.

The moon of Syria watched, uncaring. The wind sighed and tickled at the leaves of the gnarled and twisted olive trees that stood in the oasis like dark, silent gnomes. The stalker drew a long, slow and very quiet breath. Slowly his fisted hand rose, measuring, upper arm held well out from his body, forearm curved in from the elbow, the red-stained blade held horizontally. His other hand was similarly poised, slim fingers spread and slightly curled, like claws.

He drew in a long, quiet breath.

Then, in one swift movement, his left hand leapt around the sentinel, grasped and whipped up and back his beardless Norman chin. Even as the man's bulging eyes were forced to stare skyward, even as he strove to get his mouth open to cry out an alarm, he felt the icy line of the swiftly-traced dagger draw across his throat.

Spurting scarlet fountained from his neck, splashed and spread over the sleeveless white coat he wore over his long shirt of steel mail, until the crimson cross sewn there was obliterated by the new splotch of liquid crimson.

The night slayer gripped his victim firmly until the man's body had emptied itself of most of its blood. Only then did the killer lower it quietly to the ground, careful that there be no thud of slumping body, no clank or jingle of armor or arms against the reddened earth. Aside from spasmodic little twitches of his limbs, the sentinel was still.

Wiping his knife in the clothing of its second victim, the slayer drew the body swiftly into the shadow of one of the great overgrown tents called pavilions.

The camp was still. Somewhere a man muttered in his sleep, and a horse whinnied, low-voiced. There was a faint tinkling rattle of linked chainmail. The moon, measured against an extended finger, moved but a centimeter.

Then from the pavilion's shadow stepped the sentinel again, miraculously resurrected, wearing helmet over cap of mail, leggings and sleeved coat of steel links, belt and scabbard of dull shagreen leather. But now he was without tabard, or surcoat of the coarse cloth called fustian—and had another looked closely he'd have seen a darker face than that of the Norman, bearded and mustached in black.

Disguised and not quite so stealthy now, the night slayer moved on through the camp. He'd been given directions and he had not forgot; soon his keen eyes spotted the warrior's tent striped in white and blue. Beside it, he glanced about, then tugged back a corner of its flap to peer within.

Again his beard and mustache writhed, but not, this time, in a smile.

Within the tent were a man and a maid, playing the ancient game of love—though between them the term was lust, not love. He was big, a brawny near-giant with brown hair, on whose muscular body there was no trace of fat. That big warrior's body covered her darker one fully. She was writhing in pleasure, a raven-haired daughter of this land, of Islam, whose clutching hands were dark against his broad and naked back.

The night slayer watched them with narrowed eyes.

Her mouth releasing delighted and delightful little gurgles of pleasure, she snapped her hips up to meet her lover's long, fast, rough strokes. He watched the almost berserk light blaze in her wide-flaring eyes, and he loved it. He pounded into the nest of her spread crotch, fucking her way up the belly.

7

The night slayer clamped his thin lips, and he watched.

The writhing temptress held her lover between deeply tan thighs and met his slow, methodical strokes with grinding circular motions of her sweaty buttocks. She was writhing and twitching in the grip of extreme sexual agitation and excitement. All around his driving, rutting organ he could feel her channel clenching and rapidly unclenching, then clasping him again.

He began moving faster and faster. Their breathing was loud in the night stalker's ears, and he smelled their lustful sweat. Beneath the man, she writhed and jerked violently, in an utter surrender to sexuality. Panting with an uncontrollable urge to climax, he jammed his rigid penis as deeply into her petal-soft slash as he could. His powerful body hammered hers, skewered hers, shook and rocked her.

Locked in a sudden frenzy of twisting, shuddering release, she was shaken by mingled ecstasy and relief. A sensuous woman, she was forced to bite her lips against her throaty cries.

Then he too was jerking, groaning, sending his seed gushing into her in a flood, emptying himself into the channel of her slippery sex oval.

So the Christian slime waits for his "lady" to reach her release before he unleashes his, the night slayer thought, and his lips twitched in a sneer.

Even as the big man—little more than a youth—spent his lusts, the disguised night slayer swiftly entered the tent, using the singularly long, wire-wrapped bow just inside the flap, rapped the spent lover sharply at the base of his skull.

The only sound was the *chunk* of the descending blow, followed by the victim's grunt. He went instantly limp atop the woman.

Dropping the bow, the stalker tumbled the powerful

young body off the far slimmer one of the young woman. She lay tense, naked and shiny with perspiration, staring up at the newcomer with wide eyes, sprawled there on her back with her legs apart and her black pubic fleece glossy with wetness.

Then, "Yarok!" she said, her lips pulling into a smile. She stretched up her arms to him.

He drew her sinuously to her feet without a word.

Still smiling, she said softly, "I see that my true lord has made good use of the dagger I slipped him under the eyes of his whoreson jailers!"

"Aye—and I see ye've made good use of the body of this infidel swine!"

He spoke in a snarl, and even as her smile started to vanish he smashed it from her lips with a hard backhand. Her head was swept to one side by his blow, her mass of black hair flying, rustling. A little throaty squeak escaped her lips, which his harsh slap had crushed back against her teeth. Blood curled out over the full lower lip, glistened on her chin.

"My lord! I did but play the part of his captive and his woman, I swear in Allah's name, that you might easily escape their foul imprisonment. Yarok ibn-Ammar has no cause to doubt his Johara!"

"Clothe your sluttish nakedness," he said, "and help me clothe and then bind this Christian cur!"

Clothing herself was simple; not so simple was the matter of attiring the unconscious man whose great frame could bend that wire-bound bow no other man could so much as string. But Yarok and Johara at last succeeded in covering the unconscious man's body, and then they bound him. Yarok stuffed a great wad of rough wool into the fellow's mouth, then secured it there with a length of cord. He drew it cruelly tight.

"Lead me to their horse compound," Yarok ibn-Ammar ordered. The girl nodded and, as he gruntingly

9

shouldered their captive, she left the tent. Her ballooning trousers, *sarawil* in her tongue, swished as she moved, graceful as the dancer she was.

Minutes later she was swaying up to a sentry, a man with a red-brown mustache curling on his English face.

"Guy of Messaria says ye be his friend," she cooed, moving closer to the man before the low palisade. His eyes widened beneath his helmet.

"G—aye, oh aye," he said, reaching for her sinuous slimness as her own arms rose to his mailed shoulders.

Happily he accepted her advance and her embrace, then claimed her soft, parting lips, recognizing the lovely woman captured shortly after her former lord, the devil Yarok ibn-Ammar, who had been the most valuable—and most vicious—warrior of their enemy, Sultan Salah-Din: Saladin. Why she had come here, why Guy of Messaria had sent her—if indeed he had— the sentry could not imagine. Nor did he care.

He enclosed her lips with his, sipped her honeyed kiss, ran his hands greedily over her tight-skinned softness. She had been a dancer, he knew—what a woman! Supple as a serpent.

And just as dangerous, for of a sudden her arms tightened about the delighted English man-at-arms and she gripped him with all her strength.

In that instant the sword of Yarok ibn-Ammar plunged into his back in a spine-smashing, scarlet-spurting deathblow.

First bracing herself to keep her footing, Johara stepped back quickly; the guard slid dead to the ground.

Yarok swiftly wiped his bloody blade on the man's surcoat. Then he slipped into the temporary enclosure among the horses. The surcoat he had appropriated from their captive's tent, Johar noticed, was very long on him. She glanced at the captive and her scarlet-bloused bosom rose and fell in a sigh. He *was* a man, he had four times met Yarok the Butcher in battle and at last, in single combat, had made him captive. Later, seeking vengeance, she had tried to slay the captor of her lord, even as he sat with his lion-heart king and Saladin's own brother, watching her dance. But he had been too clever, too swift, too strong, and she'd been ignominiously punished by the flat of a sword across her backside—and then by his fleshy staff entering her while he rode those same sword-whipped fulsomely rounded curves.

"And what now, my *lord* unbeliever?" she murmured, her mouth losing its prettiness in a sneer.

But the sighing feeling remained. For happy as Johara was to be the woman of Yarok ibn-Ammar al-Jazzar, the unbeliever *had* personally bested and captured him . . . and her as well . . . and besides . . . he was the better lover.

Yarok's return interrupted her ambivalent thoughts. Having added three more Christian lives this night to his toll of many, he now brought an equal number of their valuable horses. Johara aided him in the swift bridling and saddling of them. They hoisted their prisoner so that he lay face down across the back of the third animal, and they lashed his wrists to his ankles with a strap that ran beneath the beast's belly.

Then they set about making good their escape from the camp of the invading men of the hated Cross, with their unconscious prisoner.

The year was the *one thousand, one hundred, ninety-first* since the coming of him the Christians called Son of God; the place was near ibn-Abrak, near the midpoint between the Mediterranean and city the Muslims called *al-Quds,* the Holy, and that the Christians called Jerusalem. The month was November; soon the winter of the Holy Land would begin with its incessant rains, and there had been only minor skirmishes of late between squadrons of the two hosts, Richard and Saladin. Security, as a consequence, was lax.

First Johara had been able to smuggle the dagger in to her man, and then Al-Jazzar—the Butcher—had slain three men in making his escape. Now, with so little difficulty that he knew the King of the English, "Malek Ric" the Lion-heart, would fly into a red rage on the morrow, Yarok al-Jazzar succeeded in riding out of the sleep-bound camp with his woman and his prisoner.

The three horses, one with its rider tied in place across its back, paced out into the Levantine night. Yarok and Johara set their faces southward. For a long while they rode in silence, wincing when their mounts' hooves struck sound from the rocky terrain, for they must make certain they had escaped both the encampment and its outlying pickets.

Then Yarok spoke, without glancing at the cloaked woman who rode beside him. "Ye have the drug to keep him kitten-placid?"

She glanced at him and nodded, though he stared straight ahead into the moon-splashed night. "Aye. He will be no trouble to us, my beloved lord."

Her beloved lord chuckled, though as ever, his eyes did not enter into that smile but remained cold and serpent-steady.

The three horses paced on into the night, drawing steadily farther from the sprawling camp of the invading host of the third great Crusade of Christendom against the Saracen who held Jerusalem and the Holy Sepulcher.

Having taken prisoner the finest of Saladin's knights and conquered and bedded his woman, Guy Kingsaver of Messaria, the Crusader, was now a prisoner of them both—a prisoner of his deadliest enemy.

12

TWO

The Butcher

The Crusader awoke to awareness of a buzzing throb in his head, a steady hum in his ears. His belly felt both empty and troubled. He could hear it gurgling. He started to lift his head; found that the movement heightened the throbbing. He closed his eyes and clenched his teeth against it.

What had happened? He'd been tupping with al-Jazzar's woman, Johara. Yes, he was sure of that—and he had finished, spent his juices up her Muslim tunnel. And after that?

He was unable to remember anything else. He had dreamed, he was sure. What? What had he dreamed?

Memory, pictures tickled at the edge of his mind, but he could not quite catch them, could not make them coalesce into full pictures. With a sigh, he started to move his arm. Only then did The Crusader learn that he was bound, and lying on his back on what felt like a wooden floor. His eyes snapped open. He stared up at the rough-beamed ceiling of a small room. Slowly, because of his headache, he turned his head sideways. He faced a blank wall, plastered in the Muslim style, and one of the small, strangely-shaped windows of this land of the enemy. Beyond, he saw only sky and clouds. There was no furniture.

Wary of the throbbing in his head, ever ready to leap into a harsh pounding, Guy moved his head to look on his other side. He saw a low couch with a rumpled spread of several colors, an equally low table on which were some crumbs, a piece of bread bearing tooth-marks, a smaller piece of dark meat, and two mugs of pottery or earthenware.

Beside them, on the sleeping couch, sat a man. One loosely legginged leg was doubled under him; the other stretched out with his soft-shod foot on the floor. The Arabic pantaloons were scarlet; the long waist-nipped, side-slit shirt was black with red trim. Guy of Messaria raised his eyes along the strong, wiry body to gaze into the man's face.

He stared at his gaoler.

Eyes flat and expressionless, like a pair of dusty onyxes set into his chiseled face, eyes that never showed rage or mirth or hate. A slender, muscular man with a silky black beard arranged in twin points. Dark he was, and falcate of nose, and thin of lip; it was a cruel mouth, a mouth capable of sneering at the living or the recently dead. Slayer of many, this man, many among the cru-sading host. Indeed, this man who always wore black armor and bestrode a superb black warhorse could lay claim to being the finest of Saladin's knights, just as Guy Kingsaver of Messaria was one of the finest of the fighting men under the Cross of Jesus and the leopard banners of Richard. Guy stared at him.

Yarok ibn-Ammar, called al-Jazzar—the Butcher—stared back.

Acting on the orders of his king months ago, Guy had "returned" one of al-Jazzar's red-banded arrows—plucked from the corpse of an English knight—by

14

driving it an impossible distance into one of the Butcher's Turkish cohorts. After that introduction, the two men had met again and again, though ever fleetingly—until that last time. During a battle, another arrow from the outsize bow of the man called the Human Crossbow had carried away the black cloth with which al-Jazzar covered his helmet. Still later, during that long march of the Crusaders down the coast of the Holy Land from fallen Acre, the two had faced one another again in the melee of battle. This time the result was that the Butcher lost a second black helmet-cloth, and his horse galloped away wearing an arrow from Guy's bow.

Their fates sent them against each other again. It was in that bloody battle near ibn-Abrak that the two, now rivals, determined each to end the other's heroic career, had met still again. This time, in personal combat and then *corps-a-corps* on the ground, the Crusader defeated his Turkish opposite and forced him to mouth the two words most abhorrent to any knight, be he Saracen or Christian: "I yield."

Thus had Yarok the Butcher become the Cypriot's captive. Only a few nights later, Johara had tried to slay the former stable boy now most often hailed as Guy Kingsaver. And Guy had defeated her, too. And taken her. Aye, and he'd thought he had tamed the slut. So much for what Guy Kingsaver of Messaria knew about women!

Now, he realized, she had tricked him. He was their prisoner, Johara's and her deadly lord's.

The Crusader's eyes rolled again, slowly, taking in what he could see of the small room. He frowned. A slight tensing of muscles told him that his ankles were as securely bound as his wrists. He returned his gaze to his captor; the Butcher was staring at him.

"These bees and the thunder in my head—you struck me . . . from behind? And where is this ye've brought me, son of Hell?"

The other man did not bother with an answer. "What think ye, Cypriot? Will Malek Ric pay ransom for the *stable-hand* from Cyprus who once saved his charmed life?"

Guy considered. Ransoming captured knights was common enough, but he was no knight. His taking of al-Jazzar *had* prompted King Richard's friend, Robert, Earl of Leicester, to offer to make him Sir Guy. *(Sir Guy, son of Peter the peasant of Messaria on tiny Cyprus! By God's holy wounds, what a thought!)* But the knighting of his newest squire was up to Richard; Guy had made the bronze-bearded giant his liege-lord the night he had saved his life from an assassin's thrust, in the stable on his native Cyprus.

"Ye've brought me here to ransom me?"

Yarok chuckled scornfully, though his eyes did not change their cold stare. "Ransom you?" he said, speaking again in the Arabic tongue that Guy now understood nearly as well as the other man, for the young Crusader had received much tutoring from the girl he made his woman one night in the palace of Acre.

"No, my unbeliever *friend*," Yarok went on. "I shall demand no ransom for you! Ah no, I spare ye the *embarrassment* of learning that a peasant's son of Messaria on Cyprus isle merits no *ransom!*"

Guy said nothing. He well knew that he was one of the most valuable men in the crusading host. Yarok knew it too, but Guy would not say it. He would not beg his captor, nor bargain with him. Though far from noble, the Crusader's blood ran far too rich for such as that.

"It is a strange place," Guy said, again glancing

about, "to have brought me to slay me then, O Butcher."

"*Slay* thee? Why should I slay thee, archer? You did offer me my life when you might have taken it; how could I slay thee?"

Guy spoke quietly, and his gaze was steady. "I defeated you in fair and equal combat, ibn-Ammar, even disarmed you sword to sword. It was honorable—and it was not the way ye've taken me."

For a long moment the Turk's flat black eyes stared into the dark brown ones of the man with the short-cropped brown hair. A dark, veined hand caressed the hilt of the Saracen dagger at his Saracen hip. Then Yarok smiled.

"Nay, uncircumcised rooter in pigsties! Ye'll not goad me into ending your life . . . I have plans for ye, ye see, and they do not involve anything so swift and pleasant as death."

"Surely ye cannot be so cruel as to plan that I must lie here bound and continue to gaze on your ugly countenance!"

"Ye *would* die, wouldn't ye!"

"I have heard it said that death cures aches of the head, and—"

"Aye, by Allah, for a headless man hath nothing to ache!"

"Look closely, al-Jazzar, and mayhap those keen butcher's eyes that have slain naked lovers in oases by night will see some tremor of my body that you can count as cringing." Guy's voice was very steady, his eyes bland.

Yarok's face had gone tight and his eyes all narrow, and now his hand was drawn into a fist around the hilt of his dagger. His knuckles paled.

Then there was a rustle of cloth, and into the room came a young woman, sinuous and graceful, in yellow blouse and sarawil of pale blue. It was Johara, who had felt the steel-hard swords of flesh of both these men up the scabbard she wore hair-clothed between her legs. She bore food, and a well-decorated earthenware jug.

"Ah, our mutual slut," Yarok said, sneering.

"My *lord!*" she accused.

"Will ye break bread with us, Frankish dog?" Yarok asked his prisoner, as though Johara had not spoken.

"With salt?" Guy asked, pleasantly enough.

Yarok laughed. "Aye, even with salt!"

"And how shall I eat, armless and legless as your cords have me?"

"Johara will feed you."

"Yarok—" she began, but he interrupted.

"Feed him! It has been three days since he's had food in that growling belly of his!"

Guy stared. *"Three days!"*

Yarok laughed again, leaning back against the wall with his two hands around one updrawn knee. "Aye, by Allah, three days! For ye be far from your doggish cohorts, O son of Eblis! Full fifty miles have we brought ye, and with Johara administering the drug that enabled us to bring ye hence meek and weak as a newborn pup."

"Fifty . . ." Guy trailed off.

Six months ago he had been a stable boy. Then, all in one night, he had become Kingsaver and squire to Richard Coeur-de-lion. Less than a month later he was a crusader, bending his great home-fashioned bow against the defenders of the lofty tower of Acre, on the Mediterranean coast. Once, wearing the armor of his fever-stricken king, he had turned a sally from that city, above which now fluttered the leopard pennons of the King of England. Neither knight nor archer nor, indeed, man-at-arms, he had then tramped down the coast with the others, fighting their way through heat and rocky land and crocodile-infested rivers and skirmishing Saracen warriors. He had slain far more than one of their number and thrust his loin-weapon into far more than one woman, including noble-born Franks and dark-eyed daughters of Islam and even the heiress to the throne of Jerusalem.

But never had he been captive of any man, and never had he been so far from his own companions.

Dully, his head still thick and full of thuds from the drug, he ate what Johara offered. And drank of the wine she brought, wondering if it were drugged. He thought not. They had kept him drugged, and now he was not, so that they must have ceased, wanting him to be in possession of his senses. Because, most likely, they had reached their destination—though they would not tell him where it was when he asked.

"Was she a good fuck, Christian cur? Remember you the warmth of the gap betwixt her strong legs, the way they rise to wrap a man with such suppleness? Remember you the feel of her hard breasts against your chest, Guy of Messaria?"

"I remember," Guy said, without looking at the anguished Johara.

"Show him again that body he has enjoyed, Johara," Yarok bade, idly sloshing the wine in the green-and-yellow jug.

"Yarok—my lord—"

He said nothing. He but stared at her. And Johara stripped, and once again Guy watched the baring of that superb body. Aye, he remembered, and even as he watched, even in his captivity, he felt the stirring of the big shaft of his loins.

While he watched, Yarok ran his hands over her—his eyes on Guy—and in between her thighs, and over her tight large breasts, and into the crease between

19

those firm-fleshed buttocks Guy had so recently sword-whipped. She but trembled when her lord and master slipped a thumb into the curling dark fur between the tops of her thighs, and then pushed it out of sight up into her quaking body.

Yarok ran that thumb in and out of her, slapping her pubis with his hand, until she shuddered and went weak in the legs. Then she begged him in a tiny voice, then broke out in sweat. At last she shuddered violently in her climax and sank forward against him.

"On your knees, woman, and fill your mouth with your lord and master!"

She obeyed without a word, and Guy could not do other than watch while she ran her tongue around and around the broad dark corona of Yarok's cock, which he liberated from his loose leggings without removing them. Guy shivered, hearing the wet little sucking noises she made all the while she licked stiffening cock like a kitten at the cream-bowl.

He saw clearly when, nakedly kneeling before the other man, she took his now-hard shaft in her slim fingers and guided it deftly between her lips. Deep into the nearly-round hole formed by her distended lips ran that thick-knobbed penis, while Yarok's hand twisted in her dark, dark hair and his eyes stared at the helplessly bound man . . . and Yarok al-Jazzar smiled.

"Suck," he bade her in a throaty voice.

With her clever mouth utterly enclosing his lusty pole, she sucked, sliding her mouth forward and back along the long shaft. She sucked and drew at it, fondling and cupping the heavy hanging ovals crowding his scrotum as she slithered her mouth and willing tongue over the saliva-wet stalk.

Fully clothed and comfortably seated, her man pressed his hands to either side of her hollowing cheeks and urged his throbbing, bulging organ even more into her face. Helplessly watching in a growing agony, the Crusader could see the way her cheekbones pressed against the tight-drawn skin, as eagerly and submissively she accepted more and more hot male meat into her straining facial hollow.

"Enough!" Yarok snapped suddenly, and pulled free of his bewildered fellatrix. "Be still," he next commanded, as he walked around her kneeling, naked body.

Standing high and hard and mouth-wet before him, his excited cock swung and danced as he moved in behind her. With ease, the powerful Turk lifted her, still in her kneeling position, and deposited her on the edge of the low divan where he'd sat. Her legs and feet extended out over its edge. Yarok moved quickly in between them, bent his knees, and guided his thick organ forward with his own hand.

Guy gritted his teeth. The long vermillion slit slung just beneath the lower curves of the kneeling girl's buttocks beckoned sexily, lewdly, a wet slash waiting to be filled.

In a lurch, Yarok al-Jazzar filled it. The girl grunted as he skewered that warm furrow and crammed himself far up inside her, all in one swift violent movement.

"Unnnngh," she groaned, quivering, planting hands and knees and bowing her head at the loud-smacking impact against her upturned butts.

"So you spread your *legs* for this whoreson *Frankish* cur, did you my . . . love!" Yarok snarled, lunging forward against the quivering girl's upturned backside with each shouted word, and slamming his long thick poker deep, deep into the quaking flesh of her cunt.

"No, no my darl—uh!"

She lurched with the power of his drives. Her hands

were planted hard to brace herself. "Ah, ah," she groaned, responding with helpless sensuality to the power of his masculinity, even in its harshness.

"Ah you sluttish *wench* . . . even . . . *this,* being fucked like . . . a *she* . . . cur . . . fires your *lusts* . . . *doesn't* . . . it?"

"Uh—ungh!" She moaned and gasped, quivering, writhing. Pushing herself back to take him the deeper into the sucking deeps of her slitted hole. "Ye-yes m-my love!"

Then her moan was even more loud, with a trace of desperation, when he withdrew completely. Guy stared at her quivering backside, at the great dripping erection that the other man pulled forth from her oily passage.

"Yarok . . . my love." she quavered—and then, just as he seized the base of his well-oiled tool, she drove herself forcibly backward, blindly seeking the warming presence of that magic masculine wand up inside her.

She obtained it, and as she did, she shrieked in pain. With her own violent backward thrust, she had split wide the flesh-ring of her anus, impaled her own squirming back-passage on that vast, swollen penis.

Before the agonized Johara could hurl herself forward as she had back, Yarok's hands had leapt to her, up past the bones of her hips. Into those hollows his fingers sank, and clutched. He held fast. Despite her cries and high-voiced sobs and pleas, he clung to her—and pulled. He drove to sear the inner surfaces of her ass with the hot, swollen flesh of his charging organ, forcing it into her. And he felt it, gasping, as reluctantly and submissively, the muscles of her anal sphincter gave way.

His thick penis slid in, opening her up into a big straining ring of stretched flesh. He held her there while she moaned and shuddered. And then, beginning again to accuse and castigate the young woman, Yarok began to bugger her rapidly, and with full strokes.

Bound hand and foot, Guy could only watch the tempo of the other man's thrusts increase as he felt her strong anal muscles sphinctering around the thick shank of his delving lance. In he stroked, until her anal mouth formed a straining circle around the very base of his tightly sheathed cock.

"Ah . . . Ah . . . does it hurt *now,* she-cur?" he snarled, pumping hard.

The fleshy masses of her buttocks danced in cadence to his strokes as he forced his prick into the pink wrinkles of her arsehole. She groaned aloud—and took it. His strong hands leapt forward and down, grasping and mauling her shaking tits as if he were trying to pull them off. His hips flattened her rear-cheeks continuously as he drove straight through the center of their sweaty valley. His cock plunged along the teasingly narrow crevice of her anus and deep into her rectum. There he agitated it with spiritedly swinging hips.

"You . . . you are hur-hurt-ing my *breasts,*" she cried out, wagging her head to and fro in pain.

"Oh—well then, I'll release them at once," he said harshly, and did.

But instantly his hands sprang to grasp great masses of her midnight hair, which he began pulling and tugging until her head was forced up and back. Her back bowed far inward.

"My woman," the Butcher snarled, "does not fuck so willingly and happily with my worst enemy!"

Johara was unable to reply. Her neck was stretched into a curve, the inner bones pressing harshly out until the skin of that smooth throat was ridged and she could not swallow, much less reply or protest.

Then he released her. Her head lurched forward; she coughed and gasped.

"As Allah is my witness and I his servant," she at last got out in an ugly voice, "I love only you. It was I who stole and gave you the dagger that enabled you to es—"

Her voice broke off in a gargling sound. Her implacable lord had grasped a sheaf of the hair dangling past her face on the left, drawn it under her chin, and caught it in his other hand. Reaching again under her chin, he caught up with his left hand another swatch of her thick jet hair, from the right side.

Then, while the Crusader watched in frozen-faced horror, Yarok continued to jerk, sending his prick deep into her, leaning back and pulling strongly as though attempting to slow a team of runaway horses.

Johara's eyes bulged. Her mouth gaped. Her lovely body shivered and twitched. Her nostrils flared desperately. Guy knew she was not able to pull in any air. Nor could she gain breath through her hugely dilated mouth. Her tongue came forth, as if in search of the air she needed. Darker went the face of that young woman, who had risked her life in trying to slay her lover's captor and in smuggling to Yarok the dagger that had enabled him to escape.

She sank forward, twitching, limpening.

Suddenly liberated from her rectum, Yarok's big flesh-shaft jerked, bobbed—and began hurling its steaming seed into her bowels. Golden-white semen trickled along the dusky skin of her back. At the same time, Guy of Messaria saw another, darker trickle from her throat.

The luckless girl's merciless lord had sawed so hard on her own hair that its fine strands had cut into the skin of her neck.

Streaming blood and semen, Johara rolled over on the floor, a staring corpse.

"Butcher!" Guy lashed out, with a voice like a cutting whip.

"So I am called," Yarok ibn-Ammar said, with a nod as equable as if the other man had complimented him. "I am foremost among the warriors of Islam . . . I keep by me no woman sullied by uncircumcised Frankish cock!"

"Best you slay the owner of that cock," Guy said in a steady voice, deadly quiet. "For I swear by Our Lady that I will have your life, Yarok, O *Butcher!*"

"Not likely, son of Eblis! You will have neither my life . . . nor your *own*. For now, my Frankish cur, it is time for your *selling*. Mayhap your new owner will wish to make a *eunuch* of you. . . ."

THREE

Slave!

Numbed by certain knowledge that he was soon to be sold like an animal snared from forest or plain, the Crusader was led through narrow streets by Yarok and the man the Butcher had easily persuaded to aid him.

All about Guy of Messaria now were dark-faced Arabs, Turks and Egyptians and natives of Palestine: the land called Holy. Their bright clothing, long robes of white and the blue of the sky and of cobalt, of olive and red and orange and of stripes of all . . . the constant chatter of their voices in their alien tongue . . . none of this did anything to alleviate the mental staggering of the captive stranger among them.

From the snatches of converse he heard, Guy learned that he was in Abasan. It was a smallish town some fifty miles southwest of Jerusalem—close onto the Red Sea and vast Egypt, land where once mighty pharaohs and spoiled Cleopatra and the arrogant Caesars named Caius Julius and Octavianus Augustus had trod, and now main source of supply for the new conqueror, Saladin. The Butcher, Guy mused, half in a trance of shock, had pushed the horses hard to have made this long trek in but three days.

Three days ago he was hero, called *tu* by Richard, the greatest knight in Christendom. And now . . . now he was to be *sold,* pushed up there onto that platform surrounded on three sides by robed men with bags of dinars for the spending on new property, human property. Smiling, grinning, gesticulating men who even now were bidding on a naked girl of their own people, a girl of no more than twelve ripening summers, whose jutting round of pubis had not yet grown the fur of womanhood, whose breasts had only just begun to blossom. She was, the gesticulating auctioneer in the green and orange and bright scarlet robe assured his prospective buyers, a virgin.

She was sold to a grossly fat creature whose citron-yellow robe hung on him like a garish tent. His swollen hand happily fondled the close-crowded high-perched bowls of her buttocks as she was led away to his . . . ownership.

Others were bid upon and bought; a knight of France who stood tall and austere as though he still wore golden spurs rather than a dirty and torn tunic that bared his powerful legs and mangled left arm; a plump scarlet-crowned woman with great loose-swinging tits and dead eyes; another European nobleman who wept openly and brought only a few dinars; others, and others.

The Crusader ascended that platform in a daze.

Thousands upon thousands of the fairer people the Saracen called "Franks" had been sold in this accursed land of heat and strange language and a strange god and his peace-hating prophet. Men and women and children too, all having come here from far-away lands where the sun was not so angry, blessed by the priests of the faith that led them here . . . to be taken, and sold, and to live and die in slavery.

Perhaps those women sold into *hhareems* were the

more fortunate; perhaps they were not. Perhaps their loveliness was a blessing, perhaps a curse. Some were sold into seraglios . . . and some into brothels in tiny towns or the squalid back streets of Cairo and Damascus.

Otherwise, man or woman, their lives were spent at manual labor under masters (or, usually worse, mistresses) who spoke an entirely different tongue. Whether they had been born to silks or homespun, to wield lance and sword or mattock and scythe, they lived lives—existences—of lowly and underfed slavery, and thus they died. For their faith. For Holy Mother Church. For the Prince of Peace.

From the platform, the Crusader gazed down at his prospective owners.

I'll not die a slave, he thought, hardly aware of his purchase by a jowly and nigh-hairless Egyptian who squinted at the world from weak eyes and scratched often beneath his mauve-and-cerulean robe. *Or . . . if I die a slave . . . I'll not be old!*

Captors and fellow captives, owners and guards and drovers noted the unusually tall man their Cairene master had purchased for so many dinars. There was much muscle on him; much work in him. Young, broad of shoulder and thick of chest, far from unhandsome, he said nothing; indeed, he moved as though in a trance.

And so he was, for four days.

Then, on the afternoon of the fourth day after his owner's caravan had left Abasan, Guy awoke from his black depression and daze. He found himself walking, his legs chained, beneath a searing sun.

Without seeming to, he took immediate inventory of his surroundings.

Mounted escort: gaunt-faced, wolfish men beneath pointed helmets of blue-clothed steel, whence depended camails like cloaks to lie on their shoulders. Camels laden with great chests and bales and parcels, tended by robed and pantalooned drovers with their staves. And other slaves—seven—shackled together in a line so that they jingled as they walked.

But Guy Kingsaver walked alone, rather than shackled to the others.

Because I appear insane, he thought, keeping his gaze down and continuing to walk as he had been, dully, automatically, like a driven cow. *I have been walking for days; I can feel it in my legs. But saying nothing, responding to nothing, and so they separated me from the others.*

I shall pretend to be the same. But now . . . from this moment forward I shall be on watch!

He was on watch, but no opportunity came for escape. The four days stretched into six, and then seven. For seven days he was forced to stagger along with the caravan, forced to walk, sun-blinded and weary, across the hot sand and scraggly-grassed earth between the southern tip of the Holy Land and northernmost Egypt. On one of those long wearisome days —he was not later to remember which—he heard one of the score or so armed escort tell another that the Red Sea was but a few miles due south. Once they had crossed, just above it, they would turn into Egypt, and then march still farther south.

Into Egypt. Into a different country. And still the Crusader shambled on because he could do nothing else, with his ankles connected by just over a foot of strong chain.

He took note of one fellow captive; a European woman, blonde, and of proud bearing. She bore up well and bravely, a woman forced to walk as Guy was. Her strong calves flashed beneath the jagged edges of her torn skirts; the fabric rippled magnificently over the churning of her buttocks. With clenched teeth, the Crusader noted how she was spat upon by her Turkish and Syrian fellow-slavewomen.

Now and again, he saw, without appearing to notice, that she shot him a look from large eyes of Mediterranean blue. Playing the dumb, trancelike role, Guy pretended not to see her.

She was slated, he knew, for a lifetime of servitude. Most likely, considering her face and figure, for someone's harem; perhaps that of their fat bald buyer.

On the seventh day, the twelve camels and nearly thirty horses—and unmounted slaves—plodded along parallel to the foothills of a long line of low mountains. It was on that day Guy learned her name; he learned much from the conversations of those who treated him as though he were not present. The blonde with the fine calves and backside was Melisende, and she was from "Frankistan."

France, then, Guy thought. Or perhaps one of King Richard's lands: Normandy, or Aquitaine, or Poitou. Poor beauty!

His feet hurt. Yet he felt now as though he could run for miles on end, so tough and supple had the thews of his legs become. He received only subsistence food; his stomach consisted of hard bands of muscle. In some ways, the Crusader was in better condition than ever in his life. But what use was it to him, with his ankles connected thus by chain?

They camped that night at a quenching oasis, with those slow-rising foothills a few miles to their right. A slave was beaten, a Muslim male. Guy affected to take no note; certainly he was not concerned with the fate of any Saracen!

As usual, he was left to himself. Once his owner came to gaze upon him from a distance of fifty paces, and ordered that a girl be first stripped and then ordered to serve the big silent Christian his food and drink.

Guy betrayed no reaction to her unclothed presence, though he was glad for his ragged tunic; it covered the iron erection her swiveling coppery hips and tip-trembling breasts and flashing black bush engendered in his crotch.

She was very young, and naked and totally desirable. She still squatted near the suffering Guy when the moon soared up into a sky afloat with clouds.

Her presence brought one of the escorts, like a mailclad dog sniffing out a likely bitch. The man was tall, ugly, and walked with a swagger. The Crusader's eyes were drawn to the sword worn by the cocky whoreson: a broad European blade! Booty, Guy mused, off some dead or enslaved knight of Christendom. It hung long and tempting as the Turk lounged nearby and spoke arrogantly to the girl.

"Best ye get far hence," she told him, "else our master sees ye at converse with me and has ye whipped the rest of the way to Cairo!"

To Cairo! Guy thought. And then, like a breaking chain in his brain: *I shall not go to Cairo!*

"I fear that fat blob no more than I do the sting-flies who buzz about us in hot Tammuz," the warrior said, with a curl to his lip.

"As ye buzz around me," the girl pointed out.

The guardsman laughed. "Aye! Even so, in Allah's name—far better me—a man, eh—than your fat owner . . . or this tongueless excuse for a man he was so unwise as to buy!" He turned about, posing, to look at Guy, who squatted dumbly a few yards away.

"Ho Christian! *Stand* in the presence of your *betters!*"

Slouched in a squat with his back against an outcrop of stone, Guy appeared not to hear.

"Idiot!" the soldier muttered. 'Christian!" You, slave—*get up!* On your feet! Show me whether ye've the horn of a man beneath that grubby tunic of yours!"

Guy was still.

The escort moved toward him, slowly, concentrating on his swagger while the girl watched. His hand was on the hilt of the Frankish longsword he wore so proudly. But it only rested there, a part of his posturing. Despite the size of the obviously witless Frank, none feared him. The Turk came closer. Behind him, Guy saw the naked girl hurry away; she well knew her fate if she were caught having to do with one of the escort!

The guard came closer. Now Guy was staring at his mailed leggings.

"Up, unmannerly hare, and stand in the presence of a real man, a *fighting* man," the guard said.

After waiting a few moments during which Guy remained motionless, the Turk drew back his right foot. It rushed forward in a kick to the shin of the big man who had seemed to become smaller in seven days of silent, bovine plodding.

The rushing foot was a handspan away when the seemingly mindless slave came alive.

His right hand leapt out. Fingers and thumb slapped about the Turk's ankle, and it was as if he had driven his leg into a blacksmith's vise. Then the powerful arm behind that big hand jerked, forward and up. At the same time, Guy rose. The guard went back, and down. The impact of his fall knocked away the breath he drew to raise a cry. His chain mail camail fell away from his throat—and was forcibly replaced in seconds by the Crusader's left knee.

"Fight then, fighting man," Guy muttered.

But the guard would fight not again; his cry had just begun when a broken-neck death took him. Twisting swiftly about, the Crusader laid hold of the ornate hilt of that long sword, pulled. The familiar broadsword scraped out of its sheath.

"Spanish," Guy grunted, rising, hefting the yard-long blade.

Be strong, Spanish blade, he thought fervently. *Ever has our steel been more powerful than the Saracen's!*

Then the sword was a silver arc in the moonlight as he swung it high over his head and brought it rushing down—to slice through the chain connecting his ankles with one great blade-notching blow. The chain parted, only two links removed from Guy's right ankle.

"Free," The Crusader muttered, and on the instant he thought of the blonde.

Free? Already the other men of the escort were calling out, running toward him across the encampment. Curved steel blades whined out of their scabbards. Others of the caravan shouted; people moved in the darkness. There was no time for the blonde, or for anything else, not even water or a sheath for his sword.

Whirling, the Crusader ran for the horses. An armored man with a ready scimitar was there before him. His eyes widened at the headlong charge of the man who wore only a ragged undertunic. The scimitar struck; the long sword of Spanish steel turned it, and bit into the hand of the wielder. The man grunted and jerked his hand away—and Guy's swift backswing, the product of tremendous strength and instant reflexes, bit halfway through the Saracen's neck.

Starting to vault into the little enclosure housing the nervous horses, Guy saw the horse outside, saddled, hitched to one of the wooden poles forming the enclosure. His teeth flashed in a grin. No matter why it was tethered here thus; one did not question gifts from heaven! Even as he pounced to the gray, an arrow thudded into the pole nearest him. It whipped rapidly back and forth. Guy hurled himself at the horse, knowing now that it was not merely human legs he raced, but arrows as well.

Another bow-sped shaft thunked into the earth where his foot had been—as Guy swung into a high Arabic saddle with a grunt. It became a moan as he felt pain; he wore only the dirty, torn undertunic.

This only clothing the tunic flapping raggedly about his legs, the chain rattling from the iron gyves on his ankles, the Crusader galloped into the night. Arrows keened about him and he leaned far forward in the saddle. The horse galloped, tearing away from the oasis, accustomed to the greater weight of a steel-clad warrior with lance and saddle-bow and shield.

With a blade of good Spanish steel and on a swift Arabian horse—nothing else—the Crusader escaped into the darkness, riding back northward and east along the mountain range.

The other horses were neither saddled nor bridled; the escaped slave wore gyves and little else, and was alone in *their* land, far and far from his own kind. There was no pursuit.

Well up in the rocks of the long mountain range, Guy halted to rest for the balance of the night. He tethered the horse with care, thankful he'd been fed, however sparely.

His brief period of slavery had ended, though brief examination of his "anklets" of iron was sufficient to assure him their removing would be no swift or simple task. Clothing and armor he had not. No bow, no arrows, not even a dagger armed him. Further, he thought as he sought a comfortable position amid the stones and larger rocks, he was a pale-skinned man amid darker people whose hair was far darker than the sun-paled brown of his.

It will not be easy, and I may have to force them to

kill me, he mused, *but by God's balls I am fr—*

The thought was interrupted by sounds, conducted to him in the mountain foothills through the clear night. From far away he heard shouts, screams. The clamor came from behind him, and he was instantly certain they emanated from the oasis, from the camp of his former . . . owner.

The Crusader sat up, frowning as he stared into the darkness. Then he rose. And he saw the flames.

"The caravan's been attacked," he murmured aloud. His new horse, a swift but smallish gray, stirred at the sound of his voice.

Guy considered, gazing back at the flames that were perhaps three leagues back.

Any enemy of my erstwhile . . . owner *is no enemy to me,* he thought, and into his mind came a vision of a more-than-comely young woman, blonde, with eyes blue as the sea surrounding his native Cyprus.

Guy of Messaria sighed, and a few minutes later he was riding back the way he'd come.

Flames still flickered and crackled when he reached the oasis, though the fighting was at an end and the attackers gone. He was too late to interfere, to join one side against the other and then discover whether that *excused* his being a foreigner and a non-Muslim. For of one thing he was certain: none of the crusading host was this far south.

All around him lay the corpses of both humans and animals, camels and horses, men and women, even a dog. Others snarled over strewn meat and the remnants of the evening meal. Dismounting, Guy tethered his gray and walked slowly through that oasis become charnel preserve, amid the strewn supplies and burning tents and the bloody bodies. He inspected every one.

Here lay the man who had bought and chained him, sliced across his great belly to a crimson depth of several inches. A few feet left of that body were the smoldering remnants of his tent; amid them was the charred body of the Egyptian's girl-for-the-night. Next sprawled one of his escort; his was the third helmet Guy tried. As had been two others he tried, it was too small. Guy walked on.

A drover lay dead in a grotesque position, as though he had been hurled off a cliff; the sword-hewn mouth in his neck was broader than that of his face. Nearby was the corpse of the naked girl sent to feed the Crusader a few hours ago. He paused, gazed at her ruined, crimson abdomen with stern eyes. And he walked on.

Behind him, she moaned.

Guy returned to her, went to one knee beside her. Several inches of pink sausage looped out of the terrible wound in her lower belly. Her eyes sought his weakly; she tried to speak; blood emerged from her mouth with her groan.

"You are beautiful," Guy told her, in Arabic, and at the word *"hacene"* she almost smiled. "Because of you, I escaped."

Then Guy ended her pain, and rose, and walked on with naked sword. He wiped the blade on the leggings of the dead drover he found but a few yards farther on. He had never before slain a woman, and fervently hoped he never had to meet one in battle, or do so again, even under these circumstances.

A headless soldier . . . and two body-lengths away the head, neatly helmeted. That one Guy Kingsaver did not try on. He walked past it, stepped across the body of one of the new slaves; the rest lay in a pitiful little line, all slain even as they remained chained together.

The attackers had left no bodies, he thought as he squatted to try on another spiked Turkish helmet. Either they'd suffered no losses, or they had carried off both wounded and dead.

The helmet was slightly overlarge. Guy padded it with a bit of cloth, fine silk curling from a burst bale of the sky-blue stuff. From that same man he gained a pair of leggings of well-kept chain mail. And a belt, though the curved scabbard would not hold his Western longsword. A few moments later he corrected that: he found the man whose neck he had broken. That dead Turk yielded up a mailshirt, too, though it was snug and fell not quite to Guy's knees.

He kicked two dogs away from a package of food-stuffs, which he shouldered.

Here was a serviceable lance, here a bow, here a quiver full of arrows, here a better bow. A leather waterbag he stumbled over; it was full, and became his. He gathered more food, scavenging with the dogs, thankful they hadn't beaten him to the savory-smelling viands.

When he had covered what had been the camp and thoroughly tramped the perimeter, the Crusader paused, gazing ruminatively down at what were obviously the tracks of the departing raiders.

Nowhere had he found the corpse of the blue-eyed blonde.

Guy pondered that, and danger, and his future and the extreme danger to him no matter where he went, which direction he took. Certainly the sensible course was to return the way he'd first ridden: northward into the Holy Land, where somewhere far north the army needed him.

At last, with a sigh and set lips, the Crusader set off on his gray Arab horse, following the trail of the raiders. And Melisende of Frankistan?

FOUR

The Handle of a Whip

Hours later, beneath a bright, fat-bellied moon risen high and sassy in the sky, Guy Kingsaver plodded along on the same broad trail.

Insanity, he told himself. *Naturally they took her. And at least two other women; I remember them. And there are many of these raiders, since they utterly annihilated the camp, escort and all. Yet here go I, as though I were an army, by Holy rood, following them . . . one man, alone.*

But had his action been more sane, that night he had dropped from the loft of the stable on Cyprus? He'd driven a wooden pitchfork through the skulking man who was creeping with naked sword, upon the woman-sated giant lying there naked and vulnerable, the golden-haired giant named Richard, King of the English.

Had it been sanity that led the young ex-stablehand to hold his own with quarterstaff against one of that same Richard's best men-at-arms, or to outshoot his best archer (who could not pull Guy's homemade bow enough to string it), or then to outshoot the lion-heart king's best *crossbowman?*

Or publicly to proclaim himself, a Cypriot, Richard's subject?

Or to accompany him here, to this unholy place called Holy Land?

Or to act as Richard's secret agent, more than once?

Or to . . . to do all the other things he had done, to become the hero of this, the third great Crusade against the Saracen who still held Jerusalem and the sepulcher in which the Savior had been laid.

Guy Kingsaver heaved a sigh, and went on, wondering about the blonde woman and what might be befalling her even while he followed her captors.

She was miserable.

Her name was Melisende de Bois-Courtenay, daughter of the knight banneret Letold de Bois-Courtenay, a third son who had followed a nobler lord to the Holy Land in search of name and fortune. Like so many others, Sir Letold had found neither; he had been slain when Saladin's Turks took Ascalon, four years ago, in September of 1187.

Melisende, thirteen then, had watched with horrified blue eyes while her screaming mother was raped by her husband's four killers, and then bloodily slain. Spent and hardly interested in the pre-nubile blonde, the men had taken her with them. She became one of many Western slaves put up for sale after Ascalon's fall.

She was bought by Zuleyka, wife of the emir Shadhy, a stern Turk of Seljuk to the far north.

Over four years passed. Shadhy's glances at the ever-lovelier slavegirl made Zuleyka increasingly nervous—particularly inasmuch as she was, after the manner of too many smug wives, putting on weight apace. At seventeen Melisende was a woman tempered in the stern furnace of horror and slavery; a lovely virgin, and strong withal; Melisende carried as many as ten water buckets daily, in addition to her other duties.

Zuleyka found it expedient to get rid of her. She

found it profitable, too; a blonde virgin with fair skin would be valuable merchandise on the slave mart at Cairo.

The profit to Melisende's mistress, who feared her beauty of both face and figure, was pure. As for her new owner, the fat and jowly Cairene, he fully expected to realize double or more the amount he'd paid for her in Abasan, on the wealthier markets of Egypt's foremost city.

But then came the attack, and Melisende de Bois-Courtenay, one of the few survivors, was only a captive slung beneath a big black Arabian horse, swinging loosely and helplessly by her wrists and ankles. Daughter of a nobleman; orphan; slave to an emir's wife; slave to a fat Egyptian; now captive of surely the strangest band of warrior-thieves in all the world.

When at last they reached their incredible destination, the sore and stiff Melisende was cut loose all at once, allowed to drop to the ground on her back.

Then she had stared up at the cat-eyed woman in the mailed hauberk: a warrior-*woman!* Her name was Subha, this daughter of Islam, and she bared her black-furred crotch as she stood over the confused captive. She displayed her loins, her pubic delta, and spread her legs—and stared down at Melisende.

A slave for four years, Melisende understood and spoke Arabic. She understood the command she was given.

"Kneel up. Lick, suck Subha's pussy."

No! No!

Melisende shook her head, switching her shoulders with fine blonde hair, gold near her scalp but baked nearly white by the fierce sun of Syria. She was aware, as ever, of the soft joggling of her breasts beneath her disgracefully thin blouse, under which she wore nothing.

Subha stepped forward to bestride her.

"You had best obey, Frankistaniyeh! Think well; refuse again and you will be very sorry indeed."

"I am no *sehhikeh*," Melisende said, in a low voice in the woman's own tongue. "Seek out one of your own kind to lick your oily slit, *sehhikeh!*"

Called lesbian, Subha bristled instantly. And Melisende screamed, her scream dying into an ugly groan, when the mailed woman kicked her: swiftly and carefully, in the soft cavity of her womanhood.

It was but the first of many screams to be ripped from the throat of the seventeen-year-old daughter of a Christian knight.

"Subha," a voice called, and Subha looked up.

The big woman flashed a smile even as she brought one hand rushing up to catch the tossed object: a whip. She hefted it. It was a wicked little instrument, its handle composed of a leather-wrapped club of wood, just under a foot long. With the black leather wrapping, it was two inches in diameter. From one end emerged, like slender serpents of shining black, its three lashes. Each was knotted at the end of its foot-and-a-half length.

Without warning, Subha brought those three hissing tails down on the pale-haired young woman at her feet, across her very round and firm calves.

Taken by surprise, Melisende screamed. Absolute pain enveloped her naked legs and made her every sense swim. Her eyes filled instantly with brimming tears.

Even as, twisting, she looked up, that hissing burning lash bit into her upper left arm and back. Tears squirted from her eyes and a soft moan escaped her compressed lips. She flung herself aside, twisting, seeking escape where there was none, in a ring of stern-faced captors.

Subha struck. The three thongs fell with another blistering caress, this time across the huddling girl's back.

She wore only a thin Arab blouse of a chartreuse color. Where one leathern knot struck, the fabric broke. Again the victim cried out, again she twisted away. This time she tried to crawl, blindly, desperately fleeing the whip. The target was obvious: the whip fell with a harsh swish to plant its burning kiss across the up-turned rounds of her backside, lightly covered in Arabic pantaloons of a medium red.

"Gaahrrgh!" Melisende throated out, and she lunged forward, her body shaking and writhing as if in epileptic seizure.

She turned over; the whip dashed down to send flame-red waves of agony through her breasts. With her face screwing up in pain, she turned over again. The whip swept down, following relentlessly, to curl wickedly from base to summits of her ripely rounded buttocks. The agonized girl rolled, still seeking the unattainable relief. Tears streamed from her eyes and she was groaning, trembling in every part of her body.

As if in a berserk fury, as if thirsty for no less than the crimson life-juices of the blonde Frank, Subha struck and struck. Groveling, sobbing, rolling, twisting, Melisende took every three-thonged blow that sliced and tore her clothing and striped and welted the smooth skin beneath.

Round and shapely, a rosy-tipped breast spilled out through a rent in the shredded blouse. One excitingly opulent buttock, well reddened by stripe after stripe, was totally bared. So was most of its twin and the deep crease that divided them. Her left leg was bare from waist to ankle, flailed by ragged cherry-colored fabric. Her navel flashed darkly through a rent in the dirty yellow-green of her blouse. A flailing knot bit into a mound below that navel, a mound of flesh lightly furred with golden tendrils of silky hair.

The whip marked her with livid red weals from its

burning caress. Elsewhere, from her groveling on the harsh ground, her flesh was fiery red, chafed and cut, bleeding.

The young woman was barely able to move when Subha ceased beating her and issued a swift directive to the others. Four of them pounced; two hands gripped each of Melisende's wrists and held them flat against the ground as she lay on her back. Two others clamped on each ankle. They drew her legs far apart.

Subha squatted in that broad V. She ripped away more red cloth, completely baring Melisende's lower belly, slave-flat, and exposing the strong bulge below its base, hardly covered by the sparse, curling fleece of her loins. With her left hand, Subha peeled aside one firm and close-gripping labium.

Then, with the whip reversed, she thrust its handle into that flaming pink cleft.

The prostrate blonde drew in a sharp breath as she went tense, all over, in a surprising display of well-toned muscles. Then she emitted a long shuddering groan that seemed torn from her throat.

Subha buried half the length of the whip-handle in that narrow flesh-tunnel, agitated it here, and withdrew it.

It emerged glistening, and dripping scarlet.

Someone laughed aloud. "A virgin! The Nazrani slut isn't a slut at all, but a *virgin!*"

"Was," another voice said, with a chuckle.

"Was," Subha said, and rammed the whip's handle back into her victim's bloody gap.

Obviously possessed of a strength that belied her apparent softness, Melisende winced, moaned, tensed again . . . and went limp.

She lay slackly in exhausted sujugation, her open mouth releasing only soft, pitifully weak little moaning sounds. In and out of that warm, narrow, throbbing sheath Subha thrust the harsh instrument of the young woman's defloration, seeking with it the very bottom of her distended slit. The muscles of her thighs tensed and quivered; pitiful little shudders ran through her whip-marked body. She only groaned, lying there in helpless defeat and acceptance of the violent rape of her previously unopened, anguished vagina.

Subha wielded the leatherbound whip handle with vicious enthusiasm. The girl had refused her. Now she'd been beaten and callously, degradingly fucked by this obscene substitute for a man. The grinning warrior-woman drove it up her victim's untrammeled nook with hammering blows, stretching wet, raw membranes with hard jerks of her arm.

Melisende shuddered. How swiftly and simply and unromantically and . . . *nothing*-ly that bit of membranous flesh had been sundered to terminate her girlhood forever!

Without love, without tenderness or romance, without her acquiescence or any semblance of honor—without even a man—she had been bloodily deflowered. And now they held her down, chuckling, while the big woman named Subha fucked her with the handle of a whip.

The cruel dildo plunged far up inside her, far up her cringing, straining cunt. She could hear the broad club sucking in and out of her body, its pathway slickened by both her blood and her natural inner juices, so that it came burrowing in far up her belly, abrading tender tissues as it expanded them, rooting as fiercely into her as the raping organ of a barbarian male. Her taut labia formed a painfully-throbbing collar around the obscene instrument.

She could feel it, feel it, the big leathery shaft stretching her sexlips and making the inner oils well in unwanted response, ramming deep, pumping her pussy deep so that she felt its broad base, way up in her belly. She squirmed, compressed her lips.

Her crotch felt as if it had been pounded with a sledge hammer.

At last, sweating, Subha ceased her brutal ransacking of the pale-furred slash.

"There," she grunted, getting to her feet. "All because ye refused to yield up your *other* mouth, bitch!"

Then, while rolling waves of pain mingled with horror, Melisende was forced to watch while four women raped and forcibly masturbated one of the three male captives they'd taken. He was not unhappy when the first woman squatted over and plunged her black-furred slot up and down the standing pole of his organ until he lurched and jerked and groaned and then his seed was trickling down her thighs.

But he was pleading well before the fourth, at last, gave up trying, with her pumping hand, to force that now sore tool to spurt a fourth time.

He was then mutilated and slain.

At that instant, all unaccountably and unbidden, the staggered mind of Melisende de Bois-Courtenay went to the broad-shouldered, brown-haired and very tall man she had been so aware of while the caravan moved south and east; her former fellow slave who had slashingly escaped just last night, before the raiders attacked.

She knew a sudden sense of terrible anguish, of having been cheated—and of longing.

FIVE

The She-Lion

When he found himself nodding in the saddle and totally unable to follow the track of those he trailed, Guy of Messaria halted his mount, slid down, and tethered the horse so that it could crop the sparse and scraggly grass. By this time they had paced far into the foothills, ever upward.

The Crusader stretched out on the bare ground, wearing the armor he had grown accustomed to these past five months since he had decided to serve Richard as squire and join the Crusade. Neither the harshness of his rocky bed nor his armor was sufficiently uncomfortable to overshadow his weariness: Guy slept and did not wake until the morning sun sought to fry his eyelids.

He rose, lowered his steel-link leggings to piss, and ate of the food he had stolen from the dogs the previous night. Of the water he drank but little, and he murmured an apology to the horse, stroking his neck, that there was no water and little food for him.

Then man and mount set off again.

The trail was difficult. Now and again a line of horse-droppings pointed the way. Sometimes he was forced to dismount and range about until he found a rock that bore the mark of a shod hoof. Another time there was only a bone, with tendrils of meat still clinging to it, not yet dried; the remains of someone's hasty, horse-back snack.

Slowly, as often on foot as mounted, the Crusader followed the tenuous trail into the mountains of which he knew neither the name nor the location.

Darkness closed down again; again he slept. The horse complained. Stroking him and once more apologizing, Guy hoped the thirsty beast understood at least his tone. And they went on.

The winding track entered a long narrow divide between towering granite walls. The rock-strewn floor rose up and up toward the white-bellied clouds. The sun rose higher, reached its zenith, and frowned down upon man and toiling beast. But it was the armored man who lost the more sweat.

What, Guy wondered, *am I doing? Guy, son of Peter, a peasant near Messaria on tiny Cyprus. Following a woman! Better I were heading north, in hopes that luck and sword and God's grace might see me through many hostile leagues and back to my companions—to my duty. Here I may well be riding to meet my death, and none will be there to offer a prayer or bury me.*

Whoever they are . . . how can I expect to wrest from them such a valuable prize in this land: a woman at once fair and blonde, young, and strong?

He did not know. But he went on, the Crusader on a new and separate Crusade.

Eventually he was pacing his nervous mount along a slender ledge halfway down a cliff that towered surely a hundred feet above his right shoulder . . . and plunged hundreds of feet when he glanced leftward and down —which he did only once. He had no difficulty persuading his mount to hug the inside of the ledge-path, though his right arm was thus next to useless, should he need it.

Then they turned a corner of that slender track—and the horse halted instantly. Man and mount stared.

They had emerged onto a broader terrain, sufficient perhaps for four horses abreast. And now Guy Kingsaver faced a leveled crossbow shaft. The bolt seemed to stare him in the face, deadly sharp. Slowly, keeping his right hand on the rein, he moved his head, looking about.

Two more crossbow-nocked arrows were leveled at him.

The wielders wore steel helmets whose sheen was hidden beneath a fluttering scarf of pearl-gray silk. Chain-mail jackets could be seen above the deeply-*v*'d necks of their gray surcoats, which had three-quarter sleeves that again exposed chain-mailed arms. From left shoulder to right hip ran the slender strap that supported their daggers; from right shoulder to left hip a buckled baldric supported the sheath of a curved Arabic sword. The skirts of the gray surcoats, slit back and front to facilitate the wearer's sitting the saddle, were long, falling to the instep.

And . . . all three deadly crossbows with leveled bolts were held in the sunbronzed hands of helmeted, mailed, well-mounted, stern-faced . . . women.

"Understand ye our language, Frank?" one of them asked, and Guy met the slitted eyes beneath well-arched brows. The eyes were heavily *kohled,* as protection from the sun.

"Yes."

"See that your hand remains on the rein."

Guy nodded and kept both hands still. *Women!*

"Why came you here, Frank?"

"I have followed you two nights and most of two days. I was captured near Latrun by a Turk, taken in my sleep in coward's fashion, and sold in Abasan. I marched with my buyer's caravan into this land. One night I cut my way free—and hours later heard an attack on the caravan, and saw flames."

One of his accosters chuckled. The spokeswoman said, "At the oasis of Kaylulah?"

"At an oasis, aye. I know not its name."

She nodded with a little smile. "So."

"Was it you who attacked the caravan?"

After a long silence, she said, "It is we who ask and you who answer, Frank. And then what did you do?"

"I was not born a slave and do not intend to die one. I returned to aid your attack on him who bought me, and I have followed your trail since."

"We left no trail!"

"I have just followed one."

Again, a long silence; the women exchanged looks. Then, "To aid us, eh? But you have not answered my first question. Why do you follow us?"

Us. Then they were the raiders . . . these women!

"With you is a Frankish woman whose hair is the color of the sun and whose eyes are like the Mediterranean. She is my sister."

"Oh? What is your sister's name?"

"Melisende."

After a moment of silence, they laughed. The spokeswoman backed her horse, gestured. "Come then, Frank. Meet thy sister. Mahara—take his sword. Easy, Frank; crossbows trigger too easily."

Guy nodded, raised his arms slowly and held them clear while the warrior woman named Mahara relieved him of his long sword. His dagger, too, she plucked from its sheath, and never had Guy of Messaria known less emotion while a woman's arm went around his waist. Then she had disarmed him and was backing her mount, turning the big bay.

Guy accompanied them, one in front and two behind him and his gray. Along the broadened ledge they paced, and into a cave that soon encompassed them in darkness, though it was short, a natural tunnel, for he could see the light at its far end.

They emerged onto a ledge above a terribly high drop, a narrow crevasse no more than twenty feet across. The ledge itself was slightly less wide. And the leader of the trio of warrior women shouted, then made a trilling bird-call.

With his captors, Guy stared upward.

High above, a pair of thick wooden poles thrust out over the edge of what was obviously the mountain's very top. From the two poles swung, on chains, a great iron-bound platform, framed with thick wooden slats like a cage made for an elephant. With chains creaking and rattling, the strange device descended to Guy and his escorts.

One of them was dismounted and ready, while her companions kept their crossbow shafts trained on their prisoner. She opened two bolts the moment the great cage was steady on the ledge. The closed portion of the cage swung downward, revealing itself to be a heavy door, like a drawbridge. It formed a ramp from the ledge into the cage. Into the structure she went, leading her mount.

Once she was inside and aside, another of Guy's captors led her horse in. And moved him aside, and turned, and leveled her crossbow once again.

From behind the Crusader, Mahara said, "Dismount, Frank. Lead your beast in."

Guy turned half about in his saddle. With a small smile he said, "After you, milady warrior."

She rolled her eyes upward. "I remain behind. In!"

The gray was not at all certain about entering the great cage, but the calm presence of the other two

50

horses and Guy's gentle words and stroking hand convinced the beast. *Clop-clop,* and Guy and mount were aboard. Mahara closed and secured the door.

Then she stepped back and shouted.

"Climb up here, Frank," one of the women bade him, and he mounted to the ledge that ran around three sides of the heavily-constructed cage, above the level of the horses' backs.

Then came the rattle and clatter of chains once more, and the cage creaked, and shifted—and began to ascend. The gray snorted and stamped, widening his stance to brace himself in his nervousness. The other two horses acted as if they had been thus rising into the air all their lives—which, for all Guy knew, they had!

Up and up they went, with much noise of metal chains and creaking wood.

Then, when they were snugged up against the two huge poles that jutted out over the crevasse, one of his guardians tripped the miniature "drawbridge" again. It fell with a heavy thud.

One by one, the three led their horses out onto a broad, nigh-flat mesa dotted with pavilions and strange structures of wood roofed with some glittering black substance.

Now Guy saw that the cage that had drawn them up was operated by means of a great horizontal windlass mounted around a pole of enormous girth. The windlass was turned by four horses harnessed to its spokes. The Crusader marveled; nowhere had he ever seen such as this evidence of ingenuity of man.

But . . . was it of . . . *man?*

The camp—or town—as he was led from the cage-lift out onto the mesa, appeared to contain nothing but women! He saw what were apparently servants, wearing very little indeed, low-slung girdles of slender plaited silk from which depended long fluttery strips of gauzy stuff in several colors. One strip hung down in front, past the calf muscles; another covered all but the outer curves of their buttocks and dangled in back, to the same length.

All wore bandeaus, again in various colors, that tied twice: behind the neck and then either behind the back or between the breast, which were in all cases, partially exposed.

They stared at him.

So did the others, women who wore long side-slit robes—slit, indeed, to dusky hips!—over bare flashing legs, drawn tight above the waist by clasped or laced vests. The robes were of a half-score colors; the vests were uniformly black. And all wore scymitars in curved scabbards on their left hips. No, two wore their swords on their *right* hips; he assumed these to be left-handed women.

It seemed to the astonished Guy Kingsaver then that he saw fifty or so women and girls, of varying ages. But none was truly old, he noticed.

He was led to the center of the mesa-top hamlet, stared at and whispered about by women, some of whom had never seen a man not of their race before. (That they had never seen a man was too much to believe!)

When his two captors brought him to a halt, he faced a strange pavilion. It had been pitched atop a great wooden platform, with three steps leading up to it. The great entry-flap of the pavilion—which was jet black, like an oversized *bedawin* tent—was set perhaps a yard back from the edge of the platform, which thus formed a sort of porch before the "door."

In that doorway appeared a woman. She and the Crusader stared openly at each other, brown eyes staring into jet black pools like oil.

52

Guy decided that she was not tall, though she gave the appearance of being so by the slimness of her hips and the length of her legs, which were emphasized by the snug-fitting leggings of dark blue-gray mail. Her torso and arms were covered by a scarlet blouse of clinging silk, with balloon sleeves and tight cuffs covered by bracers of buckled black leather. Rather than the over-the-head blouses Guy was accustomed to, this one was laced up the front by a black thong—and loosely laced, at that. Plainly visible were the fruit-firm curves of golden breasts.

Over the shirt, like the others, she wore a black vest, though hers was broidered in scarlet and hung open. Red gauntlets sheathed her hands past the wrist, and matching boots of soft leather rose just above her ankles, clasping the lower curves of her calves.

She descended the steps of her dais-elevated pavilion of stark black with the majesty of a queen. And slowly, without taking her eyes off him, she approached the Crusader.

Hers was a squared face, firmly square-chinned. Its high cheekbones were well-delineated and just escaped being sharply-etched. A gentle central declivity divided her strong chin. Long, almond-shaped eyes gazed boldly at him from beneath thick, well-arched brows with a hint of insouciant nonchalance that was almost arrogance. Her mouth was broad, firmly held, its lips neither thick nor thin but well-etched, beneath a long, haughty, and only faintly aquiline nose.

Brows and eyelids were *black,* glowing and gleaming liquidly. Her hair was invisible beneath a blue-gray helmet, its tall spike piercing a kerchief-like veil of chain mail that fell in back and on both sides of her face, to the shoulders.

There was a weird aspect to the vest; it was sewn with two breastplates of gleaming gold. Somehow Guy was certain that when this woman donned chain-mail coat, she wore the breastplated vest *outside*.

Everything about her was striking; the gold breast-plates, worn so ostentatiously and unnecessarily, perhaps drew his gaze more than anything. But she was a striking, handsome, perhaps beautiful young woman without them. Her carriage, the open boldness of her eyes, the set of her shoulders and mouth, spoke *confidence*, unusual in any woman of her time—particularly one in the land of al-Islam.

"What's this you've brought me, Aziza?" she asked, in a surprisingly high, very feminine voice, which was clear and firm of timbre.

"A Frank who claims to have followed our trail from the Oasis of Kaylulah, O Libwah."

Libwah, Guy mused: *Lioness! Aye, an she be captain-general of a band of women, the name may well fit the arrogant beauty!*

"Speak you our language, father of trackers?"

"I speak your language," Guy replied, in Arabic, though their accents were different.

"Speak your name, Frank-who-speaks-Syriac-Arabic."

The Crusader spoke the name the warriors of Saladin had given him, Son of Satan: "Guy ibn-Eblis."

She blinked, then shrugged. "So, son of the devil. And why have you come here?"

He gave her the same story as he had told her minions, adding to the truth only the lie that Melisende was his sister. What else could he say? He was fool enough already!

"Interesting. My brother would not have been so solicitous as to follow me—nor was he so expert a tracker. Know, son of Eblis, that you are among the band of Julanar al-Libwah," she told him, gazing coolly into his eyes. "There is but one way down from our great city, unless mayhap you care for a thousand foot leap! Thus there is no escape; the other sides of this mountain are sheer, and without purchase even for skilled fingers. You say that this woman is your sister —said I woman? This cloud-haired little girl of Frankistan!"

Guy noted that she mentioned Melisende at last, and spoke of her not in the past tense; she was alive, then. He noted too the satiric lilt in the voice of Julanar the Lioness when she called this strange collection of tents, pavilions, and strange houses a "great city."

"Know, O Son of Eblis, that she was a virgin, but that she is no longer. Her maidenhead was taken by the handle of this, my whip." She flourished a three-tailed whip with a long handle, thick and leather-wrapped. "She bled beautifully, and we pumped her with it until she spent her passions in sensuous climax. I believe she may wish only the company of this whip hereafter! Only the truth Julanar speaks. You understand?"

"I understand," Guy bit out, hoping he imitated well the angry brother of a European girl ignominiously deflowered by a whip handle, barely able to contain his rage.

After gazing at him a moment, in what appeared to be contained surprise, Julanar laughed. "Good! Then hear this, and only the truth Julanar speaks. You will either fuck your sister, Guy ibn-Eblis—or so ye say ye be called—or suffer the fate of Ayyub."

After a startled moment, Guy asked, "Who be Ayyub?"

"Him," she said, pointing, and, menaced by crossbows and many surrounding women, Guy turned to follow the direction of her pointing finger.

A naked man had been fetched from somewhere. He was now being stretched over a bale of some fabric from the caravan, so that his genitals were raised on high, balls dangling. Each of his wrists bore ropes, tied around wooden stakes a foot in length; these were pounded into the earth. His legs were immobilized in the same fashion.

While Guy and the others watched, one of the servants, an obviously very young girl with taut breasts like the golden cups on Julanar's breasts, stepped between his tethered legs and dropped to her knees.

The man gasped when her hands slipped up beneath his scrotum and began to toy with its twin-agate contents, kneading and pressing and fondling them lovingly. Then her pink, lasciviously wet-shining tongue began jabbing at his curled, limp member. She worked to arouse him with lips and tongue and fondling hands.

His organ, Guy saw, was beginning to straighten itself out, radiating heat and lust. A film of transparent wetness formed on the very tip of the bulging crown. Smiling, the girl bent her head to it. The man groaned and twitched; she was kissing away the glistening drops of moisture that emerged from the tiny hole in its swelling head.

"What think you of the fate of Ayyub?" Julanar the Lioness asked quietly, from behind Guy.

"Methinks I could withstand such a fate," he said, without turning.

Around him there rose scornful laughs.

Now, at a command, the girl rose fluidly to her feet. She backed away with her dark, dark eyes fixed on what she had wrought: a great thick prick that throbbed impatiently above its owner's tight-clenched balls.

One of the robed women stepped forward between his legs. She glanced about at her fellows as she opened her vest and handed it to the girl whose mouth had prepared the high-standing shaft of hardened flesh. Next the second woman, whom Guy supposed was one of the warriors of al-Libwah, doffed her side-slit robe. She revealed a good, plump body with a rounded belly and large round breasts whose brown tips appeared knotted amid their aureoles, downward-pointing.

She bestrode Ayyub's hips. Poised above his outstretched thighs, she positioned the fluffy black bush of her loins in a lascivious, parted display above that standing flesh-club. With deliberate slowness, she lowered herself, her face taking on an expression of strain as she impaled the luscious mouth of her vagina on his upstanding cock.

Her stomach's muscles appeared in its roundness, tensing and tightening as she continued lowering herself, her widening slit riding down his thick organ while he stared up at her, gasping and groaning.

Then he was enveloped inside her body. With her mouth stretched in a broad grin, she turned her head to gaze upon her companions—and Guy.

And she started to move. Up and down rose her supple body. Her calf-muscles bulged as she raised herself and then slid again down the pole of the man's organ. Guy stared, watching the big balls of her breasts rise and fall, flopping and jiggling so that they seemed to leap up and down before her.

As she rode the helpless tethered man, her own fingers rose to her breasts. Guy saw how rough she was with them, her dark hands squeezing and pinching the tight flesh, making the shapely globe shapes quiver until the fattening brown tips danced. They also swelled to an incredibly fat tumescence.

Then she fastened onto those teats and began to pluck at them, squeezing, pinching, twisting them about on the ends of her big breasts. All the while, her body rose up and down, up and down.

The man groaned, stiffened, began to twitch. Obviously he was spending, his semen spattering up into her, seemingly pumping quarts of sticky syrup into her vertical channel.

But she continued her steady, now-furious riding. Now as she pumped up and down, semen appeared and spattered his belly, trickled down his softening shaft onto his belly. Then all the watchers—some of whose hands had stolen inside their robes—were watching her with staring eyes as endless waves of climax washed and rolled over her. No one had to ask whether she had spent her lusts to the full; she suddenly yowled as though dying.

When she stood erect and backed off her well-raped "victim" at last, his liquid-glistening penis fell from her and lay limply against his crotch. He was gasping; so was she, as she took her clothing from the waiting servant and walked naked to one of the pavilions without so much as a sideward glance—or a word or glance at her choiceless partner in sexuality.

"And what think you of Ayyub's fate now?" Julanar's voice came, low and throaty from behind the Crusader.

He had to work to answer calmly: "I believe I could withstand that, too."

She laughed. Others laughed.

And then one of the warrior women came forward and, grasping Ayyub's penis and scrotum in one hand, she swiftly used the dagger in the other to slice them off. She sprang back as a fountain of blood erupted from the crotch of the hapless man, who shrieked as his spurting blood drained away his life.

Hands went to swordhilts and crossbow bolts leveled on him as Guy wheeled about to face Julanar—whose face was frighteningly impassive.

"Demon from hell!" he accused. "Either that monstrous fate or lie with my own sister?"

"Aye," she said, and nodded. Calmly, coolly.

"God! And how long have I to ponder this evil choice?"

She glanced at the shadow the sun cast from the pointed crest of her helmet onto the ground, a scant fingerbreadth from Guy's left foot. And she pointed with a scarlet-gauntleted hand.

"When the shadow of my helm falls upon your foot," she told him with utmost coolness, "you must have chosen."

Guy blinked.

SIX

The She-Demon

"You would really do that to me, a stranger, unless I agree to lie with my own sister?" Guy asked.

The beautiful Julanar the Lioness gazed unblinkingly at him. "Only the truth does al-Libwah speak."

Guy nodded. "And what if I agree to your heartless bargain, O Lioness of Egypt?"

After staring at him several seconds longer, Julanar shrugged. "You both live, Son of Eblis. I guarantee it. *Life*. Only the truth I speak: what else is there but *life*, man of Frankistan?"

"Than life? Nothing." Gazing steadily into her eyes, Guy stated what had become his own credo: "God does not care. That is what life means, and that's what death is. Death is something that just happens. I shall *live!* I shall live every day, all my life, and if it be short, then . . . I shall have *been* here!"

She blinked, widened her eyes, regarded him with intense interest. "That is what you believe, Frankistani?"

"It is what I believe," he said with a swift nod. "There was a woman, once. I loved her. She was young, a servant to a noble lady, and God saw fit to send upon the noble lady—the mistress of a king—the illness we call the Syrian fever. My love caught it of her, and they both died. I went away in despair, and I thought long and hard. And at last I said to myself what I have just said to you and it is that I live by."

Still obviously intense, seeming to strain toward him, she urged, "Repeat it."

Guy repeated the words that had become his personal philosophy and guideline.

"Guy—listen to me!"

All others were as if vanished, as though invisible or not there. Only Guy and Julanar stood there atop this mesa, and he nodded. "I am listening to a beautiful woman in breastplates of gold. I have no choice; she has power of life and death over me. Speak, Lioness Julanar."

Her eyes were dark, piercingly intense like those of a hunting hawk who sights what he has long sought.

"I have spoken, and al-Libwah speaks only truth. Once I have spoke, I take back nothing, an it mean my own death. Do it, man of Frankistan. Lie with your sister. It is not yet your time to die."

The Crusader gazed steadily at her. "Bring forth my sister. I have not seen her since you evilly took her maidenhood. I cannot guarantee that I shall be able to be . . . up to the occasion. My own sister, after all. Long have I loved her, but as my *sister*, O Lioness. I would drink strong wine, had I strong wine."

"Bring him *kahwah!*" Julanar called, without taking her stare from his. "And bring forth the Frankish . . . *keuss.*" Her eyes checked his reaction as she callously and insultingly called his supposed sister "cunt."

"An it pleasure ye to call names," he said quietly, "call *me* names, then. Elsewise it is unworthy."

Her blink showed her astonishment. "I, a woman, speak of another woman!"

"You speak only to test my reaction, to rouse my

anger and then sneer at it, for I am captive here. As to your womanhood, yours and Melisende's, she is a girl. You are a lioness, leader of this band of fierce outlaws. There is no comparison . . . as there is none between me and that man Ayyub."

She was still staring at him in silence when a plump serving girl in lemon-yellow bandeau and orange "skirts" brought him his wine. The goblet was of solid gold, and beautifully tooled with the head of a lioness; the wine was rich and good and old; better than good.

And then from one of the broad black tents came the blonde he had seen earlier, the woman he had so noted on the march from Abasan.

Guy called out quickly, in French, the language of most of Europe and most of the English and others as well. "My darling Melisende! It is I your brother Guy! This demon decrees that we lie together before them all, my poor darling, lest we die. Remember our father. Melisende—speak his name!"

For a time the blonde young woman stared at him. Then she said, "Our father, Letold de Bois-Courtenay would die rather than see what it is we must do, O my brother. But Guy, Guy . . . we *must* do what they say, or be slain. Which is worse; is there not hope while the heart yet beats?"

And in that instant, Guy of Messaria felt love for that magnificent, brilliant woman, who had become beautiful in seconds.

"What is this talk?" Julanar demanded.

"I greeted her in the language of our land, Frankish," Guy said. "And apprised her of your evil bargain. She is my sister; do you see her turn pale and sink down in a swoon?"

"A nuptial couch will be brought," Julanar said, signaling, and a pair of her warriors went away, grinning. "Son of Eblis—ye cannot lie with your waiting bride while wearing full armor! *Strip!*"

Never had Guy Kingsaver of Messaria stripped less willingly or in such discomfort. With a closely watching audience of fifty women and his supposed sister looking on, he divested himself of armor and then under-leggings and tunic. Then he stood naked before them, and of a sudden he lost his uncomfortable feeling; their eyes were in the main impressed with what they saw. He stood to his full height, conscious of showing them his broad, bulging chest.

He stared for a time at Julanar, silently challenging her to keep her eyes on his, not to drop them to his bared body. Then he turned from her, not without arrogance, and looked at Melisende. She was but a few paces away now, near where the two women were placing the divan they had brought from one of the pavilions. It was covered with a spread patterned with interwoven red and green and blue. On it lay a large pillow of white silk.

But Guy looked at Melisende, who had removed the blouse they had given her and was loosing the ties of her blousy Arabic pantaloons.

A high forehead capped a long face whose brows were nearly as straight as her longish, slender nose. Melisende's hair was honey and gold and cloud-bellies, obviously delicately thin and softly tendrilly, the sort of silky hair that stirred in the gentlest of zephyrs— and looked ever delicious, however disarrayed. Her nicely shaped but thin, in-turned upper lip was neatly balanced and set off by the sensuous fullness of the lower. Her lashes were pale, her eyes blue as the sea or a summer sky, and marked by a skittish lack of confidence, a constant fearfulness that bespoke her harsh and uncertain life of the past five years.

Absolutely lovely breasts swelled below a long, slender neck; they were beautifully rounded, not big but rather large for her narrow shoulders so that they crowded each other's inner curves. They were charmingly uptilted at the crowns. Those nipples were tiny, set like delicate pink jewels in swollen, shinily protuberant aureoles. They rode above a very narrow waist and even narrower belly, set between long, womanly hips. There was an unusual excitingly long space between her coiled little navel, almost a perfectly round and decidedly shallow crater, and a bulging pubis, only the crest of which was adorned with wavy but not quite curly hair like golden pinfeathers. The hair was very sparse, just coating the slit itself, which showed through plainly.

She stood with her arms at her sides and her eyes on the Crusader's, her bare feet and ankles obscured in a pile of her pantaloons.

He saw the distinct marks of a whip on her body, and wondered if it were Julanar's, and if she herself had wielded it.

Julanar's soprano intruded on his thoughts: "To your couch, brother and sister Frank—and couple for your very *lives!*"

Seeing the blonde tremble, Guy went to her, very conscious of the swing and jiggle of his penis, which, though not fully erect, had thickened and lengthened. Sliding his hands onto the smoothness of her hips just below her waist, he looked into her eyes.

"I will not tell you that I do not want you," he said. "I have seen you! But . . . I am sorry it must be this way."

"Thank you," she said, in a soft, muted voice. It was about the same level of soprano as Julanar's, but *so* different! And after a long moment, "Just—just *beginning* will be the hardest!"

"Are you . . . sore?" he asked.

"Ye've been told what they . . . what they did?"

He nodded.

"No, not sore, though . . . it may hurt, I suppose." Her face had been taken by a flush.

"I will try to make it so that it does not hurt," he said, terribly aware of the steady rising of his cock, "and to make you forget if it does."

She gave him the shadow of the ghost of a smile. And nodded, a barely perceptible movement of her pale-crowned head.

Behind him, Julanar clapped her hands sharply, twice.

Tightening his mouth, Guy sat on the divan, drawing the girl down beside him.

"It must happen," he said. "You . . . you must put your hand on me, so that I am hard and ready for you." As he spoke, he was gently manipulating her nipple, hoping that her once-invaded womanslit was one that readily and copiously oiled itself.

Then he grunted and twitched as her hand encircled the base of his prick.

"It is not necessary," she said. "It—you are . . . big, and hard. So big!"

Guy looked down. She spoke truth. His penis was imitating a quarterstaff, though thicker than most. Its angrily swollen, livid head pointed nearly straight up.

His hands slid from her hip inward, making her tremble, caressing, slithering over the delicate furring of her loins. He found the tight-pressed lips, springy and firm and outthrust, and the line between them that was narrow enough to have been sliced there in one swift movement of a shaving knife. She trembled, sighed as he opened her, slowly and gently, and insinuated his finger into the vestibule of her girlish cunt.

It was wet.

"In a moment," Guy murmured, "she will call out again, to order us to get on with our incest."

Suddenly Melisende flashed him a smile. "Think of it that way!" she said. "We are deceiving the bitch! Cover me . . . my brother Guy!"

Releasing him, she fell back on the divan, with her legs parted. Deliberately Guy rose, so that their on-looking captors had a full view of his mighty erection. Then he moved between Melisende's whip-marked legs, which she opened still more.

The big glans of his prick nosed up against the soft pursed beauty of her slitted vulva. For a moment he smiled down at her, then he began moving his hips forward.

"Uh," she gasped, but she managed to return his smile.

Her once-widened passage began to enclose his steely tool like warm oil as the moist, hypersensitive glans probed between scalloped inner lips.

"Better to take it all at once," he said.

"I . . . am ready," she said.

"Do not scream for them."

Her face had paled and her eyes were like those of a frightened and cornered rabbit, but Melisende said, with near-firmness: "It will not hurt!"

He nodded. And he slipped it on into her, drilling in and in, straight for her cervix, long and hard and cramming, filling and feeling the extreme constricting heat of her buried passion.

He wondered if it had ever been awakened; if al-Libwah did indeed speak only truth; if he was capable, under these circumstances with the sun and fifty or more hot gazes upon his back, of arousing and satisfying this terribly mistreated young woman who was hardly yet a woman at all.

She had stiffened, trembling, tensing, and he bade her relax, in a soft voice. He saw her trying. And he gave her the rest of himself, to the balls, and waited again until that sudden tension had left her.

"You have it all."

"I—have it all," she said.

"Lift your knees, draw up your feet," he told her. "The villainous bitches have given us the narrowest divan in all Egypt; there's no room for me to raise my self on my hands."

"Aren't you supposed to lie on me?" she asked, with ingenuously wide blue eyes.

Guy chuckled, belly against belly. "There is no 'supposed to,' " he said. "But a man worthy of a woman takes his weight off her as much or more as he lets her feel it."

She was silent, then she heaved a great sigh that moved her tits squirmily under his chest. "Let me feel it, then. Guy—*is* that your name?"

"Aye. Guy Kingsaver, of Messaria on Cyprus. I was squire to King Richard."

"The *Lion*-heart?"

"The Lion-heart."

"And you will be a knight?"

"Aye, if ever I can return to them. I could have been ere now," he added truthfully, for her sake; she was nobly born. "The Earl of Leicester in Richard's land of England offered to knight me, less than a se'en-day ago."

"Tell me about it later," she said, breathing more and more easily. "Why do you no longer feel so huge inside me?" But that question was a wondering, rhetorical one for herself alone, telling him that she was relaxing and accommodating herself to him. She followed it with another: "Why the surname 'Kingsaver?' "

"On Cyprus, my home, I saved the life of Richard the King from an assassin who'd have ended it but seconds later that night."

She smiled. "Brave enough to escape the caravan . . . brave enough to follow here and challenge all these . . . unnatural creatures; brave enough to have been offered knighthood by no less than an English earl . . . brave enough to have saved the life of the Lion-heart!" Her hands rose warm onto his hips. "Now save *my* life, Guy Kingsaver!"

He began slowly, and stepped up his pace only when he saw that he was not hurting her. Far from it; she loved what she was getting. His belly churned with erotic joys as he drilled through her now juice-saturated pussy lips. He was breathing hard and shallow under the hot afternoon sun, grunting with lust and effort in a rising, uncontrollable joy. She was very tight around his delving organ, and it was utterly engulfed in her, embraced by her sapping, humid cunt.

She gasped when he dragged all the way out, groaned when he drove it all the way back in, with lubricious ease and a heavy jolting impact.

He thrust and thrust, stirring her, opening her wide, straining her virginal track all around his great skewering sword of flesh. His cock raced in and out of her with wet slurpy sounds. Sweat beaded his brow.

Placing his lips against her warm ear, Guy whispered, "Act ecstatic."

Her hands clamped him. She strained every muscle to move beneath him. "I do not have to . . . *act*," she groaned. And then she was jerking, twitching, stiffening, and a long wailing sigh silenced every whisper and sneering voice on the mesa, for all knew the sounds of a woman who has reached the peak and the release of her arousal and need.

An inferno of sheer ecstasy spread through her system until she was so excited she was unable to contain it. She pounded the divan with her bare heels.

He pounded her silky form with his solidly-built body in a savage rhythm that smacked the gentle concavity of her belly and drove him deep, deep into the hot slick delicacy of her. Hot slippery juice flowed forth from that dilated hole onto thighs like warm satin. Her mouth was gaping and gasping in erotic abandon, her whole luxuriously formed body enveloped in wanton impulses.

Half mad with the impatience of physical demands and desire for absolute possession of her supple curves, he rode her with whipping, convulsive movements.

Then a bursting dam of thick white semen gushed into her open, swollen cunt. His jerking organ salvoed hot streams of sperm into the very depths and filled up that squirming vaginal tunnel until it leaked forth in whitish little rivulets.

He lay still upon her, holding and being held, until a hand tapped his back.

"Up, fucker."

Smiling, Guy again kissed Melisende's ear, then rose from her. Both his loins and hers were covered with their mingled juices.

"The face of one who has so delighted in the embrace of her own brother is an abomination before my eyes!" Julanar shouted in an angry cry. She pointed to a tall stake in the center of the little hamlet atop the mesa. "Bind her there, by her ankles, so that her incestuous cesspool is lifted high and her brother's sperm may flow into her womb and get her big with the child of her own father's son!"

Guy wheeled on her, fists knotting, but leveled crossbows kept him at bay. He brought himself up short.

"I remind the Lioness that she claims to speak only truth," he snapped. "I have your word . . . would you then bind her thus, in the sun?"

She nodded with a little smile. "Aye, I would. The sun is almost gone this day, anyhow. Soon it will be more than cool; it is not hot at night, atop this mountain! Her back and shoulders will bear her weight, and she will not die. I promised you *life,* and her as well. Ye still have my word, man of Frankistan. Ye both *live!* Life I promised you both, and life you retain. To neither of you did I promise freedom, or even happiness. Yasmina, see to the attaching of a *new* chain to the iron anklets this *slave* still wears!"

SEVEN

Dinner with a Lioness

Melisende's fine, almost tendrilly hair spread out over the sparse grass and granite of the mesa like a white fan tinged with jonquil yellow.

The sun beat down on her strained body, attacked her eyes so that she turned her head this way and that and constantly ran her tongue over her drying lips. Her face, like the soles of her feet, was turned straight up to the cloudy sky. Her ankles had been fastened high enough on the stake to force her weight onto her shoulders and neck.

But if her fair, delicate skin and so-pale hair made her captors think she was a soft and therefore perfect victim, they were disappointed. The upended young woman did not so much as whimper.

Around her, the business of the unnatural community went on. Scantily clothed servants laundered, and sorted out the foodstuffs and wines from the looted caravan, and carried water from where it was drawn up from the well. Warrior women sharpened their blades, carefully rubbing out nicks, checked their armor, tested and repaired their leathers.

Guy sat still while the two ends of a three-foot

length of chair were attached to the shackles on his ankles.

"You have no men here?"

"Oh, now and then," one of his warders said, without glancing up from his ankle. "Who needs men?"

Guy chuckled. "The world. Men make babies."

"Ugh. We neither want nor need babies here."

"But I saw two children!"

"Ye talk o'ermuch, big man," the other woman, older and thicker, said. Also without looking at his face.

"Oh let him talk; he'll accomplish nothing more here! Aye, there are children, Frank. We have taken in pregnant women—raped slaves."

"Can slaves be raped?" he asked.

This time she looked up at him, a chain-mailed girl no older than Melisende, with very thick eyebrows. "It is always rape," she told him, "unless a woman says 'yes' or 'weave my yarn.' "

"Umm. And is there no weaving here, no *ghunj*? For pleasure?"

The older woman looked up sharply. "We find and take our pleasures, Frank!"

"*Sehhikeh*," Guy suggested; " 'she who rubs' or a tribadite, a lesbian with a large projecting *zambur*, or clitoris.' Uh!"

She had deliberately twisted the chain so as to make the upper edge of his iron anklet bite into his leg. She chuckled, rose. The other woman tested the chain, and herself stood up.

"There, man. Would ye like to challenge me to a foot race?"

"Another time," Guy said, rising to tower over them both. He would have freedom of movement—constantly accompanied by the clink and clank of the

72

yard-long loop of dragging steel links—but certainly attempt no act against his captors.

Women smiled, and some chuckled as he was escorted, rattling, to a small black tent. He was ordered to remain within.

The tent was empty save for a worn mat of woven fibres. On it Guy sat, trying to convince himself that he was dreaming, that there could be no community of over a half-hundred armed and armored warrior-women atop a north Egyptian mesa. But shackles and chain, when he tested them, were real enough. He'd not be getting them off with anything approaching ease.

He wondered what they would do with him. If they were *male* outlaws, they'd have been raping Melisende, all of them, and he'd probably already have been killed. But . . . women?

Melisende.

Well, he had pleased her, he knew that—and she him. He thought disconsolately of her now, of the sun baking her smooth thighs and belly and her uplifted loins, so delicately furred, and the white undercurves of her lovely breasts, turned up by her position. He trembled in impotent anger; told himself it was pointless and stupid, and calmed himself.

The Crusader thought about Julanar too, and the mix of her sensuous beauty and insensitive cruelty . . . and of Yarok al-Jazzar.

"Somehow," he murmured. "Someday, somehow, al-Jazzar . . . we will meet again, and I shall not grant you life, as I did when I had bested you and set my dagger at your throat. Some day, Yarok the Butcher. *Wait for me!*"

After a long while the Cypriot rose, stretched, as was his habit, to keep his muscles ever supple and ready, and with his chain clinking he went to the tent's open entry.

Night-black eyes met his from beneath a domed helmet with a point rising from its crown like a slender, erect penis of shining steel. And her lance was ready.

"Better to guard and menace me with a sword," he advised, "and held ready to strike, not pointed at my body where I could grasp it easily as I could now snatch your spear!"

She blinked . . . and retreated a pace.

"So advise your lionlike mistress," Guy said, gazing out at the stake. Melisende was no longer there. A servant passed, the heavy ovals of her breasts trembling within a light short blouse tied beneath them in a way he had never before seen. "Where is my sister?"

"What matters it to you, Frank?" his guard sneered. "She is alive; so Julanar has ordered. Perhaps we will put a ring through her nose and hang a weight therefrom," she said, smiling viciously, warming to her taunting suggestions, watching him for reaction. "Perhaps we will shave off all that pallid hair of her head, or pluck out her eyes, or slice off her silly pink-tipped tits, or perhaps—"

"Perhaps," the Crusader said in a voice so low and full of menace that she had to cease talking to listen, "ye'd best cease your prattle, else I take your spear from ye and impale your unwiped anus on it." And he turned and walked back into the tent that was his prison.

He exercised, but the rattling of his chain only reminded him of his helplessness. He sat and gazed morosely out the open flap of his tent. Now and again someone passed, tinged red by the setting sun, and once a very pretty, very dark servant, who wore only loose trousers and unclosed vest of lemon yellow, shot a glance his way.

Or perhaps, he mused in disgust, at his guard. *Sehhikeh!*

After a time, a new sentry replaced the evil-tongued *bahglah* outside. The sky darkened.

After a time, a figure loomed in the tent-entry, and he looked up, blinking. There stood Julanar, still wearing her golden tit-cups but daringly bare of leg beneath the sleeved scarlet tunic. Almond-shaped eyes fixed him with an emotionless stare that reminded him for a moment of al-Jazzar.

"Is it true ye advised Shadi to guard ye with scymitar rather than spear?"

"Is Shadi my sentry?"

"Was. She reported to me."

"Aye."

"And is't true ye threatened, too, to impale her rectum on her own spear?"

"It be true. And did she tell ye why?"

But Julanar was laughing. "Marvelous!" she snapped. "If your life be short, then ye shall have *been* here, eh?"

"Aye."

Laughing, the lioness-queen of the she-bandits turned and left him.

Guy sat and waited. For anything; for nothing. Captivity was waiting. He'd rather have been ordered to work at some stout labor.

After a time a big woman with naked scimitar came, and with her two others, doe-eyed servants in snug-sleeved blouses and baggy trousers.

"Come, man."

Guy went. The chains clanked; watching women stared and giggled and muttered. Containing his anger, the captive was led to a bath house. There he suffered himself to be stripped, then bathed by the servant-girls, and dried. The guard sneered at his erection; the servants giggled, and one of them brushed the seated man's cheek with her pointed breast.

Then they dressed him, and to his astonishment . . .

Underpants of soft Egyptian cotton. A high-collared, long-sleeved shirt of white silk, the first Guy of Messaria had felt on his skin. Then a blood-red robe that fell past his ankles and fitted snugly to the waist. It was ornately decorated with cloth-of-gold curlicues, arabesques, and closed with loops of the same heavy stuff that slipped over sewn-on bosses of gilded bone or ivory, and cinched with a belt of braided cloth-of-gold.

He was garbed, surely, in clothing intended for an emir.

"Boots?" he asked, as the three women stared at him in awe.

His warder did not smile at the obvious taunt; to have added boots to his attire, they'd have had to remove the gyves. "Come."

Again the Crusader went. This time there were many stares but few chuckles as he crossed the camp, tall and broad and striking, in the long robe.

They conducted him to the heavily-reinforced silken pavilion of Julanar al-Libwah. Inside burned no less than two ornate oil-lamps and as many candles, illuminating divans, low tables of wood and brass that should have groaned beneath their burden of meats, dates, nuts, bread, and several strange but passing savory Arabic dishes. Pillows and tasseled cushions were scattered everywhere, in many colors and shades. There were also three silent servants, very young, all bare of arm in tightly-laced vests of red cloth and ballooning trousers white as clouds.

And there was Julanar. On her wrists silver bracelets glittered; from her ears dangled lengths of the tiniest, daintiest silver chain, with two strands of red-amber and turquoise stones.

She seemed to have been draped, rather than dressed, in several shades of flowing gauze that flashed bare coppery skin every time she moved.

Gone were helmet and gold breastplates and vest, and somehow the steel in her thin face and almond eyes seemed to have been doffed with the warlike trappings. Her hair fell in long blue-black waves.

Julanar the Lioness was both beautiful and consummately feminine.

She took a deep breath, and Guy saw the surge against the pale blue gauze of restless breasts with blood-red tips.

"Magnificent!" she said.

While he felt the word was merited by her more than himself, Guy was not of a mind to pass compliments on his captor. Instead, he replied drily, "They neglected to provide me with footgear."

Her eyes dropped to his bare feet; the robe only partially covered his iron-circled ankles. She looked again into his eyes.

"Swear to do only what I say and attempt no escape, and I shall order those chains struck off."

"And the shackles?"

"And the shackles."

He shook his head. "No. A captive makes no such promises; a captor should expect none."

She regarded him for a moment, long liquid-black lashes veiling her black eyes. Then a smile tugged at her full lips, which had been stained a violet-red.

"Swear to do only what I say and attempt no escape," she amended, "and I shall order those chains struck off—and I shall order your sister bathed, fed, and given silken pillows for her bed . . . and no torture this night."

"Done."

Julanar smiled. "Aziza—"

"Wait," the Crusader interrupted. "I agree to make no attempt at escape, nor to lay violent hands on you. But I shall not swear to do all you say," he told her levelly.

Again those onyx eyes gazed at him, wide-held and cool under brows that arched faintly. "Ye interrupt me to say that—ye would not even lie, attempt to trick?"

"Only the truth Guy speaks," he said, without the hint of a smile.

Only her eyes smiled; she nodded then, once. "Done. Aziza—"

"This night," Guy added.

The outlaw chieftain jerked up out of her lounging posture on a great tasseled cushion of purple-bordered yellow satin. Now she sat very erect. *"What?"*

"The Lioness added the words 'this night' to her pledge. I do also. Tomorrow perhaps you may decide to mistreat Melisende—and I may decide to interfere."

This time Julanar regarded him for a long, long while. Her bold dark eyes ran up and down him, his broad shoulders and unusual height. Even among his own people Guy was tall, rising six feet; among the shorter sons of Allah, he had even fewer peers in height. In the emir's robe, with the slimness of his waist and hips accentuated by the belt, he was as Julanar had said: magnificent. A man among men; a man beside whom other men were as boys. And him as yet unmarked by the wrinkles drawn by age's relentless brush!

"And were I to extend the parole through tomorrow?" Julanar asked at last, bargaining.

I have pushed her, Guy thought, *challenged her. And she, the captor, now bargains!* He nodded. "So shall I extend my pledge to act the guest and ignore the fact of my captivity."

"It is what I wish. Aziza, remove his shackles. Sakina: measure his great feet and bring him shoon of felt."

"O Lioness—" the nervous Aziza began, but the look on her commander's face closed her mouth like a trap.

Guy was soon seated on the edge of a low divan of dark blue stripes and bordered in two shades of green, with Aziza bent over his legs.

He rubbed his chafed ankles, once the gyves were off. Then Julanar ordered a servant, plump and naked but for a single broad bracelet and a low-slung girdle from which hung an ankle-length strip of sky-blue silk to cover her loins, to see to the chore. The Crusader leaned back while the jiggly-plump girl sat at his feet, rubbing and kneading his ankles.

"Eat and drink what you will," Julanar said, again lounging back and regarding him from beneath lowered lashes. "I eat little."

The servants poured wine for him, passed him this heaped dish and that. Guy ate well, indeed.

"What would you tell me of Frankistan?"

He quaffed a draught of wine to wash down some peppery dish of meat and a Syrian legume. "I would tell you that the castles, and the silken pillows and divans, and the food of your land are far superior in beauty and comfort. And, so also superior are the women of al-Islam. But what of one called Julanar, an outlaw, who lives apart and manless as queen of outlaws on this eagle's aerie?"

Julanar shrugged. "Suffice it to say that I live well and am happy, and have slain many, of both sexes— and will slay more. And you, Frank?"

"I? I am Guy Kingsaver, and my liege-lord is Richard, called the Lion-heart. I have sent many men to hell, all Turks save only one, who was of Cyprus."

"Only men?"

"I have slain two women," he admitted.

She asked, and he told her of the female attacker in that upstairs room of Acre's palace where he had found Leila, and lain with her and learned the language of her people. And he told Julanar, too, of the woman he'd found after her own raid on the caravan, and how he had ended her misery for her.

"A man afflicted with the dangerous virtue of consideration for others," Julanar commented, "as I have noted. Not an ideal trait for a warrior."

"I was human before I was a warrior."

"Umm. A little wine, Zo," the lounging Lioness said, extending a jeweled goblet of well-shaped gold without glancing at that servant, whose shoulders and chest were broad, but whose hips were narrow; she had breasts like eggs, tiny and stiff.

"You ignore the Prophet's mandate against strong drink," Guy observed, suffering his cup to be filled, too.

Julanar al-Libwah pretended to spit. "Muhammad was a man; Islam is a faith for *men,* with no place for women save as slaves. I believe neither in his rules for the worship of Allah . . . nor in your faith of a dead carpenter of the Jews."

"And God?"

Julanar flashed him a smile. "Who can say? I have never seen . . . Her."

Guy had to smile, too, at the pronoun applied to the Deity.

"And those who have felt the bite of your steel were all Turks, Guy of Frankistan?"

"Aye, all save one. It was he sought to slay my lord the King of the English, master, too, of lands in Frankistan, he whom Saladin calls Malek Ric."

"The Lion-heart."

Guy nodded. "The same. And *he,* Julanar, has sent headless to hell far more men than you or I will meet at arms in this lifetime."

"And you slew one who sought to slay this mighty lord?"

"An assassin, aye. I am called Guy Kingsaver, of that deed."

She asked him about that night in the stable on Cyprus; with more wine, he told her of it, though he neglected to mention that he was of Cyprus.

"And ye have loved many women I suppose, saver of a king," she said, watching him from beneath veiling lashes like raven's feathers.

"Not *many,* Lioness of Egypt, but always well."

They gazed at each other in silence.

Then she said, "Ye brag like a Turk!"

"You like not the Turks?"

"Pfah! No! My family is of Egypt, nowhere else."

"We have that dislike in common then, commander of she-warriors."

She chuckled, studying him from under her lashes. "You fancy yourself quite the lover, then?"

"No," Guy said, though he did; before she had turned traitor, the Lady Luisa Vermandois had taught him what it was that women wanted of men—not always what men thought, and usually more than men gave. Thus he was not so selfish a lover as were most men, and a champion in the lists of love and lust. "I am good with sword and quarterstaff, and I know none better with a bow. That other is merely something else I do, now and then."

She smiled then looked challengingly at him. "Ye fancy yourself an archer?"

He nodded. So he had said, and he saw no reason to repeat.

"We shall see," Julanar said. "And perhaps about sword and stick, too."

"And the other?"

"The other?"

"The weaving and pulling of yarn," Guy said, speaking her language and using a common euphemism in it for the way of a man with a maid.

"My yarn needs no weaver to tug it into new shapes," she said, rather sharply.

Guy nodded without comment, and again sipped the wine forbidden by the holy book of Allah and his prophet Muhammad. Calling their names one by one, Julanar dismissed the three nearly-naked servants with a little gesture of her fingers. Lying languorously back in the plushy buoyance of her cushions, she stared at Guy until he met her piercing gaze.

"Guy, son of Eblis, Saver of a King."

"Julanar," he acknowledged, "surely daughter of Eblis, Lioness-who-slays-lions, and surely the most beautiful woman in Egypt."

She did not so much as blink. Without preamble she returned, "Stay with me this night."

"So," the Crusader said, "I appear to be doing."

"*Kabul!*" she snapped. "You know my meaning."

"Ye ask me to remain with ye, Lioness, and practice *ghunj,* and ye call me *kabul* . . . one noted for buggery? Your desires are unusual, Julanar!"

She leaned suddenly forward with restless movements of her scarlet-crowned breasts beneath their gauzy covering. Her voice was low and intense: " 'God does not care. And if life be short . . . then I shall have *been* here!' " she said, quoting him. "But toy not with me, smirking hulk, or your life may be shorter than ye'd wish!"

"I made the mistake of forgetting we were captor and captive, spider and fly, O *mistress,*" he said drily.

82

She started. "You *are* a man!" Julanar breathed at last.

The Crusader did not bother with replying to the obvious.

"Stay with me this night, man among men."

"Provide clothing for my sister, woman of women."

"Ye . . . ye *dare* bargain!"

"It is not meet that the sister of Guy Kingsaver be naked, as a child or the lowliest of slaves," he said, watching her carefully.

The wings of her nose flared with her angry breathing and her eyes seethed. For a long moment she stared thus at him. Then she shouted, "AZIZA!"

Aziza came. In his resplendent robe, wearing only the tiniest of smiles, and wondering if he were not perhaps insane to have thrown away a night with a woman by challenging and crowding her too far, the Crusader was escorted back to his prison-tent.

EIGHT

Virgin!

In the morning Guy was brought food and water by a girl he recognized as one of Julanar's trio of personal servants. She spoke no word, but swayed swiftly from his prison tent with her tight little buttocks pumping on either side of the long strip of cloth that slung from a girdle so low on her hips as to show rearward cleavage.

He ate and drank, wondering what sanctions Julanar might take for his insult last night. He sighed. He'd pushed and pushed—and at last pushed her too far.

Well, at least he was not chained. Yet he knew that he must be docile, so long as they and their strange leader showed no menace to Melisende or himself. So long as he was their prisoner, and hadn't wings to fly to freedom, he'd bide his time—and search for a means of escaping this falcon's nest!

He smiled a secret smile, wolfishly. A man knows when he is attractive to women. Guy of Messaria knew that Julanar was interested in him, as a man. And he had shown her he was no fawning slave, by Satan's scarlet pizzle!

Aziza came for him; he was told to wear only the dirty undertunic he still possessed, not last evening's finery. His mail they had taken from him, naturally, along with his weapons. Guy accompanied her.

Fifty female warriors were gathered, some mailed and all armed, and a halfscore of the servants. One of the former stood with her gaze fixed on him. A red-leather quiver was slung on her left hip by a narrow strap that was buckled betwixt her breasts. She held a short, curved bow of the desert. Neither Julanar nor Melisende was in evidence. Three crossbows were, though, and their shafts remained fixed on the Crusader as he walked to the archer.

"Observe," she bade him. And in a few swift motions she drew and nocked and drew string three times, loosing three shafts at a bale of straw many yards away along the mesa. All three arrows drove deeply into the target and stood there quivering. Only then did she return her gaze to the near-naked man.

"You are convinced that this is a worthy bow?"

"Aye. And that its wielder is worthy of it, as it is of her."

His pretty speech brought a mingled reaction of glances, smiles, sneers, titters, chuckles, mutters, and rolled eyes. The archer's reaction was among the last-named, that and nothing else. With a single brief nod of her black-banged head, she handed him the bow. Automatically, he tested its strength and suppleness a few times.

"You are to shoot against me, Sitt al-Shihah," she said, holding out a hand; a servant girl in white bandeau and scarlet "skirts" hurriedly placed another, more ornately-worked bow in her hands.

"At you?" Guy asked innocently.

"You heard her," Aziza said. "The Lioness has said that you admit to no peer with the bow. We would see proof of your archery."

"You are best among them, Sitt al-Shihah?" he asked the archer.

"I am."

"I, Guy Kingsaver, am called the Human Crossbow. This toy is shorter than my bow, and lighter, and gentle in the pull," he said, and he pulled the bow, and broke it.

Amid murmurs, Aziza bade that he be brought another. The second was slightly more powerful. "And what be the prize in our competing?" he asked, getting the feel of his new weapon.

There was a moment's silence before Aziza chuckled: "Clothing!"

"Since I have so little, then I must take care to win!"

They nodded and chuckled their approval of his lighthearted words. He held out a hand to Sitt, palm up. "And may I have arrows for the testing of this bow?"

Her eyes swerved uncertainly to Aziza, who said, "He has eyes to see the crossbows. Take care, Guy Kingsaver."

"I am not stupid," he said, and in seconds he too had placed three arrows in the bale, without difficulty.

"Well shot," Sitt al-Shihah said. "And how find ye the bow?"

"Serviceable," he said, and after a pause, "and weak."

She cocked her head. "Ye be so strong?"

Guy nodded, without further comment.

"I fear ye must needs content yourself with that bow, man of Frankistan," a clear soprano called out, and all eyes turned to the speaker: wearing helmet, mailed leggings and coat, with the golden breastplates worn over it, Julanar descended the steps from her porched pavilion. The morning sun flashed fire from the breastplates as she waved a hand. "On with it."

"A gong will be struck," Aziza said, while two warriors plucked the six arrows from the bale, and stood well back. "Sitt will then draw and loose arrows until its tone has ceased. Then it is your turn, Frank."

Guy shrugged. A test of both speed and accuracy. "Arrows missing the bale count nothing?" He was looking at Sitt; she nodded.

None saw the gong. The black-and-scarlet-clad Sitt took up her stance, turned slightly leftward to the distant target, bow in left hand, both arms full length at her side.

The brazen note of a gong pealed out. Sitt moved swiftly. Arrows rattled out of her quiver, hummed away like bees with the twang of her bowstring. Under his breath, Guy counted, a steady beat. When the gong's uluating voice was no more, a voice called *"Stop!"* Sitt, with a seventh arrow nocked and bow half-pulled, froze. She had loosed six arrows; all six stood from the bale of straw.

"Twelve," the Crusader said aloud.

"What said you?" Aziza asked, while the arrows were plucked from the target and Guy adjusted the strap of the quiver he was given.

"I said 'twelve.' It is as high as I counted while the gong resounded. I shall count again, during my turn. And I shall feather my man in the upper chest, seeking his heart. I am ready."

He barely was. Someone was swift: the gong's deep voice boomed out the moment he'd said the words. Counting in his head, Guy plucked arrow from quiver, nocked, drew, let fly, plucked, nocked, drew, let fly. "Twelve," he muttered, nocking the seventh arrow.

"STOP!"

"Fairly struck," he said, with a nod, and let the arrow fall to the ground. His six shafts were in the upper portion of the bale, closely clustered, at center or just left of center. The competition was a draw, though all knew that he had placed his arrows where he had promised, and with a strange bow at that. He nodded respectfully to Sitt, who hastily returned the gesture of acknowledgement to a fellow archer.

"And now a *head* for your foeman!" Aziza said.

Not only was a head-sized melon set atop the bale of straw, a helmet surmounted the melon! There was to be ho timing, no gong. Each would loose three arrows, alternately. Again, Sitt would shoot first.

Sitt drew, nocked, pulled, aimed, and her arrow whished away as the string twanged. The arrowhead rang off the helmet. There were cheers.

"He is yet unharmed," Guy muttered, and an instant later sent an arrow into the melon. There were no cheers.

Biting her lip and aiming carefully, Sitt sank an arrow into the melon beside Guy's. And then he did again. And Sitt did, this time splitting the melon—one falling piece of which was pierced by Guy's third arrow before it struck the ground. He had won, a clear victory. But now, amid murmurs and frowns and looks both admiring and unhappy, he backed ten paces and sent a fourth shaft into the melon's other half as it lay on the ground, a very poor target indeed. Then he nocked a fifth arrow—and deliberately overdrew. The bow snapped. He tossed it to the ground.

"I said it was weak," the Human Crossbow said into silence.

"Bring Guy Kingsaver a stronger bow," Julanar called out, and he waited, trying to look natural while striking a nonchalant pose, studiedly looking at no one. As the bow was fetched, he turned a brown-eyed gaze on Aziza.

"I have won clothing?"

"Aye," she told him, with but little grace.

Without a word, he tore off a strip of cloth from the hem of his tunic. "Do you dagger this to yon bale," he said, extending the bit of fabric to Aziza. She stood stiffly, wearing an unfriendly face.

"Hamama," Julanar said, "pin that cloth to the bale. Here."

A dagger whipped past Guy, who managed not to flinch. It sliced into the ground a hand's length from the bare foot of a plump serving girl. Swallowing her shock, she plucked it up. Then she took the new target from Guy's hand, which was broader than the wisp of dirty white cloth.

Guy tugged and bent the new bow, arrowless, while Hamama swiftly walked the many yards to the bale. When she stepped away, he hoped he had not gone too far; the fabric was a tiny target indeed, at this distance. His little finger, held before his eye, obliterated the target! For the first time since he had bested her, Guy glanced at Sitt. He raised his brows questioningly. She looked unhappy. Then Julanar the Lioness spoke again.

"Ye've fairly bested her, bowmaster. Now it is demonstration."

"I would test the bow for distance first," he said, looking at the lovely bandit queen and thinking himself a great fool for having left her last night. "It is strange to my hands. I shall loose three shafts; the third will be directed at the target."

She nodded. All eyes watched the ragged man on whom their leader had conferred the title "bowmaster." Then heads whipped away to look at the bale. The first arrow struck it a foot below the white spot that was the cloth. The second clove into the bale a few inches above it, and slightly to the left. As Guy drew his third arrow, the cloth fluttered. He waited, motionless. Second after breathless second passed.

"Have ye lost confidence, O Human Crossbow?" al-Libwah demanded.

"He waits for the breeze to abate, O Lioness," Sitt unexpectedly said. "See how the target flutters."

Guy glanced over to give Julanar's best archer a tiny smile and a nod with his eyes. Then he turned his glance back to the cloth. It was still. The Cypriot drew string immediately, back past his cheek as he tilted the short Arab bow slightly—and then the string snapped forward with its *fnggg!* sound and the arrow whipped up and away.

It pinned the cloth to the bale of straw.

There were excited murmurings and some cheers; some of the women could not restrain themselves. Captive or no, he was *good*. Before Julanar or anyone else could comment on the superb shot, a small shadow appeared on the ground before Guy, moving. His right hand rushed across his muscled belly even as he tilted back his head. Above flew an Egyptian buzzard, soaring so high as to resemble a large insect, black against a high-sailing white cloud.

Sitt al-Shihah was saying, "A magnificent bowshot, Guy Kingsaver. I acknowledge ye—"

She broke off as he whipped up bow and nocked arrow, let fly, and without lowering eyes or bow drew the last arrow from his quiver. This was not his great wire-wrapped bow; a thin line against the sky, the first arrow fell short of the carrion-eating bird, which immediately pulled out of its soar and began to flap its ragged-edged wings. A bowstring twanged; another dark line raced aloft, and Guy held his breath.

The buzzard jerked in air. Two dark feathers flew, and began to flutter down. The buzzard itself dropped like a stone, transpierced by the Crusader's arrow.

Of the sixty or so women, only a handful failed to

cheer or cry out excited congratulations. A bird on the wing!

Guy threw the bow to the ground. "It, too, is weak," he said disgustedly. "Two arrows for such a large bird!" He swung on Julanar. "And now a test of swords, O Lioness?"

She almost smiled. "Fetch him a goodly *quarterstaff*."

"A *goodly* quarterstaff," Guy echoed.

The long stave was brought. It was nearly two inches thick and just his height, as was the one wielded by the big woman called Subha. She wore a coat and leggings of linked chain; Guy wore only the undertunic.

"Signal to commence," he said, noting the two women who stood ready with drawn swords. They took no chances, with him "armed!"

"He has no armor, no protection!" Aziza called.

"BEGIN!" Julanar commanded.

The armored woman and the nigh-naked man circled and paced, eyeing each other. Each gripped quarterstaff in both hands, though less tightly with the left. Subha feinted; Guy tucked his left elbow in to his body and shoved with his right. The stout staves clacked together, then again as Guy jerked back his right arm and slammed forward his left. He followed up with a stride. His left hand slid back along the thick pole as he thrust it forcibly forward; Subha only just blocked, with a loud rap of wood on wood hard enough to break bones.

Guy spun completely around, the staff extended from his right hand, at the end of his rushing right arm. As he whirled back to face the big cat-eyed woman, she was swinging her stave to meet his, which was a racing blur. But his right leg seemed to go limp, and as he dropped his knee to the ground, his hard-swung shaft, now on a lower trajectory, struck her mailclad left calf.

Subha grunted. She staggered, her face twisting. Guy danced away from her two-handed thrust, then struck her staff with most of his strength. Her arms were hurled rightward by the impact, her body partially turning. One of the sword-armed guards was forced to leap back. Then a great cry of laughter rose: the Crusader's quarterstaff impacted Subha's mailclad butt, *hard*.

Even while she was stumbling forward, off balance, Guy half-turned to slap his stave into the curved sword of one of the two guards. She groaned, then went to one knee when he thwacked her broad hip. Aziza, looking alarmed, reached for her curved saber.

The other swordswoman was springing forward, swinging a great overhand cut, clearly having lost her head. Gripping his quarterstaff in both hands, Guy thrust it up and forward in the manner of a weight-lifter. At the moment of impact, he let his arms drop, and sank into a crouch. The maneuver caught and cushioned the swordcut, also saving the quarterstaff. Then the Crusader, rising and lunging simultaneously, sent the woman sprawling backward.

Ignoring the circle of naked swords, he leaned casually on his great stave and directed an equable smile at Julanar al-Libwah.

"Return my mailshirt, and ye may bid them seek my death!"

"*I* did!" cried the woman he had downed, scrambling up with murder in her eye. "And I shall!"

"HOLD!" her chieftain called. She stared at Guy, who noted that her color was high and her eyes asparkle; her gold breastplates rushed visibly up and down with her rapid, excited breathing. She gasped, "Aziza! Go to the Frankish woman with the cloudlike hair and see that she is clothed as befits the sister of a man among men!"

Then, after another long glance into Guy's eyes, the armored outlaw queen whirled and strode to her pavilion. She mounted the steps and disappeared within.

Guy watched grinning, then turned to apologize to the swordswomen he had attacked. Next he spoke to Sitt: "If there be a stronger bow, a longer bow or suitable piece of good wood, I should like to see it, archer. And is there any wire about?"

"Wire, bowmaster?" She was the sort who acknowledged defeat and showed her respect for the victor; a good loser.

"My own bow, archer, was the length of my body, could not be strung by two such as Subha, and was wrapped all over with *wire*."

Sitt al-Shihah blinked. "I think I believe ye," she said quietly. "I shall look personally. And what, bowmaster, do ye *not* do well?"

"Lose," Guy told her, and she believed that, too.

Then Melisende de Bois-Courtenay was walking through the mountain-perched hamlet, her hair a pale bright cloud about her face. She was attired in lurid scarlet blouse with broidered cuffs and neck, vest of yellow felt sewn with glimmering pearls, and ballooning orange trousers that clung to her thighs and billowed about her calves. Guy went to her, took her two hands in his. Both were very aware of watching eyes and listening ears.

"Thou art well, my sister?"

"I am well, my brother," she said, smiling quietly as her blue eyes met his brown ones.

"I hope that the wicked plan of our captor did not succeed, and that thou art not with child, my sister."

She lowered her pinkening face. "My thoughts and desires on that matter are . . . mixed, my brother."

Around them, the outlaw women laughed. The Crusader was not unaware of the open looks that had been lavished on him.

He was provided with leather-soled boots and snug white leggings and a knee-length Arabic outer shirt of deep blue, and a broad leather belt. Sitt found and brought to him a stave nearly six feet in length, along with a strip of gut. She watched with eyes of both an archer and a woman as he bent the stave, his arms bulging, and nodded; aye, it would make a fine bow.

There was more. Last night Julanar had said, "Stay with me this night, man among men." And Guy had responded by pushing still further, bargaining: "Provide clothing for my sister, woman of women." And now, obviously excited by his prowess and the bit of violence, Julanar had ordered Melisende clothed "as befits the sister of a man among men."

Guy had assumed those words to be a signal to him, and that he would be called again to her pavilion this night—for the weaving and pulling of her yarn. *"Akhmitu ghazla-ha,"* Arabic men said; "Thicken her yarn (or thread)" was the literal meaning. But the slang usage meant "Fuck her well." Another weaving term was applied as well: *" 'award o burd,"* "brought and bore away" applied to the to and fro movements of the loom, and to *ghunj,* the movements in fuckery.

He requested a shave or a blade, to rid his face of a fortnight's growth, but word came from Julanar: denied. With that word came the expected: his commanded presence in her pavilion.

"Only fourteen days?" she said, when he was there. "Ye raise a respectable beard in a fortnight, Guy Kingsaver. It is the way I know you; I like it. When it grows out more, it can be trimmed and shaped. For now—keep it." And on this mesa, with escape dependent on the horse-operated lift-cage and with Melisende to consider as well as himself, Guy had to accept Julanar's word as law. Until . . . opportunity arose.

This night she wore a bandeau, similar to those of the servants; the snowy silk contrasted beautifully with the bronze rounds of her bosom. A chain of slender golden links encircled her neck, depended upon her chest, vanished excitingly into the cleavage between the boldly high-perched thrusts of her breasts. A jeweled girdle supported what Guy eventually learned was a voluminous skirt, not pantaloons.

Their meal was a prelude, and both of them knew it. Their conversation, the movement of their mouths and tongues, was a prologue to their coming movements together. And then the meal was finished, the tables cleared but for a bowl of dates and wine, and the three servants again departed at command of their mistress. She leaned back, directing her smoky gaze at the Crusader from beneath glistening, night-black lashes. Her hand stretched out blindly, the three gold bands about her wrist clinking, and returned with a large date. As she set it between her lips, Guy moved from his divan to hers.

"That should be shared," he said quietly.

After he'd bitten half of it from her teeth, their lips remained together, moving together as they chewed. Her hand slid up his back; his went to her supple waist. Their mouths opened to unite restless, probing tongues. The kiss lengthened, warmed, grew more and more animated. Guy felt the familiar stirring of his own organ against his thigh.

His hand slid up over a silk-contained breast, firm and full and flawlessly rounded. She sighed into his mouth; suddenly her hands became claws that sank their nails into his back. At the same time, with a

95

sound that was neither a moan nor a growl but that contained the elements of both, she sank her teeth into his lower lip.

For many, many long minutes they fondled and caressed and embraced and kissed. Guy was intent on being the lover, not a mere cocksman. Most men were the latter; few filled the former role.

His tongue stroked her nipples, back and forth, from one to the other, until they were thick and hard and quivery. His teeth teased with a light nibbling; his hands massaged the virginally-hard ovals they decorated, arousing them until the fat centers contained every micro-inch of her aureoles and were thrusting eagerly into his mouth.

By this time she was moaning and writhing openly, and her hand was busy in his crotch, tracing out the great swollen length of the quarterstaff that had developed there.

The time for doffing clothes came. Their eager hands stripped each other—and Guy found that the Lioness of Egypt had still more surprises for him.

Her vulva was not available. Over it she wore a gleaming shield of padded, beaten gold, with a single toothy hole—that would admit no cock, even one far tinier than the big erection with which he saluted her. Frowning, his eyes met hers.

"I am virgin still," she said quietly, fondling his great swollen bollocks and sliding another hand over his massy chest. "And I shall remain so. But . . . I am open to thee, O my lover." And she turned over, so that he gazed down upon the naked, swollen summits of her arse, and its enticing peach-cleft.

The bands that encircled her thighs below those finely-molded buttocks were of gold; the one that encircled her hips above their swell was of black leather, broad as his thumb. She had sealed herself, but offered instead the garden gate, the channel up into her bowels.

His hands molded and manipulated the spongy cheeks, traced the warm crevice separating them, and he planted a kiss on each trembling summit. She sighed, squirmed, arched their superb curvaceousness up to him. Then she was sucking in a swift breath and releasing it in a long, vocal sigh, as he tested her openness with a spit-wetted, gently pushing finger.

It slid easily up into her rectum, a tribute to her powers of relaxation.

"It is the way I . . . excite and give myself release," she said softly, against the divan.

"It is the way I shall excite myself, and gain my release," he promised her in a voice as low, as he circled the finger inside that hot snug channel.

And he did, first arranging her comfortably with her upper body resting on elbows and forearms and her legs spread well apart, her lovely stern lifted to receive him. The cheeks of that velvety rump thus jutted out and up at him in pouting, long ovals.

She trembled, feeling the pressure of his swollen, blood-filled glans nudging at the tight elasticity of her clenching anus. Then she was breached, her flesh dilating and spreading all around his incoming meat-shaft, and his flesh-loving cock nosed hotly all the way into her rearward passage.

She moaned, deep in her throat. Her lithe hips began to undulate in time with the strong pumping strokes that drove her passion to a seething pitch. More and more swiftly, the turgid hugeness of his cock slid steadily and easily out of the little amber hole, and she felt it all the way along the hallway to her liquid bowels.

The buggering man trembled. The tight, clinging membranes of her arsehole were molded tightly around his imbedded stalk and his lunges flattened her broad, fleshy rump. Shiver after shiver of delight and arousal swept through her.

Delighted, he held her with both hands on her firm, flaring buttocks while he thrust in and out of the warm and super-tight chamber in an attempt to rush himself to the very pinnacle of sexuality—and over the edge.

Insurmountable lust sent sizzling sparks of desire charging through her. She snapped her supple body back and forth, riding the thick organ filling her anal hole. Behind her, he chuckled aloud in sheer delight. Now she fucked herself savagely on him, her rectum an expanding, welcoming cunt, she groaning and squirming as he fucked strongly, almost brutally up her widening arsehole, into her squirming guts.

She was an unashamedly passionate woman. Her belly rippled, filled with a sexual magic. She bounced up and down and twisted her hips to meet and take the powerful hips that pounded her and crushed her buttocks while driving their hot appendage between the quivering cheeks.

He knew that she reached her climax, an anal release, when she squealed and her body lurched into a series of massive, convulsive jerks and contractions. He pumped faster, harder, thumping her head and jiggling her body with the impacts of his hips on her butts.

Then his hips were jerking without control, and he was groaning, and his seed leapt from him, warm semen spewing into her in a series of jerking spurts that filled her encompassing arsehole's narrow tubeway to the bursting point with thick hot liquid.

He sank upon her, enwrapped her with his arms, and they lay panting and gasping, with his spent prick still up inside her dilated anal ring.

So tight was she that he did not lose his erection, and after a while he began pumping again, and they paused after a while, and with great care to move without losing their connection, they turned her over to face him her legs high and her rectum still impaled, the gold shield covering her vulva hard and chill against his lower belly, and then they fucked still more, until they were exhausted and fell into a sweet sleep.

NINE

Girls for the Sultan

Intoxicated with his lusty Egyptian paramour, a woman of less than twenty-four years, the Crusader—who was younger still—hardly noticed the passage of four days.

Nor, in his enchantment and since he and his "sister" were not allowed to converse, was Guy aware that Melisende de Bois-Courtenay was receiving no wine, and food of considerably lower quality than he; further, the lovely blonde had been set to work. In the wood-reinforced cave wherein were kept the horses and camels, she joined others of lowly station, in tending the beasts.

Guy learned that the captoress of his body and now of his mind was not only not a follower of Islam, she was *anti*-Muslim. Muhammad, she told him, founded a faith in which men were gods and women no more than slaves. She did not hate men, as men; she hated the faith, and what the men stood for. And above all, she hated the Turk.

Nay, above all, she loved Guy's body against hers, Guy's hands on her, Guy's charging penis hard and thick and long, up her back.

Then came the day when, as he sat working at turning the thick stave given him by Sitt into a bow, an excited scout raced into the camp to make her report. He noted well the subsequent excitement and activity in the camp, while pretending to devote all his attention to the task of laboriously wire-wrapping the powerful bow that would replace the one so far away in Richard's encampment.

Late in the afternoon, the Crusader was called to the great black pavilion of Julanar al-Libwah.

His Egyptian paramour wore the tightest-fitting shirt and leggings he had ever seen. He realized immediately that they were designed to be worn under armor.

"A Turkish caravan rides northeast from Cairo," she told him, excitedly. Her black eyes seemed to glow like moonlit pools of pure oil. "It is not huge, so as to attract little attention. A guard of thirty mounted men, with five camels and five wagons."

"Turks!"

"Aye. As you once said, my lover . . . that which we have most in common is a hatred for the Turkish overlords!"

Guy nodded. His brain began to work furiously, excitedly.

"Four of the five wagons," she said, "contain a *special* cargo, my lover." She paused, then flashed him the almost frightening grin she had shown him a few times previous; the grin of a predatory cat, intent on its soft prey. *"Women,* Guy! Girls, really. Girls, young and soft—for the soldiers of Salah ad-Din, the Kurdish peasant; *thirty* of them."

Salah ad-Din. It had been many days since Guy had thought of the conqueror Saladin. His breathing was rapid, his mind awhirl.

"Julanar!"

"My lover?"

"Do you keep Melisende here in the camp as hostage.

And return to me the mail I wore when I came here, and the long Frankish sword. And let me ride with you!"

She studied him for a few moments, then grinned lazily, like a well-fed and smug lioness. Certainly her sexual appetites had been fed well of late! "The girls," she told him, "are for *us*. Some will be servants . . . but some, surely, will become *members* of my band!"

He stared at her. "Allah's eyes, woman! Could I lust after soft little kittens when I have lain with a lioness? It's a tug at Saladin's beard I want . . . and Turkish blood on my blade!"

Again the slender outlaw studied him for a time in silence. Then, "Guy, my lover . . . if you ride at aught but Turks, slay aught but Turks, Melisende of the cloudlike hair shall die many deaths, hemorrhaging from a camel's cock up her belly, toothless, each hair of her cunt and then her head plucked forth, one by one. Only the truth I speak."

"Play at frightening me another day, Julanar. You insult me, and so I say: So be it. But it's fighting the Turks I lust for. When do we ride?"

He suffered another long, thoughtful scrutiny from her clever black eyes. Then she nodded, briefly. "At sundown."

"At night? No man fights at night!"

Julanar the Lioness smiled. "Women do," she told him.

Working swiftly in thin leather gloves, the Crusader completed the wiring of his new bow, then checked the Frankish armor he was brought, link by link. The previous owner had been not so tall as he, but as broad of shoulder and chest, and thicker through the gut. The steel shirt would fit.

The hot blood surged in Guy Kingsaver's veins like

mulled wine set fire to a man's brain. Ah, to fight the Turks again! To snatch from under his pointed vulture's nose Saladin's own playthings! To jerk his biforked beard . . . Guy grinned wolfishly and whistled through his teeth.

What a shock for them, he mused in high excitement, *when those enslaving Turks hear the cry* "Dieu le Veult"—*in Egypt!*

"DIEU LE VEULT!"

Just at dawn, five-and-forty yelling women, mail gleaming in the rising sun, charged down onto the Turkish camp. Julanar rode shrieking, waving her curved sword, surging forward on her big black horse, Guy on a superb roan, long bow in hand, shield on saddle, longsword of Spanish steel at his side.

A dozen men died bloodily in that first mad charge, which they were totally unable to meet. Pounding hooves and flashing scymitars tore through their ranks.

The nubile young maidens destined for Saladin's men tried to conceal themselves, shrieking and cringing, behind wagons and the trees of the oasis, or ran with flashing legs to take shelter behind rock outcrops.

Chopping away most of the face of a warrior-woman from his rearing gray-white horse, a snarling Turk swung his mount even as its forelegs touched the ground, and away he galloped, obviously without stomach for battle. In headlong pursuit pounded a roan horse carrying a silent man in armor of gray steel. Guy bent low, squinting his eyes against the wind of his own fleet mount's passage and against the beast's flying, whipping mane.

Within less than a league, he overtook the Turk. In passing, without so much as engaging the man, Guy sent his head arolling with one terrible sweeping chop of his long sword. Helmeted head went flying in a shower of blood to bound over the sand, leaving a red wake.

The horse galloped on for several yards before the headless rider toppled sidewise from the high-pommeled saddle and added a fresh spot of gore and crimson liquid to the thirsty sand.

Wheeling back to re-enter the fight with the joy of battle singing inside him, every muscle tingling, Guy saw ugliness. It must all have been a trap!

For now, bucketing down the long hill toward the oasis where Julanar's triumphant band was already dismounting to inspect bloodily won spoils, came a contingent of well-armed cavalrymen, mounted on fleet steeds and obviously intent on massacre . . . a squadron that was fully a hundred strong!

Guy's dark eyes swept about, taking stock of situation and terrain. Then he twitched the rein, turning leftward from his intended course, and bent low again as he spurred his roan into another stretched-out gallop.

Even as he fled across the Egyptian sands, the Crusader's slitted eyes picked out the leader of the ambushers: a man with silver-glittering armor and heron plumes cresting his helmet, waving and streaming in the breeze stirred by his loping mount.

The ambushing squadron was upon the warrior-women when Guy's horse attained the same hill over which the Turks had silently sped. He sped just as silently, hurtling down upon their rear.

Even as he rushed down the slope behind the new attackers, his enormously powerful new bow drove a feathered arrow into the back of one cavalryman with such force that the gore-smeared point tore through his armor in front and stood before his belly.

Then with shield up and heavy sword whirling in a silvery wheel of steel above his helmeted head, the

Crusader smashed into the Turkish rear. Aye, and Turks they were, not Cairenes at all; the ambuscade, then, was of the devising of Saladin's men, not the native Egyptians.

A short-bearded man with a scarred cheek fell before Guy's chopping blade, cloven through his chain-mail shirt from shoulder to nipple.

Another man spurred about to meet the maniac charging their rear, and in seconds his sword-grasping hand sailed away in a welter of liquid scarlet. A third Turk tried desperately to rein aside to get his shield up; Spanish steel chopped into his thigh to the bone. Guy twisted and jerked his blade free and spurred on into the mass of Turkish knights.

The sword whirled; a headless body toppled from a silk-streaming saddle, fountaining blood that splashed Guy's horse and the skirt of his surcoat. At the same time a scimitar rang off his shield on the opposite side. The berserk Crusader rammed mightily with that arm and set the fellow reeling in his saddle so that a screeching woman found him easy prey for her chopping, crescent-curved saber. Guy spurred on.

Then it was a squat, broad-shouldered man in silver-chased mailshirt and helmet decorated with nodding heron plumes that the Cypriot faced, both with swords dripping crimson.

" 'Tis a MAN-N-N ye face, son of a barn-cunted whore!" Guy bawled in filthy Arabic. "Guy Kingsaver —son of EblI-I-I-IISSSSSSSS!"

The heron-plumed leader of the ambushers might as well have tried to stem the fierce desert sandstorm as to meet the berserk, iron-muscled attack of a man gone happily mad with battle's lust. His shield was struck so hard that it was torn half away and his arm sprung from its socket; his scimitar met another whirling, slashing

105

chop, and its last six inches were sheared through and went flying away to scar the cheek of one of his own men.

Seconds later, the man in the plumed helmet, commander of men, was a man no longer but a corpse, and his slayer was slashing away at the shield of still another man—and then at his mailed arm. It flew from his shoulder, still gripping that torn and bent shield.

Splashed with blood, his chest rising and falling in great lung-swelling breaths beneath his shirt of gray steel mesh, the Crusader sat his horse in a space clear of all but corpses and blood-pumping men becoming corpses. As he swung his head in search of a new direction in which to launch his attack, his eyes went wide.

Even as he looked, an unhorsed Turk stabbed upward with his curved scimitar—into the belly of a great black horse. The animal screamed out its agony and its life poured out in a twisting spaghetti of looping intestines that dangled to the ground. Its rider, wearing flashing breastplates of solid gold over her mailshirt—and jet-black tabard, plunged forward over the beast's head as it went to its knees. Its slayer died, pop-eyed, under the body of the falling horse.

And the sprawling Julanar looked up at a saber of Damascene steel that was already starting its downward rush toward her neck.

Guy Kingsaver dug in his spurs to the blood. His horse shrilled a cry, then, as if hurled from a catapult, it careened forward to slam into the mount of Julanar's nemesis. The path of the sword descending upon her was changed; the hardswung scimitar rang off her helmet in a shower of sparks, rather than sheared through her throat.

Before the reeling man knew what had befallen him to spoil his murderous aim, his Saracen soul went flying down to hell, aided by Guy's comet-rushing sword.

"Onto that horse, lion cub!" the Crusader bawled.

But the woman on the ground was beyond mounting or hearing, sagging to earth to lie prostrate. The chain-mail kerchief binding her helmet was torn; the helm itself bore a goodly dent. She lay still.

Hurling aside his shield and clinging to his rein, Guy swung down from his high-curved Arabic saddle. Even as his feet struck the ground, he was scooping the limp body up in his sword arm, not knowing whether she might be dead or dying, but determined that she should not be trampled by the eddying tide of the battle.

Then he was forced to drop her again to the ground, in order to parry a blow and to chop a knee into splinters mingled with twisted chain mail, sword-torn like cloth. The man plunged by on his bay horse, screaming; Guy again picked up the fallen Lioness.

This time he boosted her across his horse's saddle, her head dangling off one side and legs down the other, her mail-shining butt high in the air. With the flat of his sword he gave the animal a mighty blow on its heaving, sweat-shining haunch. With a squeal, the beast bolted forward and was a hundred yards away in seconds, still galloping.

The fallen body of a woman nearly bowled over the Crusader as she was toppled from her horse with her mailshirt and the breasts beneath in crimson tatters. He let her fall, and was in her saddle seconds after she had slammed to the ground. Guy's sword swung, chopped; the woman's slayer joined her posthaste.

Then Guy Kingsaver of Messaria, unaware that he had put fully nine of their number out of the battle, was watching the mad flight of the remaining Turks. Nine . . . including their leader . . . but without taking into account the three he had slain of the little caravan's original escort.

Fully sixty men lay dead or quickly pumping out

their lives from wounds that no one would staunch or treat. Perhaps dead or dying, Julanar al-Libwah was out of the combat, and so was a ghastly toll of her female warriors: no less than twenty-one of them lay bleeding.

As the battle madness began to fade from the Crusader's eyes, he found himself staring at Aziza across a carpet of cooling corpses.

"The wagons," he said, and she nodded.

"I saw all, or nearly," the woman who had never warmed to him said, and she added, *"ya layth!"*

Then she was spouting orders, and the remnant of her command as Julanar's second were checking their dead and wounded and hurrying about to round up the wagons and the terrified girls that Saladin's men would now never see.

For a moment Guy sat still atop the horse he had commandeered, his eyes bemusedly following Aziza.

Ya layth, she had called him: *O Lion!* His proving his prowess with bow and quarterstaff in the camp, his being the obvious favorite of her commander, none of these had won the faintest glance or word of respect or friendship from her. But his actions this day had, and she admitted it with those two words bestowed upon the man worthy of playing the lion to her chieftain's lioness.

Hoping his roan horse with its limp burden had been headed straight back to the mesa of the outlaw encampment—and without losing its senseless rider along the way—Guy at last awoke and galloped off in its wake.

Within a league, swaying and afflicted with a sore headache that had her cursing with the vehemence of a Pisan sailor and the eloquence of a knight of Thuringen, Julanar came cantering to meet him, astride his horse.

She stopped, reining in to stare at the big blood-spattered man riding toward her. Like Aziza, she well knew that the Frankish knight they had made their prisoner had saved them all from annihilation, as well as Julanar's life, personally and alone.

TEN

Idyll

"Thou art my lion," the proud commander of that army of female outlaws said, once they were back atop their fantastic aerie-nest. And she dropped to her knees before Guy of Messaria. "I am thy woman."

The Crusader stood over her, gazed down upon her. "Mine?"

She met his eyes with the black pools of hers. "Only the truth I speak, *ya layth*."

Guy did not smile. "On your feet, woman—lionesses do not kneel!"

She rose slowly, her mouth uptilting at the corners. She had been knocked unconscious in the battle, and that only. As tokens she retained a lump on her head and an ache within, under her mass of night-black hair. Now, slowly and with her eyes on him, she peeled off surcoat and armor and then the snug-fitting clothing beneath. Again the dark-tipped thrusts of her breasts braced him, joggling softly with her movements. Again the golden shield she wore over her untrammeled vaginal depths glinted and flashed at him from the base of her near-flat belly.

She came to him, walking naturally as a confident and competent woman, rather than swaying seductively.

Her hands rose to him as the tips of her breasts touched his surcoat.

"My lion wears too many clothes," she said, and together the two of them remedied that.

"I am no longer a captive?" a naked Guy asked a naked Julanar.

Meeting his eyes directly, she spoke without hesitation: "You slew more than any of my pack of she-wolves; you destroyed the trap and in all likelihood saved us from annihilation . . . and you saved my life. You are no longer a captive, Guy Kingsaver. You are my man, my lion and my love." Her eyes were bright with the fervor of her words.

He nodded, noting that though she assured him he was no longer a captive or a slave, she made him sound like a possession. . . .

"Aye," he said. "Julanar . . . I am also squire to him the Turks called Malek Ric, my liege-lord. I cannot remain here, Lioness of Egypt."

After a moment of wide-eyed staring, she lowered herself sinuously to her knees and spread wide her arms.

"Slay me! Strike here, between these breasts I offer you! Slay me physically, Guy Kingsaver, for by talking of leaving you slay my mind and soul!"

For a moment he considered laughing at the melodrama. But he did not; could she be serious? He went to her discarded clothing, slid her dagger from its sheath, and returned to set its point between the mouthwatering pears suspended on her chest.

"You are ready to die then, woman?"

"What other man could there be, for such a woman as I am?"

Guy touched her naked skin with the point of her dagger; she continued only to gaze steadily at him. Then, swiftly, he lowered the blade and sliced through

111

first one, then the other of the leathern cords that held her self-imposed chastity belt in place.

Her eyes flared wide as that padded golden shield fell, like a dropped drawbridge, to bare the defenseless triangle of her loins. Soft fleecy curls of jet black completely obscured the furtive crevice he knew nestled there. Unopened, as she said?

He found out, on the instant. Her dagger was not the only object he'd fetched from her discarded clothing. He had, also, her three-tailed whip, and while his left hand pushed her over backward, his right thrust it at her. The thick, leather-wrapped handle of her lash rushed toward the valley of her belly.

The back-sprawling Julanar started a cry that broke off into a gasp of pain and shock as he thrust it into her puckered, hymen-sealed cunt.

The whip handle tore its way into her, splitting those tight-clenched lips wide and creating its own blood-lubricated tunnel as it plunged in with the force of his arm. She cried out at that brutal first invasion of her cuntal canal. Her body squirmed desperately as the coarse handle of her own lash seared fiery pain through her unused passage. Her mouth dribbled moans that she tried hard to keep him from hearing.

"You invited me to strike, to slay," he told her hoarsely. "I have, Julanar—but it is not your death I want, lioness!"

He pulled the cruel instrument of her defloration out of her. Blood drooled forth with it. Then he jolted it in again, increasing the rawness of tormented inner membranes. Trembling violently, she writhed her gorgeously curved body in burning pain. But she did not seek to escape, or to oppose him.

"Now," he grunted, holding the savage cock-substitute well up in her, "you know how Melisende felt, daughter of Eblis!"

112

Her eyes were full of pain as she looked up at him.

"All . . . right. I invited you to slay; you slew only the bit of skin I have kept intact all these years, since my father lusted for it and I slew him and fled. Now you have your revenge for your sister's maidenhead. I suppose it is justice. And what now, my lion?"

"Now, my lioness, you experience what else she did—though immediately, not after two days."

He pulled the whip handle out of her. It was red-smeared. He discarded it, and moved swiftly.

One quick movement sent his violently erect organ into her crimsoned cleft and the burning circlet beyond, unheeding her groans and pleas and threats. A flood of virginal blood enveloped his turgid prick. It was considerably thicker than the handle of her whip, and she emitted an un-pretty grunting noise as she felt herself stretched anew, now around a throbbing sliding hardness that enforced all her attention on her crotch. Every nerve in her body seemed to end there, in that tortured hole.

He plowed in deep, pushing with his toes in an effort to pierce her very womb. Her cunt was like the hungry, fur-rimmed mouth of a lamprey eel, feeding, sucking away at his engulfed tool. She was very, very tight inside.

She ran her tongue nervously over her lips, staring fixedly up at him. Her lithe belly and legs quaked. Long tremors ran through her. But he remained still within her, holding his weight off her slippery, sweat-soaked body by propping himself on his elbows, lying there gazing into her face while his big shaft stretched her supple labia.

For many minutes he eased it in and out of her, in long, slow strokes that made her feel the constant lascivious distention of her fluid-filled niche, the slippery gliding of his great staff of manhood inside that natural channel she had so long kept closed, like a treasure vault, whilst proffering the unnatural one in the division of her backside.

Minute followed minute as he carefully, slowly, gently plied her with his prick.

He knew when her face changed, when her reactions and responses changed, when her natural sensuality took over within her. He could see it, in the tremor of her skin, the twisting of her face, the surprised look in her eyes, the way constant erotic thrills jolted the long-virginal beauty, until she was shaking and shivering.

The heaving turrets of her breasts swelled, heavy with passion and humid carnality. He pushed and pulled, pumping her now-welcoming chalice with steady strokes that suffused her face with joy. She moaned in a helpless, feverish ecstasy.

And then Guy pushed back, and back, and drew his wet-shining staff totally out of her.

For several seconds she lay there, blinking in surprise, staring up at him. Her tongue came out, slicked over her lips. They gazed at each other in silence.

At last she said, "I . . . have been fucked."

Almost, he smiled.

A little frown worried its way over her forehead: "You have not spent?"

"You know I climax like a storm!"

Her breasts heaved, jiggled liquidly as she sighed. She turned her face aside, started to speak. Then, with obvious warrior's resolve, she faced him again.

"Then finish what you've only begun, my lion."

He smiled, bent to plant a kiss on each of her nipples. His tongue coursed over them until they glistened brightly, wetly as they jutted pinkly forth in strong erection.

"Ah," she sighed, half closing her eyes. "They feel swollen to bursting!"

114

Then he set about finishing what he'd begun, having met a worthy warrior in combat and, as so many times in past, having conquered. He positioned himself between her splayed legs, staring down at the burgeoning pole that jutted forth from the auburn mat of his loins, to touch the parted vermilion lips behind her own thick forest of jet-black curls.

He stuck her with it in one good swift lurch, and in an instant her excited and welcoming cleft had taken it all, all the way to his hairy scrotal pouch. She groaned and shivered; the blood pounded at his temples. They were again united, and this time her virginal belly had accepted and swallowed his full breadth and length, all at once.

Smiling, she put her hands on him, began jogging her rump, seeking still more prodding of that hot maleness, loving the throbbing invader that cruised her warm, dark depths. His hands swept beneath her, warm on her teasing buttocks.

He probed his cock into her fully open vulva and began jackknifing his hips, clenching his hands on the supple mounds of her nether cheeks. He poled it to her, good. She began writhing her smooth belly under him, against him, grinding her butt into his clenching fingers and slapping his furry pelvis with hers.

He released those sexy cheeks and propped himself above her on both hands, as if exercising.

"Move!" he commanded. "Shake that pretty arse! *Grind* that sweet ass, woman!"

She grinned lewdly and obeyed with fervent enthusiasm.

He could hear the susurrant hissing sounds as the clenching half-moons of her rump glided back and forth. He could feel her thighs against his, her soft-skinned belly rubbing his, and the strong suctioning pull of her cuntlips around his penis.

Her steaming passage felt as if it was trying to come together, to crush his big driving bone in a vising grip. Inside, she had become a frenzied well of desire in which he submerged his virile meatstaff.

She was ready for more; he gave her more. He slammed his hips forward, his nakedness glistening with a coat of sweat. Pure ecstasy streamed through the length of his encunted shaft. The little jerks of her agitated body added to the delight, increasing the friction around his encompassed erection. He squirmed atop her in a transcendent rapture, loving the feel of her belly's satiny smoothness.

She accepted it, she took it, she gloried in it.

Their bodies slapped together loudly, hands moving and seeking, hips writhing against each other. Her breasts were like hard tight fists against his chest. Her breath hissed between her set teeth in panting gasps. She jerked and plunged, screwing herself with squealing gusto, and he grinned, enjoying her wild thrashing beneath his plunging body.

His heart was pounding wildly as he humped her, driving his thick knight's lance deep into her now-gaping lower mouth—which was gulping down, inch by inch, all of that swollen staff he could stuff up her.

He shuddered. His organ was being gripped by excruciatingly powerful muscles, deceptively sheathed in soft wet silk.

He could not hold back any longer; she was far too tight and far too exuberantly cooperative.

A groan escaped him as he tried to stem the sudden rushing tide. As well try to blow back the wind. His aching cock began spitting forcefully into her. The milkish fluid of his boiling load shot into her tight, clenching cunt. She cried out as she received it, and gripped him tightly.

He lay for a time on her, while her hands and arms strove to crush his body.

Then, aware that she had not spent, he moved, letting his emptied penis slide from her inundated slit, and with his fingers he rubbed and circled and pressed her clitoris, while she moaned and twitched and tossed her head.

It took a long time. His wrist grew tired, but still he strove to give her release, and at last she filled the air with shivering squeals. She lurched, jerked, groaned, and her hand rushed to remove his as she slid into the soft sweet daze of final consummation.

After a time, she rose and performed the necessary ablution to avoid that which she feared most, getting with child. She returned, beautiful and glowing, to where he lay. She dropped to hands and knees beside him, her breasts jiggling wildly beneath her.

For a long time they stared into each other's eyes.

Then Guy pulled her down onto him, and her hand slipped between them to encircle his cock, and they began anew.

ELEVEN

Murder

In the morning she was relaxed and warm and open when he bored in between her soft labia, spreading the supple folds farther and farther as he pushed his churning tool into her. Totally exquisite sensations raged through him like a fever as he sank between her legs.

They parted, widened. Her desire rose ebulliently. Her arms leapt up to encircle him. Like twin mountain peaks beneath his hard chest, her quivering breasts surged their sherry nipples. She groaned. Her belly seemed to knot up with an intensity that matched that of the thick rod he sank into her body.

Her cunt tightened up, milking him in unbelievably ebullient contractions. Again he spurted her full; again he fingered her gristly, wobbly little clitoris until he was tired. This time she stopped him, apparently needing no release.

They lay naked, toying with each other.

Her servants called her in soft voices without daring to enter; Julanar ordered them away. Aziza came, requesting audience to discuss yesterday's booty; Julanar bade her return later.

"Much later," Guy whispered.

"Much later," Julanar called, and rolled giggling onto him.

They did nothing that day, lion and lioness who had discovered each other. She brought him dates and nuts and meat and Guy called her *jariyah:* slavegril. She laughed at that, and they laughingly dressed her in white bandeau that barely contained the dazzling swells of her breasts, and loose trousers of some transparent stuff of pale blue, and jingly bracelets. And she fed him morsels of meat and nuts and dates, bite by bite, with her own fingers. With her dagger he slashed her trousers, then ordered her to her hands and knees as if she were indeed his slave. Chuckling, she assumed that unfamiliar posture, and he crouched and entered her from behind.

"Ah . . . ah! Put it into my anus! Up my back!"

"No," he said, and he did not.

Neither of them left her pavilion that day, nor did anyone enter. They slept away much of the afternoon; awoke hungry. They cleansed each other with wet cloths, giggling, and dressed. She called for her servants, who brought them dinner. Guy ate ravenously, and drank deeply of the good aged wine from Shiraz.

She bade the three girls leave then, and took a great mouthful of wine, which she transferred to his mouth in a long heated kiss of lingering sensuality and promise.

Suddenly she drew back to stare excitedly at him. She looked . . . girlish.

He put his head on one side to give her a questioning smile. "Julanar?"

"I . . . have thought. Yes! Yes . . . I shall give you a present!"

"You have," he told her quietly.

But she bounced to her feet, wearing voluminous white pantaloons and the breastplated vest over a blouse the color of polished new gold. "Ah, but you will *love* this present!" she assured him, and the Crusader sat wearing a whimsical smile while she hurried out of the pavilion that he had not left in more than twenty-four hours.

She returned, smiling smugly, secretly, and sat opposite him. He did not speak, though he looked questioningly at her. But she also remained silent, maintaining her secret, though she was obviously full of it to bursting, nervous and fidgety.

The secret came. Two secrets.

They were nervous, and shy, and fearful, and they looked at him and at her and all about the pavilion. This within the first few seconds after they had entered. Then they stood straight and still, seemingly examining their feet.

Girls. Two of the newly-gained girls from Cairo, those intended for the recreation of Saladin's men until Julanar and Guy and her band had stolen them from the caravan. Both of them appeared quite young, indeed.

The one with the extravagantly curly hair that seemed flecked with red in its twisting, convoluted mass of black, wore a tight-cuffed blouse with broadly belling sleeves. It tied behind her neck and beneath her breasts, and it was sewn with pearls and semi-precious stones in several colors; the color of the blouse was rose. An expanse of surprisingly pale skin stretched between the ties of the blouse and the thick, jeweled hip-band of her ballooning *sirwal,* which were partly transparent. She was very slender, though she was far from boyish or breastless.

The other was plump; had she not been, her breasts would have been ridiculous. They were huge, bulging out against the fitted top of her caftan-styled dress, which covered nearly all of her body. Her face was round, full of cheek and lips, and both mouth and eyelids had been tinged with *surmeh,* a preparation of crude antimony that, unlike kohl, imparted a purplish hue. Her long coal-black hair decorated her shoulders so far down her back as to caress her buttocks.

"Had you reached your destination, you would have provided pleasure for the soldiers of Salah ad-Din," Julanar said quietly. "All your days and nights would have been filled, and so would you have been, with a progression of erect cocks jutting from nameless and faceless bodies. It was your destiny, or so Salah ad-Din thought. Eventually you'd have become unattractive, or cavernously large between the legs and in your bung-holes where, too, they'd have used you—or with child. Then you'd have been discarded, and only Allah can say what you might have had to do to gain a bit of bread daily."

They stood unmoving, but Guy saw that each of them was taken by a tremor at her harsh words.

"Here, we are free women, who live and eat well and answer to no man. As to this man: he be a Frank, as ye can see. He defeated my best at archery and at quarterstaffs, and he it was yesterday who spoiled the trap the Turks had laid for us. Hear ye both: he slew no less than thirteen men, and was unscathed, for no sword can come within the silvery circle of his great blade."

They blinked. The plump girl lifted her lashes to dart a look at Guy; saw his eyes on her and swiftly veiled hers once more. They stood still, hands behind their backs.

"He is Guy Kingsaver, of Frankistan, a warrior of Malek Ric of the lion's heart. I am Julanar the Lioness, and he is my lion. And tonight you are ours. You are here for our pleasure; you two I have chosen from all the others. What are your names?"

Their names, they advised in subdued voices, were

Miska, she of the curling hair, and Shemselnihar, the plump one, whose parents must have welcomed her indeed; her name meant Sun of Day.

"You will divest yourselves of your clothes," Julanar told Shemselnihar and Miska.

Both shot Guy glances from beneath their dark lashes; Miska turned a frowning face on Julanar. That swiftly, Julanar's three-lashed whip whushed out to enwrap the young Egyptian's hip and snap its nasty kiss onto her lightly-pantalooned buttocks.

The girl's face twisted and she jerked, clapping her hands to her burning bottom in a way that made it hard for Guy not to grin, despite the swift and surely unnecessary meting out of cruel pain to her slim young body.

"We are not cruel," Julanar assured, "but I am sole commander here, and I am accustomed to being obeyed, not stared at."

Plump little Shemselnihar's enveloping gown was half off, and before her sullen companion had begun untying her blouse, the darker girl with the long straight hair stood naked before Guy. Though her loins were shorn and her bulging cunnus thus invitingly displayed, all raw and naked and inviting and most vulnerable in appearance, it was her breasts that drew his eyes; they were very large, far too big to stand up and brace the world, but great naked ovals of shining flesh that dangled like elongated melons ready to be picked from the bough. Large, red-brown aureoles extruded tiny nipples that were even darker.

"I chose one slender and one otherwise," Julanar said, paying no attention as Miska divested herself of blouse and trousers. "Like you her with the cow's udders?"

Guy nodded. "I would not call them so," he said, with a catch in his throat; the sight of such immense tits made his mouth dry, made him anxious to suckle at their nipples, drawing them out longer.

Julanar stood, nodding. And she began stripping.

With a little smile tugging at his lips, Guy also stood. But he did not touch his clothing. "Shemselnihar," he said, "strip me."

She trembled, licked her lips, blinked—and stepped quickly forward to obey, her great breasts dancing and jiggling with every move she made. They brushed him again and again, as she removed his clothing, gazing admiringly, appraisingly at his rising cock in a way no virgin would have dreamed of.

When she was before him again, he seated himself—and reached for her breasts. He clutched them in both hands, cupping the soft, swollen undercurves in his big hands and lifting the little nipples with their large settings to his mouth. She sighed as he suckled impatiently at each dainty protrusion, pulling and drawing strongly to make them fatten and lengthen. Her hands came to his head, her fingers slithered through his hair, she sighed, and held his face against her huge melons with their tiny centers.

"Do that to me," he heard Julanar's voice, and when he lifted his head to glance around Shemselnihar, he saw that slender Miska's rounded little buttocks were turned up at him, bowls placed in the center of the flare of her hips, and tightly cleft. She did as she'd been bid, bending her curly head to kiss the other woman's breasts with her soft lips, her tongue licking and swirling over the tips of those shapely tits.

Miska sucked and licked Julanar's jiggling beauties until the nipples were superbly diamond hard; Guy drew and sucked at Shemselnihar's extraordinary eminences, working to draw out their nipples, which were recalcitrant.

123

"Umm," she sighed, "ah—oh my lord . . . let me . . . let me . . ."

He lifted his head from his saliva-wet feast. "Let you —what?"

She smiled, caressed his face, and slowly began shrinking. Or so it appeared; she was bending at the knees, going to them before him.

"Ah—ah, suck, you sweet little bitch!" Julanar throated out to Miska—and Shemselnihar obeyed.

She went after Guy's swollen prick without urgency, raising and lowering her hot wet mouth over it, steadily lapping it with her slithering tongue as she eased it slickly in and out of her face. Her full lips made smacking noises as she drew them up and all the way off over the big red head, then thrust them back down again until she endangered her breathing.

The girl sucked the thick staff deep and hard, in a seeming effort to strangle herself with it, to engulf its entire length inside her bobbing head. She sighed around that great mouthful as she moved her head gently up and down, up and down.

"Kneel," Guy heard Julanar say, excitedly. He glanced at her, over Shemselnihar's head; saw that the lioness was avidly watching him and his fellatrix. She flashed him a smile, thrusting Miska down with her hand on each of her slender, narrow shoulders. The curly-haired girl went to her knees; Julanar's hands slid into her hair, tugged.

The girl's back bowed as her head went forward to nestle between Julanar's clasping thighs. Guy stared at the kneeling girl's widened arse-crease, at the dark shadowy cleavage between those small buttocks, at the tuft of black hair that curled back at the very base of that long fissure. He saw that Julanar was tensing her legs, tightening and relaxing her buttocks in unison so that she was fucking herself up and down against the girl's face.

Julanar's head went back; she emitted a long, throaty sigh.

"Ah yes—lick deep, deep, little slut—ahhhhhhhhh!"

Guy was trembling at the delicate friction of Shemselnihar's lips as she sucked, her head pumping up and down. The muscles of her throat worked smoothly, drawing at his enormously swollen glans. He surged helplessly forward, straining her full lips as her mouth willingly accepted and engulfed even more of his broad, bulging organ.

His hands slid down onto the grandiose curves and radiant warmth of her breasts. He caressed the milk-soft bulges, molded them, pressed them together and sank his fingers into the resilient flesh, his hands roaming back and forth and over them, teasing and arousing their delicate little nipples.

Above Miska's bowed back and enslaved head, the crowns of Julanar's breasts were violently, quiveringly erect; she was watching all that Guy and the other Cairene girl did.

He tried to imagine what it was like to be a woman, to be Julanar at this moment, the unbounded delight as her lover began lapping, licking and sucking at her soft-furred cunt, feeling a sweet busy mouth making oral love to the musky, squishing slit, feeling the slithery tongue gliding over her twitching love-button. . . .

He was sure it felt as good as the oscular and lingual attention he was receiving.

Enveloped in the soft inner caress of loving mouth, his cock twitched and flames of lust rose in him. He was wild about the way her pretty purple mouth seemed to pulse teasingly up and down the full swollen length of his pecker. His body was coated with gooseflesh; his prick was more than half swallowed by that sweet mouth.

His hands clenched around her huge tits; she shivered and sucked with all her strength. Noisily, fervently, the sensual little bitch sucked cock. His hips pushed automatically, helplessly forward in short fucking motions.

He fucked her face.

Then it wasn't enough; he had to be inside her body, wallowing on that plump flesh and feeling the fat give of her tits beneath his chest. In seconds he had tipped her back and over, and was on the floor with her, heedless of the guttural grunting, gasping noises Julanar was making.

Shemselnihar smiled up at him: the sensual maiden lay wantonly squirming, shaken with tremors, shaking her tremorous mountains of tit, her legs shifting so that his eyes were drawn by the play of the muscles along supple, butter-soft thighs. Even as he loomed over her, the misty languour of rising passion dewed her dark eyes.

He pushed forward at her nakedly shorn loins, and quivered when he felt her hand enclose his cock, guiding it to its nest. The soft little sex-lips closed hungrily around the crown of his incoming prick. Immediately, she pushed herself onto it.

Little sounds of effervescent rapture gurgled up from her throat as she felt the relentless, pleasant distending of her delicate inner layers of spongy flesh. Her entire desirous organism seemed to rush out to pull him into the waiting oval slit of her loin. Holding onto him with a shocking strength and fervor, she pushed until she felt his pulsing male strength deep inside the haven of her pelvic basin.

He began moving hard and fast, immediately. His prick was hot and hard in the tight grip of her cunt, which he pumped rhythmically, loving the luxurious feel of her heaving flesh under his. Her breasts were like two great silken pillows for his comfort; her thighs were a fine padding for his lunging hips.

He rose, got himself onto his elbows, got his hands onto those outsized breasts. He commenced mauling the soft nipples with enveloping intimacy, so that she writhed and wriggled violently. She hunched to him, levering her pelvis up while he continued kneading the soft tit flesh. Her well-rounded, squirmy ass was pounded into the pavilion's carpeted flooring as he stoked her inner fires with the poker of his loins.

A few steps away, the other girl was working at Julanar's soft loins with lips and tongue. A surging cataract of lust rocked the naked body of the woman called lioness. She was gasping for breath, so desperately that there was the sound of voice in every intake of air. The kneeling girl who mouthed her crotch deliberately let her hear the soupy slurping noises she made around and in that flowing slash.

Julanar groaned, jerked, bit her lips to keep from crying out. The rising and falling of Guy's muscular body, the pumping of his hips and small, tight male buttocks, became a misty vision she was not sure she saw.

And of a sudden her lover ceased her oral ministrations, and looked proudly up at Julanar's face, between her swollen, hard-tipped tits.

"My mistress is pleased with me and my mouth?" she asked, in a purring voice.

Julanar stared down at her. Her eyes blazed; she quivered. The girl was so smug; she sought control, and now interrupted so as to prove it, to be begged to continue.

"Little *slut,*" Julanar the Lioness hissed, and Miska had no time for any reaction but enormously widened eyes as the other woman's hand rushed down.

Into the kneeling girl's fist-sized left breast plunged Julanar's dagger, and blood spurted, and Miska's eyes rolled and her mouth went slack as she jerked and quivered, like a leaf in a rising wind. The breath gushing from her mouth was the only sound she made. Her eyes remained wide and staring as she sagged.

"Ah—ahhhhh," Julanar al-Libwah gasped. She screwed up her eyes as it happened, her body seized and gripped and shaken in the physical and emotional power of orgasm. Her body seemed to fall in on itself in uncontrollable and overpowering climax that left her weak with rapturous satiation.

She glanced down at the huddled girl, at Guy and the other one on the floor. He had not seen; neither had Shemselnihar. They did not know that where there had been four there were but three; that one had died in a moment of anger and passionate lust for satiation, and in dying had provided the outlaw queen with the most marvelous orgasm of her life.

"P—" she gasped, and had to swallow and take a breath before trying again to form words. "Please, my darling lion—roll over so that I may see her great bobbing rump as you lance her womb!"

Without looking up, the Crusader grinned. He was no follower of Muhammad and Allah, to be shocked and horrified at a woman's coming between him and heaven! Without losing his penile anchorage in the plump, gasping girl, he enwrapped her with his arms and rolled onto his side, then onto his back. He grunted; she was no lightweight burden, stretched this way atop him!

He could not see what Julanar was doing.

First she tipped Miska sidewise, so that the curly-headed Cairene flopped onto her back. Then, crouching, Julanar withdrew her dagger. It was followed by a great swelling of scarlet. Into that growing pool of blood the Lioness dipped the handle of her whip. . . .

Shemselnihar wriggled her rump up from the man beneath her, gasping and pounding at him, taking his mighty wand of masculinity deeply up her belly every time his powerful body lunged up to hers. His arms were warm around her, big and enveloping, his hands fastened on the buttocks that thrust up and out in majestic mounds above her, opening them, spreading them, widening the crease between them so that she felt the kiss of cool air in that hot, heaving crease.

Then Shemselnihar shrieked, and Guy groaned as she slammed down against him. Her rectal tunnel felt as if it had flamed up and was afire.

Something big and thick, and slick with wetness, was being crammed up into her from behind, scraping her sensitive inner walls and grinding along them against the mighty cock thumping her from beneath, slicing and sliding in the contiguous hole of her agonized body.

With a wild light in her eyes, with her hips jerking orgiastically, Julanar forced the blood-greased handle of her whip farther and farther in between the plump, clenching cheeks of the girl.

Shemselnihar shrieked, jerked wildly, desperately strove to escape the burning invader of her bowels. But then Guy was supporting even more weight; Julanar, sprawling on the girl's back, held her in place atop him—and kept the searing whip handle in place with her own hunching cunt.

It hurt, it hurt—but Julanar sighed and groaned and twisted, loving even the hurt, loving the knowledge that she was giving the other girl both a thrill and pain. . . .

All three of them hurtled into orgasm, groaning and gasping and lurching about. Their sweat poured, streamed, mingled.

Shemselnihar cried out when the weight left her back, but fingers slid into her hair and jerked. Her eyes bulged and squirted tears when Julanar dragged her off Guy and dumped her on the floor on her back—with the whip still implanted up her rectum.

"O my lion," Julanar panted, kneeling to suck the cream off Guy's subsiding penis, "my darling, my life . . . we shall love and fight and raid and kill and kill—and love again . . . and if our lives be short, why then we shall have LIVED!"

The Crusader was a long while assimilating the scene. Then he knew; Miska was dead, her chest and abdomen covered with blood, and Shemselnihar had turned onto her stomach and dragged the bloody whip-handle out of her arsehole.

Julanar had spent, hugely.

He stared down at her bobbing head, and he shuddered. He had known she was an odd mixture. Now he realized that she was stranger than he had thought; the Lioness was not wholly sane, and therefore terribly dangerous.

TWELVE

Duel to the Death

Miska and Shemselnihar, Julanar told the others brought from the caravan, had sought to attack her in the night. And then she, along with Aziza and two others, began the recruiting process with those frightened young women. The quiet converse went on for a long while.

Guy occupied that time in thinking.

He had to get away from this place. There was not just the matter of trying to make his way back to the crusading host that was the hope of Christendom. In addition to that, there was the plain fact that Julanar al-Libwah was more than erratic; she was obviously less than fully sane.

One moment she was his lover, the next his slave, the next an excited girl with a surprise, like a child about Guy's present. And then she was the stern and powerful lioness, ruthlessly using her whip on Miska for a misdemeanor, then sharply ordering the girl to suck, first her tits and then the slash of her loins. And then, swiftly, with seeming uncontrollable passion . . . murder. Miska was dead, for no reason!

And later, while Guy was out behind the pavilion relieving himself, she had slain Shemselnihar!

Julanar had patiently explained to him that there were thirty of the girls, that they must not know of this night; she needed them. Shemselnihar would certainly have told them of Miska's death and her own sadistic buggery with the whip handle. Thus, naturally, Shemselnihar had to be silenced; surely Guy could see the obvious!

He had to leave this place.

But there were two complications. First, Melisende. He could not leave a Western woman here, could not leave *her* here. The second complication, though, thrust all else into the background. There was no way for them to leave this mesa together. There was one way down. Whether she called him lion or lover or master, Julanar was not likely to permit him and Melisende to descend at the same time.

It was to continue the waiting game, then. The dangerous waiting game. Meanwhile, he could observe, and remember. A time would come, surely.

He knew that were Julanar to order Melisende slain, or to start to do it herself, he could and would attack. Otherwise . . . no. Guy was not so constructed; he knew he could not even hold a knife at her throat and demand his and Melisende's release.

The others? No. A man must accept responsibility—and know where it ends.

He would wait, then. At least he had partial freedom, so long as he was cautious. The Crusader entertained no notion of trying to learn how far he could go with her before Julanar curbed him. No, he could not utilize his lack of chains to wander too freely about the camp. But he did decide to tell her the truth about himself.

He did, that night, in a strange situation: he knew Julanar was to be feared. He no longer wanted to make love with her. On the other hand, how could he refuse her? That might well return the shackles to his ankles, or bring worse down upon Melisende, despite his having saved Julanar's life. Besides . . . he was a man.

Thus he again enveloped himself in her hot and juicy interior, pushing hard and deep as though he were raping her, his cock rolling juicily in and out of her, pounding with a maniacal lust into the deep narrow channel while his hands maltreated her breasts, squeezing the eminently squeezable tit-flesh all the while his body pounded hers, surging forward and back, in and out, until he had spurted a tidal wave of warm milky juice into her and then was lying upon her, gasping for the time required for his heartbeat to return to normal.

Then he told her, told her that he was from Messaria on Cyprus, and that Melisende was not his sister.

She came fluidly to an erect sitting position. "Not your sister?" she said, with an odd light in her eyes, and suddenly he saw her mouth curve into that smile of the predatory cat she was named for. "Then . . . she does not *matter* to us!"

Guy knew instantly that he had erred, and he tried not to talk too rapidly.

"She doesn't," he said. "She is a Frank, a Christian, and so am I. You must not do her harm, Julanar." He fought his desperation; kept his voice calm. "I have not spoken with her or asked to, and I have shown no interest in anyone save you." He stroked the smooth flesh of her bare thigh. "You need have no fear on her account, my lioness."

He was aware that he was talking to someone whose moods and mind were as changeable as the weather, as a child's.

She was silent a long while, her eyes dark and steady and unpredictable. "I will make you a bargain," she said at last.

"Another?"

She nodded, smiling. "Aye. Another. I must be sure, you see, my lion. None has ever affected me as have you—and ye know that. Only the truth I speak!"

He nodded, stroking her. "Aye, and there be no reason to—"

She interrupted. "You have proven yourself a man, then fought as the best, and conquered my heart and then my body, as a man should take a strong woman—with strength."

"Then why a bargain? What have I to prove to you, Julanar?"

"That you have no care for her, my lion. You see? I must have that. You will sit beside me, as my lion, while she is scourged—for she be only a captive, Guy," she added, warningly, "and then while she is fucked by one of the captives."

"You—daughter of Eblis! Why must you try to make me hate you?"

"*Son* of Ebliss . . . I *love* thee! And I must know that you love me, and have no care for that pallid daughter of Frankistan!"

Guy squeezed her thigh reflexively, then released it and pounded it in frustration. "You owe me a *life,* Julanar—your own! I claim that life!"

She had become the ingenuous child again, gazing into his face with wide eyes. "Mine? You would slay me?"

"Of course not. I claim life—for Melisende!"

She shook her head. "Not necessary. Only the truth I speak: She shall not die at our hands."

He nodded, bent to touch his lips to her soft nipple, still trying to persuade. "Then she need not be whipped and raped."

She stiffened. "You *care?*"

"Of course. I cared last night, about those two girls."

134

"They were only worthless girls; only cunts. We saved them from whoredom in the camp of the sultan . . . their lives were ours to dispose of."

"Then yours is mine to dispose of?" Guy put in swiftly.

She shrugged in a way that made her naked breasts quiver beautifully, made the rising twin swells roll from side to side. "I offered you my life, but two nights removed from this!" She turned, stretched sinuously for her clothing, turned back to him with her dagger. She offered it to him, hilt-first.

The Crusader stared at the sliver of steel, at her twin-pointed chest. He thought of Miska, stabbed just there. And of Melisende.

But he could not do it.

And surely, though he were able to bring himself to slay this strange woman, he could never gain Melisende and then lower them—and two horses—to the ground below, past all her warrior women!

He heaved a sigh. "I do not want to take your life, Julanar."

"You cannot."

"I cannot."

She hurled the knife away and embraced him fiercely. "My lion! My love! Love me! Enter my body with yours—bruise me, as a man with a woman, just a woman!"

He slid his hand over the warm, tender skin of her lush haunches, between which he had thrust his skewering organ so many times. "Then we need not prove anything."

She stiffened, eased back, stared into his eyes. She said, "She will be scourged and raped."

Guy raged inside. But he could *not* cause himself to be shackled or incarcerated. He had to try to do it with

135

words. "Mother of God, *why?* And—" He paused, stopped. He temporized. "While I look on, as though I had some part in it? WHY?"

"Because," she said with intensity, "both she and I must know that you have no care what happens to her, *ya layth.*"

For a long while he was silent, in frustration and exasperation. Then: "Julanar—sometimes I think you are *mad!*"

Her eyes blazed. She thrust him back and bounded to her feet. Her breasts heaved up and down with her infuriated breathing, and her eyes seemed to flame as she stared down at the seated man, for a long while.

Then, like a summer storm, her rage subsided. She knelt gracefully, then sank to her haunches before him again.

"Aye, I am mad. Mad over Guy Kingsaver of Messaria, lover of Julanar, and great lion of Egypt!"

He turned away. "You said a *bargain,* Julanar," he said quietly. "A bargain involves agreement and profit on both sides. What is to be the profit in this for Melisende, and for me?"

Her chuckle brought his face around, swiftly. "You persuaded me to take her out of the stable, Guy, my lion. But—perhaps she longs for those horses and camels. Perhaps she is hot of blood . . . as I am. Perhaps the pale-haired slut who is *not* your sister would like to return to *visit* her former charges . . . and to get a camel's cock up her slit!"

He thrust his head forward, and his voice came low and intense and menacing with barely-controlled anger. "Do that, and you will never have me. Do that, and I will feel nothing for you but hate and horror, Julanar, and I shall think of nothing but revenge."

"Perhaps she would not die," she said, teasing now. "Mayhap she would merely have great pain, and a cunt

136

like that of a whore of sixty, like that of a she-camel! And you have no feeling for her, why should that affect . . . thee?"

"She has done nothing to you, Julanar, *nothing!*"

The naked woman's nostrils flared. "You are a Christian, even though from Cyprus close by, and a Frank who fought with the Franks against the sons of Allah. How know I that you may not decide you prefer the blond Frankish woman and her softness to . . . a lioness?"

I do, he thought, *now.*

In the end, he agreed to her ugly bargain, though he gained a bit more. After her ordeal, Melisende would have freedom of the camp, and would be treated as were the servants, which was well.

Thus it was that the Crusader, not sure that he did not despise Julanar and himself as well, sat beside her next day, she in her golden breastplates and he in emir-like splendor, while a wretched and completely uncomprehending Melisende was stripped and whipped.

She was lashed rhythmically, with long spaces between the strokes. Weal after red weal appeared on the snowy flesh of her thighs and hips and buttocks. Her wrists, as she twisted helplessly at her bonds, were cruelly chafed by the slender cords. With each falling lash she gasped through parched lips, her bared breasts rising and falling in shallow, chest-lancing breaths.

The whip Subha wielded with such obvious pleasure and expertise made a vicious singing, hissing sound as it clove through the air. Guy's hooded eyes watched the way she huddled her poor buttocks, the way the whip slithered obscenely off their slopes after Subha had struck. He knew that sharp spasms of pain were ripping through her, stabbing as if a thousand needles slashed and rammed deep. And each leather-strapped blow left a bright red welt on the soft, quivering flesh.

137

Tears poured down her flushed face as the nervous spasms of pain filled her with shudders. She was unable to be still; she had to writhe her burning body in agony. Now the lash had marked the swelling halves of her backside with vivid lines.

But they could not make her scream. Guy could not understand whence came Melisende's strength. Again and again the whip hissed out and bit into the soft flesh of her shamefully denuded body. Shudders and tremors rocked the hanging globes of her breasts. She moaned, she groaned and grunted, and tears like diamonds glistened on her contorted face.

But she did not scream, even as Subha turned this way and that and struck with great care, etching that tight-clenched, twitching rump with red weals that swelled and swelled and took on a transparent, too-tight appearance.

Then the cruel lash split the swollen flesh, and blood oozed redly from the raw wound.

Guy was tensing to leap forward and take his chances, when the woman beside him called a halt to the beating.

Melisende sagged, panting, sobbing as she gasped, weak and swollen and cut and yet grateful that it was at last over.

She well knew that Guy of Messaria sat there beside the leader of this unnatural group, and that he was still there when the big Turk was brought out from his prison, escorted by two women with drawn swords. His dark eyes twitched about, taking in the bruised, whip-streaked bottom of the blonde, the tufts of nearly-white hair curling back between her thighs, beneath those excoriated cheeks; taking in the ring of warrior women, their chieftain . . . and the man beside her, a Frank who was richly clad in Eastern garb.

He was told what he must do; fuck or die.

They then turned him to face the helplessly proffered, swollen backside of the Frankish woman, whom they bound into a new position——on her hands and knees, so that she could be fucked like a dog.

The Turkish captive's wrists were freed. He was unbound, and naked, with a naked sword on either side of him. He stared down at the kneeling body, the upturned bottomcheeks, and then he squatted. He began to run his hands over them and between her thighs and over the light-furred, resilient bulge of her vulva.

His cockstand came. The moment he had got it up, he guided it forward with two fingers, between the backs of her red-striped thighs. And he plunged it into her.

Grinding his teeth, Guy of Messaria sat beside Julanar in her breastplates of gold, and he watched as the Turk hunched hard, thrusting his thick cock into Melisende from behind, slapping her burning arse with his thighs and jarring her body.

He groaned, tensing his own buttocks and banging strongly into the soft trembly cheeks of her broad-flanged rump. The humid walls of her vagina caressed his shaft all the way in, as though trying to suck him off in her pussy's warm, mushy wetness.

Guy well remembered how tight that recently virginal channel was, and he knew the Turk had not been with a woman for several days. As he had expected, the man came swiftly, grunting, grinding, then weakly half-lying across Melisende's poor bruised, welted, bleeding ass.

The Turk recovered swiftly——and moved with the speed of a striking adder.

He was rising to his feet even as he lunged leftward. The warrior woman there grunted as his body slammed into hers and his hand easily plucked her sword from her fingers. The man spun, whipping up the crescent-curved blade as the other guard started at him. He lunged, scimitar extended.

The blade ran deep into her belly, was jerked out even before she she began sinking. Then the naked Turk, wearing an expression of wild desperation and determination, swung again—and sprang toward Julanar.

Already Guy had marveled at the man's swiftness and courage; he must have assumed that he was a dead man, one way or the other, and had decided to go down with a bloody blade in his hand, as befitted a warrior of Saladin.

But the Crusader, too, was a warrior, and his courage and swiftness were no less. He had no thought at all of allowing the lunging man to succeed in his attempt to plunge the stolen scimitar through Julanar's body. Perhaps he should have allowed it to happen; the thought did not occur to him. Guy Kingsaver moved, and no roused lion ever took action more swiftly.

All in the same motion, the Crusader rose, pounced, and clamped a big hand down around the wrist of the Turk's sword hand. Then he jerked, and twisted, and let go.

The man was hurled backward. Even though he recovered swiftly, he came up to a crouch to find himself facing an Eastern-dressed Westerner who was now armed with the sword from the dead fingers of the woman the desperate Turk had slain.

"Get back, Aziza—have at him and I'll carve off your head!" Guy Kingsaver rapped out, without taking his eyes off the wildly burning ones of the naked man facing him. "You want death—here it is!"

"Idiot!" the Turk said, circling warily, half-crouching. "I am dead already—but you have no reason to feel this blade!"

"I do not intend to," Guy said quietly, half-smiling.

Ah, God, how good it felt to be facing an enemy again with a steel sword in his hand, though the blade was short, and curved, and his foeman was naked, and Guy without armor. Too, neither of them bore a shield. It was man against man, vulnerable body against unarmored flesh and bone, scimitar against scimitar.

The Turk lunged forward in a driving thrust at Guy's middle; he beat the blade aside even as he moved rapidly leftward. The Turk recovered before Guy could bring his blade up and back in a return cut. The two men circled, crouching, within a circle of staring women.

The Turk feinted; skipping back a step, Guy grinned wolfishly. Had he parried that pretended lunge with his blade, he'd have been a dead man.

This was no way to fight. A man should have a shield on one arm, so that he could cut viciously, widely, trusting in his strength and skill and the shield to turn the other's blade while his own great slash fell. This business of dance and thrust was—unworthy. Childlike.

Accordingly Guy thrust viciously, swinging his blade as he did. But the other man twisted his body sidewise so that the rushing steel actually touched his side as it plunged past, and his blade came rushing down at the Crusader's head. With all his strength and in pure desperation, the Crusader twisted his athletic body in midlunge and hurled himself aside. Pain leaped through him as he forced his body to vie against itself, moving in two directions at once, and new pain flashed when he struck the mesa's hard ground.

The Turk, too, was swift and athletic, and he managed somehow to stop his terrific cut before his blade bit the ground. Whirling even as he raised the scimitar again, he whipped it above his head and began what would obviously be the final slash of this strange duel, at the man lying on the ground, unarmored and without even shield to protect himself from the down-rushing sword.

A woman shrieked; Guy realized only later that it

141

had been Julanar. But it did not deter the Turk's death-chop—or Guy's swift upward thrust, a thrust that sent his point driving into the man's lower belly, slicing through skin and intestines and bringing forth a sheet of blood that drenched his recently-spent penis and black-furred balls.

There was a second shriek; this one came from the dying man. What had begun as an attack ended in a toppling, and Guy rolled aside to avoid the bloody body, not the blade that now slapped down without force and bit the ground. The Crusader rose victorious. . .

. . . and found himself staring at a ring of scymitars, each backed by a wary-eyed, staring warrior woman.

He made his sneer implicit as he half-turned and tossed his bloody Saracen blade to the ground at Julanar's feet.

Julanar's arousal was obvious in the dilation of her eyes, the flaring of her nostrils with her agitated breathing, and the heave of her bosom.

"Come with me to my pavilion!" she said hoarsely, staring at Guy.

He took a deep breath, gazing at her. Then, with his eyes meeting hers, he said, "No."

And the Crusader turned and walked from her, across the outlaw camp, to spend the night in the tent in which he had originally been a prisoner.

With each step he took he felt his back crawling. Would an arrow or spear come plunging between his shoulder blades? True, he had saved her life. But . . . he had also scorned her couch, scorned *her*, given her an unqualified No. He had no idea how many people had said that word to her. He assumed very few—and he wondered if any of those were alive. Would she order him slain, now? He was sure she was standing there in a rage, with all her women about her, watching her, waiting, having seen their indomitable and unrefusable leader refused, and insulted.

The distance across the outlaw "hamlet" seemed tremendous to the pacing man.

But he traversed it, with neither shout nor arrow nor spear from behind him, and he entered "his" tent. There he spent the rest of that day in thought. And that night, alone, Guy Kingsaver was a long while getting to sleep.

THIRTEEN

Ingenious Plan—or Harebrained Scheme?

Next day Melisende was obviously free, and well clothed besides. She was just as obviously looked upon with respect by the other servants. She had taken the whipping, she had taken the brutal fucking; she had earned status.

She also would not so much as look at Guy Kingsaver. All she knew, he realized, was that he had sat there, by Julanar's side, while the blonde was lashed and then dog-fucked in a public display.

The same was the case with Julanar; she refused to see the man who had refused her.

He wandered about, taking careful note of the whole camp without seeming to do. Without stopping and making his interest obvious, he particularly examined the great windlass that raised and lowered the lift that was the only means of access to this mesa—and of egress from it.

He watched the windlass and its operation that afternoon as an excited spy was drawn up. She raced across the camp, and entered the big porticoed pavilion of the Lioness. A short time later preparations were got under way for a new raid of the band of female outlaws.

Guy waited to be called.

He waited in vain. He was not summoned to Julanar.

At last the raiders, fully armed and armored and leading their horses, massed before their leader's headquarters. Guy of Messaria was striding that way when Julanar emerged, in full battle dress. He moved through her followers to confront her at the base of her pavilion's steps.

"A raid? Why have I not been called?"

Her eyes met his coolly from beneath her camailed helm; eyes that seemed to cut and slash, to stare through him. God, he thought, how totally and unreservedly magnificent this warrior-woman was!

"You," she said, "are not going with us. We warriors go to fight more Turks and strip them of their burdensome booty—but *you,* lion-*cub,* remain here with the servants!"

Guy stood alone while she led her horse to the mesa's edge. All her band but three followed, nearly cleaning out the camp save for the servants and the new girls from the recently-robbed caravan. And then the draught-horses were plodding round and round, and chains and cables and wood were creaking and rattling, and warriors and horses were going down, and . . . and then they were gone.

The Crusader stood alone.

There were none left in the camp but three of her warriors—one of those limping from a recent wound—and the servants, and the captives . . . and Guy Kingsaver, who was none of those.

The sun was approaching its point of disappearance on the horizon; it set a bit later, seen from here atop the mountain. Guy bit his lip, and his brain worked.

If I go now and talk with Melisende—wherever she is, he thought bitterly, *Julanar will be told of it, seconds after her return.* And though he hadn't seen Melisende for hours, he knew that knowledge of his having conversed with her so soon after Julanar's departure would endanger the blonde.

He chewed on that for a long while, like a dog seeking to break open a huge bone to get at the marrow. *I shall have to take that chance,* he decided at last. *I must tell Melisende I was forced into . . .*

And then the Crusader knew. Julanar had made it easier.

It will not matter, he thought, with his heartbeat quickening, *what Julanar is told . . . if Melisende and I are not here when she and her raiders fly home to their vulture's nest!*

One of the new girls, won from the caravan meant for Saladin's warriors, was, Guy knew, more than passingly interested in him. It was to her that he imparted his wish to talk with Melisende.

Kelmoune looked at him strangely. He watched her take a deep breath and hold it, to impress him with the swell of her bosom, which was already more than half exposed by her skimpy halter. At last she told him, reluctantly, that the *skinny,* pale-haired Frank with the *washed-out eyes* was in the stable.

"Guy Kingsaver thanks Kelmoune of the beautiful bosom," he said, and started toward the stables, which were at the far end of the mesa from the lift.

"Wait," she said after him.

Guy paused in mid-stride, looking back over his shoulder without appearing to have been stopped. He directed a questioning look at her, without speaking.

"You—you cannot go in there," she said, her face and dusky breasts strangely blood-washed by the setting sun.

"Can't? Why not?"

"She is . . . guarded."

"Guarded? And what is she doing?" he demanded, turning back to her with anger in his eyes.

She raised a staying hand. "I know not, Kingsaver. I am not allowed in there, either." She gave him a bold look. "But there are . . . other secluded places here."

"Aye . . ."

But that was all he said, and the girl heaved a sigh and gazed after him as he strode past her and went to the warrior-woman Julanar had left in charge in her absence: Yasmina. She was just emerging from the Lioness' pavilion; Guy met her at the foot of the steps. He told her he wanted his armor, which was kept inside.

"You need no arms and armor, man of Frankistan."

"I think I might," he said, letting his eyes run up and down her chainmailed form.

Her eyes narrowed. Her voice, her face, her question were a challenge? "Why?"

"Consider, Yasmina. Suppose it is another trap. Suppose those in Cairo, or in Saladin's force, know even more now than they did before when they sought to annihilate your band with the decoy caravan. Stare at me and keep high your head, but let me remind you that all are alive only because of me. My problem with Julanar is personal and none other: I refused to fuck with her after I slew that Turk yesterday. You know how the sight of blood excited her. . . . Well then. Suppose this was another ruse, this caravan they go to attack? Suppose they are followed when they return . . . or suppose that all of it was a ruse only to get them off the mesa so that soldiers may come here!"

Yasmina glanced around in the dusk. "But—none can climb up to us," she said, not without nervousness.

"True, none can," Guy said. "But they could wait below and massacre Julanar and her band as they return, or attack just as we start to bring them up. . . .

Yasmina stared at him. Her tongue came out to lick her lips, suddenly dry.

"We are not many, Yasmina," he said, "but you and

I are surely more than any ten of *them!*" And he ascended the steps, and entered the pavilion of the Lioness.

Guy got his armor—and a bit more. When he went out to the brink of the cliff near the lift, bow in hand, he sat down as if to keep watch. He had taken a dark cloak, which was obviously to pad his rear as he sat ... though he was careful not to sit on the several days' supply of dried meat wrapped in it, or the full canteen of water.

Kelmoune came to bring him food, which Guy gratefully ate. She remained there before him, the heavy ovals of her breasts much on display in her kneeling position, with her buttocks on her heels, her upper body tilted slightly his way. Her dark gaze was for him only, and all for him.

She intended to stay, he saw. If he sent her from him, she would watch him: either because he was angered, or to seek another chance: she wanted him.

Without preamble he said, "I am armored, Kelmoune, and will not remove any portion of it so long as there is a possibility of attack."

Her dark eyes steady on his, she shrugged. The movement darkened the cleavage of her smooth fleshy breasts and rippled their surfaces, bulging above the cuplike portions of her halter.

I will drive her from me with callous roughness, he decided. He was a warrior: to think was to act. He reached out.

Seizing upon her halter, he twisted and pulled until he had torn it and the girl's pretty, tip-tilted tits came jumping out into his hands. She gasped. Her mouth writhed. Her eyes flashed. But she said nothing, and she did not jerk back or flee; she leaned farther toward him.

His hands moved over the firmness of those ripely

148

outsurging ovals and slid beneath to cup their under-hang. He tugged them out into large, dusky ovals and smiled at the result of his sensuous whim, her breasts all stretched and taut and standing straight out from her chest. Fiery thrills assailed Kelmoune's well-padded body, and she gasped.

His hands moved, roughly, callously, as though he were kneading dough. Her moans were not all of shame and horror as he toyed with her, watching her face for her reaction. Nor did she draw away, or raise her hands to interfere with the harsh manipulating of his. Yet his hurtful attentions had her whining, twisting un-controllably, shivering. He hardened his heart and the pressures of his hands, squeezing and pressing as if he meant to destroy the youthful firmness and muscularity of her sumptuous mounds.

His thumbs slipped out to the tips, found the firming little nipples. With his fingers clenching the curving sides of her breasts, he pushed with both thumbs. She gasped and quivered, rolling her eyes down to watch the erotic rigidity of her nipples vanish into the strain-ing, forced-in, unfolding flesh of her sensitive tits.

"Uh—unnnngh . . . oh, oh!"

Her nostrils flared and her eyes bulged. He had shoved her nipples deep into the balls they crested, and it was a weird experience, feeling her own bosom-crests rubbed around over her ribs! He grinned down at them as he continued moving his wrists, circling, circling. . . .

Shivering spasm and tremors rippled through her voluptuous young body. Her rounded belly was amove with a constant twitching in convulsive reaction to his irrepressible manhandling of her breasts. Her luminous eyes sparkled in the light of the up-soaring moon; he could see that her forehead was beaded with lust-sweat.

He had discarded his notion of driving her from him

149

with cruelty, now. He knew that he must finish what he had begun. He was aware of the ecstasy that grew and swelled deep in her body. Her lithe, sumptuously rounded thighs were shaking and jerking in erratic movements, as utterly delicious sensations assailed her.

Guy whipped back his thumbs, releasing her breasts. The full tits juddered and shook, bouncing; their bulging, distended very dark tips thrust thickly forth, swelling still more at contact with the cool night air. Her eyes misty, she swayed forward to collapse against his armored body.

He thrust his hand in between her thighs, found the slash of her filmy scarlet pantaloons, pushed in. He discovered a thick forest of curling pubic bush that covered the full mount of her genital bulge. She groaned when his finger found the sweet crack and ruthlessly pried it open. The soft folds of that heated cavern were already moistened, ready to be parted and entered.

"Unh—AH!" she gasped, shuddering in pain and pleasure as he jammed his finger up into her. It slithered through soft cloying membranes like a handful of wet worms fresh from the ground after a rain.

He began running his finger in and out of her.

She squirmed, gasped, rolled her eyes in rising sensual pleasure and helpless lust and love of what he was doing, not with, but *to* her. With the tip of his finger and its harsh nail, he tickled the trembling, cringing head of her cervix, far back inside her dilated hole.

Then she was sprawling, unaware of where she was or what she was doing, unaware of her fingers clutching her nipple, pinching it viciously, while he fingerfucked her cunt into a boiling cauldron that spattered its sizzling juices out onto her thighs. His constantly-moving hand thrust aside satin-sheathed inner tissues and mashed the delicate little lips framing the slit he filled and battered.

She rocked her hips, loving every lunge that drove his finger ever deeper until he was teasing the tiny mouth of her womb with the tip of it. Squishing, sodden noises arose from the base of her belly as his fingertip skidded repeatedly over her cervix. She mewed in whining pleasure.

Guy kept at her, treating her as if she were a captive to be spun down in to a giddy vortex of deep sensual joy. Then she squealed, totally astonished.

Her belly exploded in fiery and convulsive throbbing that made her contracting cunt squeeze his engulfed finger like a hot fleshy vise.

She lay there limply, sighing, for a long while after her climax. When she showed signs of returning to awareness of her surroundings, the Crusader seized one of her now soft-nippled tits, turned her roughly over, and landed a harsh swat on one upturned buttock.

"Until tomorrow night," he muttered. "Next time it will be more than a finger, darling little whore. Now get to your quarters."

She lurched away into the night, staggering a little. Guy stared after her. The unpredictable variety of women; the manifold manifestations and needs of sexuality!

The moon was two hours high when he rose. Wrapped in the dark cloak that prevented any flash of his armor in the silvery light, he slipped around the perimeter of the mesa, to the stable. Then, looking all about, he emerged from shadows and walked boldly to its door.

Armored and with helmet in hand, a guard challenged him. It was Mahara.

"The Lioness left orders," she told him. "No one enters until her return."

Guy opened his cloak to show her his chain-mailed body—and his bared sword. "Do not cry out, and do not think to cross blades with me, Mahara—you know better. Now turn and lead me in to Melisende."

She neither cried out nor reached for her sword. "Go back now, O lion," she urged. "I shall tell no one you came here. Otherwise, when Julanar returns, she will slay the Frankish woman and make a eunuch of you."

"It is what she said?"

"Aye. And well you know that al-Libwah speaks only the truth; she makes no idle threats, and her word is as constant as the sun."

Guy kept his gaze fastened on her eyes. "Lead me, Mahara."

She looked at him for a long while. Then she sighed. And turned, and led him into the hay-smelling, manure-and-sweat-and-leather-smelling darkness of the stable. There was no trickery; she led him to Melisende.

The girl was naked, bound with strips of harness leather in a stall—where she lay face down in a pile of straw-threaded manure.

Guy hoped he struck hard enough but not so hard as to kill: he used his swordhilt on the back of Mahara's head. And caught her as she started to fall. He had gauged aright; she was still breathing, but quite unconscious.

He gave Melisende a brief explanation, leaving out much but letting her know that he had bargained with Julanar for her life and had been forced to agree to her being beaten and raped—whilst he looked on. This, as he raised her and freed her of the binding straps.

"She loves you?" the blonde asked.

"Perhaps. Who knows, with Julanar? Here, cleanse yourself," he said, handing her the handsome dark cloak he had wrapped himself in.

The naked blonde, wrinkling her nose but showing

great pluck, used the cloak to rid her body of the horse-shit, calmly enough. Meanwhile Guy was undressing, then binding Mahara.

"Dress," he said, and Melisende began, without a word. But he did not leave Mahara naked, or return her to the pile of manure where Melisende had lain. There was no viciousness in Mahara. She had been doing as she was ordered, guarding the girl, just as it was Julanar's orders that had the blonde bound and in such a stinking, sickening cell. After gagging Mahara, Guy wrapped her in the cloak. She did deserve a *bit* of discomfort. . . .

Melisende had donned all the women's gear, and now she and Guy spent several minutes tucking her mass of blonde hair up into the helmet. The Crusader was glad for the camail of steel mesh that fell from the helmet like a curtain of supple steel links to cover most of her head except her face.

Astonishingly, she did not look tiny or swallowed up in the body-encompassing mail that left bare only her face and hands. Melisende de Bois-Courtenay looked . . . warlike.

In the moonlit darkness, two warlike figures strode openly across the mesa to the edge of the cliff. Some saw them; none paid overmuch attention. They knew the big one was Guy Kingsaver of Messaria, he whom Julanar had dubbed *lion,* and a few knew that the armored, helmeted woman beside him was Mahara. But as they were not rushing, there was obviously no imminent danger. The other inhabitants of the aerie returned to their previous activities—which, in more than one case, were soft girl-to-girl games.

Four horses remained at the cliff, day and night. They were there to turn the windlass that raised and lowered the cage-platform that was the only way the aerie could be reached, or escaped. All four horses wore halters, and lead-straps of slender leather were provided.

Using his dagger, Guy cut and prepared reins that would make riding horses of the draught-animals. From the harness they wore, a system of leathern straps from chest to rump, he created a sort of stirrup. One horse he left as it had been accoutered.

The dried meat and canteen were where he had left them concealed.

"We will have to ride bareback, you know," he told Melisende, smiling.

"But—how are we to get *down?*"

"Pray," he said. "And not so loud. I *think* that if I prop open the brake on the windlass, the one horse we leave attached to it will not be able to prevent the platform's descending—once you and I and three horses are on it! Yet his presence, harnessed to the windlass, will serve as a sort of brake, to slow the descent. He may have to run—and we may well drop very fast. But with God's grace and the luck of Cyprus and of Bois-Courtenay, we will win freedom!"

With her help and the aid of the leading straps, he propped open the brake on the windlass. Then he created a *sort* of brake, so that he could start their descent from within the cage, at the cliff's edge. For a moment he and the girl looked at each other in the moonlight, two pale faces surrounded by chain covered with cloth. A smile flickered on her face, though it was a pallid one.

The wood creaked, the cage-platform rocked, and the chain tautened once the Crusader and Melisende and the three horses were on the platform. Guy secured the door. The makeshift brake of leather was a quivering taut line.

Then, with a last glance at his companion, so warlike in her militant garb, her face so wan in the moonlight beneath the camailed helmet, he bade her climb up on the cage's slat framework. She did, and the Crusader lifted high his good Frankish sword. . . .

And chopped through his makeshift brake.

The platform began dropping; the horse above was forced to move, snorting, for its tugging weight was more than he could withstand. The platform wanted to drop. The horse could not withstand that pull. But he could slow it, Guy hoped. . . .

Down they went, to freedom via an ingenious plan . . . or death on the rocks below, via a harebrained scheme.

Once the platform swung so violently that Melisende cried out—and swiftly clamped her mouth—and had to hold fast to the framework to keep from hurtling into the abyss.

Their hearts pounded. The air of their own rapid downward passage whistled in their ears. The three horses squealed and moved nervously about.

Then they struck bottom, with a frightful jarring and a crash. Wood groaned, creaked, and some slats splintered with cracks loud as lance on shield. The horses neighed and stumbled; only their being up on the framework saved Guy and Melisende then.

But they were down, and alive, and so were the horses. Even the platform had survived the swift drop, though the horse above, Guy thought with a grim little smile, must have his tongue hanging to his knees from the enforced race around the speeding windlass. Guy was down in seconds, opening the gate that fell forward to form a drawbridge.

"Now we must get ourselves down the *rest* of the way," he said, well remembering the narrowness of the ledge they must tread . . . in the darkness broken only by the moon whose rays now only just found them, halfway down the gorge and far below the mesa.

They departed the lift. Guy walked first, leading one

155

horse. Another horse followed, hanging close to his fellow so that his nose was switched by its tail. Then came Melisende, a noblewoman in the armor of an outlaw. She led the third beast.

It seemed to them both that they walked for hours.

They were out of the gorge, with the mesa far behind them, and open country ahead, past the foothills they must first cross through.

"Safe," Guy said, expelling a long gust of breath.

"My thanks to Our Lord's virginal mother," she said, with the piety of her people—or the vocal piety, at any rate.

"Now we mount and *ride,* Melisende, *ride,* and hope that we and these animals can find our way, and survive days on the desert ahead, without dying from the sun, or from lack of water, or being discovered and slain—or worse."

He boosted her onto one of the horses.

"I have already experienced the 'or worse,' " she said, taking up the reins he had made. "I shall not return to it, nor shall I be slain." And she showed him Mahara's dagger, which was now Melisende's dagger and *coup-de-grace.*

"We will see," Guy said, swinging onto his unsaddled horse and getting his feet into the (very) makeshift stirrups.

And they rode.

It *had* been hours; it *was* hours.

The sky was commencing to go gray with the coming of dawn when they were at last riding out into the open, out of the long gulch and the foothills that disguised the way to Julanar's aerie.

"Now, by heaven," Guy Kingsaver said, sitting tall on his converted draught beast as though he were a king mounted upon the finest of warhorses. "We are *away,* and we shall—"

156

He was interrupted by the going up of a shout from many throats, and he and Melisende both whipped their heads to the side to see them: fast-galloping horses. Julanar and her returning raiders!

FOURTEEN

The Field of the Dead

The galloping mass of warrior-women, led by their gold-breastplated leader, waving her scimitar and screaming her rage, looked to comprise some twenty-five of her band. They had completed their mission, presumably, and sustained losses. But this quarter-hundred was alive, and well-mounted—and angry.

They bore down on Guy and Milisende, who sat staring, frozen.

The the Crusader jerked his heels. "FLY!" he shouted. "Hang on, and grip with your knees, and *bend low*, girl, and *use* those spurs! FLY-Y!"

The two horses bolted forward as armored heels slammed into their flanks. They galloped.

Behind them, Julanar's warriors gave chase. Sensible or not, she wanted the two captives *back*. The burly form of Guy Kingsaver was easily recognizable; she could well guess at the identity of the armor-clad woman with him.

While the pursuers' horses were not so fresh as those Guy and Melisende bestrode, their mounts were without saddles and were draught-animals, not trained war-houses. But they were powerful animals, long accustomed to release or pull or hold back the windlass controlling the horse-laden lift, and they galloped well enough.

They fled, a man and a woman in armor and helmets, mounted on horses without saddles, and behind them streamed a long line of five-and-twenty women. That pursuit was silent now, determined, bent on vengeful murder, and preferably not swift in nature. Doubtless Julanar entertained hideous thoughts of tortures and the slowest of deaths. But the Crusader knew that if they were overtaken, he would draw sword and his arm would not cease swinging and hacking and chopping until he was dead. He'd have no compunction about fighting women this time, and to the death!

Now and again an arrow whished by or clattered beside or behind the fleeing couple. But the warrior-women of the mesa were not so strong, or so expert at loosing their arrows from galloping horses as were the Turks, and they knew it. Guy was sure that even if an arrow found him, it would not pierce his armor—and thank God for the knight from whom it had been stolen that night in the oasis of death.

That hopeful surmise was soon corroborated: he felt the blow in the back, heard the arrow rattle away. With a wolf's savage grin, he galloped on. Both he and the girl who was his companion in flight bent low over the flying manes of their mounts.

A mile, two miles, then three fled by beneath the pounding hooves of the horses, who stretched out and *ran,* as if delighted at the relative freedom after their long captivity as mindless drawers of a horizontal wheel.

The rolling ground became a plain, stretching far before them and now basking in the glow of the rising sun.

Then came the second great shock of this new day, for suddenly their way across that plain was barred . . . by a long rank of many mounted men!

Automatically reacting, Melisende cried out and drew rein.

We are lost!

Behind came racing the female fiends of Julanar the Lioness; ahead ranked a broad line of well-mounted men, with the sun glinting off the spike peaks of their helmets . . . Turkish knights!

"Follow!" Guy snapped, without slowing his horse, and then the Crusader raised his voice in a loud cry: "LHAMDULILLAHHHH!" he cried—Praise be to Allah! And, still in his Turk-accented Arabic, still at the top of his lungs: "SUCCOR! SUCCOR!"

The cavalrymen ahead of them were pointing, jabbering—and not only at Guy and Melisende who rushed toward their ranks at the gallop, with a seeming fullness of confidence, but past and behind them.

The wind rushed past the ears of Guy and Melisende. They raced nearer and nearer the massed enemy in still another desperate gamble that might well be an ingenious plan . . . and might well be a horrible mistake that would soon end in their bloody deaths. Their galloping mounts covered precious feet at a stride.

A hundred yards from the ranks of the newcomers, some threescore armored Turkish knights in pointed helms, Guy tugged the rein of his careening mount rightward. With Melisende following his lead, galloping behind, he cut across the front of that mass of men. They sat their horses and watched him and his companion and their onrushing pursuit, a squadron of cavalrymen three deep and twenty across.

The moment the fleeing pair had cleared their left flank, the Turkish knights charged the oncoming band of raider-women!

Sixty powerful knights of Saladin directed their plunging warhorses at the racing band of twenty-five

160

women—who had been out on their all-night raid and could not possibly be fresh.

Guy reined in, thrusting his feet forward and leaning back as he tugged the straps of leather, but it took many yards for his snorting, excited horse to slow and come about. Melisende was still with him. He smiled, admiring her courage and skill in remaining on a galloping horse without benefit of saddle.

They sat their restless, heaving horses and gazed back down the long gentle rise they had just topped. Below, the dawning sun was already flashing like white storm-fire from armor and bobbing helmets and whirling, chopping swords. Curved blades of Damascene steel clashed and rang from spike-centered shields, chittered along the circles of close-linked chain. Horses neighed and screamed, men and women shrieked out their hatred and their death-cries.

"Guy. . ."

"Aye, I know," the tortured man said, sitting atop a hill watching the destruction of the outlaws; the destruction of the life and dream of Julanar al-Libwah. "We should be riding on. These men have saved us, all unwittingly, for those be warhorses and I've no doubt Julanar would have followed us clear to Jerusalem, if she had to. And now, she's met by men on fresher horses, men who have not been fighting, and who outnumber her force by more than two to one."

He sank his teeth into his lower lip, a fighting man watching a massacre.

And abruptly he decided.

"Melisende, stay you here. Watch. If the women win and I come not galloping back—fly, fly! And remember your dagger, and your vow. And if it is the men who win—then I shall certainly not be coming back, and your course is the same. Fly, ever north and east. Accept help from no one save Christian knights, girl—

and then be sure you doff your helmet so they can see the flying of your blonde hair!"

"Guy—*no!* You *can't!*"

But he could. His legs were already twitching back and up, teasing his mount's flanks with his spurs.

"*Shouldn't!*" he corrected, dust flying from the hooves of his horse as it hurtled forward toward the battle. His voice floated back to her: "But must!"

Melisende de Bois-Courtenay was almost of a nerve to gallop after him, regardless of her lack of skill with sword. But, to what purpose? She could not help that noble madman, and scimitar-wielding combatants of both sides would be cutting at her; the men because she was a woman, and the women because they would recognize her as the Frankish woman, as the renegade whose pursuit had got them into this one-sided combat, on this horse without a saddle. Too, despite all the sun she had taken, her face was far from dark as most of theirs; Melisende had the blonde's tendency to freckle, rather than to tan. And her eyes were blue.

With tears slipping from her eyes to sparkle on her cheeks, furrowing the dust, she sat her horse and watched as Guy Kingsaver plunged like an enraged lion into the sword-slashing melee on his unsaddled draught-horse.

A broad-swept scimitar struck blue sparks from his helm, and the Crusader reeled. But only for an instant. Already he was past that man, and deeper into the steel-shining host. His own sword battered a helmet, struck partway through it, and splintered the Turkish skull it housed.

Already the bodies lay beneath the horses' feet like ripe grain, oozing their crimson sap upon the earth of Egypt. Over those mangled shapes of once-men, and those they should have been loving rather than slaying, drummed the slashing hooves of the warhorses.

With his sword a blur of silver, the Crusader struck, and struck. Around him rose the screams of horses and warriors of both sexes, the horrid clanking sound of heavy steel blades biting into flesh and blood, its terrible crash and screeching, teeth-edging scrape along shield and mail. Dust rose about the battle, dust rose within it to clog the mouths and dim the vision of the combatants, and blood spattered that swirling dust and carried it scarlet to the ground.

Heads and hands sprang through the air, fell to the hoof-torn earth to roll and lie forever still, pounded and slashed beyond recognition by straining warhorses. Obviously the Turks were winning, though Julanar's women—and the berserk ex-captive who now took their part—were taking a heavy toll of the knights of Saladin.

The battle flowed across a hundred yards of plain, tearing up the ground as though it had been plowed, sowing it with bodies and soaking it with blood. The Crusader saw Aziza go down, her face a streaming cauldron of crimson. He hacked and slashed, grunted and ducked and hacked on. A crescent-curved blade struck his left arm, but failed to bite through the linked steel covering it. Yet that shield-arm was limp and tingling for many minutes, so that he was forced to let his horse take its own course and defend himself with sword and weaving body, for his sword arm was constantly amove, far too busy to bother with reins.

A blade came rushing at him when his own was at the end of its sweep in the opposite direction. Desperately Guy hurled himself leftward. At the same instant that his saddle-less horse plunged to the right. Unable to recover, he plunged to the ground. His knee drove down into a blood-smeared chest. Then he was up, dodging a vicious cut, diving aside from a great black horse and dragging himself into the empty saddle of a roan who seemed happy to bear his weight.

His sword flashed and glittered like balefire, and in seconds the world boasted two less followers of Allah and his prophet Muhammad. Then the Crusader was somehow side by side with a fire-eyed woman in golden breastplates. In a momentary lull, she cut viciously at him. Only his mail and the jerk of his arm saved him from being chopped through the shoulder. With a grunt, Guy sank in his spurs. His horse bolted ahead, nearly bowling over another, whose rider Guy struck so hard in the back that the man pitched forward to the ground, though his armor had held.

Seconds later that warrior was a mass of red jelly beneath the hooves of more than one lunging, staggering, blood-sliding horse.

A man rode at him, sword high as he stood in his stirrups, and Guy's vicious, full-force backhand chopped the sword-wielding arm from the Turk's body. Shrieking, the man plunged past on his snorting mount, to prove easy prey for the first woman he met.

The horses plunged and braced and skidded over a carpet of blood-spattered steel and bone and flesh tattered like ancient cloth.

Within the melee, concentrating only on staying alive and reducing the number of those bent on the opposite end, Guy hardly noted that the battling mass became less noisy, that somehow it was less crowded, that horse after horse was riderless and retreating from the scene of carnage. In a superhuman effort that should not have been possible save for his battle-rage and berserk lust, the Crusader hurled himself onto one of those beasts as his own second mount was cut from beneath him.

He chopped and chopped again, slashing and swinging, slicing armor and flesh, chopping into necks and arms and legs and notching his Spanish blade on shields and spike-surmounted helms.

Then the Crusader realized that there were but three women left, and himself, and more than a half-score of the men.

He plied his shining blade with throbbing arm in a way that sent three more of the enemy racing down to hell. He saw a warrior-woman slain, back-chopped while she killed another. Both fell and rolled together on the ground, as if armored friends overcome with amorousness.

Yet again Guy's horse was cut down, falling with a wavering scream more piteous than a human's. He fell, rolled, saw another unhorsed man rushing him with extended scimitar . . . and saw the galloping woman lean out of her saddle and send the fellow's head rolling. Her golden breastplates flashed in the sun, and then Guy of Messaria rolled again, desperately—for, having saved his life, Julanar now sought to ride him down!

To his left, a woman screamed out a gurgling death-cry and fell in a spurting gout of blood like molten lava.

Afoot, the Crusader looked swiftly about from within a low-walled castle of bodies, horses and humans alike, all smeared with the ruby juices of life.

Now there were five men, four of them mounted, and Guy Kingsaver, and the woman called Lioness. And corpses, a carpet of corpses and crumpled, writhing, blood-streaming forms becoming corpses.

A Turk screeched and his hands shot automatically to his face as Julanar's sword slashed across it. The curved blade took away an eye even as it left behind a deep blood-welling gash. Guy sprang for another man, trying to topple him from his horse; the knight's scimitar slammed down on his helmet and the Cypriot rolled, dazed, among the dead.

He looked up into the face of a bleeding Turk, kneeling over him, swinging down his sword. There was no time to roll or meet that descending blade with his own. Guy's hand shot up and his big hand slammed into the downcoming wrist with a shock that rattled both men's teeth. Guy yanked, twisting. The man fell half across his legs. The Cypriot slammed his sword down onto his upper back. The armor partially held; the back did not. It cracked loudly, and Guy struck again in something approaching mercy for an agonized foeman with a broken spine.

A riderless horse plunged by. Guy sprang to grasp the stirrup—and cursed his folly, as the horse continued moving, seeking escape from the awful scene of carnage. But it was slowed by the armored body it was now encumbered with, the Crusader's feet dragging the ground. He continued shouting the Arabic "WHOA!" until the beast at last came to a stop.

The handsome black horse turned its head to look curiously back at the man it had dragged a hundred yards.

In seconds, that man was in the saddle and turning back.

Even as he charged, he saw that Julanar was unhorsed. A man on a plunging bay swung a mighty scimitar blow that sent her helmet rolling. Hair so black it shone blue in the sunlight sprayed out over her mailed shoulders in a great mass. Then she was falling backwards over a dead horse, her legs flying high. The Turkish knight reined, wheeled his horse to return and finish her.

"GOD AND FRANKISTAAAAAANNN!" Guy bawled, in a desperate attempt to distract the three remaining cavalryman from her.

One of them turned, grinning under his spiked heel like a gaunt brown fox, and spurred to meet the insane Frank on the black horse. His rushing sword struck interposed shield with a sound like fifty such impacts. The off-struck shield buckled, bent back half over

Guy's arm, and he groaned—even as he clove through steel-mesh camail and neck in a great sidearm slash that sent the Turk lurching out of his saddle with the tremendous impact.

Then a fallen war-woman rolled over, groaned, with blood bubbling from her lips, and thrust her sword blindly upward.

Guy's new mount emitted a hideous scream as the curved blade slashed into his ponderous sac of balls and on up into his intestine. He wrenched sideways, staggered. Kicking free of the stirrup, the Crusader swung his ironclad leg over before the agonized beast could fall on it. Hurling himself from the screaming animal even as it fell, Guy plunged headfirst to the ground.

He groaned as his body rolled over fallen weapons and legs and the leg of a death-jerking horse and the mailed leg of a dead man.

The world was a kaleidoscopic rush that left Guy's eyes useless. But he heard a galloping horse, heard without believing his ears the high-screamed words, "GOD AND HOLY SEPULCHRE!" shouted in French, heard the crash of forged steel on steel mesh and a man's hideous dying cry.

The the Crusader was on his back, up on an elbow that tingled from being slammed against something unyielding, and staring.

A new warrior-woman had joined the dying battle, and added to the carnage. As Guy looked, her horse plunged past that of a man who was toppling sidewise from it; she must have slammed her sword into his back at full gallop! Now she reeled in the saddle, sawing at the reins of her still-racing mount.

Melisende had joined them.

The man she had slain fell, and beside him rose up an unhelmeted woman in gold breastplates and gore-smeared surcoat. Her raging eyes followed Melisende's horse, carrying her out of the body-strewn battle area. Then the Lioness's dark eyes dropped to fix their gaze on Guy of Messaria.

Julanar rushed at him, swinging her sword up.

Guy tugged at his own blade, wondering even then if he could strike her—and learning that he would never know. His sword was caught. The horse over whose twitching leg he had rolled had jerked and thrashed a last time in its death-throes, and now its great body pinned his sword to the ground.

So I am to be slain by her after all, the Crusader thought, and he released his grasp on the useless sword to paw out his dagger—which would be of as much value against her scimitar as a Christian life in Damascus.

Then the swift-moving horse of the last cavalryman slammed into the running Julanar, intersecting her course so that she struck it like a wall. The woman called Lioness went flying like a doll made of rags and old cloth.

The eyes of that last Turk swung to Guy. His lips peeling back in a grin, he jerked his horse's rein.

"DIE, MANGY DOG OF AN INFIDEL!" Melisende's voice screamed, from somewhere behind the Crusader's supine form.

The Saracen's eyes jerked up even as he started the charge that would end with his sword smeared with Guy's blood. It was a moment of respite, and moments, in battle, were as golden hours to a man such as the Crusader. He hurled himself sidewise with all his strength, grunted in pain when his knee came down on something cylindrical, something that rolled. . . .

Then he was twisting, pawing up the lance that had fallen from some dead hand, and running with it stretched before him.

The Saracen was in the act of turning his mount, having smilingly allowed the charging Melisende to sweep harmlessly past him. His eyes went huge, and then his horse screamed as the lance slammed into its neck just above the shoulder. The beast reared, attempting to get away; Guy groaned as the lance's haft came up in his armpit with sufficient force to lift him off his feet. He fell sidewise as the Saracen fell backward off his scarlet-welling mount.

The ground was soaked in blood, littered with the bodies of men, women, and horses, and weapons. The Cypriot's mailed hand snatched up a curved Damascene sword as he dragged himself to his feet. His armor now seemed to weigh a hundred pounds; surely it was only a matter of minutes before his muscles collapsed into jelly. . . .

Surrounded by bodies, both without horses, the last two men on that tiny battleground of ferocity and carnage faced each other.

"So ye fight with these women spawned of Eblis, do ye, Frank?"

"I did," Guy told him, the words emerging through gasps. He had lost pounds this day, in the coursing sweat that slimed his armor-clad body. "It was only meet that I did—I am called Guy, Son of Eblis by the lord Saladin himself, little man—and I have sent many of his men off to the cold hell!"

The man blinked. His face twisted, and he charged.

Guy took a vicious chop on his ruined shield, gritting his teeth against the pain to his left arm. Twisting slightly, he sheared away the arm that had wielded that sword. The Turk staggered back from the short-lived duel, staring in horror and disbelief at his blood-gouting stump. Seconds later Guy put him out of his misery.

He heard Melisende's shout as the last enemy fell, but the Crusader ignored it.

Slamming his sword down so that it stood quivering in the ground like a solitary marker for all these dead, Guy of Messaria ran, staggering and stumbling in weariness over the corpse-covered ground, to where lay an unhelmeted woman in breastplates of gleaming, shining, blood-spattered gold.

There was blood on her lips when he slid an arm beneath her shoulders and turned her onto her back. Dark, almond-shaped eyes stared up at him, and there was no hate in them now, only wonder. Her steel-mailed body trembled in his arms. The gold breastplates were suddenly hard, harsh, ridiculous, a travesty of the woman she was.

"My . . . lion!" she gasped. "I'd have . . . killed you willing . . . ly!"

"You'd not have done it, *ya libwah*. A lioness does not slay her mate." He gazed down at her face. It twitched in pain.

She coughed; bright blood burbled over her lip and stained her chin. Within her carapace of linked steel, she had been crushed like a beetle by the racing horse and the impact of her flying fall.

"M-ate?" She blinked, blinked again, rolled her eyes, which suddenly widened.

"Aye," Guy said quietly. "Only the truth I speak. We are mated in blood and spirit, in love and hate, Julanar my lioness, I who have saved your life and you who have saved mine. We—"

"The sun!" she gasped, and blood covered her chin. "It . . . dims, it fades . . . oh my—my li-on . . . I am *cold,* and the sun fades from the sky."

He glanced around, realized with horror that she was looking directly up at the blazing circle in the sky, which

170

had not faded at all but had surely cost him ten pounds in sweat this day.

"I will warm you," he said, holding her close, heedless of her blood and the pressure of one ridiculous breastplate of gold.

"No . . . let me . . . look at you . . . see you . . . Allah help . . . me . . ."

"Aye," Guy murmured, staring down at her face, "Allah help this—"

She interrupted. "Allah does . . . not care," she gasped, and blood slid from her mouth with every word. "This is what . . . life means . . . and . . ." she coughed. "That's what de-death . . . is. Death is some-thing that ju—*ungh!*" She shivered violently and her face writhed. "Just happ-ens. And if . . . if my life is short . . . th-then . . . then I shall have . . . ha-have . . . *been* here!"

"We have lived, Julanar," Guy said, feeling a tickling behind his eyes, "you and I. Oh we have lived, my lioness, and fucked like children who have just discovered it, like a lion and lioness in perpetual rut, and we—"

He broke off.

Julanar had gone limp, after a long aspiration. Her eyes stared up at the sun. She did not blink.

He stared down at her face for a long while, holding her.

"Did you love her, Guy Kingsaver?"

He looked up, blinking against the moisture in his eyes, to see another warrior-girl-woman bent over him, gazing into his face with eyes more blue than the sun-splashed sky.

He looked again on Julanar's face; closed her eyes with iron-clad fingers she did not feel.

"No," the Crusader said very quietly. "We were animals together, and she . . . frightened me. But we were drawn to each other. Animals, lions, and our love-making was as full of fire and fury as a battle. I smashed her maidenhead, Melisende, did you know that? For you, I used her own whip, the same plaited leather handle she used on you—in you. We were magnificent, she and I, and we were hideous. We loved, and we hated. Neither of us was ever sure, Melisende. She was fierce, and cruel, and loving, and confused, and not quite sane. Rushing to kill me was her last act . . . I wonder if she'd have brought that sword down?"

Melisende said nothing. The Crusader was sure the blue-eyed blonde had no doubts; she had known only Julanar's viciousness.

Guy rose to his feet. Now that the battle was over and the need for adrenalinized super stamina had faded, his legs trembled and the muscles twitched. His right arm seemed to weigh fifty pounds. He was aware, too, of a throbbing pain in the left.

"We must get from this place." He looked about. "There are provisions behind many of those saddles, Melisende, and we will need robes or surcoats, and a Saracen helmet. And look, only a few of the horses have really fled. We have our pick of the animals. You take one, and I shall, and we will lead a third."

"A third?" Glancing about, the mail-clad girl seemed to realize for the first time what she saw. She shuddered. They stood in a great charnel house that was already attracting flies and dark circling shapes in the sky.

But there was no way, now, for him to wrap a comforting arm around her; no way either that she could have accepted such a gesture.

"Aye," he said. "We must *ride*. We must soon be far from here, for the buzzards will attract the attention of all within miles. But, her we take with us."

She stared at him, blinking, uncomprehending.

"I have to bury her, Melisende," the Crusader said.

FIFTEEN

A Town with No Name

Long days had slunk past, with Guy of Messaria and
Melisende de Bois-Courtenay riding across the forbidding plain.

Perhaps it would have been better to travel by night
and sleep by day, but other travelers were abroad
then, too, and Guy Kingsaver had rather be surprised
in the saddle than on the ground in the shade of some
great rock or dune.

They rode, and the sun lashed at them, and sweat
sloshed when they moved in the saddle. Each of them
was in an oven of steel links.

And then there was the rain. Guy was sure it was
December by now, and the Levantine rainy season was
under way. It rained every day, pouring out of sullen
skies where moments before there had been the flaming sun-ball. They huddled, muffled their heads and
armor in the great cloak he had taken from behind a
Turkish saddle, and the voluminous robe of dark blue
she had taken from a similar source. The sun was
agony; the rain was misery. Surely God hated this land!

They had seen a caravan once, southbound, but they
had given it wide berth and the column had paid them
no attention, two lonely riders in robe and cloak and

Saracen helms. Surely, in such weather, there'd have been no caravan, but for the war and Saladin's necessity of supplies from his base in Egypt.

Daily the sky attempted to dump down rain enough to see this ugly land through the long summer of total dryness; daily the sun attempted just as assiduously to suck up all of yesterday's rain, so that the horizon and the very ground only yards before them seemed to tremble and waver. And then the darkness chased the sun, and the clouds rolled in, and again the rain came crushingly down. The horses slipped and slid and complained.

Guy paid them little mind. Accompanied by the ghost of the woman whose captive they had been, whose tormented victim she had been, whose lover he had been, Guy and Melisende hardly spoke. Nor, when they rested, did she seek shelter nearer him than a yard.

The way became harder. The rainy season was deepening, coming down swiftly, for it was late in the year in this land called Holy where even the seasons were confused.

Meals for the horses were whatever scrub grass they found. Their riders were forced to let them tear at the scraggly nourishment as they plodded on, ever northward. Meals for the pilgrims were the dried meat Guy had brought from the mesa, and the few dates and nuts they had discovered in a fat saddle bag on a horse that must have belonged to the Turkish leader.

Guy rode him now, without giving the great black beast a name.

And it rained.

On what he thought was the eighth day, they came to a town whose walls had been breached in more than one place. They approached slowly, and with caution, though there was no sign of life within those smashed walls. At the tumbled gate, he glanced at Melisende; she was looking questioningly at him.

Freeing his sword arm of his cloak and bracing his shield, the Crusader shrugged and made a clicking noise in his cheek. The black warhorse paced forward into the town.

Wary, their eyes rolling this way and that, they rode down muddy streets between silent houses with gaping windows and flapping doors. The horses paced with care, just as wary of the sucking, slippery mud that threatened to slide their hooves from beneath them. The noise of their passage was loud and wet and sloppy.

There was no one. Not even corpses, or bones, not even vultures or buzzards. These people had fled. There was no way to know whether from Christians or Saracen, or whether on command of Saladin, who had emptied so many hamlets and towns and even cities, ruining their defenses against the relentless advance of the moving wall of mail that was the Third Crusade—King Richard's Crusade.

Guy had no way of knowing where they were. He was sure they had once again crossed up into the Holy Land from Egypt, into Syria or *Falashtim,* but he could not be certain how far they had plodded northeast. Certainly their daily total of covered miles was miserably low.

They came to a wall once more; they had paced the length of the deserted, mud-streeted town.

"We need rest, and so do the horses," he said, checking the rein. "Let's check the stables for fodder, and find a house with carpets left behind."

She agreed in silence, giving him only a weary nod.

Within an hour they had stabled the delighted horses, who were feasted on a small amount of grain and on dry, long-dead but not mouldy hay, and the two pilgrims were themselves in a cozy home whose owners had left behind both carpets and cushions. One fat cushion with a cover of third-grade silk, dirty yellow, was leaking its stuffing on the brown-and-blue carpet.

Outside, the rain, which had abated for no more than a half hour, began anew. Heard from within the shelter of a house, it was not nearly so dreary a sound, that steady beating and pattering and the heavy splashes where it ran from the roof.

Melisende said nothing as he began stripping, but when he was down to his underclothing, sodden and discolored, she frowned.

"What are you doing?"

"It's raining, and there's a barrel outside. I am going out to wash all this."

"Naked?"

He nodded. "I have nothing else to wear."

"You'll get *wet!*"

Guy laughed. "Aye—and I am going to love it!"

She turned away when he began stripping off his drawers. Then, gathering up his clothing, he gave her stiff back a smiling glance, and curbed his sigh. He went outside into the rain.

It was as he had thought, though it brought goose-flesh to his skin: he loved it! The encrusted sweat of many days began running off into the mud, which did not notice. When he looked upward, grinning, a harder stream of water ran from his beard onto his chest and plunged down to feel cold on his pubic hair.

He was wringing out his clothing in the overflowing barrel when he heard the little squeal. He turned swiftly, instantly ready for anything, even naked. His smile returned; he saw that he had been joined in the cleansing rain by another naked form.

But it was, to his eyes and mind, a far more interesting form than his, with sleek-curving hips and broadly rounding backside and jostling, shaking breasts that looked very white and as succulent as fresh dangling fruits.

The rain plastered her nearly-white mane to her within seconds, so that she was streaming water when she came to where he stood at the barrel, staring.

"Stop staring," Melisende admonished, dimples creasing her cheeks as she smiled, "or I shall blush, and that will make me angry—and I feel so *good!* Isn't rain *wonderful?*"

"We'll not be saying that by March," he said, in a sudden attack of practicality. "I am told it rains every day here, this time of year."

"Oh it does, and it's miserable, but it is wonderful now, and you are an evil, terrible old man to remind me of it!"

Stricken with remorse, he muttered an apology. He hardly felt an *old* man, though, as he took his clothes inside.

In the back room of the little house, the cooking room, he wrung out his clothing again, then spread it over a low table to dry. He searched, but the abandoned dwelling contained neither food nor clothing. His surcoat was both dirty and wet, but he drew it on over his nakedness before he went to inspect their little store of food. Enough, he thought, for two or three days more—with a little husbanding.

At least there was no problem now about *thirst!*

He transferred the cushions to the back room, all of them, and dragged the small carpets from the front room back there as well.

Then Melisende came in, carrying her clothing. She stopped short to stare. She had lost weight as well as he; there was little padding on her hips now, and she seemed to possess no stomach at all. Riding through rain and then blazing sun that sucked up that water —while wearing full armor—was a miserable proposition, but an excellent means of producing figures worth a troubadour's rhymes.

"How dare you have put on clothing!"

Guy blinked. He said nothing, merely continuing to stare at her. He felt a stirring along his inner thigh. She was beautiful. And ten days had passed since he had lain with a woman.

She extended a hand, making her breast jiggle and rise slightly to aim its sugar-pink nipple at his shoulder. "Give me that surcoat," she said imperiously, "I'll take it out and wash it."

"It will serve," he said. "When we leave, the rain—"

She wiggled her fingers. "Off with it! I washed mine, and you shall not be clothed when I am not!"

At last he gave in and removed the surcoat—to bare an erected penis that stood before him like the strong bough of a tree.

"Hmph," she said, and took the surcoat, and went outside again, with a great churning of her naked and almost snow-white buttocks.

He stood there and tried to take his mind off her nakedness, and he succeeded only in reducing his prideful, needful cock to the point of standing straight out from him, rather than aimed upward. It was at that level when she returned, looking thoughtful. She spread out his surcoat, then stood and gazed into his eyes for a time.

"Guy? Do you think we will make it? Will we find our people? Or die on the open land, or be slain because this is enemy country and we have been blessed so far?"

Good, he thought. *We will talk of something else, and trouble our minds, and I shall be rid of this cockstand! Arrogant bastard, to rise and point so rudely at a woman who does not want it!*

178

"We may," he said truthfully, for he was not a man to dissemble about danger.

He had no idea. Perhaps this was his last adventure. So far as he knew, this night, as might have been every other since last July when he had come to this barren land of the enemy with the different god, might be his last on earth.

Just now he was far more concerned with her seductively lovely nakedness and with his own obvious response. It was standing high again, that uncontrollable response. He wished it would blow away; that he could slap it down into wormlike quiescence. He could never initiate anything with this woman, this girl, really, of only seventeen years. Not with what there was between them. Not after what she had seen, and perhaps heard; not with what she knew of him and that magnificent lioness he had once known.

Melisende sighed and lowered her chin in a faint nod. "You do not lie, even to me. We may live, and we may not. Perhaps I shall be eighteen, and perhaps never. Well, thank God I shall not die a useless virgin, for I have learned that the nun's life is not for Melisende! That vasty bludgeon standing before ye was my first, Guy, and since we may not see so much as another sunrise, it might well be my last as well."

Naked and slender and white, with her pretty breasts swaying and softly rippling, she came swaying toward him. "Come, warrior . . . plunge that sword of hard flesh into me!"

Still he hesitated, the hero-son of a peasant possessed of more nobility than most highborn. "Are you sure about this, Melisende, gentle Melisende?"

Her eyes met his steadily from a distance of less than a foot.

"Only the truth I speak," she said.

SIXTEEN

In the Mud

Without another word, the naked man drew the naked woman to him.

His descending mouth found her full lips wet and parted. His arm encircled her slender waist. He ran his fingers titillatingly over her sleek, still wet flesh, while he pressed his mouth to hers. The slow, gentle grinding of his hips made her profoundly aware of the blood-bulged staff rising up from his loins. It was a hot bar that beat steadily against her with a pulse that seemed to make it a live thing.

That, and the penetrating kiss, sent shivers of excitement racing all through Melisende. She filled his mouth with a long, uninterrupted groan and grasped the thrusting hardness of his buttocks, pads of muscle that felt as if they could impel him all the way through her vagina and nail her on the spike of his groin.

He maintained the kiss, making her feel small in his arms, until the inner churning of sexual desire had her grunting and gasping and sweating. She pressed against him, arching up her cunt and ripe bowls of her breasts. The inquisitive squirming of her tongue became a flogging urgency between his lips. Her hands clutched his muscular buttocks as though she sought to bruise

180

them. Deliberately tensing those cheeks, he lowered his hands from her waist. Thrusting deeply with his tongue, he placed both big hands over her backside and gripped one plump cheek in each.

"Um-mmmm," she breathed into his mouth, flexing, squirming the shapely, opulent rondures in his grasp. Her words were uttered into his mouth, barely coherent: "Hands so *warm!*"

His hands continued to roam the rainslick hillocks of her rump, fingers pressing the spongy resilience of its cheeks, teasingly tracing along her tight crease. The sudden delving of an errant finger into that warm division of her buttocks brought a startled gasp from her. She rubbed the root of his thick erection and the heavy pouch beneath it with the soft prominent bulge of her mound, so delicately feathered with sparse, nearly white hair.

She hugged him sweetly close, rubbing her vulva against him in open provocation.

He was very aware of her silken, honey-skinned breasts against him, pressing their crests into his flesh. He could feel them, two separate points, thickly erect and warmly pulsing. And urgency was overwhelming him. He had to have her, though he knew that he would be fast, too fast.

With shivering willingness, her sighs emerging as little moans, she allowed herself to be backed to the pile of three cushions on the three small carpets from the other room.

Once on that pallet he had created on the floor, Melisende went wanton, afflicted with an insatiable itching between the very firm tops of her thighs.

Guy could see that her nipples had stiffened and lengthened to throb fatly erect, standing atop the smooth summits of her perfect tits. Her thighs were well open, a blatant sexual invitation. Her eyes, the flushed heat of her face, and the lustful, abandoned aspect of her posture invigorated him and spurred him.

Her Mediterranean blue eyes rose from his heavy erection, standing high before him, throbbing with its engorged blood in a series of lewd salutes to her loveliness. She met his gaze. Her breath was coming fast and her eyes seemed to house flames behind their blueness.

"Must I say it again? Come, warrior, plunge that great sword into me . . . fuck me!"

With a smile, he dropped swiftly to his knees between her thighs, which were wide apart, the pouting, slitted niche of their juncture well parted by her uplifted knees.

He used his fingers to guide his stiff and distended organ between the juicy outer lips of her vulva. Her hands leapt up automatically, voraciously, to his neck. She pulled him strongly onto her, into her. The oval ring between her inner labia grabbed his swollen glans, stretched around its sensual girth. She pulled as he pushed and his sweltering cock was quickly wedged deep in her.

His kisses and caresses had built her desire to the fever point. Her rage to quench her own flaming desires made a chaotic shambles of her mind. She seemed borne up by wings of ecstasy, completely abandoning herself to the delicious sensations.

The thick shaft was searing and skewering in her. She could feel it all, with an intense awareness of his cock's forcing her warmly clinging lovelips to dilate around its lecherous breadth.

Her legs snapped wide, quivering with tensed muscles, and he had to lie on her and reach out with both hands to drag them back. He felt their shivers of sensual response. Their warmth was an erotic joy against his palms.

He was too aroused; it had been too long. He could not hold back, could not cruise his thick cock slowly in and out of her to make it last. No, he plunged and lunged like a raping barbarian. He had fought that last battle with a berserker's fury; now, a week later, he fucked the same way. He pounded throbbingly into her with a male vigor that shook her and made her squeal.

Her restless hands prowled his back, his hips, the lewdly thrusting bowls of his muscular ass. A sudden hot current of wanton need took her and she thrummed her heels, rubbing his humping hips with her thighs, then planted the soles of her bare feet on the carpeted floor. She exerted herself to arch her wet-thatched mound up, while she pressed down with her soles, in a lust-dictated effort to draw and force him deeper and deeper inside it.

"I—I can feel it! I can f-feel the head of that marvelous truncheon of yours . . . right in the very bottom of my—*ah!* My CUNT!"

Grunning, he swiveled his hips to heighten the raking of his deep-seated glans over her cervix.

She squealed in delight, then seemed to go all weak and flaccid. Her legs slid out to lie flat. Her eyes became huge azure marbles that stared glassily up at him.

He began pumping hard and fast. His flesh slapped hers with loud sounds. The throbbing shaft of his turgid cock plunged and plowed into the juicily luscious recess, a warm wet cocoon well-greased with sweat and his pre-seminal juices and her own inner lubricant.

Riding her fiercely, unable to hold back, he gasped and grunted at the feel of the pounding heat of the blood rushing through his veins.

"I—it's going to," he gasped, stiffening, "to happen!"

"No!" she cried, but instantly clamped her lips so as not to spoil it for him by betraying her own disappointment. She needed more, more.

He went taut, groaned. A fiery torrent of sperm went rushing, cascading in to mingle with the seething juices flowing in her eager slit. He continued, jerking in love spasms, squirting out his semen while the fleshy warmth of her cunt remained like a powerful, satin-covered vise all around his plowing organ.

He filled her utterly with bubbling, seething sperm.

He continued pumping his spent cock into that slimy pool of his own liquid seed as long as he could, while she held him with fiercely tight arms and strained the seething pudding of her loins up to his. Then he was panting, too exhausted to continue moving.

His body sagged upon hers. The gasping girl held him clamped there, happy beneath his weight.

Happy, he knew . . . but wanting. He felt no shame, no guilt. He knew that he would soon be ready again; there was more than one arrow in the quiver of Guy Kingsaver of Messaria!

Carefully keeping his emptied but unshriveled penis in her, he began to play. He nibbled at her sweat-damp breasts, licked them, tasting the salt as his tongue traced over the swollen, jiggly, pink-tipped turrets until they were coated anew, this time with his saliva.

She seemed surprised, but she responded, stroking him even as she sighed under his gentle lips and tongue. She felt his teeth, inflicting little love-nips all over her breasts. Then he was cupping them in his hands, crushing them together in the center of her chest, lowering his onto the upsurging masses, lowering his mouth to hers.

"Uh-ummm," she groaned. "You're . . . my breasts are bursting! *No, no*—stay where you are! Crush them!"

They kissed. They kissed a long while, and their hands were ever active. Then his tongue was imitating a cock, plunging strongly in and out of her mouth in a steady, deep-thrusting tempo. She loved it. She shivered in excitement. She squirmed; moaned when his penis slipped out of her sperm-filled gap.

Immediately, her hand worked its slithering way between them to enwrap the slippery-sticky staff. As their long kiss continued, as he squeezed her wet pubic mound until she twitched at the pressure, her hand squeezed and slipped up and down his limber wand.

"Keep at that," he murmured into her mouth, "and you will soon have that back inside you."

"I want it back inside me!"

"I know," he told her. "It's been long days, over a week, and I was too fast. This time you will have it much longer, Melisende. I'll give you a ride on my cock-horse until you're saddle sore!"

Her belly trembled with her throaty little chuckle. "I have it longer, already," she said, steadily yanking that lengthening shaft. They laughed together, in delight.

Had he not just spent in her so that his penis was coated with both her sticky juice and his, he would have suggested that she take him in her mouth. But he knew her not well, and he would not ask or suggest something she might find repugnant. She was still poor, gentle Melisende to him, despite her joining the recent battle like one of those pre-Christian warmaids of the Norsemen; he could not remember their names.

And as they toyed with each other, they re-erected together, her nipples and his prick. Both became thick pink extrusions standing from their bodies.

And she surprised him, astonished him: "Am I very wicked if I say I want to taste it?"

"Yes," he told her. "Marvelously wicked. Delightfully wicked!"

He rolled onto his side, then his back, watched as

185

she floundered down along his body on hands and knees, the quaking masses of her tits lovely white cones swinging and jumping beneath her.

Then, without any sort of preamble at all, his still-swelling penis was trapped tightly in her sweet young mouth. It was, he had to assume, a virgin chamber.

He groaned and quivered. To his ears came her slurping, sucking sounds as she slid her head back, and back, and then swooped it down again, with him watching her take his broad length into the well of her face. She pumped that well on his flesh. Now she was able to feel his very balls against her face, so much mighty male organ did it contain.

She slid it forth only long enough to say, with a happy smile of completely ingenuous salaciousness, "Mmmm—I love it!"

Then she claimed it again. With the head of his penis firmly captured between her soft lips, she massaged its very tip with her darting tongue. Her hands slid around him, under him, to knead and caress the hard cheeks of his butt. Then he was shivering as she began sucking more and more stiff cock into the sweet moistness of her mouth.

His hands stroked the silky softness of her hair; tugged it lightly, and pulled at her earlobes. They had long since been pierced, after the manner of the people who had made her a slave for five years, but there were only the holes, no rings. He resolved to get her a pair, if they lived, as he thumbed the puckered little punctures.

She began sucking at the big, still-growing penis imbedded in her oral grip, pressuring it with lips like warm elastic. Her eyes sweetly shuttered, she swiped her tongue around and around in a constant motion that worked his need up to a frenzied pitch.

"Enough," he groaned. "Both of us want it *in* you."

She slid her mouth lingeringly up off his standing tool, a great angry-red pole now, and she gazed at him up the length of his torso.

"Guy . . ." She paused, ran her tongue over her lips. "I . . . I think . . . I need . . . um, Guy . . ."

He stretched out an arm to press her thigh in the big warm clamp of his hand.

"My very first time," she said, not looking at his face, now. "I was raped, wickedly, with that . . . that whip handle. Then it was you, and though you made it so lovely, there were still all those people around . . . all those staring, sneering women . . . we had no choice, neither you nor I. And then it was the Turk . . . you know. After the . . . the whipping. He was rough—"

"Brutal," he said, stiffening his lips.

"Um. Well . . . I think maybe I . . . maybe I like it, uh . . . well . . . could we try . . . a, a game?"

"A game?" He was bewildered, though he had an idea that she must mean—but she was talking, nodding, talking excitedly.

"Suppose . . . suppose you came here just as we did, except that you were alone, and this was my home—I was still a slave—and they left me behind when they fled . . . whatever they fled. And you came in, and made me do what I just did, put this lovely thing in my mouth. But then I ran, and you had to chase me down, and . . . and . . ."

"Rape you."

She nodded, still without looking up.

His big chest rose and fell in a sigh. "No man would turn down such an invitation, Melisende. But I may have trouble being rough with you. I've seen you hurt, I know what sort of—*owww!*"

She had looked up sharply, with anger flashing in her eyes, and then: "Don't you feel sorry for me! I took it, I took it all—and I galloped in and *killed* a man, too!

187

Don't feel sorry for *me*, Cypriot pig!" she cried, and she slapped his balls sharply, and then was on her feet and running out into the other room.

Guy lay screwing up his face and squinting his eyes for seconds, pain tightening his stomach and intestines, surprise and then anger ramming through his brain.

Then he was thrusting back the pain in his mind, getting swiftly to his feet and charging into the other room after her.

She was not there.

"God's balls!" he snarled, and with his own sending him little messages of pain as they swung, he charged out the door after her, into the falling rain and the mud. It was ankle-deep in that dark street, and he slipped and slid just as much as the fleeing white form he saw just ahead through a curtain of rain that was chill on his sex-warmed body. Once he slipped and went to his knees, plunging into nearly four inches of mud.

She fled without squealing, without laughing, but with frequent backward glances. That slowed her, and his legs were longer and far more muscular, and in seconds he was just behind her, then reaching out for her. He realized he could not just hurl himself upon her, or bring her down with both arms wrapped around her thighs—she'd fall face-down into the mud.

So, skidding, slapping his feet about for balance, he wrested her to a halt, half spun her, and slapped her sharply across her naked bounding breasts. She squealed, her face screwing up, and then he wrapped a big hand around each of those juddering firm-fleshed thrusts. He clamped.

She was instantly still, shivering at the flow of sharp, lancing pain that radiated out from his fingers through the superb masses of rounded girl-flesh.

"Down, bitch," he snapped. "Kneel! So you're a trembly snivelly little virgin—that's of no interest to me, save that I *like* breaking the dams of stoppered pussies and hearing silly little blonde virgins squeal! Now kneel—I have a lot of cock that wants to warm itself up your belly!"

For a moment a smile tried to tug at the corners of her pink mouth, as she realized he was playing her game, and embellishing upon it. Even as she hesitated, though, he was mauling the swelling contours of her ripe, soft breasts, and it *hurt*. She sagged, whimpered, and went to her knees.

The rain pelted down on them as her knees sank deeply into the oozing mud. Strangely, it was a soft caress on her flesh, like softly-stuffed silk. He surprised her by stepping *behind* her—and then she was emitting a fearful squeaking sound of shock as he tipped her forward. Her hands leapt down desperately, catching her so that she rested there on hands and knees, with the mud from her down-slapping hands dark and slickly sliding on her dangling breasts and arms.

"AH!" she cried, for his hands had come down onto the outthrust cheeks of her bare rump with force enough to make the sound echo and re-echo from the little houses lining the street.

Then she cried out again, for the swollen crown of his tool entered her coral cleft in a great slamming bubbling searing rush. It pressed strongly on down the gliding furrow of her cunt. But the pain was not great; her excitement had had her damp there, and his seizing her breasts and the rough rape talk had made her positively wet. As he urged himself deeper up into her, his body pressed against the firm canteloupe-halves of her butt.

Instantly, orgasm lashed through her in a blinding delight. She tilted up her head and cried out her pleasure to the rain-fulled sky.

She could feel the tight bag of flesh cradling his big

ballocks slapping her lower thighs as he dug and rooted between the lower curves of her white, silken buttocks. Waves of fire rippled sensuously through her. She was very aware of his hands, grasping and clutching at her hips as if he were trying to drag her back to cram all of his cock and balls up into the slippery tunnel of her vagina.

He was jerking roughly, his body slapping her buttocks and jarring her so that her breasts danced wildly under her, while he plunged his pike in and out of her from behind, around and around in her until a cataract of pure rapture coursed blissfully through her and she was suddenly hot, kneeling in the mud beneath the chill rain.

She worked to match his motions, rotating her hips in the air as he lunged against her rump with slapping, splashy sounds. Her belly was filled with heated tingles from the magnificent maleness filling its liquid depths. Her vagina clutched him in a sinewy embrace as, on her hands and knees, she squirmed and struggled in a desperate attempt to satisfy the burning itch inside her wet love-mouth.

"Lied about that virgin hole, did you, slut? Wide open as though it's been plowed by dozens . . . I should reward you by knocking the arms from under you and fucking you face down in the mud!"

The voice was snarly in her ears, hardly his voice at all, and she trembled with a mingling of fear and delight. And it began again. . . .

The muscles of her creamy-sheened thighs flexed and twitched, rippling as shudders raced through her and set the blood pounding hotly in her head.

He was writhing against the perfect curves of her rump in an accelerating tide of sensual desire. Flames of passion flickered in his hotly swelling balls as he hung onto her squirmy arse-globes and probed her cunt in riotous, burning need. His hair was plastered to his head, streaming down his forehead; water flowed over him and from him. And it was glorious, all of it. He loved her game as much as she.

She was hunching backward in totally wanton response, making whimpering sounds of unrestrained excitement and need. Again it happened; a fabulous climax slammed through her and she screamed aloud in massive sexual gratification. Her back sagged. . . .

But he enwrapped the cradle of her hips with both arms and big hands, and holding her close against him, continued to hunch strongly into her weakening body. In her orgasm, her cunt closed and sucked around his plunging, ramming tool, greedily engulfing and holding it deep inside her slippery gash. Where it belonged. Where she wanted it. Where both of them needed it!

The rain washed down on them, and it was only one more addition to the experience of pure sensualism. The rain . . . it washed from them the dark shadow of the mesa, and of Julanar, and of his relationship with that strange woman.

A groan escaped him and he ground in strongly, feeling himself spiraling steadily to soaring heights of carnal joy.

Lust swept over him, and he tried to saw her in half. His cunt-engulfed cock jerked, a big wedge that rubbed every surface of her slick, quivery channel. He lunged violently in and out, plugging and plunging as he plumbed her, moving himself to the brink of orgasm and dragging her ass more tightly back against his sweaty, rain-soaked loins.

When he felt it about to happen once more, a maximum exertion of will was necessary for him to do what he wanted to do. But he did; with his teeth in his lip, he jerked his hugely swollen prick out of her.

The girl cried out—then squealed loudly again as he

raised her, tipped her, and forced her backward. With a great splash that sent nearly liquid mud over both of them to be washed swiftly off by the rain, she dropped onto her back.

"Unnh!" she grunted, as he slammed himself again between her legs. Then his chest splatted down onto her breasts, and she made no sound at all, for she hadn't the breath.

"How," he gasped, "do you—like—your . . . *rape, beautiful lady?"*

"Oh, my darling!" she cried out. Her face was a joyous smile as her arms flung themselves about his neck. Even the mud was a soft caress under her squirming buttocks.

His flesh slithered over the superb sculpture of her body, rooting into it like a wild boar in undeniable rut. She dug her nails into the wet, water-running flesh of his shoulders and strained to arch her pierced pelvis up to meet his grinding, viciously powerful thrusts.

It came surging up to pour into her, and the Crusader laughed aloud as she shrieked in joy, receiving his seed.

Tomorrow, he told himself, grinding himself into her. *Tomorrow, we shall saddle the horses and ride forth again in search of King Richard and the army—and to find . . .* what?

Well, he mused, *if it be death . . . then I shall have lived, I shall have been here!*

And he picked the dripping, sighing, laughing girl up from the mud of the street and, with his seed running from the reddened slit of her belly, he staggered back into the house that was theirs for the rest of the night.

BOOK IV:

My Lady Queen

ONE

Duel in a Stable

Her hair was the color of gold and honey and the bellies of sun-gilt clouds. Even disarrayed as it was now, it looked delicious; silky, tendrilly, delicate hair that stirred in the gentlest of zephyrs.

Lightly shaded by pale lashes, her eyes were as blue as the nearby Mediterranean. They held a growing confidence, her eyes, but the old nervousness was still there, for she was still skittish, ever wary, after her harsh and uncertain life of the past five years—even now, in the protective company of The Crusader.

Her forehead was high and smooth, her brows nearly as straight as her longish, slender nose, and she had recently experienced two firsts: she was no longer a virgin, and she had killed another human.

Her name was Melisende de Bois-Courtenay. Her father had been a third son, a landless knight banneret who had followed a nobler knight here to the Holy Land in search of name and fortune. He had found neither; following in the footsteps of so many other Europeans, he had found only death in the land the crusaders sought to wrest from its Saracen conquerors.

Saladin's Turks slew him when they took Ascalon, over four years ago, in the eighty-and-seventh year of the twelfth century since the birth of him called the Prince of Peace—in whose name this war was being fought, in whose name Melisende's father had died. For now the Sultan Salah ad-Din and his Turks held the city both they and the invading Westerners called Holy: Jerusalem.

Melisende had watched with horrified eyes while her father's four killers raped and then bloodily slew her mother. Spent by then and little interested in the pre-nubile blonde of thirteen, they sold Melisende as a slave —one of many Christians thus sold, of both sexes. The wife of an emir bought her, and over four years passed.

At seventeen, the girl was attracting more and more of the emir's hot-eyed gazes, and his fattening wife frowned. Melisende was a lovely young woman, and strong withal; a girl-woman who carried as many as ten water buckets daily. Her mistress found it expedient to sell her again. Tempered in the stern furnace of horror and slavery, the Frankish blonde with her fair skin represented a valuable commodity on the slave mart at Cairo, down in Egypt.

But Melisende de Bois-Courtenay never saw Cairo. Her fate was linked with that of the outlaw Julanar the Lioness, who attacked the caravan and made a prisoner of the girl with the fascinatingly unusual skin and hair; and with that of a former stable-hand from the isle of Cyprus, he who had saved the life of Richard of the Lion's Heart and was thus dubbed Guy Kingsaver of Messaria, later called the Human Crossbow, one of the heroes of this third great crusade, The Crusader.

Treacherously betrayed and stolen by night from his camp-tent by his own worst enemy, a man he had bested in personal combat, The Crusader, too, was sold and destined for Cairo. And Guy and Melisende became fellow captives of Julanar the Lioness and her outlaw band. It was among them that Melisende's virginity was torn from her, by the leathern handle of a whip; that Guy Kingsaver became her first man; that he lay, too with Julanar; that Melisende was beaten, and raped, and made to clean the stable housing the outlaw's swift horses.

But now Julanar was dead and buried, and Guy and Melisende had won free, and fought and slain the Turkish cavalrymen that destroyed Julanar's band. Long days had slunk past, with the armored pair, well-mounted on Turkish warhorses, riding ever northward in that forbidding country, seeking to rejoin King Richard.

The month was December, the rainy season in this unpredictable and unholy land called Holy. Daily the rain fell, and then the sun slashed at them, sucking up that water only to hurl it down once more the following day. Sweat sloshed with each of their movements in the Turkish saddles. They suffered, in chain-link armor become ovens of steel.

On what The Crusader thought was their eighth day of riding north from Egypt, they came to a nameless town. Its walls breached in more than one place, it had been bloodlessly deserted. Guy of Messaria had no way of knowing whether the former inhabitants had fled Christians or Saracen. Perhaps they had precipitately departed on command of their lord Saladin. The sultan had emptied many hamlets and towns and even cities, ruining their defenses against the relentless advance of the moving wall of mail that was King Richard's crusading army.

The Crusader hoped to find and rejoin his chosen liege-lord's army. He was sure he was out of Egypt by now and in the Holy Land—Syria, the land its people called *Falashtim,* Palestine. But both he and Melisende were tired and rain weary. In the town of no name and no people, the two took refuge from the constant rain.

They had hardly rested. Last night they had made love, with the full realization that they might not live past the dawn, alone in enemy land. Then, in the tiny house they had decided upon, they slept, well into the day. This day they had spent talking, mainly, getting to know each other and rubbing their armor against the dread death of rust. They had fed the horses on the small amount of grain and long-dead hay, and had themselves eaten from their dwindling supplies.

Now night had returned. The Levantine moon hung round and white as a maiden's breast over the little town. Its silvery rays picked out rain-streaked white walls, reflected from puddles of water like polished shields amid the mud of the streets. A gentle breeze rustled through pines and gnarly olive trees dotting the surrounding terrain like gnomish sentinels.

Tonight, in this cozy little house whose owners had left behind both carpets and cushions, Guy and Melisende had begun again. With her lying back on the carpet and the old cushions they had found and collected together, he had held her in powerfully possessive arms, cock-stabbing her until she became a tigress of passion and wailed out her satiation while her body was rocked by absolutely stormy sensations of blissful passion.

Now the slender blonde from France was asleep, happily sated, with The Crusader's seed cooling in the silken-walled sheath of her lower belly. She sprawled atop a fat cushion with a cover of third-grade silk, dirty yellow, with its stuffing leaking out onto the brown-and-blue carpet. As naked as she, and as spent, Guy Kingsaver gazed at the loveliness of her very slender body.

Strange thoughts crowded his mind. It never occurred to him that there was responsibility in being a woman's first man. *A girl's first boy,* he thought with a little smile, for they were both youthful, despite The Crusader's powerfully muscled body and unusual height; he was rising six feet.

Quietly, so as not to rouse her from the sleep that was sweetest, he stood and drew his surcoat over his nakedness. The horses must be checked; no need to don underclothing, and leggings and then coat of silvery mail. But habit prevailed: he drew on his great broad belt of black leather, with the scabbarded sword of Spanish steel swinging from it, and the smaller suspended sheath, too, of a Saracen dagger. He grinned at his own thought, as he started to leave the two-room house. But he obeyed the thought, returning for his Saracen helmet with its curtain-like camail of fine steel links, for, ridiculously, he did not want to get his head wet.

Quietly, the tall man went out into the muddy town, under the steady gray drizzle. He sloshed down the street to the stable with the mud seeking to hold his feet with loud sucking noises.

He had just stepped inside when he heard the horsemen come riding. Instantly Guy wished he wore full armor. How could the riders of those approaching horses be those of his kind the Saracen called "Franks;" Westerners, Christians?

No, that creaking leather was the hide of the animals of this land, the clank and jingle and metallic scraping were of curved swords and the lighter chainmail of the sons of Allah; the enemy. And aye, now he could hear them: they spoke not the almost universal French, or any other Western tongue. Their words were Arabic. Thanks to the tutoring of a dusky girl who pleased to call him "master," and to much practice, Guy Kingsaver understood that tongue. Pressed against the inner wall amid the aroma of hay and animal sweat and old urine and excrement, he listened.

They were three, those Turks, and they were on their way south into Egypt, the base of Saladin's power and the source of his supplies of men and food and horse and arms. The Crusader's eyes narrowed. He held his breath lest he miss a word. For they were soldiers, Saladin's warriors, and he was hearing information of military value. Immediately Guy of Messaria, recently slave and outlaw and even more recently lover, became soldier once more.

Saladin, he heard, had taken refuge in Jerusalem from Richard and the crusading host. But the Turkish conqueror was far from hopeless. He expected reinforcements from Turkestan, and with those additional horse and men-at-arms, the three men Guy overheard assumed that their lord and commander would break the back of the besiegers, the cross-bearing unbelievers. Certainly with the Turkestani would come provisions—but they were hurrying, and thus were lightly laden, and thus Saladin would need much more supplies for the even huger army he was soon to command.

These three men were on a flying mission to Egypt, to arrange a great caravan. A mission for Saladin; a mission, then, against Richard.

The Crusader's heart beat the faster. He and Melisende must resume their northward trek at once, now, to warn King Richard. *If only I'd worn my armor,* Guy thought, *if only I had my wire-wrapped bow, a shield* . . . but he had not—and he was going to have to fight anyhow, for one of the men was now bidding another to stable the horses.

"An there be fodder for them there, Ayyub, feed them well, for they may go days before their next bellyful. If there be none . . . then make apology, in Allah's name, and be certain the poor beasts are well secured."

Then there were sloshing sounds in the watery mud.

"I have to stable the flea-infested horses whilst *they* hie themselves to shelter and comfort," Ayyub grumbled, in the manner of soldiers of all times and all places, as he approached the stable—and the silently waiting Messarian. Well concealed in the darkness, Guy allowed the man to lead the three animals inside and close the door after them.

"At least it's dry in here, praise be to Allah," Ayyub muttered.

"Aye, and ye'll not have to work long or hard—not in *this* life," a voice said from the darkness, in barbarously accented Arabic.

Ayyub's hand was tugging forth his scymitar even as he swung about.

A smile twitched the Saracen's thin-mustached face

12

as he saw himself set upon by a shaggy-haired, bearded man wearing only a surcoat, a white robe designed to be worn over armor as protection against burning sun. Despite the man's considerable size, Ayyub knew that the fellow had no protection at all, neither armor nor shield. Sidestepping quickly, he braced himself and prepared to meet the attack with ready scymitar.

Guy cursed himself mentally. He should have slain the other man without a word, merely hacking off his head or slamming his sword straight into the Saracen's back! Yet that was not the way of The Crusader, whose personal code transcended that of most nobler-born men.

He had to abandon his rushing attack, for without armor or shield he could take no cut of the Turk's sword. A scymitar-cut to an arm covered by linked Frankish steel was a heavy blow, perhaps a bruise; nothing more. But now even a half-blow would cost him the use of his arm for life—and perhaps the arm itself.

The two men faced each other in the dimness of the stable, staring with eyes held wide in their attempt to defeat the darkness and see the more clearly.

I am too vulnerable, Guy thought. *I must let him come to me—and I must be swift!*

"So ye speak our language, Frank, and ye deemed it prudent to come at me without armor, did ye? Well, ye'll not be the first Frank I've sent off to hell!" With those words, Ayyub lunged with his crescent-curved sword held so as to pierce his antagonist's unarmored belly.

The Frank, though, was considerably faster than Ayyub might have expected, considering the other's height and muscular bulk. He danced away, swung half around, and his long broadsword came rushing around with a force and speed that made it hum as it clove the air. There was a great clang as blade fell upon blade, and the Turk grunted and winced with the shock that

13

ran up his arm. The Frank was as strong as he looked
—and even faster!

Hard-struck by the other sword, Ayyub's blade
thunked loudly off the wall of a horse stall. Within, he
heard a horse move and utter a nervous whicker. But
the Turk did not trouble himself with that; his only
concern was to regain his balance and the position of
his sword, for the big Frank was twisting his own wrist,
arresting his stroke, and starting the backhand movement that would bring that long blade rushing back.

Ayyub moved, and Guy's backhand stroke struck
sparks from the Saracen's armor. Ayyub's teeth flashed
in a feral grin; it would take more than that! He backed,
grateful for the blade-turning strength of his light mailcoat, and swung his own shorter sword in a vicious
chop to carry away the other man's swordarm.

And Guy Kingsaver did the totally unexpected. He
did not duck aside, or dance back, or attempt the impossible: to get his blade in the way of the oncoming
steel. He drove forward, straight at his attacker. Ayyub
grunted when his rushing forearm slammed into the
upper arm of the other man, who immediately whipped
his elbow up and out from his body just as if he had
worn a shield. The Christian's face writhed in pain as
a hardswung arm clad in silvery mail impacted his own
unprotected one. But he made no sound. Having sprung
in too close to be sword-cut and having whipped his
arm out to deflect the chopping stroke, he again did the
unexpected.

Guy of Messaria dropped his three-foot sword! Down
sprang his right hand even as his body slammed into
the other man's with a force that brought groans from
both their lips. And up came that right hand, empty of
sword—but no longer completely empty. Ayyub had
only an instant to be aware of the sliver of steel thrusting from the fist that rushed upward at his chin; only an
instant to try, desperately, to flail his sword into the
attacker's back.

14

Then The Crusader's powerful underhand blow terminated up under the other man's chin, and the Saracen dagger he had drawn slid in easily through unprotected skin, between the bones of the jaw, and drove on upward to burst into Ayyub's mouth. The Saracen's teeth clacked together and bit off the cry he should have loosed long ago.

Now he died in the darkness of the stable, his mouth full of blood that flowed out between his lips and rushed down his throat and into his windpipe, and without having either called or warned his two companions. His swordarm dropped beneath the weight of his scymitar, his other hand clutched weakly at his opponent's big shoulder. Ayyub swayed back. For a moment a stall propped him up, while he stood staring in shock and surprise at the other man, strangling on his own blood.

He fell. Guy left the dagger where it was, pinning the man's jaws together. He paused for a few moments, listening. He heard only restless horses; the other two men had apparently not heard the almost silent fight.

They will know about me soon enough, The Crusader thought. *But I shall be better prepared to face the two of them!*

The man he had just slain was not so big as he, not so burly or well-muscled.. But Guy worked swiftly at ripping away the dead man's white robe, and then at getting the mailed coat off the body. The leggings, he knew, were hopeless; the Turk was too short. But the mailcoat would afford him at least partial protection, provided it did not hamper his movements.

Swiftly Guy stripped off his swordbelt and surcoat; hurriedly he drew the padded Saracen mailcoat about himself. It would not quite meet across his powerful chest, and he sighed and buckled the other man's belt tightly around himself, in order to hold the chainlink jacket nearly closed and so afford himself as much protection as possible. The dead man's shoulders had been broad and his upper arms thick, and a couple of practice

15

swings of his arms told Guy that he was only slightly hampered. But he would certainly be better equipped for a fight wearing the ill-fitting armor than without it.

He drew on his surcoat again, thinking it important to cover up the fact that a two-inch expanse of his bare flesh provided an excellent target from neck to knee. Then he buckled on his own swordbelt, sheathed the broadsword, and slipped into his own sheath the Turk's unused dagger.

Murmuring soothingly to the beasts, he moved among the horses and took from one saddle a round shield with a pointed steel boss set in its center. *Now for the other two,* he thought, with a smile that was not pretty.

At that same moment, he heard Melisende's scream.

TWO

Rape

Melisende woke from her happy sleep to rough hands and leering faces. By the time she had assimilated the facts that Guy was nowhere about, that she was naked and defenseless and entirely at the whim of two armed Saracen, one of them was behind her, kneeling with one leg on each of her arms and thus pinning her. The other was on his knees between her legs, grinning as he gazed down at the pale-haired bulge of her vulva.

She cried out when he thrust at her with a rough-skinned, callused finger, and in one painful drive imbedded it in her wet slash—wet only because it still contained the semen of Guy of Messaria. She was otherwise unprepared, and the gouging finger *hurt*.

"Unnngh!" she groaned, and jerked violently. Instantly a dark Turkish hand came down to cover her mouth. Try as she might, she could liberate neither her hands nor a sound from her throat. Huge-eyed, she lay there quivering and panting.

"Ready!" her tormentor grunted, roughly jabbing deep.

"Then hurry and fuck her, Hassan. My need for this Christian cunt is great!" This in a tight-throated voice from the man holding her arms motionless.

Hassan grinned, clamped his hands to her hips, and held apart her restless legs with his own. He came into her with a big, driving entry that seemed to be splitting her tender passage as the fat crown of his circumcised Saracen prick opened the way for his thick prickshaft that lunged into her in search of her vaginal depths. Rooting hard into her, grunting like a pig at the trough, her rapist jammed himself into the warm niche between her spread thighs and far back inside her clasping, clutching gash.

She moaned and twitched, trying to tug her arms free of the numbing pressure of the other man's legs. He chuckled, watching his companion shove deep into the blond Frankish woman, and, keeping his hand over her mouth, reached down with the other to maul her pretty, startlingly white breast. It was the first tit of such color he had seen, and the first nipple of so pale a pink. It fascinated him, that nicely rounded, quite firm mound of white flesh with its twitching coral crest.

Hassan slammed into her with bold thrusts of his jerking pelvis. His lust-mad brain was unable to dictate other than a precipitate rush to orgasm. There was no regular rhythm to his lunging strokes up her belly, no tenderness in the way he cock-battered her squirming, soft-fleshed interior. Despite her lack of cooperation, her own body came to her aid, and the arrogant soldier of the sultan chuckled aloud.

"She's flooding inside," he advised his companion. "The Nazrani she-cur loves it, Saif!"

"It isn't that little poker of yours she loves, Hassan," the other man grinned, "it's the attention her white teat is receiving!"

"Hmp," Hassan grunted, humping, gasping, grunting, jerking in slobbering lust. His dark body slammed against the pale, sumptuously curved form of the Frankish slut, filling him with scalding streams of voluptuary pleasure as, helplessly and unwillingly, her wide-open pussy embraced his throbbing tool.

He jerked hard, sending his frantic penis far up into her, seeking her cervix, her womb, her belly. What a

18

joy to fuck this unwilling Christian cesspool of a cunt! Again and again his pelvis drummed against hers, with loud slapping sounds. His face glistened with sweat. Like fine silken cords, the inner muscles of her vaginal canal gnawed at the prick sliding so slickly and easily in and out.

At the same time, his partner crushed his dark fingers deeply into the pliant softness of her firm white breast. She groaned and writhed, dashing her legs up and down, suffused with shamefaced blushes. She stared with dilated eyes at her savage ravisher's lust-twisted face. She had known cruelty and humiliation for year upon year—but she had thought it was over, that with the big man of Cyprus she was surely safe forever. Now he was nowhere to be seen and she was prey to vicious rape. Had he abandoned her? Had they slain him?

Melisende did not know. She knew only that she was a vessel to be used, a cunt with body incidentally attached, and that the moment Hassan had sped his slimy seed into her the other man would take his place—and by the time he had fucked her and spurted into her ravaged channel, Hassan might well have produced another erection by watching and by painfully mauling her breasts, as Saif was now doing.

Hassan's hips pumped rhythmically with surging stamina into the snug fit of her hungrily absorbing trench. The hot tingle was building, building, rising like sap in his tightening ballocks.

Saif's big hands squeezed and pressured and pinched the taut skin of her breasts, dimpling it deeply so that dead-white ridges of straining breast-flesh rose up about his fingers. She whimpered, her lips quivering, as she felt his horny nails digging cruelly into tender, spongily-yielding flesh.

"Gahhh!" Hassan throated out, in the wordless lust-sound of an animal. And he ground in deep, his face suddenly twisting, his body going rigid. His liquid lake burst into her as he groaned and shuddered in a crash-

19

ing climax. The clutching cavern he had widened to take and hold his semen took it now, all of it. She writhed miserably as her body accepted his spermy reserves. Then he was gasping and grunting, sagging onto her, heedless of his weight and the mailshirt he had not troubled to remove.

The man kneeling on her arms suddenly set the point of his dagger against the curving expanse of one perfect breast, its whiteness deeply pinkened now by his mauling fingers. She jerked, moaned, for he pressed the point just firmly enough to bring a tiny trickle of blood.

"Scream when I remove my hand from your mouth, Christian whore, and I will lean on this dagger, slowly, and you will feel its cold steel slide deeper and deeper into this milk-bag! Do you understand? If you do, *lick my palm!*"

She understood both his words and their meaning, this girl of seventeen who had spent over four years as a slave among his people. She lay still and, shivering in disgust, performed the demeaning act of response he demanded.

Saif giggled like a girl of ten. "She licks," he said gleefully. "Raise your dead weight from her, Hassan, and make way for a real man!"

With a sighing groan, the spent Hassan did. Melisende felt an instant chill as the sweat coating her body was exposed to the air. Then, after a brief consultation, Hassan moved up and clamped his hand around her neck.

"Turn over," he ordered her. "Turn over, and be silent. Cry out and I will squeeze this pullet's neck of yours! Saif must be accustomed to *boys*—he wants you from behind!"

"Allah yenik," Saif muttered obscenely, but with little anger. Hassan chuckled, Saif chuckled.

The slender blonde turned over and obeyed the rough command to get on her knees with her backside high and her legs apart. Kneeling behind her, Saif grinned

20

broadly as she arched her backside to expose the deep warm cleft between its halves, between the tops of her silky and incredibly white thighs, presenting her soft Christian pussy more accessibly to his big, hard, male bone.

Her cunt-lips were violently red and parted, from the other man's recent rummaging between them. Saif saw the evidence of Hassan's passion, in the thick long drop of white syrup that seeped from between those strangely colored lips and plunged down to stain the floor beneath her. He moved closer, the glistening round knob of his cock aimed at that slit, his glans nakedly exposed by their Allah-mandated rite of circumcision. Guiding his erection with one hand, aiming its broad tip downward though it wanted to stand high and stiff before him, he drove suddenly forward at the kneeling girl.

She remembered the hand menacing her breath and Hassan's threat as his rutting comrade came plunging into her ravaged slash, and she made only a throaty groaning sound. The man behind her pushed, in and in, opening her up again—and with ease—until his polished cockflesh had vanished beneath her quivering arse-cheeks.

Saif grunted happily. His hairy crotch thumped into the nicely rounded cheeks of her rump. He had imbedded his full distended length inside the embrace of her pussy. It was slick with the other man's sperm and yet surprisingly, delightfully tight, that pink-cunted embrace.

Saif began moving. He hunched under and up with his hands pressing her hindcheeks, pummeling through her vulvar lips with a savage rhythm dictated by the fact that he had been days from Jerusalem and its willing, camp-following whores.

Melisende could not see this fucker. She was not only no virgin, she was a consummately sensuous woman indeed, who had reached an orgasm her first time, that

21

day on the outlaw mesa when Guy had been forced to tup her while Julanar's entire band looked on. Now, staring down at the floor of the little house and feeling that big fat-knobbed organ drilling in and out of her from behind, opening around it and feeling no pain whatever, she realized that it was not unpleasant and that, if she put out of her mind the circumstances, she might well enjoy it.

She tried. Closing her eyes, she concentrated only on the slick, swift cruising of lust-bloated maleness sawing in and out of her pleasure-slash.

The man behind her ground into her squirming arse-cheeks and pumped her girlish hole with great lurching strokes, like a rutting animal. Her breasts swung wildly beneath her, their soft resilience turning into hard firmness, swollen with pleasure and lust, the nipples springing out hard and excited.

Saif grinned. Her lubricating oils and Hassan's semen coated his gliding organ. It was slick enough, slimily-coated enough to rend the puckered and hairless little *feurdj* of even a nine-year-old. It was certainly hard enough and slippery enough to breach the hole he had begun thinking about and coveting even before this cross-following slut had assumed the position they had demanded and turned it temptingly up at him!

Accordingly, Saif leaned back, whipping his slime-glistening cock out of her. She trembled as it left her, with a slurping popping-forth. But he gave her no time to wonder; the raping Saracen ensheathed his prick between the excitingly compact ovals of her backside in one hard lunge.

The kneeling blonde shivered at the dilating, flesh-spreading sensation of his great pole of lust forcing its relentless way past her tightened sphincter. Flesh-spreading—and agonizingly flesh-*tearing!*

As a blazing fire of pure agony tore through her, Melisende tried desperately to lunge forward. She screamed at the utmost capacity of her lungs and throat.

Instantly hands seized her hips to stay her attempt at a forward crawl; instantly relentless fingers tightened about her throat to shut off further cries. With a gagging, retching sound, she was forced to accept the heartlessly forceful breaching of her rectum. She could only moan piteously as hot waves of burning agony erupted in both her anal mouth and in her throat.

He had breached the closed hole between her buttcheeks, driven up that sweet, tiny hole as if it were a hot and vehemently tight cunt, and now he was sunk far up her back. Her tremorous rump wiggled high in the air, shaking its creamy halves, its slick humid furrow caressing the fiery pole embedded in it.

New pain lanced when he withdrew, his prick oozing back and back until only its bulbous head remained within her, propping open the strong muscle of her anus. Then he rammed it into her again, and only Hassan's constricting, ever-menacing hand stilled her shriek.

Saif's hips began jerking frantically back and forth. With the hot blood pouring into his groin, he buggered her fast and hard. His cock was assailed by the heat of that deep chasm, and he could feel the wildly agonized shivers that passed through her. Moist, tender rectal walls were incredibly tight around his organ, and he paused for a moment, holding himself motionless inside her.

His pause was not dictated by mercy or concern for her poor strained rectum. He thought only of himself, wanted only to savor the sensation of that tight anal grasp, and to look down at the tiny hole he had enlarged to the circumference of his circumcised horn. He gazed down into the hot valley that parted her quivering oval cheeks, and he could see the hairy base of his tool rammed in tight to the valley floor, its entire length invisible in the hole between her beautiful cheeks.

"Move, O buggerer," Hassan snarled. "Fuck, man, for soon Ayyub will return from the stable and want his turn—and I feel new life in my *zubb* already!"

Saif laughed aloud. His lust-mad body crushed his groin against her buttocks with each new lunge, forcing her open, wider and wider for his thick grinding cock. The huge poker throbbed hard in the grip of constant prickly sensations. His thighs slapped her butt with repeated slapping sounds each accompanied by his pounding tool rushing up her moist, burning tunnel. Her body quivered and shook as he pounded its soft white rearcheeks. She whimpered, writhed, shook with repeated tremors. He was forcing wide and taut her dainty anal tissues with a cruel vengeance and an apparent fixation on driving himself through her very bowels.

"Ah," he grunted, "ah, ah—arrrrrghhhh!" His suddenly larger prick began spitting and he began grinding in as he climaxed, voiding himself up her bowels. He groaned and hung on, his body quaking, as it streamed from him into her.

He was just pushing, coaxing out the last few droplets of his semen, when all three of them heard the sound of rushing footsteps, squelching muddily across the other room of the little house.

"Ahhhhh," the sated, emptied Saif happily sighed, and turned his head with a grin to the doorway, to catch that first glimpse of Ayyub's face, which he expected would show first astonishment and then delight. It was Saif's face that registered astonishment, though, and shock—but not delight.

Horror was his expression, his last expression. His features remained frozen in that expression as they flew across the room to be smashed against the wall, so violent was the sword-blow that severed Saif's head from his rapist's body.

Melisende cried out as the still-hard organ that had violently breached her anal passage was jerked out just as violently, tugged forth by the collapse of the headless, blood-gouting body behind her.

She fell forward as Hassan's hand left her throat.

Desperately, the Saracen scrambled away from the great blood-smeared broadsword in the hand of Saif's killer.

"Ye've had your turn with her already, Saracen slime? Then fetch out a sword and die happy, man!"

Melisende gasped. She was dizzied by a sudden flow of adrenalin. Her stomach felt as if she'd been struck at its base. Relief made her go limp, as she heard the voice and twitched her hair-streaming head around to look up at Guy Kingsaver of Messaria.

"Rehhman—" Hassan began, shaking violently.

"Speak not to me of mercy, sucker of Allah's scabby prick! Your sword!" The Crusader's voice rang in the small room.

A moment more Hassan hesitated; then he snatched the hilt of his curved brand from the floor where he had abandoned it with belt and scabbard. They rose with it as he whipped up the blade. He slung away sheath and belt and faced the big Frank holding the terrible sword, dripping with Saif's blood.

On The Crusader's left arm was strapped a round Saracen shield that Hassan recognized as his own. He knew that Ayyub had gone the same way as Saif, that the woman they had sported themselves with was the woman of this big man with the fierce eyes—and that this man was bent on the death of Hassan, as he'd already slain Ayyub and Saif.

"Allahumma!" Hassan gasped.

"He will not help you," the other man told him, and struck.

Desperately Hassan essayed to meet that ferocious sword-cut with his blade, since he had no shield for defense; indeed, it was his own good round shield he faced! He might as well have attempted to spit into the *zoba'ah,* the dread black sandstorm of the desert.

A terrible pain jolted up through his arm, his scymitar snapped off halfway up its blade, and the mighty stroke of the Christian's sword sent that sliver of steel flying across the room where, as if aimed, it struck point-first into the wall and remained there. Again Hassan started to plead for mercy.

And in the most vicious swordcut of his life, The Crusader inflicted a suitably Saracen punishment on the other man for his rape; his sword clove down into the split at the front of Hassan's mailskirt, the slit that enabled an armored man to sit a saddle and still keep his legs covered. Hassan shrieked, as half his penis was carried bloodily away to drop bloodily onto his left foot—at the same time the heavy Frankish sword chopped deep into that foot.

Moaning in awful pain, the Turk sought to strike at his attacker with the jagged stump of his ruined sword—and lost his hand in a new gout of blood.

"GUY!" Melisende shrieked.

The desperate cry of his name slashed through the berserker rage shrouding The Crusader's brain, and he knew why she cried out, and that she was right. He was not a Turk, to torment a man with a slow death of many cuts, even a craven whimpering man who had raped her and held her by the throat whilst another buggered her.

Guy struck again, in another iron-shearing blow, and Hassan's head leaped to roll on the floor near that of his comrade.

With his sword in his hand, Guy swung to the girl, bent over her.

"I'm sorry," he murmured, and then drew her up in one arm.

He carried her from that charnel house and into the one next door, where he stood her weakly in a corner, so that the two walls braced her shivering nakedness. He returned to bring carpet and cushions, clothing and armor from the house where she had been twice raped. The bodies of her ravagers turned the floor dark with blood; that of Hassan still jerked as its shredded neck vomited forth scarlet.

Dropping everything he carried as soon as he re-entered the little house where he had carried Melisende, Guy enwrapped her in his big arms and held her for a long, long while.

THREE

The Palace of Ascalon

In the morning, they rode.

She was the daughter of a French knight, a slave of the Saracen for nigh onto five years, lately a slave of the outlaws of northernmost Egypt; a blooded warrior and a victim of beatings and rapes. Her mass of blond hair was tucked up into a pointed Saracen helmet, and she was disguised in a long white robe, split front and back for ease in the saddle. On her saddle's horn a round Saracen shield with a pointed boss in its center. A Saracen scymitar hung from a taken-in belt that was buckled around her hips, since when worn baldric-style it brought discomfort to her breasts. Eyes as blue as the Mediterranean gazed outward from her oval face, ever wary—and often directed to the man beside her. A woman at seventeen, without family, with no friend save her companion.

He was the son of Peter, a peasant of Messaria, a tiny town on the island of Cyprus, where Richard the Lion-heart had tarried on his way to the Holy Land, last year in May. He had tupped a local lass in a stable, was marked for slaying by a paid assassin, and was saved seconds before his death by the young Messarian; Guy had dropped from the loft onto the black-clad assassin and plunged a wooden pitchfork into the man. That had been seven months ago; to the young man who had earned the name Guy Kingsaver, it seemed many years.

He was older in the ways of war, for he had proclaimed Richard his liege-lord and come on the crusade with him, and with his legendary longbow and sword and dagger he had slain many dark, twin-bearded sons of Allah. More than once had he been hero, and more than once had he been promised knighthood, despite his most humble birth. When he had defeated and taken captive Saladin's best knight, Yarok ibn-Ammar al-Jazzar, slayer of many good crusaders and most notably the Viscount of Ellandun, it was the king's righthand man who had offered knighthood on the spot. But Guy had said nay to the Earl of Leicester; he would wait until Richard himself saw fit to dub him Sir Guy.

He was wiser, too, in women, for there had been many, and not all common, as they had not all been of his own people. There was the widowed Luisa de Vermandois, who had made the hero of Cyprus her goal and had easily captivated him, and who had taught him much in the ways of a man with a maid, so that he was a knowledgeable and often solicitous lover—another characteristic that set him above most of those around him. And there was Rosamonde, the lady's maid he had wooed and perhaps loved during the long siege of Acre, and who had died of the Syrian fever. There was Leila, daughter of an emir, whom he had been forced to best at arms and then to sword-spank, in the palace of Acre. After that she termed herself his woman, and from her he had learned the language of her people. There had been others, here and there. . . And Lady Blanche of Tyre, and that stranger whom he had twice loved in the darkness before learning that she was Isabella, heiress to the throne of Jerusalem and wife of the lord Conrad, Marquis of Montferrat and Protector of Tyre. There had been Julanar al-Libwah, "the Lioness," as fierce and giving in their coupling as

29

she had been fierce and unyielding in battle, commanding her band of all-female outlaws.

And there was Melisende.

He was far wiser in the ways of the world, for he had seen the unworthy quarrels that had split the ranks of the crusading force and made it less effective, finally resulting in the decamping of King Philip Augustus for his own France, so that Richard of Normandy and England remained supreme. Yet even in that supremacy, King Richard was constantly challenged and made to wring his hands. Philip had left behind the Duke of Burgundy, Hugh, who seemed bent on destroying Richard's generalship and the crusade. Too, the thrice-arrogant Leopold, Archduke of Austria, was a constantly twisting thorn in the side of the red-bearded Richard. Nor would Conrad, safe in Tyre, lend aid to these men who were widening his area of defense and thus strengthening his rule.

Now Guy and Melisende rode. They had turned the faces of their mounts north by west at first, until they were sure they had crossed, north of the Red Sea, from Egypt into the Holy Land. Now their course, north by east, was made treacherously difficult and dangerous by the daily rains that made raging torrents of little streams—and impassable running lakes of the rivers. In many places the way was impassable not only because of the rain-swollen streams but because of the marshy ground that threatened to suck up horses and riders, to swallow them without remorse or belch.

When they stopped, it was to inspect and work away at their armor, ever in danger of rust. Their outer clothing, Guy's surcoat and Melisende's robe, clung soddenly to them. It increased the weight of the armor they wore by, seemingly at least, another stone. They spoke but little, in their misery. But they plodded ever northward, for now Guy had information of value to impart to the kingly lord he sought to rejoin.

One day Melisende's horse plunged a foot through

into the sucking marsh, and with a cry she slipped from the saddle and plunged into the awful muck. Guy of Messaria would rather have fought ten men than to have spent a long, danger-fraught and disgusting hour winning her free. And that was hardly the end of it, still. They spent the rest of that miserable day holed up as best they could, huddling together without enjoyment or romance, cold and wet and slime-streaked. Neither of them knew until much later that the date was December twenty-fifth, Christmas of 1191.

Weary riders on weary horses, they turned coastward and came plodding up to Ascalon, on the Mediterranean coast. The town was deserted, its walls ruined; it had been both emptied and rendered indefensible by Saladin, against the coming of the crusaders at the end of summer. Cypress and mulberry trees, bereft of their green cloaks, erupted forlornly among the buildings of white and colored stucco.

As she had on their arrival at that nameless town of a few days past, Melisende turned her eyes hopefully toward her companion, though she said nothing. If he should say they must forge on, she would nod and twitch her rein, though she were forced to tie herself in the saddle to remain ahorse.

But he did not so decree, and they rode into a city of mud and empty houses, windows and gaping doorways like the hollow eyes of skulls; a city inhabited only by ghosts. And perhaps the Arabic *ghul* . . . and more than one brave mongoose, for there were many snakes. To Ascalon's palace they rode, and into it, and within its ornately painted walls and on its tiled floors they stabled the animals.

With sword in hand and Melisende five paces behind, her blade also bared, The Crusader roamed the tesselated tiles of those halls and peered into every silent room. Only when he was satisfied that the large building was indeed deserted did he turn to Melisende with a smile.

31

"Milady, regretfully we are without servants this evening, but our lodgings are warm, and dry . . ."

She doffed her Saracen helmet and tossed it from her so that it rang and clattered on the floor. Then, despite her martial attire, she dropped him a curtsy.

"Milord . . . I am enchanted. And now shall we inspect the larder to choose our repast this e'en?"

"Methinks our larder is in the panniers on the backs of our horses," he told her ruefully.

Straightening, she shot him a look. "It is what I meant," the blond Frenchwoman assured him.

And he was right; there was no larder amid the magnificence of the place. What food had been left behind by the fleeing citizens of Ascalon had long since turned to rot and mould. Yet their own food, newly replenished from the packs of three Turks so recently met and slain, would taste better within this small palace of a small city on the southeastern coast.

Most of the furnishings remained behind, including low Arabic couches and beds, pillows, carpeting, even lovely wall-hangings . . . and Melisende found a partial bolt of cloth, a very busy paisley pattern of pastels: yellow and gold and blue and green with threads of white snaking all through pattern, separating the colors. In that same chest she discovered, too, a broken bracelet of silver; a single earring of great size, set with bits of colored glass; what had been a jeweled girdle, the stones having been pried out before the owner had abandoned the thick, refulgent belt of cloth-of-gold; a pair of shoes of scarlet felt, one of which was worn through at the heel; a fat woman's tent-like robe of tan and blue vertical stripes, well-worn and with a tear just behind the right shoulder; finally, there was a silver comb minus three teeth.

Happy as a child with the "treasure", she shooed Guy from the room, after begging him to don the striped robe of worn silk.

He saw to the horses, callously quartering them in

a carpeted room, and he himself went over their armor with great care for every possible droplet of moisture. It was he, too, who washed her robe and his surcoat in the shrub-surrounded pool behind the palace. It was long since full and overflowing, so that he stood in water to his ankles. The naked branches of mulberry and orange trees scraped cratchily together when a little breeze rose.

One wall of a large anteroom bore naked hooks where once had hung tapestries or perhaps arms; across four of these he stretched their wet outerclothes, to drip on a floor richly carpeted in hues of wine and wheat. Padding from that room, he wondered what he must look like: a great near-giant of a man, thick and broad of shoulder and massive of chest, almost flat of belly, bearded and overlong of hair—and naked but for the baldric-slung sword and a dagger at his lean hips!

With a little smile, he donned the striped robe. It was snug on him nowhere, though short of sleeves and skirt. Then he walked out into the long cool hallway of alternating pink-red and white tiles.

"MILA-A-ADY-Y-Y!" he called, and his voice echoed and re-echoed.

She came, descending that broad staircase with its crimson marble steps, and Guy was astonished at what she had accomplished. Her hair, free of snarls but full of long gentle waves, shone lustrously from its combing. Caught somehow at her left shoulder with the single earring, the paisley cloth she had found was wound and gracefully draped about her slenderness, leaving bare her right shoulder and a scandalously great expanse of her left leg. The garment was girt with the cloth-of-gold belt, handsome despite its gaping jewel-settings. The soft scarlet shoes encased her feet prettily without showing their worn soles, and she had somehow persuaded the broken silver bracelet to cling around her right ankle.

Guy imitated a lordly bow. "My lady is beautiful in

her finery," he said. His wet hair dripped.

"My lord is more than passing handsome in his new robe of state," she told him.

Without so much as a smile, they went regally, hand in hand, into a dining hall of low tables and carven, high-backed chairs. There they ate their meager repast, exclaiming over its richness. Rain water was their after-dinner wine, dried figs their fruit.

Guy surprised her, when they were done, by singing a portion—all he could remember—of King Richard's lay, "Red Was His Sword." His lady exclaimed over his good voice. That much was not fantasy; many had remarked the similarity between the voice of Guy King-saver and King Richard's bard, Blondel de Nisle.

She grew silent then, as their pretending ended with their meal. Both knew it was time to retire, and Melisende was no practiced temptress.

With her hand on his arm in manner most noble, they walked the dark hall and entered a room of two broad divans, still covered with deep-hued velvets, and one table carved of some dark wood. The whole was silverily lit by the moon that had burst through dark clouds and frightened away the rain.

"SEND ME IN A COUCH-GIRL," Guy bellowed suddenly, gazing out the window at the moon's reflection on the flat roofs surrounding them.

He heard her gasp, then the whisper of her worn felt shoes, joining in this new fantasy. Instantly he whirled, doffed the robe, and lolled on one of the low beds, with his legs well apart in a deliberately lascivious display. His hand played between his thighs to make himself appear more ready for the advent of a "couch-girl."

She came, silent and with bowed head in the moon-light, and stood before him in the same manner. He leaned out slightly to run his warming hand up her left leg.

"Ah—it is *Kimri al-mukarremeh*," he said throatily,

34

calling her "Dove the magnificent," after the Arabic manner.

"My lord *Akbar al-aqib*," she murmured, giving him too a grand name in the continuation of their pretense; *Akbar* was "Mighty" and *al-aqib* meant "the wonderful." And she pressed her bare leg into his hand.

A little gasp escaped her when he ran that hand on up, pushing up the folds of her makeshift gown, and tickling the fine soft bulge of her vulva.

"My heart is gladdened," he said, gently fondling and making her sigh, "that I have been sent my favorite girl, this night. I would see her naked of her finery."

Slowly, without moving from where she stood, Melisende stripped until she was clothed only in her long hair of honey and sunshine, and in the moonlight.

He sat up, tugged her forward with a hand on each of her hips, fingertips resting on the swells of her shapely backside, and pressed a kiss to the lightly furred, full round mount of her genital bulge.

It was a more than unusual act for a man, and a great tremor went all through the standing girl. She gasped and slid a trembling hand through his hair.

Encouraged by her reaction to do that which many men would have considered both revolting and demeaning, he lengthened his kiss between her thighs. The pretty pink lips were moist and parted, and he ran his tongue teasingly up and down between them.

The astonished girl emitted a high, sighing squeal of rapture and nearly fell. A fiery, melting sensation thrilled within her, and spread out in warm waves throughout her body.

He pressed his lips forcefully against those soft, very springy lower ones of hers. The fragrance of rising cuntal sap rose to his nostrils with the aroma of woman, and sex, and then there was the sensation of the viscous fluid on his tongue. It was not displeasing in its flavor. He sucked it up, being noisy about it in a deliberate titillation of her senses, and he smiled at her new squeal

35

of surprise and happiness. His mouth was assaulted by more and more fragrant vaginal liquor.

His tongue, caressing those softly encircling flanges of her womanhood and the wet cleft that divided them, licked titillatingly up the entry of that heated cavern until it was tickling maddeningly, teasingly at the barely perceptible little nubbin set high within the liquid crack.

A great shiver took her. Her hand tightened in his hair without her knowledge, tugging him closer, pressing his face and welcome tongue into her furrow.

He sensed her excitement and extreme response; her body was shaking and pearly juice ran in rivers from the steaming chamber of her wildly aroused cleft. Like a pale cloud, her hair cascaded back and forth as she tossed her head almost hysterically and kept the air filled with her constant moaning.

His fingers kneaded her tensing buttocks. He licked her clitoris, sucked that stiffening, twitching little woman-cock, and delighted in the obvious pleasure he was giving her.

It was greater than he realized. Of a sudden, both of them felt the sweat streaming down her sides. Her quaking body exploded into a climax of cataclysmic proportions, and cry after cry erupted from her throat. Her eyes flaring wide, she hunched desperately to him, while her interior became a lake and contracted fiercely in cherished agony. Then she collapsed, as though she were made of unbaked dough, and he had to catch her sagging body and swing her onto the bed with him.

She was long minutes recovering.

For another long space after that, she stared at him, unbelievingly, adoringly. And then she was racing her fluttering hands over him, raining kisses on his face and neck and shoulder and chest, sucking swiftly at a nipple, flicking her tongue over it, gliding her face and mouth and pleasantly tickling hair down his hard belly.

Her wet tongue flicked over the swollen bulb of his high-standing, lust-hardened organ. Pursing her lips as though for a tender kiss, she instead slipped them over that helmet-shaped glans and let it coast into her face.

The Crusader groaned aloud. The sensation of ravenous mouth voraciously engulfing his prick was so poignant, the sight of that thick hairy shank sticking lewdly out of her parted lips was so beautiful, that he felt in danger of spurting well before he wanted to. His cock was consumed in moving, enveloping, saliva-moist flesh that was a net of sensation all around the hardened flesh. Pleasureful quakes jolted through his belly and stabbed into his guts.

He stood it as long as he could, and then he thrust her face back from him and dumped her unceremoniously, roughly onto her back. He moved swiftly after her, between her splaying thighs, and even in her surprise she thought to send one hand leaping down to clasp around the precociously swollen prick that came rushing at her.

She tucked it into herself. The warm inner walls of her pussy stretched to accommodate the bulbous head of that slippery length of maleness. A great sigh escaped each of them as he seated himself far up inside her.

He was unable to be still. He began moving at once. His body slithered on the satiny white nakedness of the excited woman hunching beneath him. Every lurching instroke squashed her lovely tits wetly under his chest—and banged his balls, just as wetly, into the crater of her loins. Wider and wider spread the soft tender lips of her clutching channel.

She groaned. Incredible . . . but the great delving spear of his penis was growing still more!

She shivered again and again, thrilling to the big slab of ultra-masculine meat that slid so forcefully up her. Her temples and her twitching clitoris pounded feverishly. Her hands wandered rapturously over his rising, falling body. Their pubic hair entwined and sweat flowed from both their whipping bodies, mingling and making them slippery.

Caught up in a maelstrom of sexuality, he slammed

his body down onto hers. He rammed hard into her crotch in a delirium of joyous rapture.

Her sex juices churned and leaked from the inner layers of sinewy flesh as his cock furled and spread her. The warm flow came trickling out between blood-swollen labia. Her body churned up and down. Flanking his meaty ones, her thighs seemed burning with her sultry need and the constant abrasive movements of his body against their soft inner surfaces.

A tremor of blazing lust racked her and she revolved her hips, straining to move beneath him, thrusting with her loins at the strong and turgid spike foraging her cunt. Her eyes were filled with the hot glow of desire.

He began pounding her, his body slapping hers loudly in painful impacts that drove him far inside her heated hole and let him feel the pressure of her cervix against the tip of his prickhead. Groaning, her eyes flaring, she dug her fingers into his upper arms, then let them leap inward to seize and worry his tiny masculine nipples.

She hunched him in a desperate animal abandon, as wildly excited as he, her cunt a seething, boiling, bubbling cauldron of arousal and sucking desire.

Wedged way inside her, his searching, probing tool strained and stretched her pussy's lush pink lips with its thick base. Curling and wiry, his pubic hairs abraded her. She could feel it, grinding into the softness of those widespread labia.

Every movement he made slashed his cock deep into her, seeking her womb as he rode her with deliberate up and down movements. Intense lustful pleasure surged through his sweat-wet form. Signally aware of her breasts, like over-filled wine pouches beneath him, he arched his body and strained his neck to suck at their pink spouts. She cried out as sweet joy flooded her and those upthrusting buds prickled, swelled, stiffened into hard pink points.

His teeth nipped her, teasingly, in tiny love-bites.

His hard length of cock sluiced in and out of her, striking deep. She jerked in ever rising delight and, her movements freer now with him arched above her, she shook her sleek breasts so that they appeared ready to tear loose from their moorings.

Abruptly he released his toothy hold, jerked himself all the way out of her, and in one swift rough movement turned her over.

"Ah!" she cried out, as her sensitized nipples dug into a soft coverlet that felt as if it had been sorcerously transformed into chainmail. "Put it back, put it back, I want—annngh!"

He put it back, in a swift rush that smacked her upturned bottomcheeks, hard, with his lunging body. He drove hard and fast, thumping and bumping against her bouncy behind, driving deep into her steaming depths while lying atop her back in a way that made her utterly powerless to move. Nevertheless she squirmed and thrust herself back in a paroxysm of passionate need.

Oh give it to me, she begged mentally in a mad welter of sensations and thoughts, *let me feel that wet cream filling my sluttish chasm, make me scream as I receive it!*

He groaned loudly in her ear, went plank-stiff atop her, and strained as if attempting to puncture the floor of her stomach with the huge head of his cock.

His exploding groin drenched her inner flesh with waves of steaming seed that flowed like a gushing hot fountain into her welcoming body. Relentlessly jerking, his organ pumped and pumped warm milk into her until there was nothing left in his emptied, flaccid penis. Both of them lay still, as it began shriveling in the lake he had made of her expanded channel, shriveling and creeping slowly back out of the flooded funnel to her womb.

They went to sleep that way, both of them, and she awoke only because of the discomfort of that great

39

muscular body crushing down onto hers. Yet there was such security in it, such warmth and the marvelous feeling of protection, that she hated to move.

She did at last, and he rolled onto his back and was still. For a long while, she sat up on the Saracen bed beside him and gazed down at The Crusader's powerful body in repose.

They rode on next day, and reached Ibelin, just up the coast from Ascalon. The sight in the gray rain was the same: ruined walls seeming to stagger around a deserted town. Guy shook his head, and they rode on, ever north in the awful rain.

They did not reach Jaffa that day, but had to camp out in the open again, and there was no repetition of their marvelous and fierce sexual encounter of the night before. Again she was awake after him, wondering: Did she really want to reach Jaffa, others? Was this not the good life? Might she not on the morrow lose The Crusader?

FOUR

The Palace of Jaffa

Astonishment was broad-writ on the faces of the men on the walls and attending the gate of coastal Jaffa.

They soon learned that the man who had returned from the dead had brought with him no Turkish prisoner, but that the Saracen-armored rider with him was a young Frenchwoman, whose cloud of blond hair cascaded and swirled once she removed her camailed helmet.

"Nay, Guy Kingsaver," one short sentinel from Normandy said as the two were admitted, "King Richard has not been here these many days. He has taken the army inland, westward, to that place called Bayit Nuba. From thence, they plan to attack Jerusalem itself—and here be I, poor Fulk Fulk's son, tarrying idly about this peaceful city whilst such great deeds are done!"

Guy nodded. "I will be setting out for Bayit Nuba this after—" He paused, glancing up at the sky, and sighed. "In the morning," he amended.

"Give such instructions to those at the stable, Kingsaver, and forget not that Fulk son of Fulk of Verneuil would fain ride with you to where aught is likely to happen!"

"I have no say over the defenses of Jaffa, Fulk, but am only a common fighting man like yourself," Guy told the stumpy man. And with a glance at Melisende, The Crusader twitched his rein. The two horses paced into Jaffa.

People stared as they rode at a sedate walk through the streets of the city: people of both East and West, Syrians and French, men from Pisa and Genoa in their strangely different clothing and with their own rapidly babbled language, shopkeepers and good wives, wine sellers and occasional knights or their ladies in their bright finery. These last, too, stared at the unusual: the huge armored man on the spirited Arabian horse, the slender figure beside him also Saracen-mounted, with her pale hair spraying out over her Saracen-mailed shoulders.

There was no challenge at the gates leading into Jaffa's white-domed palace; the man there was Alf the Small!

"GUY! By'r Lady—it be the Kingsaver himself and *alive!*"

"Alf? Is that you—aye, I am alive, or mostly. But what does the redoubtable crossbowman do here, lurking about Jaffa like a merchant whilst our liege marches on Jerusalem?"

"Give me a moment with your questions, you great Cypruser child!" the diminutive Englishman cried, smiling. He swung to his cohorts. "Ho, open these gates, devil rot ye—'tis Guy Kingsaver of Messaria, see ye not his awful bow?"

Guy chuckled; long ago, on Cyprus, he had shot against Alf the Small of Rough Lee in Lancashire . . . who had first made fun of the Cypriot's overlong, wire-wrapped bow . . . and then had been unable to bend it so that it might be strung . . . and then had participated in the archery match that had resulted in Guy's being dubbed the Human Crossbow—rather than "stable boy"! But the short Lancashireman from England and the tall Messarian of Cyprus had been nought but friends after, shooting side by side against Acre and its Accursed Tower soon after they had disembarked from their liege-lord's ship in this land. Less than a month later, in late June last year, Alf had been one of the many who succumbed to the ravages of the strange sickness they called the Syrian fever. He had also been one of the few fortunate ones, along with his king: he recovered.

The great gate creaked open, with the other armed and armored attendants directing far more of their attention to the silent and unintroduced Melisende than to Alf's big strapping friend—a friend some had already decided was mythical, as well as legendary. Into the walled enclosure before the lovely Syrian building rode Guy and Melisende, with Alf at Guy's stirrup.

"Now to your question, Guy—the fever returned upon me but a few weeks ago, and I was left behind to recover. Will Fourfinger himself assigned me to castle duty, that it might be good Englishmen who protected the wife and sister of the king!"

"I see nothing feverish about ye," Guy told the scarlet-tunicked man.

"Hmp! Recovered, 'swhat I am, by God's grace! Now to *my* question—how is it ye return when all thought ye dead, and on a Saracen horse at that, and accompanied by . . ." Alf trailed off, rolling his eyes in the blonde's direction.

"The daughter of a French knight, and him slain and her sold into slavery, as I was," Guy told him, "through the treachery of al-Jazzar and his whorish woman. We've been in Egypt, Alf, and—"

"Egypt!"

Guy nodded. "Aye, Egypt, though not quite to Cairo. And we've been a long time returning."

"Rot your soul—ye'd not blush to jest wi' me, would ye?"

"No, but I am not jesting now, Alf," Guy assured the other man, swinging down and turning to put up his hands to Melisende.

Alf chuckled, watching the armor-clad woman swung down from her horse, and wondering if he should touch his forelock or make a knee. He decided against it; she was, after all, daughter of a *French* knight, not a real fighting man—not a real knight! Grinning, the little crossbowman said, "And ye left the way betwixt here and yon strewn with Saracen corpses, I'll wot, or I be not Alfred son of John of Rough Lee!"

"We did break a few skulls, Alf," Guy told the other man, "and—this armored woman did save my life, as well."

Alf stared.

"While he saved mine on several occasions," Melisende said quietly, keeping close to the big Cypriot.

It was Guy's words, though, that decided the son of John of Rough Lee; Richard's best crossbowman solemnly bowed. "My lady, then ye've saved and been in the company of the best man in Christendom." With a glance at Guy as he straightened, Alf added, "Though he do be a barbarous Cypruser."

Guy laughed, laying a mailed hand on the other man's mailed shoulder, with some force. "Surely I have instincts of Englishness, though."

Alf's smile vanished, and he looked very solemnly into Guy's eyes. His own hand rose, extending well above his shoulder to rest on Guy's. "Aye," he said, "ye have that, and more, by Holy Rood."

After a silent moment, Guy nodded, shortly, and lowered his hand. "We must within, Alf," he said quietly. "I've returned with news I must impart to the king with all speed, and I'd share it with—his sister, perhaps? At any rate—"

"Aye, she be within, and the king's lady wife, too," Alf said, biting out the last words. "But come, I'll take ye to the palace commander, my friend, my lady. We—Guy! She's weeping!"

Guy turned to find that Alf was right; two bright tears traced down the girl's cheeks, and her compressed lips quivered. "Melisende—what is it? We're safe now; among the best of friends, I assure you. What's amiss?"

"Alf," Melisende said, extending her own hand to his shoulder, which was on an approximate level with her own, "I was sold when I was thirteen, and have been slave ever since. And Guy has rescued me, brought me hither . . . and the first man I meet bows his English head and calls me 'my lady.' I—" Unable to continue, she lowered her head and turned partly away.

"Uh—" Nervously Alf the Small glanced to Guy, then across the stone-set courtyard, back to Guy. He took a half step toward the white building with its strangely shaped windows and gleaming domes.

"Aye," The Crusader said, and they started for the palace.

They were not yet to the door, flanked by men-at-arms, when Melisende stopped, tugging back with her hand in Guy's.

"Alf," she said, and when he turned to fix her with a questioning look, "Alf of Rough Lee, ye're the friend of my—my friend, and champion, and . . . and ye're not to call me aught but 'Melisende,' ever. D'ye understand?"

Alf's eyes widened somewhat as he stared at her. Then he bobbed his head in assent. "Aye, my la—Melisende," he said, albeit uncertainly. Then he swung quickly back to face the pikemen at the door of Jaffa's main house.

"An ye recognize not Guy Kingsaver of Messaria, he who saved the life of the Lion-heart and hath within the year rejected knighthood at the hands of milord of Leicester, it be your own great loss! Now stand aside, Bertran . . . and you, Godric you ugly Saxon, get inside and call forth Sir William to greet a great warrior and a Christian lady returned from the clutches of Saracen slavery!"

With a glance at the tall man with the unusual adornment of hair on his face, the slender man on the left nodded and hurried inside. The other stepped aside—and stared.

"This be Bertran, from some unpronounceable place in Anjou, whence came the king's ancestors," Alf explained, with a small smile.

"Bertran," Guy said, inclining his head an eighth of an inch to the Angevin, and after a moment of flustered hesitation, Bertran also nodded, considerably more deeply.

"William, Viscount Braintree, is commander of Jaffa, Guy," Alf said, and he remained there to provide a suitably magnified introduction of his friend to the brown-locked man who came at last, a man of perhaps thirty, wearing a side-split, round-necked tabard of yellow and brown over rusty brown leggings and a close-fitting blouse of dark green. He wore a jaunty velvet cap of the same brown as his tabard, with a yellow feather.

"I need no introduction to Guy Kingsaver," William of Braintree said, with his blue eyes meeting Guy's dark ones full on. "Ye've returned from what we all thought was death, Kingsaver; are ye unhurt and in good health?"

"In good health, my lord, and pressing anxious to betake myself and the information I have to Bayit Nuba. I will impart it to you—and beg a boon. Could ye prevail upon someone within to find clothing for my companion, suitable to her station; this is Melisende de Bois-Courtenay, whom I—"

"GUY!"

The name was shouted out, and in that peculiar pronunciation the Messarian recognized; the owner of that womanly voice was the daughter of a Frenchwoman and of the grandson of William of Normandy, him called the Conqueror, and she had spent years on Sicily, as that island's queen. The shout came from above; Guy stepped back a pace to turn his gaze upward.

"Aye, my lady queen," he said, and bowed, and then gazed up again at the freckle-spattered face under the wimpled mop of orange-red hair.

"My lord William—surely military matters can wait," Queen Joanna cried, "while you bring that man and his companion to me, who am his friend!"

Muttering something about duty, Alf hurried back to the gate. Bertran and Godric had gone all rigid at attention—and milord William's bony face wore a look of surprise and respect as he looked at Guy.

"Kingsaver, my lady," he said, "come with me."

A few moments later, first the astounded Guy and then Melisende, despite their armor, were being roundly hugged by the slender redhead in the enormous-sleeved overgown of bright, grass-green wool, and a few minutes after that not one but two ladies-in-waiting were taking the mailclad blonde away to provide her with clothing, while the gray-green eyes of the freckled woman were gazing happily into Guy's.

"My lord brother may have wept once or twice in his life, Guy," Joanna told him, "but not within recent memory—recent being within the last forty years," she said, with a flash of a smile. "But he was moved close onto tears that morning he found you gone, and he did bellow and roar like the beast whose name he bears. He will be overjoyed—as I am." And Richard's sister made as if to hug him again—which only increased The Crusader's nervousness; he was not unaccustomed to the sensuous embraces of noblewomen, but he had never before been hugged by a queen, widowed and off her throne even as she was.

Later, the king's bride of less than a year, dark and beautiful Berengaria of Navarre, also welcomed him— though with considerably more restraint. And there was a feast that night, for a goodly excuse had been provided for these nervous non-combatants to make merry. Guy told his story, and Melisende some of hers, both of them handsomely turned out in courtly clothing, and Melisende more lovely than Guy had seen her.

He did not ask about the woman who called herself both Guy's woman and his slave, the dark daughter of an emir, Leila. But he was told of her. In disguise, Joanna smiled, lowering her voice, the girl had gone with the army in hope of some sign or word of him.

"All any of us has known," the freckled sister of the Lion-heart pointed out, "is that the camp awoke one morning two months ago to find both Yarok al-Jazzar and yourself vanished."

Guy nodded, understanding, though it had not occurred to him that many would have thought him dead. Indeed, he had expected soon to meet God, once he had awoken in Yarok's hands, helplessly bound. But the Saracen had sought to make his vengeance more cruel than that, by selling into slavery the man who had bested and captured him—and who had enjoyed Yarok's own woman. She had paid with her life; Guy had survived because Yarok had not summarily slain him, rather than seeking to prolong the Cypriot's misery.

And now Guy renewed his vow; he and Yarok the Butcher would meet again, and next time The Crusader would not offer the Turk a choice of captivity or death, but would see the treacherous devil's blood flow!

Certainly there was no disagreement with Guy's wish to depart Jaffa at once for Bayit Nuba. They agreed that a Templar named Joscelin would accompany him, and five yeomen and Guy gained approval that one of them would be Alf the Small. If the foreshortened Lancashireman had not been in good faith about his desire to return to the area of combat, Guy mused, Alf would certainly learn not to dissemble again with his friend from Cyprus!

Called "my lady" and "Lady Melisende" by all, including Joanna, as though the blonde were accustomed to a station she might well no longer hold, Melisende was made much over by all in the great banquet chamber. Especially attentive were a handsome young knight from Aquitaine, and an older Frenchman with a small beard Guy thought was far too effete for a knight. (The Crusader had decided to retain his beard long enough for his fellows of the crusading host to see it, for he was no longer above a bit of vanity he had not possessed eight months ago when he was but a stable hand on a tiny island hardly noticed by the broad Mediterranean it rode.)

Unfortunately, there was no way he could interfere with Joanna's generous offer, as there was no way Melisende could be aught but grateful: not only would she be a maiden-in-waiting here at what passed for a court in Jaffa, but this night she would sleep in the queen's own bedchamber. The blue-clad blonde cast a glance back at her rescuer as she left the hall for bed, and her lip trembled.

Tired, and well wined, Guy thought only briefly on her before he succumbed to sleep.

Just after dawn, a small company left Jaffa and headed inland, westward toward the mountains and ancient Jerusalem. Above the seven men fluttered only one pennon, the cross of the crusaders.

Five were yeomen-escort, in scarlet tunics and hose and in shirts of chainmail, with short swords sheathed on their left hips and feathered shafts slung so as to ride across their backsides, the nock ends at their right hips. One was a tall and thick man who wore a new surcoat of plain white muslin over his old armor—and a Saracen helmet. Bearded, he rode in silence, gazing straight ahead, thinking of the blonde he left behind and of the dusky Syrian maid who waited ahead. The seventh man wore over his blued armor the white surcoat emblazoned with the stylized red cross of the Knights of the Temple of the Holy Sepulchre; he was Joscelin, of Perigueux.

Hawk-nosed and very thin, Joscelin made no secret of having fled his native land thirteen years ago, a fugitive—and having journeyed here with no intention of devoting his life to God and cross. But he had become a Templar who would fight his God's enemies until his death—in atonement for the murder of another squire. Now twenty-nine, Sir Joscelin was a seasoned warrior, twice wounded, and more reliable in knowledge of this land than any map.

Inland toward Bayit Nuba they rode, with one yeoman riding ahead and one behind, mounted because it was Guy's wish to make good speed through the mucky land that was bad enough for horses, let alone men.

"The rain rotted our stores and rusted our armor and broke our tent poles," Sir Joscelin said, as they rode. "The excitement we all felt when we gazed upon the Holy City from the tableland at Bayit Nuba soon faded. Men and horses died, sick from the constant wet and cold—and from the food; putrefying pork and biscuits become yellow mush. The king did study maps of Jerusalem and question us all, and decided there could be no successful siege; Saladin was safe within the walls of that mountain city. We could *see* that twisting road up the Judean hills, Guy, and we knew it led to Jerusalem. But—Christmas came and went, and though we had all been primed for it, we did not attack."

"The Lion-heart is as wise as he is valiant in battle," Guy said.

"Aye, but that did not prevent much muttering against him. Jerusalem is in all our hearts. It is there that Our Lord died, there that his Holy Sepulchre lies, and . . ." the Templar heaved a sigh. "It is our symbol and our goal, Kingsaver, and it is Jerusalem we all dream of taking. If only we could—spirit would be as high among all men as when first they landed on these shores."

Gazing ahead toward the distant hills, Guy asked, "And you, Sir Joscelin?"

"King Richard was right," Joscelin said without enthusiasm, and he fell silent.

So did Guy of Messaria, cloaked within his thoughts . . .

Suddenly the yeoman who rode before them as scout emitted a loud cry that was recognizably one of both shock and warning. The wordless shout was followed by another yell, this time enunciating a single word: "SARACENNNNN!"

"Ah, by the good God," Joscelin of the Temple muttered, and his spurred heels clapped to the flanks of his big gray horse. A slight smile touched Guy's lips. Joscelin was a man like himself, thanking God for the presence of the enemy and the opportunity to ride redsworded among them—and charging even before the scout's cry had ceased wavering on the air!

Guy's was an Arabian, a big horse and black, and so The Crusader had given him an Arabic name: *Deukkak,* "Crusher." Nor did Deukkak wait for his own rider's heels to set him in motion; he lurched forward in a war charge even before the big right haunch of the Templar's mount was level with his nose.

Shields up and lances lowering, the two men galloped up the short slope and bucketed over it—to face no less than a half-score enemy.

Three Saracen were lifting their bows; two were already in the act of speeding shafts at the Christian yeoman-scout. The other five were couching their lighter lances to meet the charge of the two mailed knights—even though one of them, Guy Kingsaver, wore no golden spurs and held the official rank only of squire to King Richard.

One dark-bearded son of Allah covered a distance of perhaps ten feet in his charge before Joscelin's lance slammed into his shield with a great booming sound and sent the man hurtling as many feet backward, to crash unhorsed to the ground. The man beside him batted at the Templar with his shield as the monkish knight drove past, but to no purpose.

Guy's shoulder moved, his shield tilted, and a leveled lance careened off it and away, while his own stout iron-tipped stave drove though the Saracen's armor and cut off his warcry as it destroyed chest and lung. With his mouth pouring blood, the man was torn from his saddle by The Crusader's lance, for neither horse so much as slowed. Guy released his grip on the lance and tugged out his long broadsword. One sweep and a Saracen lance was but a stub of wood; another and the man's arm joined his lance-tip on the soggy ground. Fountaining blood, the man galloped on past—and caught two arrows from the yeoman that sent him to meet his god.

The yeoman scout had managed to stick a feathered shaft into the arm of one of the Saracen knights, but the fellow seemed not to notice. Roaring out an angry yell and spurring on, he chopped the English archer half in two with one sweep of his scymitar. Then the Saracen ran afoul of the other four archers, and suddenly sprouted two more arrows, one in his left arm and another in the right hip.

"He dies hard," a voice shouted, and though it was behind him and he was using his sword to strike away another lance, Guy recognized the sturdy voice of Alf the Small. It was followed closely by the sound of the Englishman's crossbow, and The Crusader assumed there was one less foeman; the chances of Alf's missing at anything under a hundred yards, mounted or no, were closely equivalent to that of a mare's birthing kittens.

Now Guy heard only the pound of hooves, the cries of men and horses, and the terrible grating clash of metal on metal.

As if acting on its own, his shield sprang leftward to deflect and short-snap a slim lance, while his sword sprang out on his right to turn slit-eyed man into wide-eyed corpse. He only grunted when an arrow struck through his surcoat and partway lodged in his mail. It would leave no more than a bruise. But it had been a new surcoat, unmarked, and he spurred angrily toward that archer, all heedless of the man who strove to strike off his leg. The scymitar rang and screamed along the mailed legging, and then Guy was away.

The archer sped another shaft with commendable swiftness—and blinked in astonishment when his target whipped up his shield with even greater speed to deflect the slender shaft of death. He nocked another arrow to bow without taking his eyes off this weird knight who wore a Turkish helmet with a pointed spike on top, rather than one of the new kettle-like helms that had been appearing on more and more Christian knights of late.

The arrow went keening past Guy's face, between cheek and shoulder—as his scarlet-smeared sword sheared through bow and hand and into the man's chest with a hideous split-melon sound. That done, The Crusader tugged rein, pulling Deukkak about to return to the fray even before his sword was jerked free of the dying man's body.

Joscelin, Guy of Messaria saw as he swung back, was reeling in his saddle—but beside him another foeman was falling, hacked through the face by the Templar's sword. Only a few feet away lay another of the Saracen, with Joscelin's lance standing above him like a grave marker.

Two of the enemy remained as Guy charged. But the man he galloped for sprouted, in an instant, an arrow in his right side and a crossbow bolt in the face. Groaning but flailing still with his sword, he tried to meet Guy's whirling sword. It fell to cleave his helmet and then his face, from forehead to nose.

The tenth Saracen booted his mount wildly, swerving around Joscelin and heading back the way he had come.

Arrows rushed after him. One made a tinging sound

when it caromed off his helmet; another brought a squeal from his horse when it sank into its haunch; a third slammed into the man's back. He rode on, swaying, and a crossbow bolt thunked home just above the arrow the fleeing Saracen already wore. He fell forward, then slipped sidewise and fell to lie very still with his face sunken in a great pool of muddy water.

Joscelin was wounded, bleeding through a rent in the mail that covered but had failed to protect his left leg, and two of their yeomen were dead. None other was so much as scratched, and Guy was shouting a triumphant cry when Joscelin swung down from his horse beside the man he had just slain. The Templar winced and bit into his lower lip when he set down his left foot, but he hardly deigned to favor it. Stretching the leg out oddly, he squatted beside the dead man.

"—even had they been *twenty*," Guy was crying out to a grinning Alf, "with yeomen such as ye three about!"

Then Joscelin rose from the corpse and shouted his news, and it was not in the same triumphant tone.

"These men are from Turkestan! Saladin's reinforcements must have arrived!"

FIVE

Homecoming

He was a giant in every way, this man with the unruly shock of hair the color of an autumn sunset. Without doubt, he was the greatest warrior of his time.

He was the great-great grandson of William of Normandy, that same William who had sailed across the channel and subdued Saxon England to become William the Conqueror. He was the grandson of Geoffrey Plantagenet, Count of Anjou, and the son of Henry of England, who had declined the crown of Jerusalem . . . and the vaunted title of Holy Roman Emperor. He was the son, too, of Elinor of Aquitaine, that same strong-willed woman who had accompanied her first husband, the King of France, on crusade to the Holy Land—and who had divorced him, in a time when women were subservient chattel-things, to marry the King of the English.

He stood two inches over six feet, when a man was tall at five feet and ten inches. His shoulders and chest were broad and massive, and he'd been seen to fight for hours with an ax whose broad head of English steel weighed full twenty pounds. He had carved out lands for himself on the European continent, a demesne greater than that of the France it bordered. He had conquered Sicily in less than a month, aye, and Cyprus too. His bravery was legendary, bordering on the foolhardy—save for his immense strength and his un-equalled prowess as a horseman, and with lance and sword and ax.

He was captain-general of this crusade against the Islamic conqueror, Salah ad-Din. He was Duke of Normandy and Aquitaine, Count of Anjou, King of the English, and he dared wear a ruddy beard when many men were at pains to shave, daily. He was Ricart Rex, Richard the King, Malek Ric to the Saracen enemy, and he was called the Lion-heart by friend and foe alike.

And he hugged the son of a peasant of tiny Messaria on little Cyprus as though they were brothers.

Jubilation flowed through the camp as news spread of Guy Kingsaver's return from the dead, for these men had need of heroes and symbols—amid tattered tents and mouldering food and the shallow-buried corpses of too many companions who had died not of wounds but of ignoble causes: bad food and water, and exposure and pneumonia. Bedraggled men smiled. And they gazed across the bare, rocky slopes of Judea to their goal of Jerusalem with new hope.

King Richard and his barons had just planned a desperate attack on the Holy City, despite the odds and impossibility of surrounding the ancient city with an impenetrable line; they were too few.

Now, in his own scarlet pavilion, the king's face fell while he listened to the news of Guy and Joscelin.

Again, the Lion-heart called council of his barons. Those stony-faced men listened to their leader, and to Guy of Messaria's story of the three Turks along the road to Egypt. Cries of "well done" applauded his single-handed smashing of Saladin's plans for swift new supplies from Cairo. Then they listened to Joscelin, and their voices fell silent and the smiles left their faces. Saladin had been reinforced. Saladin was too powerful, now, and all knew that he was safe from them, behind Jerusalem's great walls.

The barons of the third crusade agreed, reluctantly and with bad grace, that they must not try to take the Holy City. Even Hugh, Duke of Burgundy and spy for King Philip of France and a constantly irritating thorn in the side of Richard Coeur-de-lion, agreed. But in manner surly and churlish he expressed his dislike for the king's suggestion that they abandon Jerusalem and go down to Ascalon, there to restore its defenses.

"Too oft and for too long," the Burgundian duke said, "have we been reduced to miners and engineers and carpenters!"

The Lion-heart nodded. "That I neither deny nor disagree with, milord of Burgundy. But here we can do nought of import to our cause, while with a refortified Ascalon in our hands, we shall at least control the whole coast, and thus ever threaten Saladin's line of communications and supply with his home base, Cairo."

Heaving his mailed shoulders in a disgruntled sigh, Burgundy rose. "Well, I like it not," he said with sheer petulance, and with his two lordlings and the Bishop of Beauvais, he left the pavilion.

"Nor I," another powerful baron—and another thorn in the Lion-heart's flesh—muttered. He rose, a burly man, thick and broad even in this time of short rations, with a broad and thick mustache and a hairline that was ever retreating so as lengthen the space down his forehead to his stubborn chin. He was Leopold, Archduke of Austria, and now he too led his knights from the great pavilion of the commander.

"It is only God's truth and good sense, lord King," another said quietly; he too was losing his hair, and a bit of paunch tightened the front of his dark robe. This was Hubert Walter, Bishop of Salisbury, friend and close adviser to the commander.

Richard sat gazing down between his big feet, not visibly cheered by the bishop's support.

In a corner, sweet sound flowed from the strings of a vielle; Blondel the fair-haired, too, sought to cheer his lord and friend and singing companion.

Guy Kingsaver stood silent, suffering for his chosen liege-lord. The churlish barons had well known they must decamp, and they had not gainsaid Richard's pointing out that to stay on and seek to attack, even menace Jerusalem, were pure folly. But then they had mouthed their surliness, loading onto the king's great shoulders the burden of responsibility and an undeserved feeling of guilt.

Guy had by now discovered what the crusade with its bickering barons had accomplished since his unwilling departure from among them, back in November: precisely nothing. Skirmishes, minor triumphs and minor losses, accompanied by a feeling of powerlessness against both weather and Jerusalem's walls. These had lessened even more the spirit of this army that was not an army, but bands of men each loyal only to his immediate liege-lord—and some not even that, but hopeful of carving out their own demesnes in this strange land.

"Lord King," Guy began, frowning a little.

The king looked up at him, and his orange-red beard twitched as he strove to smile. "We thank you again for your information, Guy, and for quashing the enemy's plans to replenish his supplies. At least he'll not be able to sally out against us from behind those damned walls! Dare not feel sorry for your liege, great Cypriot hulk; 'tis a king's lot to bear the world on his bowed back!" He reached up to tug off the slender gold chaplet he wore, and gazed dolorously at it as he turned it about betwixt his fingers. "Strange that headgear so tiny can be so heavy, ever heavy!" His blue-eyed gaze lifted to The Crusader. "Get ye to the pavilion of milord Leicester, Guy Kingsaver. There is something of yours therein; go and repossess yourself of it."

The king had spoken; Guy departed.

He nourished within himself ugly and sanguinary thoughts as he walked, cloak-wrapped against the vi-

58

cious wind, through that rock-perched and forlorn camp.

What this world needs, The Crusader thought bitterly, *is barons who are more noble and kings who are less—that he might smite them as they so deserve! How I should like to see my dear lord Burgundy's face mudsmirched!* He stamped viciously, splashing mud broadly to spatter the tents between which he wound his way. *As to my lord of Austria—what he wants is a slap across the face—with a hand gloved in linked steel!*

He cursed himself mentally for a fool. What thoughts, for a peasant's son! Why, he had just attended a meeting of noble lords, great ruling barons of property and responsibility for many lives and crops and the entire future; he should count himself fortunate indeed to have breathed the same air as such! Guy of Messaria spat into a mud puddle.

The sun had never appeared this day, though it had at least existed, somewhere, so that the sky had been gray. Now it was black with night, a cloudy and moonless night. None recognized or took note of the stalking, cloak-wrapped man. This gave The Crusader some idea of the morale of the others; surely the way his cowl was lifted high by the spike of his Saracen helm should attract a challenge!

It did not, and he arrived before the entry of the brown and gold tent of Robert, Earl of Leicester, the man the king called his "good hired hand," and the man who had offered Guy knighthood, less than two months ago.

"Milord Leicester is not within," the guard said. He was a short man whose face was invisible within his cowl.

"I am Guy Kingsaver, and—"

"Kingsaver! Aye, and ye be thrice welcome back among us, by Our Lady!" the sentry interrupted, with high enthusiasm.

Guy smiled. "My thanks. None is more glad to have me back here than I, by God's balls!"

The man-at-arms chuckled, recognizing the king's own favorite oath.

"Ye may be wrong, I warrant," he said, with a sly note in his voice. "Into the pavilion, Kingsaver, and through the heavy brown arras of Syriac weave." He stepped back, and Guy heard the warrior make a sound unbecomingly close onto a giggle.

The Crusader entered the pavilion, looked about, decided he did not feel like making himself known to any of the squires and pages sitting about in the dim glow of but a single fat candle, and picked out the dark curtain with the Arabesque design.

"Ho there—that portion of my lord Leicester's pavilion be off limits to all!" one of the lollers shouted, glad for some distraction.

The tall, cloak-swathed man before the brown and green arras paused, turned, and threw back his cowl.

"Would ye seek to halt a man in a Saracen helm, fellow?"

Men came to their feet instantly, and there was the noise of scraping swords. Then grinning, Guy doffed the spiked helmet and swept it across his middle in a courtly bow.

"Fellow squires, I have come from the tent of the Lion-heart, and I have been told to enter through this arras."

"B'r lady," someone muttered excitedly, "It's—"

"GUY!"

That cry came from a different throat, in a feminine cry that was almost a scream, and Guy whirled to find himself rocked by the impact of a flying missile that enveloped his wet-cloaked form with a great squeeze he could feel even through his mail. The squires and pages chuckled, giggled, muttered this and that, and frankly stared as Guy was hugged ferociously by the dark woman who had so long awaited his return.

"She did dispute us all, Kingsaver," one of the others called, with laughter in his voice. "She's sworn daily,

60

aye and thrice daily, that ye were not dead and would be back among us, and betimes we began to fear saying aught than agreement, so ferocious is that heathen woman of yours!"

"I wish him good luck of that firebrand," another voice muttered darkly. "Surely no man could handle such a fierce witch!"

In the face of such doubts and surmises, Guy could not resist: he swung the clinging girl up, balanced her in air with one big hand and forearm under her midsection, and landed a strong slap on her backside. The pages and squires of the Earl of Leicester were struck silent on the instant.

"Inside, girl, I'd be out of this wet cloak and this steel turtle's shell I wear!"

"Body of Christ!" That from the same throat of him who had assumed that no man could handle the "fierce witch" whose well-rounded rump the Kingsaver now slapped and to whom he spoke so sternly.

They heard her tiny voice too: "Your pardon my lord—oh, my *Lord!*" And she nearly fell in her eagerness to strain herself to his wet self again.

Guy swept back the arras and entered a little chamber that was redolent of the scent of woman and a perfumed candle. Still cloaked and armored, The Crusader strained to him the body of her he had first met at arms, and conquered, both physically and mentally, that day the army had at last smashed its way into Acre. She was Leila, and her father had been an emir of Mosul, slain by Saladin's Turks.

"You Franks defeated us," she had told him that evening long ago in July, "and you have conquered me personally. I am yours." And so had she been ever since, and more than just the language of her people had the small dark girl taught the man she called her lord.

He had disputed her then, reminding her that he was no lord, but a callow youth from Cyprus—who, now, seemed to have aged ten years in but six months.

"You have conquered me," she had said softly, gazing at him with large, nearly-black eyes set in the heart-shaped face of a child, all surrounded by a mass of wavy, blue-black hair. "I have felt your bow on my bottom, and it made me desire you. Saw you not the stripe it left? I can feel it—I bear your mark as a brand! You *are* my lord!"

And so Guy had become her lord, and had let her feel that great wire-bound bow of his again, on her plump-cheeks rump, before he had entered her body and they had pleasured each other for what was the first of many times to follow—and he had told her that he would fight even Richard for her.

Now, after hugging him for many long moments with all her strength, Leila of Mosul at last loosened her grasp enough to allow her to look up into his face.

"I knew that your God and mine would send you back to me," she said softly. "You are not harmed?"

"Stronger and healthier than when I was struck by al-Jazzar from behind and carried off to be sold," he assured her. "And you, Leila? You have been well seen after? How is it you are in the pavilion of men, and the English lord?"

"I am well, since you are back," she said, rubbing her cheek against the smelly wet wool of his cloak. "And I have not been here in this pavilion, until tonight. I—we have a tent of our own, my lord, and with carpet and cushions of our own. I have not known why I was ordered here but a few turns of the glass ago, by a messenger from the Lion-heart himself. I have been at once hopeful that he had word of you, and miserable because that word may have been . . . ill."

"The devil," Guy muttered. "And where is this tent of—ours?"

She stooped to snatch up a long cloak that enveloped her like a tent when she swung its dark blue folds about herself. "Just without. There is a flap, here," she said, and showed him the exit.

Swiftly extinguishing the candle, Guy followed her out into the dark, wet night—within seconds they were in a cozy tent of considerable size, floored, carpeted in a happy light green, strewn with pillows, and aromatic of both incense and the aroma of herself. She had a candle aflicker even as he flung his wet cloak from him.

Her inability to keep her hands off him slowed his undressing, but he was naked soon enough, and shivering, so that she showed him the great blanket and bade him enter. But she could not allow that; in a breathless flash she was on her knees before him, running her hands over him, pressing feverish kisses upon his penis —which responded by taking on an aggressive aspect, throbbing higher and higher in pulsing hardness.

She strove to choke herself on it, taking it deep and contentedly nursing at the swollen shank of heated flesh inserted so rigidly in her face.

She wanted no attention, no lovemaking; she allowed nothing but the wedding of his flesh with hers and the encompassing of it within her body.

He was unable to resist or prolong. He covered her, roughly and totally as she wanted. He drove hard, matching and overshadowing her own almost berserker efforts, groaning and plunging deeply into her, working to make her groan as well.

She grunted and shivered, burning with a lustful fever that his plunging organ goaded into a rapturous frenzy. Her rump squirmed as she clutched him, thrilling to the feeling of his virile organ pounding into her lust-ravished body. And he jerked his hips, grinding it in, parting the firm, tensing lips of her cunt more and more as he dug into her liquid shelter.

All too soon he liquified it still more, flooding her grasping depths with his warm, sluicing flow until there was a pool of it sloshing around in her cunt.

Weary, he fell asleep atop her. Leila made no complaint, but clung to him and stared gratefully up into the dimness overhead. When he awoke in perhaps an hour and slipped from atop her with a groan, she at once scrambled down to get at that part of him she loved most.

He tugged at her, slipped his fingers around her breasts as she burrowed in his loins, and he sought to pull her face up to his. But she refused to let his limp organ escape her soft-lipped embrace. He trembled, knowing she wanted more—as he did—and that she was determined to suck it up again, to get herself stuffed with it.

Her mouth was a snug sheath, as if a receptacle expressly designed for his cock. She licked and lapped and slurped and sucked, she tongued and bobbed her head whilst her fingers kneaded the large eggs of his testicles. He knew that she loved it, that she was a cock-loving woman, that she was pleasuring herself as much as she gave pleasure, sucking his root so avidly and sweetly.

He tried to talk; she ignored him. His voice wavered, for the delightfully lewd fluttering of her clever tongue made his hot flesh quiver and twitch as it swept over the hard pillar of his erecting penis. With her stiffened tongue, she pressed it firmly up against the roof of her mouth, then bobbed her head to rub the sensitive corona over the fleshy corrugations there. Guy trembled. The powerful shaft she loved lurched and trembled in her face, longing for her throat.

At last he forced himself into a half-sitting position, holding himself there by straining the muscles of his midsection until they might have turned a heavy blow, and seized her by her waist and one dark-tipped cone of breast. He pulled, and she twisted so that his thumb buried her firming nipple in the resilient bulge of flesh it adorned.

He remembered something she liked, and he heard the wet *splop!* and felt her teeth as her mouth was dragged reluctantly off his new erection. Swiftly he swung her across his thighs, and now he sat erect with one hand in the small of her back.

Deliberately, she wiggled her backside, swayed the

deeply-tan cheeks, tightened them together and then let the muscles go limp so that they sagged apart and widened, enticingly, the deep crack between those pretty ovals.

"Welcome home, my lord," she murmured.

Pinning her helplessly into an enforced submission that was not at all necessary, since she found great pleasure in the experience, he assailed her upturned bottom with a series of rapid-fire slaps that jiggled both cheeks of that plaintively writhing rump. He watched them, smiling, seeing the pretty buttocks flinch, and tremble, and redden, and commence to glow as the little tent was filled with the splats of resounding smacks.

Writhing and moaning, she deliberately thrust her bottom up to his flailing hand even while tears began to fill her eyes and threaten to spill down her contorted cheeks. Sigh after sigh came pulsing up from her throat, punctuated by a grunt each time another smack fell.

The man she called master paused to run his hand over those bare, much-warmed slopes, caressing the dark skin. He leaned forward as he tugged one youthfully firm cheek aside, and she reacted with a little twitch to the string of spittle falling into her heated crack. He smiled, seeing her relax, for she knew what he was going to do the moment she felt that lubrication.

He did not disappoint her, but tickled his spit-wet finger into the tiny anal opening so that it was forced to dilate. Like a vising ring, it hugged his finger's embedded joint. He wiggled it; she moaned and jerked in the throes of pleasure. He added pressure; she sighed out a long vocal sound as his rigid finger pushed past the muscular ring and into the softness of her hot tight rectum. He did not cease pushing until it was embedded all the way, deep and tight and far up her arse.

With his left hand set in the small of her back just above the twinned dimples, he used that finger to rape her slender orifice then, until it opened more and more and grew wetter and wetter and she jerked and made little squealing noises as the force of her voluptuary joy convulsed through her.

He knew her; knew that flaming lust slashed through her body like fire. Even though his arm grew tired and strained, he continued the whipping of his finger in and out of her until she was a wild, sex-abandoned creature who groaned and grunted and jerked and lunged, but was totally incapable of forming coherent words.

He knew when her own hand doubled back under her to seize and pinch her own hardened nipple viciously, groaning in excruciating ecstasy. And he knew when the wave of fire passed through her, and—because she was who she was and the way she was, a way that other women might have found incredible—she groaned and shuddered in blessed sexual relief, from having her backhole swiftly fucked by a relentless finger.

Sagging weakly after that soul-satisfying orgasm, she begged him to stop. She could stand no more.

For a long while they lay in the candle-flickering dimness of that tent while they kissed and murmured to each other. Then he released her, bade her turn over and elevate her backside. She gave him a last lingering kiss.

"Aye, oh aye my lord!"

Guy rose to his knees behind the dusky, beautifully uplifted moons of her rump. His own asscheeks tightened together into hard balls. He gazed down to watch the bulgy head of his cock, so long erect and pulsing, approach the lower curves of her proffered bottom. It glided under them, between them, into the warmth they radiated. She twitched, with a little gasp, at the heated touch of a long, stiff erection like a thick lance of hardened flesh.

She was ready, bending forward and jutting her rump, both hands firmly planted. He knew that her resolve was strong, that she would take it no matter what. Nevertheless he wetted his palm with saliva and smeared his prick before setting its bulging tip against the little crater of her anus. He pushed.

"Ah-*ahh!*"

She trembled. She felt the pressure mounting and concentrated her entire organism on relaxing the finger-plumbed anal pocket he now coveted with a far thicker probe. He pushed. And slipped steadily and relentlessly within. Her anal sphincter was forced to open, to dilate until it became a thin amber ring squeezing his big goring horn. He was slow and gentle with her, for he was no rapist and she no unwilling "victim" of sodomy. He knew that the slowly gliding advance of his cock into her tiny channel, even though it hurt a little, was indescribably erotic to this woman.

When it was half buried in her, he withdrew slowly. Her hand came back to seize his thigh; he paused, waited, withdrew some more. And he then pushed back within, just as slowly, this time not ceasing until he was sunk all the way and his scrotum was wedged against the soft bulge of her ignored vulva.

Once again he withdrew with care and slowness; again he sank himself into her, again he eased slowly back. The way grew less tight, more moist, far more willing.

Then he was hunching hard and fast, spearing her up the back, gazing as if in trance down the long line of her back, its loveliness deeply etched by a center crease that vanished into her jet-black hair. And his cock drubbed the inner walls of the hole within the luscious, perfectly-halved sphere of her ass.

She moved, too. The kneeling woman met his deep plumbing of her rectum with backward thrusts and swings of her hips that smacked her buttocks against his loins and stuffed her to the bowels. Hot rippling waves shot through her belly, tightened by that big log of rock-hard flesh impaling the tightness of her grasping anus.

"Fuck it," she groaned out fiercely, pillowing her face on her forearms and pushing backward. "Oh, yes, fuck it, fuck me!"

And he did, thrusting hard and ever faster and filling the air with the sucking sounds of his heavy organ sluicing in and out of that expanding tube of cock-hugging flesh. Eventually he grunted and stiffened and, hanging on tightly to her hips as he strained forward, he filled her bowels with gushing sperm.

After that they slept, exhausted and sated.

SIX

Ascalon

The tortuous way to Ascalon seemed to stretch on forever. As the men of the Hope of Christendom plodded on wearily, bitter snow drifted in their faces. Men fell. Thick hailstones rattled down, and men were injured. Pouring rain enveloped them, and men coughed and sneezed and wheezed and moaned softly in their misery. The horses plodded, staggering, and it was King Richard who set the example for the others: he treated himself no better than his Fauvel, by dismounting and walking along beside the great bay warhorse.

During the rain-shrouded days and black nights men vanished, fading away, deserting. They had never known such misery or such a feeling of hopelessness. Jerusalem was the symbol, and they had wanted to attack the ancient city no matter what their leaders said of the impossibility of taking it.

Beneath their feet, the marshy land gave way with the treachery of a bitter enemy. Baggage-horses and men sank into the swamps. The more they struggled, the more deeply they became enmired. The hours spent in dragging them forth extended into days, and the awful trek west by south to the coast lengthened even beyond their expectations.

Malcael of Langton, who had left his young second wife and their infant son and his peasant's thatched-roof hovel to follow his liege-lord and their mutual king to this horrible land, was not even missed until two days after his vanishing forever within a deep clutching pit of watery mud. John de Lovetot pitched headfirst over his horse's neck when the animal stepped onto a mud-covered stone, stumbled, and went to his knees, and the golden spurs of knighthood he wore did not save Sir John from strangling ignominiously in the muck that swallowed his head.

The King of the English himself dragged forth his clerk, Master Philip, from a swampy mess that Philip swore was embodied with a great sucking mouth. One man died, and three others succeeded only after great effort and peril in gaining the release of Archduke Leopold from a similarly disguised death-pit of mud and last season's dead grass and murky water.

Days dragged past; nights slid by all too fast for men desperately in need of rest. And days became weeks. It was a new year, but the weather of January was no different from that of December. Cursing the day of their birth, the bedraggled warriors of the third crusade staggered and dragged themselves on.

"Sensible men," treacherous Burgundy said in manner most lofty, "seek shelter in winter!" And the duke, with a large contingent of his knights, yeomen and men-at-arms, rode off to winter pleasantly up in Tyre with Marquis Conrad. "And to plot," Richard the king muttered darkly, watching the Burgundian French depart.

"So battered, so weary and worn, smiting ourselves," the king's clerk wrote down with shaky hand, "we at last reached Ascalon, only to find it in ruins so that we could barely struggle through the gates over the heaps of stone."

The Crusader arrived in tumbled Ascalon nearly a month after his one-night idyll here with Melisende. The date was the twentieth of January. Less than a year had passed since he had gazed back at the shores of Cyprus from King Richard's flagship, but now began his second year as a soldier—with little promise.

By the time the great mass of men and horses and wagons reached Ascalon's ruined walls, their number was considerably less. Too many had died along the way; too many had deserted.

But the great machine of unending energy that was Richard Coeur-de-lion set to work. Money and time were short. Ascalon's defenses, he announced, had to be reconstructed, and all must take a hand in the labor. As before, he saw to that by leading the way; the king himself set his great shoulders and mighty arms to moving huge stones and replacing them with others for the refortifying of a town become suddenly valuable to the war.

Gray days passed no more swiftly and little more pleasantly at Ascalon than they had on the trek here. The rain fell.

Richard knew as well as the others that their numbers dwindled by a few men daily, as disgruntled French and Normans and Germans and Austrians and even a few English sneaked off by night to avail themselves of the notorious "dancing women" who lurked in perfumed welcome in old ships just offshore at Acre, and Jaffa, and Tyre. As ever, there were those who were glad to profit from war and the misery and death of others; merchants in human flesh accepted recruits and did not flinch from buying and kidnapping women to serve as whores to the woman-hungry army.

Guy Kingsaver was straining at a taut cable attached to a stone no ten men could move without the application of cable and leverage, when he heard the bellow of his king.

Richard had just been told the reason there were less workers this morning: Archduke Leopold not only refused to labor at the construction, the arrogant Austrian was holding back his men. Sweaty, dressed in a workman's smock that bared his thick-calved legs and mighty arms, the king strode to his own pavilion in what for others would have been extreme rage; for the Lionheart it was merely high dudgeon. Work slowed.

Muttering, grinning at the confrontation they knew was soon to come, the men of the crusade waited. They noted well the horseback departure of Richard's chief squire, along with a lesser squire and a page clad luridly in particolored scarlet and jonquil. With the king's triple-leopard pennon fluttering above their heads, the trio cantered through the sprawling camp to the sprawling pavilion of the leader of the Austrian contingent. Leopold's headquarters was set up as far from that of Richard as the Austrian had been able to manage.

He was in no rush; fully two-thirds of the sands had run out of the glass before a sumptuously attired Archduke Leopold rode majestically through the camp, accompanied by a contingent of ten mounted men, all of them as handsomely attired and caparisoned as their liege-lord.

They were met and passed by a mounted man in scarlet; it was Henry the Teuton, Richard's standard bearer. Workmen looked up, all eager for any distraction from the unwonted physical labor. Henry the Teuton rode straight to where Guy was standing erect, arching his back after having aided in the placing of another stone. The thick ugly man with the battle-broken nose and the stertorous breathing leaned down.

His voice was carefully low: "Milord King has need of you, Guy Kingsaver. Quietly now, swing up."

Guy mounted behind the man; the horse grunted. Rather than guiding the beast straight back to the great scarlet pavilion, Henry wove through other tents. He spoke quietly to Guy over his shoulder: "My lord Leopold as you see has brought no less than ten knights with him, and certainly he and the king will have harsh words. The king wishes you nearby, with your bow, Guy, unseen. Just if need be."

Thus did Guy Kingsaver enter the king's pavilion secretly, from the rear, to stand motionless behind a thick hanging arras. With bow in hand and arrows ready, he was witness to the stormy meeting of King and Archduke.

Richard asked; Leopold answered coldly. Richard explained, cited his own participation in the labor; pleaded. Leopold, standing in his arch-baronial finery before the carrot-haired king in his dirty smock, lifted his chin and puffed his chest. His eyes were unwavering and cold; his mien haughty and his voice as though he spoke to a peasant.

"My knights and I are neither masons nor carpenters and we will not conduct ourselves as such. As for the business of digging in the ground and sweating over the mounting of stones one upon the other—we are willing to let the baseborn do such work!"

Guy gasped. He could not understand why the king did not do more; surely Richard was both shocked and rightfully enraged, and that whoreson Austrian's head was there to be cloven . . .

With no more than a very faint nod of his head to serve as a bow, Leopold turned to leave the pavilion. He took a step, two, three, four. Behind him, Richard seemed to come alive as though from a trance. Six steps the archduke took toward the pavilion's entry. Behind him, the bare-legged king took but four, but they were long and half-running. His right foot did not come down in the fifth step; it continued rising in a line from his hip.

The King of the English kicked the Archduke of Austria in his noble and arrogant arse.

Leopold rushed forward, propelled, with flailing arms. He whirled, his face empurpled and his hand on his sword's gleaming hilt, his left behind him, touching the source of his mortification. He stared with blazing eyes at the worker-smocked man who had dared what no man might dare. With his brawny arms folded over his massive chest, Richard stood impassive, linking their blue-eyed gazes.

Guy Kingsaver of Messaria thought it politic to jostle the curtain, to allow the Austrian noble a view of himself and his great bow. Leopold saw. Then he whirled and quitted the pavilion.

Richard turned both hands to his head. "Ah God, why do you not grant to kings the patience they need? I—" He caught sight of Guy, and broke off. Instantly he was a king again, besmirched workman's attire or no. "A king's thanks, Guy Kingsaver. Let your lips be sealed. And leave me."

Taken by surprise, Guy hesitated for an instant before he bowed. "Lord king," he said. "My lips are sealed." And he, too, left the pavilion of the agonized monarch.

Leopold of Austria and all his men departed for home as soon as they were able to arrange ships. Another nail had been driven into Richard's cross; another thorn gouged into his forehead, and, as Guy was told Hubert Walter had said, "Another piece of God's Crusader flakes away like overdried bread."

The work of refortifying the city went forward slowly; there had been too much of this sort of unwarlike work already, and none had his heart in it.

At last the king, after conferring with Walter and Leicester, decided to send the two of them, his closest and most trusted advisers and friends—if a king may possess friends—up to Tyre. Their mission was to persuade another haughty man to send help: Conrad of Montferrat, rescuer and now ruler of Tyre, husband of the heiress to the throne of Jerusalem—and thus the man who stood to gain most from the crusade.

Guy Kingsaver had been to Tyre previously, with the late Ellandun, and too he was a hero with exploitable public appeal. The king himself advised the Cypriot that he would accompany the expedition to Tyre; the king himself provided Guy with courtly clothing from the great trunk of the dead Viscount of Ellandun.

En route, the little party dropped off a more-than-reluctant Leila at Jaffa. From there, the diplomatic delegation took ship up the coast to thrice-ancient Tyre. Guy Kingsaver stood at the forward rail, gazing ahead, reflecting on his previous visit to the city that was old before the birth of Jesus the Christ.

It had been one of the strangest experiences of his life; *the* strangest amorous experience. A courtier named Lady Blanche had sent a woman to fetch him to her quarters, after exchanging looks with him at dinner. Guy had gone right willingly, to enter a darkened room and a waiting woman already abed. He had shortly joined her, they had played their pleasant game of loveless lust in total darkness, after which she had signed him to wait; she would soon return. Swathed in a great hooded cloak, she left the room. Soon the cloak-shrouded form was back, and again Guy sank his prick deep into warm, soft woman-flesh and filled the hungry pocket with his seed. When he awoke next morning, she was gone.

The same events were repeated the following night. By that time he was sure of what he had suspected; he proved to himself and then to the "returned" Lady Blanche that he was being used for some sort of stud service. The first woman, both nights, had not been the blond Blanche of Jerusalem.

She had begged him not to ask; she could not tell him the other woman's identity, a woman as ruddy of hair as Blanche was blond. She vowed, too, that he would be given a sign. In the bazaar The Crusader bought identical scarves of blue, which he gave to Blanche. And then Richard the King had come, and Conrad had steadfastly refused to aid the crusading effort, and soon all were leaving. A palace page had rushed down to the quay to hand Guy a present even as the sleek ship began making her way out of the harbor. Glancing up at the citadel a last time, Guy saw on a balcony the Lady Blanche, and beside her another woman, red of hair.

75

Each of them wore an identical blue scarf.

The second woman was Isabella, Marchioness of Montferrat, wife of the Protector of Tyre, daughter of the King of Jerusalem, and thus heiress to that throne and title.

Guy's hands ran over their gift now, as he stood at the prow of Leicester's galley. The gift was slung by a strap across his back and chest so that it presented its mouth just behind his right hip: an arrow quiver of superb workmanship. It was of leather ornately decorated with strips of colored leather and wound about with a band of curious construction. It was a slender little braid of long human hairs, mingled blond and dark red.

As the favorable wind sped the galley northward along the coast, Guy stared ahead, thinking, wearing a slight smile on his lips. And wondering.

SEVEN

Tyre

Once again Guy of Messaria trod the narrow streets that had been laid out fourteen centuries before the birth of God's son. In Christian hands for a scant eight-and-sixty years, beauteous old Tyre was a great seaport, a trading city, and its way was Syrian. A city of great memories, it brought together peoples of several races and religions, including veiled women with eyes like pools of oil that shifted to the visitors from the sea—and the tall, short-bearded man among them, he with the outsized bow and the ornate quiver.

As before, Guy ate at table in the main hall that night, below the salt but among these nobles because he was a member of the deputation from the kingly commander of the crusade.

He was able to keep from staring at the woman beside Conrad, a woman both regal and beautiful, with a great mass of pearl-bedizened hair the color of rich wine beneath a chaplet of gold—Isabella, looking every inch the queen she had been born to become. Present too was Blanche, a blonde of French parentage who had been born in Jerusalem when it was Christian held. She was lady-in-waiting to Princess Isabella and, as before, she smiled and fluttered her kohl-brushed lashes at him from her position farther up the long table.

He saw too another noblewoman he knew, a beautiful

77

one—and sight of her definitely affected his equilibrium and his ability to eat.

After the meal, Guy betook himself up the table to advise Leicester and Bishop Hubert that their board had been shared by none other than Luisa de Vermandois.

Robert of Leicester blinked. He knew the name, he knew the woman. He knew that she had shared both Guy's tent and the king's, that she had betrayed them all to a Saracen lover, that Guy had discovered her, slain the Turk, and taken the traitoress to the Lion-heart. Certainly Leicester had heard how she had been punished in manner entirely cruel by the king—and by thirty-seven of his men-at-arms. After that massive rape, the king had caused the treacherous beauty, all semen-smeared and with her cunt sewn up around its packing of wine-soaked sand and mud, to be dumped on the plain before Saladin's encampment.

All this Leicester knew; knitting his brows, he spoke quietly. "The Frenchwoman my lord king presented to Saladin her master—with the gift-note pinned to her breast?"

Guy nodded, thinking, *her big, right breast, of which she's so proud!*

"Aye, milord. Naturally we thought that was the last of her. It was at our camp before Aisuf that I discovered her again. All unwillingly because I knew not it was she. Alfred Longshanks the Scout and I saved her from a band of Turks, for Saladin had only given her to two of his men, who used her up and were going to pull all her teeth out so that—"

Leicester nodded, raising a russet-gloved hand, glancing about; the great torchlit hall was now a hubbub of many voices engaged in many separate conversations.

"Yes," he said, "I recall. The king then sent her out to serve on one of the whoreships."

After Alf and I each fucked her face and cunt—and after the king eased his pecker in her asshole, Guy thought, but he kept that to himself.

78

He said, "It was the night of the storm, and Saladin's attack. The ship was blown in to shore, and broken up on the rocks. I saw a German knight rescue her from the waters, but then the Turks attacked. Next day I asked Sir Geldemar of Wertheim about the man. He recognized my description of the fellow's armorial bearings; the knight was dead, and the Lady Luisa was nowhere to be found. The king sent word to search Jaffa for her."

"And she was not found?"

Guy shook his head. *No,* he thought, *and now I've found her again, dressed in costly silk, at Conrad's board!*

"This woman seems to haunt you," the earl said thoughtfully. "Her presence here may well bode ill for you, Guy."

"She and I have ample reason to hate each other," The Crusader said, through set teeth.

Robert of Leicester looked about, as if casually. "I said that I know her, Guy . . . I am sure I would not recognize her. Where is she now? What does she wear?"

"A silken gown the color of Christian *blood,*" Guy said very quietly, and with his teeth still clenched, "all sewn with pearls, as though she be some wealthy man's toy, which she probably is. As to where—my lord, she is now at the left hand of Montferrat!"

Leicester continued to study the people swarming the hall; his eyes hardly lingered over the bosomy woman with the soft brown hair, who stood, gowned in scarlet, beside Conrad. The earl heaved a sigh.

"Forget not, Guy, that we *need* that bas—that man. You are expressly forbid to breathe word of that *lady* to him or anyone else. Now I will move that way and see her reaction to an introduction."

"Unless it be Montferrat himself who's her patron, my lord, her reaction will be to fling herself at you."

Robert of Leicester swung his head back to give the other man a whimsical look. "I could do worse," he

79

said, but he also smiled ever so slightly and touched the dagger at his belt. Then, in beryl-hued tabard and hose, he went to join the Protector of Tyre and the Lady Luisa de Vermandois, traitor, and one of Guy Kingsaver's two most bitter enemies. That she looked beautiful only made Guy's hands become fists.

"So we are favored with your presence in our city again, Kingsaver," a cool feminine voice said, and Guy turned to face a blue-swathed blonde, Blanche of Jerusalem. "Surely ye've not so soon forgot how I congratulated ye on your prowess these few months past?"

Guy bowed low, straining the silken tunic of deep green he wore, the property of an English lord slain by The Crusader's other deadly enemy, Yarok al-Jazzar.

"My lady Blanche," he said, and straightened—to smile at the scarf of sky-blue silk she wore around her throat. "I hope that my lady is not suffering some affliction of the throat."

"Nothing a thorough swabbing will not allay," she told him innocently. "Is't true, these things that have come to Tyrian ears, that you did single-handedly capture that Turk Yarok, him called the Butcher, and that no less than Robert, Earl of Leicester, did then offer you the golden spurs of knighthood?"

"Aye, my lady," Guy said, with his mind upon the swabbing of her throat. "These things be true, though I was foolish not to slay the base villain, rather than treat him with Christian courtesy."

She smiled, nodding. "It is also true, then, that ye've since been enslaved, and escaped to ride alone into Jaffa, accompanied only by a beautiful young woman with golden hair, and both of ye in Saracen garb?"

"My lady is well informed," he said. He was not comfortable; this courtly pretending for others' ears was not something he had been trained for, as had these nobles. He wondered if he should say something of a tryst or if he must wait to hear from her, later.

"The saver of a king will not take offense if I tell

him he is a fool not to have accepted the 'Sir' before his name?"

Guy shrugged. "I have heard it afore, my lady. Perhaps it be true. I am squire to the king, and if the king decides I am ready, then I shall kneel to be struck and dubbed . . . Sir Guy." The words tasted strange; sounded strange in his ears. *Sir Guy! God's blood, I? The son of a peasant?*

Her voice dropped. "You exhibit more nobility than most of the nobility, Guy Kingsaver." Her hand rose to touch the fluttery scarf. "But I must cease talking . . . I think it best if I betake me to my bed." Her eyes rose to meet his directly. "Are you weary from your journey, Guy Kingsaver?"

"Passing, my lady. I hope to be abed early, too."

"Good."

She smiled, and left him without another word. He saw her pass out of the hall. He was wondering how long he should wait, when he remembered Luisa. While a young Tyrian page fawned over him, seemingly a boy who liked those of his own sex, Guy's eyes roamed the room. Despite its great size and the press of brilliantly dressed people, he assured himself that the traitor was no longer present. He returned his gaze to the little group around Conrad—and Leicester beckoned.

After a proper re-introduction and formal exchange of words with the Protector and his regal wife, Guy was prevailed upon to sing.

"I—sing with Blondel, admittedly," he said. "But— alone, I am not . . ."

But they insisted, and he sang what he remembered of "Red Was His Sword" and of "June-sky Lady", and once again there were applause and compliments. More than a few persons had of course to tell him how like Blondel's voice his own was. Guy accepted with proper demurrers; he had heard it before and the singing King of the English himself had assured Guy that he and Blondel sounded much alike in the raising of their voices in a lay.

He saw Luisa no more. Far longer than an hour passed before he was able to quit the hall of empty talk, and then it was with misgivings. He was forced to wait for Blanche's old woman, if she came. The Crusader was well aware of leaving behind a number of amply, even blatantly available young women. Not to mention a baron's wife of surely five-and-forty years— and surely two hundred pounds of porridge-soft flesh.

The Crusader made his way through the resplendent palace to the quarters he was to share with two squires of Leicester. He did not reach that carpeted room.

Guy recognized the woman, a fat one of fifty or more years, as soon as he saw her. She stepped out into the hallway from a deep wall-niche where she seemed to have been waiting for him.

"Welcome to Tyre once more, Guy Kingsaver," she said. "My lady Blanche bids me invite you to share a cup of mulled wine."

"Right willingly," Guy said, and she nodded and turned, and he followed her.

This time the room to which she led him was not so dark as before, and he assumed that he would not enjoy the favors of the princess this night. But this time, as previously, the woman awaiting him was already abed, and it was not mulled wine she was interested in sharing. The old woman closed the door behind him; Guy smiled at Blanche; returning his smile, she stretched out her arms to him. The coverlet of dark blue wool with its design of Arabic flowerwork plummeted, and the rose-tinted nipples of her naked breasts pointed rudely at him. There would be no courtly repartee this time!

"I was about to give up and go to sleep," she murmured, after they had kissed. Fully clothed, he sat on the edge of the broad bed.

"The Protector of Tyre," he told her dryly, "remembered that I can sing."

She laughed, and he enjoyed the sight of her jiggling breasts. "If milord Conrad only knew *all* your accomplishments!"

"I'd not leave Tyre alive," he said, sliding his hand up under her loosened hair, in back.

"Perhaps you won't after all," she said, archly.

He thought instantly of Luisa. "Someone plans to slay me?"

"Last time you were here, an effort was made," the Lady Blanche of Jerusalem and Tyre said, "to fuck you to death!"

Guy chuckled, then suddenly tightened his hand in the hair at her nape so as to tug her chin upward. He lowered his face to her neck, kissed the hollows of her throat, teased her with his teeth at the slim cables attaching her head to her body. His hand rose up beneath her right breast while he let his lips trace a damp path down onto the other. As his hand covered the one nipple and his mouth the other, he released her hair. And felt her arching, and felt her lips in his hair.

"Your beard tickles a little," she said, in a voice already becoming strained with growing excitement.

He drew back his head and wagged it, deliberately rubbing the growth she mentioned over her saliva-damp nipple. She trembled.

"Ummm! Oh, I love that! I am glad you have joined these Syrians in raising a beard, Guy Kingsaver!"

"I had no choice in the matter," he muttered, using the ball of his thumb to rub one standing nipple gently. "It grew whilst I was captive down in Egypt."

"And were you a good—ummm!—slave?" she teased, sighing and making little humming noises as he began rolling the fat red nipple between his fingers. It had been artificially tinted, so that it was darker than a blonde's bosom crest might be expected to be.

"I was not." He returned to kissing the capstone of her left breast again.

"So I'd have predicted," she said. "And how is it

you've not shaved it off, now you're among Christian folk again?"

"I left it to tease milady's nipples," he told her, and did.

She seized his head by its hair and pressed it hard into the full round of her breast. "Ahhhh," she groaned out, and then one hand slid down to brush over his crotch.

She found what she was seeking without having to search; it was thick and hard, pressing against his clothing and hard as a bowstaff. She sighed and moaned, squeezing that swollen shank while she shoved her chest forward so that her nipple was encompassed far within his mouth and the dark brown hair of his beard scrubbed the surrounding pink flesh.

He drew back his head. "One of us is overdressed."

She looked wide-eyed into his face, then raised her brows as her hand hurled the coverlet from her. "Not I!"

"No," he said smiling, and he let his hand rest on the furry little mountain of her vulva, "not you."

He rose and stripped quickly, aware of her eyes, knowing she was as happy with the body he revealed as he was. Naked, he swung to her, and her eyes dropped instantly. His cock jutted from him like a third arm, surging upward and slightly back-curving, like a Turkish bow.

He approached the bed; she met the deeply pink branch jutting before him with a warm hand and then with warm lips.

His loins stirred and his belly trembled when she pressed a heated, wet, soft-lipped kiss to the fat crown of that intimidating length of sheer masculinity. Withdrawing her lips slightly, she licked the glans and slicked her tongue up and down on its silky bulge. Like a greedy cat, she licked it until he trembled and slid his hand into her hair. Then she withdrew her head, rolling her eyes up at him.

84

"Is that good?"

He gave her a satirical look. "You needn't ask."

"Ah, but I did ask!"

"It is better than good," he told her, "and well you know it."

With a smile, she moved her head forward enough to let her tongue whip over the very tip of his organ.

While she teased him with delicate little licks, he bent over her and slid his hand again onto the silkily furred bulge between her thighs. They parted swiftly to afford him greater access to the hair-coated pink skin there, and for a long while he teased her as she did him, trailing his fingers over her mount, tweaking the hair, sleaking it down, slipping just a fingertip into the firm-lipped slit, tickling it upward, then squeezing her springy-plump vulva with thumb and all four fingers—while she licked the head of his cock as though trying to decide if it would prove tasty.

He tickled a finger between the lightly furred pink lips once more, and this time he continued pushing. She was very warm there, and well oiled, and he sank the finger up inside her, utterly.

"Unnngh," she moaned, shivering, and she pressed another of those fervent kisses on the head of his cock.

He ground his finger around and around in her sensitive gash then, constantly changing the shape of the softly yielding lips and pressing against every damp surface of her inner pocket. She shuddered as lustful warmth welled up. Her fingers pressed his scrotum, rubbed its twin globes together gently.

Around his embedded finger, the sensitive interior of her moist pink slit moistened rapidly and copiously. His swirling, dripping finger began drawing slippery fluids out of the elliptical sex-hole he excited and probed.

With her lips enclosing the head of his prick, she groaned all around it. His hand teased her, excited her, made her sigh and groan and twitch her parted thighs restlessly. They stole farther and farther apart.

The Crusader remembered the astonishing and totally unfathomable miracle of this palace: the system of conduits and pipery that brought water actually running in, a phenomenon that awed its European visitors, used to chilly, bare, rush-strewn castles in which the only water was the eternal dampness and that fetched from questionable cisterns. These people, he knew, bathed frequently—and in addition to that, he detected perfume amid the effluvium her moistening cunt was sending up to titillate his nostrils.

He remembered, too, that sudden impulse of his that had so surprised and delighted another blonde, Melisende . . .

The effect on this sophisticated courtier was the same. Women were accustomed to men who were fuckers, not lovers.

Bending far over her, Guy breathed and blew and finally licked very lightly over her furry vulva and luscious steaming cunt—and she screamed and collapsed backward on the silken bed. Smiling, enjoying her reaction and the perfume cloying his nostrils and the clean woman-smell of her as well as the satiny softness of her pubic hair, he swept her legs wide apart and sent his tongue whirling in to find the dewy fluid that rose and flowed.

She moaned, jerked, cried out, and shivered as he turned her slippery inner organs into an inferno of burning boiling membranes.

"Mother of God," she squeaked out, "what a man!" A *man,* a warrior respected so much by the enemy that they called him *ibn-Eblis,* son of Shaitan! And yet how he treated a woman! No queen, the squirming lady-in-waiting to a princess was sure, knew such soaring pleasure!

Giving way to the strong emotions that churned inside her and flowed deeply through her tremulous belly, she surged her humid, juicy slit against his face and tried to clamp his head with her thighs.

Her thighs flexed turbulently, muscles tensing as he tongued her hot, slippery rift. Now and again he would tongue-tip the ultra-sensitive little organ whose head emerged just at the apex of her cleft, and each time her entire body would jerk and her hands clench. She hunched, sliding her red gash down onto his mouth forcefully.

He tongued and sucked her flowing, twitching opening until his tongue and jaws ached. He spent long minutes tongue-flicking her clitoris, until he could not do it any more. She cried out when she reached the peak of sating ecstasy and jerked and twitched helplessly. Her flushed face was heavy with her spending lusts.

Her vagina contracted chaotically, again and again. And his tongue probed the length of its rosy lips again and again, running up and down her juicing, clenching cunt and tasting the slippery salt of her secretions. Her feet pounded; her hands pawed at his head. Then he heard her sobbing. She begged him to stop, to put it in, to fuck her until she couldn't walk.

He did not. He made her moan and gasp anew, by extending two fingers and watching the soft little labia fold in, resisting without avail as he pushed both thick fingers up inside her.

"Arr-rrgh!" she throated out. She pressed with palms and feet, and she hunched.

His fingers jammed deep. With swift strokes, he whipped them in and out, fucking her with joined fingers that he parted each time they were well within that spasming well of sensation. Another orgasm flowed through her and she groaned as though in pain.

Whipping out his fingers so suddenly as to wrench from her another gagging throaty groan, he moved into position with the speed of a rapist. He had enjoyed all he had done and her responses. And now he was as eager to be inside her as she was to have him there.

Her long-manipulated vaginal hollow hung open, like a hungry mouth. Cramming his cock between the wide-parted lobes to vent his passion in her depths, he groaned and sagged onto her. Her legs flung wide and she sighed happily. Thick, spongy lips gripped his big horn and seemed to pull damply at it. He began pummeling her mount, streaking in and out of that hot, slippery furrow.

She moved too, spiraling those clinging lips of elastic flesh up and down his hard-probing bone. She was trying to absorb him utterly in her eagerly clutching vagina, worming her smooth butt beneath her. Her hips ground wantonly. Her legs thrashed and kicked. Her clitoris was pounding and the walls of her stuffed cunt twitched and squeezed, seeking to suck out his semen. The randy young woman's body was racked as the full force of his pounding prick drove again and again into the wet throbbing slit.

The fervidly, gloriously erotic feel of the voluptuously proportioned temptress writhing beneath him spurred and fired him. He plunged his ripely swollen prick deep, again and again, feeding the scorching needs of her ravening cunt. His sensual partner thrust back with furious jerks of her pelvis as the sensation of lust clutched her more and more intensely.

Rising above her, he began rocking back and forth on his knees. Slapping her inner flesh with the pulsating weight and fiery flesh of his cock with each hard stab, he reamed her almost viciously. Beneath him the crooning blonde squirmed and murmured rapturously along the slippery avenue to complete carnal fulfillment, pumping her hips as if in a sensual daze.

Lowering himself again onto her perspiring flesh, her virile lover relaxed for a few moments atop her. Prolonging it; soaking his fervid meatstaff in her; enfolding her warm softness in his arms.

Impatient, she sought relief of the new sexual tension boiling in her by tightening up her strong vaginal muscles and squeezing, until he shuddered at the sweet pressure all around his deep-sunk cock. Again he lifted himself above her on his palms, and he smiled down at the fiercely gyrating girl.

Her movements stirred her sweat-sheened tits wildly. The snowy, rounded hills jiggled and quivered fluidly on her chest, flaunting the livid beauty of their upstanding nipples. He bent his head to send out his long tongue to wriggle deliciously over each tit-tip. She squealed, seized his head, and churned her hips.

"Move, move! Fuck me, mutilate my insides!"

With his hands clamping her upper arms and his thumbs gouging into her armpits, he tried. The blood pounded heavily at his temples. He gave it to her with ramming sexuality in a reckless invasion of the farthest precincts of her silken-lined purse. Grinding and slamming, he pummeled and punctured her, made her groan, watched her face writhe, and jarred her entire body with his charging hips.

He would feel this insane despoliating fuckery tomorrow, in his thighs. And she, he knew, would be cunt-sensitive for days.

Such activity could not be long maintained, and soon he stiffened, shivering. It was happening, happening . . . He was going to spurt, to void himself in her like a rutting bull . . .

And a perverse new notion took him. Swift as it flashed through his mind, he yielded to it. First he had to force her clamping legs off his back. She groaned and jerked when he tugged backward and his blood-red organ snapped out of her with a juicy plop.

Then he was hurrying, on his knees, up her body, bestriding it, grabbing his suddenly pulsing cock in his hands. He began gasping out his semen onto her passion-swollen breasts.

She raised her head to stare, with lunatic eyes, at what was happening. She saw hot spurts of white liquid come leaping from his jerking prick to coat her left tit. With a cry, she let her head fall back in a swirl of pale hair. She stared up at the ceiling while his torrent of sperm sluiced over her heaving tits and ran slowly, oozingly off the distended demiglobes.

When he had finished and knelt gasping over her, sagging weakly in his satiation, her hands came up to slide over her breasts. He watched her rub his sticky semen lasciviously all over the succulent bulges of woman-flesh, and down onto the soft plane of her belly, thrusting her semen-slick hand into her wet pubic hair to make it still wetter.

No one, she gasped out, pressing herself strongly to him, had ever ever given her such pleasure; never had she been treated so gently and sweetly and then with such totally delightful violence.

Both of them awoke in the same positions next morning, having slept like the dead.

EIGHT

Wrath of a King

Before he left her, Guy, who had not promised Robert of Leicester that he would tell no one at all, apprised Blanche of the history of Luisa de Vermandois:

That the lovely noblewoman was worse than untrustworthy and was a spy for Saladin; that she was responsible for Christian deaths outside Acre before its fall last summer; that she had been rescued by a German knight and had repaid him with murder, so that she might escape Richard's wrath; that it was unlikely she had changed and ceased her scheming with her own gain ever uppermost in her mind.

Blanche of Jerusalem promised to learn all she could of the woman who had somehow got so close to Conrad. And then Guy sank himself into Blanche again, from behind, with him on the edge of the bed and her seated comfortably on his standing organ. Her feet against the floor provided the leverage that bounced her up and down on that fulfilling shaft.

It was a well wearied and limp-peckered Guy Kingsaver who learned that the Earl of Leicester and the Bishop of Salisbury had not been so successful on this visit to Tyre as he.

Hardly so malleable and welcoming as his lady wife, Conrad of Montferrat and Tyre continued his refusal to send aid to the Hope of Christendom, either in combat or in the reconstruction of Ascalon's defenses. The man who had wed the heiress to Jerusalem's throne and yet had spent the night betwixt the legs of a whorish woman of Vermandois, however, did make one agreement that enabled the deputies to allow King Richard some hope.

Doubtless seeking to strengthen his own position in the eyes of others, Conrad agreed to personal negotiations with the King of the English. For meeting place he suggested Castel Imbert, near Caesarea. He evidenced good faith by agreeing to appear there with only a small escort befitting his rank.

Back to Ascalon went the unsuccessful diplomatic deputation, with Guy thinking of the lustful woman he left behind in Tyre, and the princess he had not again lain with. But that was past, and soon he was back at work, a laborer who had worn silk within Tyre's twice-ancient walls and spurted his seed between the clasping thighs of a lady-in-waiting.

Days dragged by; days became weeks.

Hugh, Duke of Burgundy, returned in early February with his men and the French knights King Philip had placed under his command last summer. Once again Burgundy demanded financing; once again the King of the English refused him. The money was not there, and besides Burgundy had never seen fit to repay or even discuss repayment of a previous loan. Ask Philip or Conrad, Richard advised the duke, certain that Hugh had already done so.

Burgundy then made it obvious that he had returned only to attempt to gain the loan, not to help; within a few days he was leading his men back to Jaffa. This time, several French barons and their followers remained behind with the disconsolately toiling Hope of Christendom.

"At least some Frenchmen," Guy Kingsaver muttered, "are aware of their duty to the cross."

"Don't be such a naïf boy," Alf the Small told him

sharply. "They are here for two reasons: to spy, and because there may be an attack or some opportunity to gain spoils!"

The new year plodded on, with the members of the noble crusade occupied ignominiously in restoring Ascalon's fortifications and in skirmishes with the Turkish squadrons that came flying out of nowhere to harry them and slow the work. Along with other archers and most of the crossbowmen, Guy was taken off labor duty, in order to maintain a constant watch for the skirmishers—and to arrow them out of the saddle before they were near enough to loose their own shafts to any effect.

The Crusader would as lief have been breaking his back in manual labor; this new duty was egregiously dull. Hour after hour was spent in watchful inactivity, to be rewarded with a few minutes' rapid-fire loosing of feathered shafts at galloping Saracen. And then it was back to waiting and watching again.

Scouts reported little activity on Saladin's part, and no major activity of his main army. Others reported strange events from the coast.

Because of the weather, Richard's wife and sister and entourage moved up the coast, from Jaffa to Acre. That walled city on the very water itself had been long besieged, and had at last fallen last summer, on the arrival of Richard's forces. Now, refortified and safely in Christian hands, it was under command of old Guy de Lusignan, still called "King," despite his utter lack of lands or throne. In order to free every available fighting man to enlarge his army, Richard had made other arrangements for a garrison at Acre. The city was protected in the main by sailors and marines from the seafaring Italian states, Pisa and Genoa.

The Pisans and the Genoese, Bishop Hubert Walter had said, got on together like brothers: Cain and Abel. The men from Pisa supported Richard because he had the power and hopefully the money, and thus they supported, also, Guy of Lusignan for the crown of Jerusalem—the Lusignans were originally from Richard's European demesne of Poitou. The Genoese, meanwhile, supported Conrad for the same title, for reasons known only to themselves—and perhaps to the pope.

To this city of bubbling turmoil and constant tension repaired Richard's sister Joanna and his unloved wife, Berengaria of Navarre. With them went, among others, Leila.

A message to Richard advised that Hugh of Burgundy had turned his cavalcade from Jaffa to ride northward to Acre. After a time of thoughtfulness and a conference with Hubert and Leicester, the King of the English wrote his lady sister that Burgundy might well be en route to enlist her aid in squeezing money out of her brother. Carefully reminding her of the fealty she owed himself, Richard wrote her that he would consider any attempt on her part to persuade him to loan Hugh of Burgundy so much as a bridle-strap—treachery and meddling not to be conscienced.

Not long after that, Guy Kingsaver received some fascinating information from the king's page, Yves, called "know-naught," for he was longer in wind than in brains and sense.

"There was the devil's own uproar when our darling Burgundy appeared before Acre, with steel flashing and banners streaming in the wind," Yves said, with a great rolling of his eyes. "The Pisans refused him entry!"

"Pisan sailors denied entry to the *duke?*"

Yves nodded solemnly, proud to be able to impart information, and more than willing to be coaxed.

Guy shook his head. "And King Guy?"

Yves snorted "My lord *'King'* Lusignan cannot control those sailors any more than he could keep Jerusalem from Saladin!"

"And the Genoese? What did they do, whilst the Pisans were holding Burgundy at bay?"

"They interfered all they could," the page said

excitedly, "without going so far as to open war with their fellow noses. There were . . . scuffles."

"Noses?"

"Haven't you ever noticed how all those Italians have big noses?" Yves asked, tugging at his own proboscis—which was, in truth, passing long and large. "Have you ever heard of a small-nosed *pope?*"

"Oh," Guy said.

"Well then," Yves said, with a great air of superiority and triumph, apparently thinking the other had said *non* in the French most of them spoke.

Not only had the "noses" from Pisa refused milord Burgundy entry, Guy learned at painful length, but one of their number had actually bow-shot the duke's handsome white horse from under his noble arse.

Guy was shocked—and delighted. He smiled. "Too bad."

Yves frowned, studied his face, then laughed when he realized he'd heard a jest. Guy returned to the drab but vehemently necessary business of examining his armor, link by link, for any sign of weakness or rust. On the morrow he was off on another mission for his king, this time as a part of a small retinue Richard was taking to his meeting with Conrad.

They departed next day only after the Lion-heart had left careful instructions for the continuation of the slowgoing work. Then the King of all the English and the putative commander of all the Crusaders rode east and north, with twenty knights and an escort of yeomen and men-at-arms.

At Caesarea, they learned the latest news from festering Acre. This time Burgundy's friend Conrad had sailed angrily down from Tyre. But the Marquis of Montferrat and Protector of Tyre had received similar treatment; his ships were kept well off shore by a veritable bombardment from mangonels manned by the Pisans.

"God's balls!" Richard stormed. "The scabby whoresons!" He snarled a fervent anathema on them and their progeny and their "gape-rectumed women." Then, "Devil rot them all! GUY-Y-Y! HENREEEEE! Yves —Yves you idiot—to me!"

Within the hour the red-faced king was galloping north from Caesarea, accompanied by an escort hardly large enough to honor a king, though his squire Guy Kingsaver and his standard-bearer Henry the Teuton were along. They were hard put to keep the pace set by the leggy warhorse Richard had appropriated from the former ruler of Cyprus, but they accomplished the king's goal. The entire contingent reached Acre the evening of that same day.

Astonished gatemen admitted them, while others raced off to apprise their leaders of the king's unannounced arrival.

"Lodge the horses and see Fauvel's fed not overmuch," the dusty king called, swinging down onto Acre's moonlit main street. "Guy—with me!"

Guy strode long-paced of a necessity; the king seemed bent on outpacing a cantering horse as he mounted to the battlements and bulled along the seaside wall. There wide-eyed men from Pisa gained a story they were not anxious to tell, though it lived long: how a red-bearded giant with face to match swept among them, followed by another big man with a bow of prodigious length; how the first man roared at them in the French many of them did not understand that if one more mangonel arm groaned and thumped and one more stone were wastefully hurled out into the Mediterranean, by God's balls, they would spend the rest of their lives walking on stumps and trying to get their own severed fingers out of their mouths.

The mangonel bombardment ended. Richard and Guy left the parapet of the seaside *enceinte* and descended again into Acre. With a pace no less precipitate, the armored king strode to the palace, through dark streets doubtless infested by dagger-clutching rogues to whom a man's life was of far less importance than the price of a mug of wine. The two men saw none of them.

Richard the King reached the chambers of "King" Lusignan only minutes after news of his presence in the city. Then there was loosed upon that tired old man a tirade such as he might well not have inflicted upon an an errant page.

"And if you cannot in future control those barbarians from Italy, my lord of Poitou," Richard summed up, reminding Lusignan of his family's fealty, "I shall send someone to act as your chamberlain—my page Yves Know-naught, perhaps!"

"Rick!" a glad female voice cried as the king and his bow-clutching squire stormed from the palace of Acre.

"I am busy, Joanna; later!" Richard called without slowing the pace that whirled his surcoat about his mailed legs like a small tent in a high wind. As an afterthought he threw back, "You might go and offer to dry the eyes of my lord of Lusignan!"

A sentry snickered as the two men boiled out of the palace amid those words; next instant he grunted and began doubling over, for a heavy bow of good wire-wrapped wood had been snapped across his belly.

"Lord King!" A man called a few moments later, on the street well outside the palace grounds.

The king and his single escort swung about to face the accoster. A string of bobbing torches approached along the street, accompanied by the clopping of horses' hooves and the creak and jingle of harness.

The approaching man was no fool; he was off his horse and afoot, on the same level with the apoplectic king well before his party reached Richard and Guy. The man was portly, mustached but unbearded, his hair black and glossy beneath a strange soft hat of something scarlet and shiny. He wore a flowing robe to his insteps, quilted scarlet, broidered and girt with gold. Richard's arm shot up to aim a pointing finger at the richly attired Italian before the man could say whatever it was he intended.

"Guibert! Lusignan has heard from me, and the Pisans have closed down their mangonels on pain of gelding by my own hand. As for you, I congratulate you on having sufficient control over the men of Genoa so that they haven't fallen upon the Pisans and slain them."

The man flashed remarkably good teeth in a smile of pleasure.

"Thank you, lord King! Admittedly it hath not been an easy matter, but we Genoese—"

"—are a tribe of plotters," Richard interrupted, "whose fame for constant snooping and twining of schemes surpasses that of your seamanship! I warn you, Master Guibert, that a few more reports to me of your conniving with Conrad of Montferrat will convince me that you and your men and indeed all Genoa are no friends of mine—and by the time His Holiness hears of your disruption of God's holy work here, you will all be anxious for recall and excommunication as being of lesser moment than my wrath!"

The eyes of the commander of the Genoese popped wide and his hands trembled. His mouth moved, but words refused to issue.

"If you will wait here, Master Guibert," Richard said in a wholly different tone, "for but a few moments, my trusted squire and friend Guy Kingsaver of Messaria will return your horse to you." And the King of the English mounted into the saddle of the Italian's big roan. He swung to the mounted man on his left.

"Get down there, and attend your lord! Guy—mount up, my old friend Conrad is waiting for me, out there on his ship."

Restraining his smile, thinking about the words "my old friend Conrad" that must be clamoring through Guibert's brain, Guy swung into saddle still warm from the backside of Guibert's astounded retainer.

"Andiari! Andiamo!" Richard snapped, thumping the horse with his heels.

Whether the king had hit upon the proper word for the imperative or not, the roan obeyed; he went, a-clatter. Guy followed after; the men from Genoa stared after them. Master Guibert had still got out no more than his first "Lord King" and his interrupted acceptance of the compliment. Guy was sure the man could have done without the compliment to have avoided the tirade and the commandeering of his horse, and wished he'd stayed at table this night.

At the quay, the lion-voiced king first roared at astonished boatmen to ready their oars, then turned to his companion, who had accompanied him on his whirlwind assault on Acre without a word.

"Return Master Guibert's horse, Guy, with thanks. Tell my sister and my lady wife that you are badly in need of nourishment, and tell them what you please. All of you are to remain here whilst my old friend, the cur of Montferrat, and I discuss this matter of his contribution to the extension and safety of *his* frontiers."

Guy nodded, still holding back his smile. He watched the tall king step down to the boat, wave off a proffered hand, and start to enter with the four oarsmen. Then he twisted his head around, and after a moment flashed a conspiratorial smile. Guy grinned in response. Richard entered the boat.

"Well, God's balls, *pull!*"

The Crusader stood on the dark quay and watched the boat skim out to the waiting ships, anchored just outside what they had established was the reach of a mangonel-hurled rock; a stone's throw, as it was put. He tried to visualize the expression on the face of the Protector of Tyre when the King of the English came over the side and onto his galley—in the middle of the night, and wearing dusty traveling clothes over full armor.

Leading Guibert's horse, Guy returned to where

the Genoese waited near the palace. He conveyed his king's thanks to a stony-faced Guibert, complimented its owner on the horse he had ridden, and walked away.

An hour later, he had eaten and enjoyed some ale that somehow manifested itself, reduced Joanna to laughter and then mirthful tears with his description of her brother's actions this night, passed the word to the king's meager retinue, and obtained from Joanna directions to the small room occupied by Leila.

Their kiss of reunion lengthened, Guy's armor and Leila's clothing were got rid of, and despite her complaints Guy had soon sent Leila spiraling off into the climactic jerks and whimpery sighs of orgasm. Then he plunged his swollen organ into that spend-wet cunt and drove deep.

Her dark eyes gazed up at him, full of love and pleasure. Her tongue came slicking over her pouting lower lip as she squirmed her deliciously formed body, rocking him in the cradle of her hips. He pumped, swinging his hips forward and back, delving far into her clasping cavern.

The juicy tenderness of her cleft . . . the warm and luscious inside of her cuntal walls . . . the sounds of her heavy breathing . . . the way her hips surged at him with undulating rhythm . . . all whirled together into a single entity of sheer beauty that sent jolts of pleasure through him. He poked it into her again to the balls, riding her deeply dimpled belly in intense erotic communication, riding her with an increasingly rapid gait. His muscular body squirmed over her, sliding in and out of her, mashing the squashy fullness of her tits, twisting and plunging in high, lustful delight.

And all the while he held himself back as he had never done in his life, until she spent again with a series of shivering spasms and a sighing little scream.

Then he groaned, pulled free, and told her sorrowfully that he was not free of the king's orders and had to be elsewhere. Naked, open-mouthed and very tiny-looking in her silent acceptance, she stared while he again clothed himself, gave her a last look from the doorway, and left her apartment.

Feeling more guilty than ever he had in his young life, The Crusader walked the airy corridors of Acre's palace to the chamber he had asked about only secretly, of a cook's assistant. Glancing up and down the hall once he was there, he smiled and pushed open the door to Melisende's room.

The couple on the bed did not waken.

Melisende lay on her back, her legs apart, her hair directly in a shaft of moonlight from the narrow window so that it was a fan of gold about her lovely face. Her right hand lay between the thighs of the man stretched beside her, also asleep in the obvious aftermath of orgasm. He would not sleep peacefully long. His left arm still pillowed her neck; his clothing lay rumpled on a chest at the foot of the low Syrian bed. The stylized lilies combined with his own armorial bearing assured Guy that the man was a knight of Melisende's own France.

His face no less shocked and crestfallen than the several he had seen this busy night, The Crusader pulled the door quietly after him as he backed again into the corridor. He made certain it closed without sound.

He had taken three slow steps along the carpeted hallway when the blackhaired daughter of Islam appeared before him. "I could have told you she slept not alone, most fickle of lords!" Leila snapped, and stalked away to her own chamber.

Guy did not follow. He crept into the room where slept Henry the Teuton and the new junior squire, Roger de Loches.

Henry snored.

NINE

The Lion at Bay

It was a morose and chastened Richard Coeur-de-lion who returned from his parley with Conrad. The Protector of Tyre had remained steadfast in his refusal of aid, and Richard had lost temper and dignity, advising Conrad loudly that he had forfeited his rights and should be denied the considerable revenues of Tyre—and those of Isabella as heiress to Jerusalem's crown. Wrapped in a cloak of indignation and anger, Conrad returned to Tyre, to resume plotting with Burgundy and, according to some, even Saladin.

When the defeated Richard reached Ascalon with his company the Tuesday before Easter, he discovered that messengers from both Conrad and Burgundy had arrived before him: The King of the English was just in time to watch the departure of no less than seven hundred French knights and their squires, men-at-arms, and yeomen.

"They've broken the back of the holy crusade," Richard whispered, looking worse than he had last summer while he had suffered the ravages of Syrian fever. But after a time the gold-chapleted head came up with a jerk: "They are traitors to Christ and Holy Mother Church and thus all Christendom!"

Going directly to his pavilion, the beleaguered commander of the third crusade dictated a letter to the pope and saw to its dispatch coastward that same afternoon. With the sun striking glints of gold and bronze from his hair, King Richard then inspected the progress made in repairing and replacing Ascalon's fortifications. It could not satisfy him; it was not finished, but the rainy season was over: It was time for war.

That evening he learned that word of life in Tyre had been well bandied about the camp, in a further eroding of morale.

"The French there in that city of ancient wickedness." the florid report read, "have abandoned themselves to wantonness, women's songs and banqueting with harlots. These recreants have amused themselves with applauding bands of dancing women, and the luxury of their attire bespeaks their indolent effeminacy."

"God's balls," the king grunted. "They have fallen into Syrian ways without benefit of its warlike qualities!" And he read on, muttering the words aloud to Hubert and Leicester:

"Round their necks are jeweled collars and on their heads garlands wrought with every kind of flower; goblets they brandish in their hands stead of swords; their nights are consumed in potations and profligacy."

He hurled the report from him, stormed around the pavilion. Eventually he began to look thoughtful, and at last turned smiling.

Next day his plans were announced for a suitable Easter celebration, and the announcement was greeted with the smiling faces and cheers he had expected. Richard was the compleat king in his wedding clothes of a surcoat of rose-hued satin, a soft cap of scarlet, and a cloak of a rich, dark blue, sewn all over with half moons in cloth-of-silver. Blondel strummed and sang; Richard joined him; Guy, too, became an entertainer that day of flowing wine and, as if God were vaunting his power over this land, bright sunlight.

On Monday every man was set back to work on the walls, headaches notwithstanding.

Now it became obvious that their time should have been otherwise occupied during the horrible season of the rains; completed work had to be undone, while the construction activity in general went much more swiftly and certainly with less grumbling.

Nevertheless, never had Guy Peter's son of Messaria known that so many weeks could pass so dully and slowly, or that he would work harder at physical labor as a defender of the Cross of Christendom than he had done as a peasant on Cyprus. March died; April was born in sunshine.

It was on the fifteenth that all paused in their stone-mason's labors to witness the arrival of a pot-bellied cleric accompanied by an escort of brightly clad men: Pisans, recruited in Acre. The cleric was Robert, Prior of Hereford in England, and the news he bore was not pleasant.

Richard the King read the letters red-faced. He heard the reports and answers to his questions with a growing realization that he had set forth on God's work only to abandon his lands to jackals and incompetents. There was, as he had long known, but one Richard Plantagenet, and his presence was absolutely necessary everywhere at once.

On setting out on this ill-omened crusade, the king had left his younger brother John Lacklands wearing a chaplet of gold—but not wielding the power. As a sort of unnamed regent, Richard left the Bishop of Ely to administer the island kingdom in his name. Now Ely, having fallen into the inevitable quarrel with John, urged the king to "return on the wings of the wind."

That part disturbed the King of the English but little; foreseeing it, he handed the Archbishop of Rouen a letter that gave him extraordinary power as justiciar, in the name of *Riccardus Rex*. Archbishop Walter had already arrived from Richard's duchy of Normandy on the continent, presented the letter, sent Ely packing to his tithes and mass-saying, and begun the effort to govern both the Saxons and the Normans, neither of whom had forgot the conquest of William the Norman in 1066. Meanwhile, overburdened Walter of Rouen had the tasks of attempting to placate Prince John and of raising more revenues for the crusade.

But there was still a third overseer, and it was her letter that tightened Richard's lips and washed the color from his face. His own brother John, Elinor of Aquitaine wrote her son the Lion-heart, was in close communication with King Philip of France—and she was sure their plan was for an invasion of Normandy. That strongest of women urged her son to fly back to England "with all speed to save your own."

The king clutched the papers to him and, bearing an expression of anguish, stalked to the most privy of his pavilion's curtain-doored apartments. There he sat in silence, and he accepted neither food nor drink nor interruption. Yves Know-naught swore that the king slept not at all, all that long night.

Two days later a shocked assembly of barons and prelates listened to the reason for their summoning.

"You see that I do not lie to you, my lords," the king said, standing before them in naught but a loose-girt tunic of white muslin, as though doing penance before these landed lords and churchmen who had delved into their traveling chests for proper finery on this summons to council.

"In this land I am hampered by the plotting of Pisans against Genoese, of French and Burgundians against us all, by the departure of petty lords who abandon God's work to the littleness of their souls."

There were gasps; in so few words the king had accused and condemned departed Leopold and his Austrians, the absent Duke Hugh and his men, as well as those French knights left behind by Philip of France—and indeed, King Philip himself, as liege-lord.

"At home my chosen justicar labors against a princely brother of mine who lusts after the lands that are mine by birth."

Another gasp and more exchanged looks; the king

was damning his own younger brother. But what could silly little John Lacklands do?

"Yet there is more, my lords. Now it is beyond doubt that the promise made me by the King of the French last year—when he departed this land, claiming illness as his reason for abandoning us all, aye, and Our Lord too—meant nothing to him. He looks with longing at the lands I won by dint of my own efforts, at fair Normandy—and he conspires with my own brother John to STEAL THEM!"

Uproar greeted those words; never had they heard such frank accusations and names-naming even from violent and outspoken Richard, whom some had called —very privately—the "lion-mouthed."

They heard more, then, and it was no less shocking. Richard the Lion-heart of Normandy and England was leaving them, he declared; he would leave behind three hundred knights and no less than two thousand men-at-arms, for he assured them he was not abandoning their noble cause, but was being forced by the machinations of others to follow the advice of his own lady mother. And he read off her words:

" 'Fly home,' she urges me, 'with all speed to save your own!' "

But it was not to be so simple. Man after man rose, to make plain his intents and wishes, and the council stretched on into the afternoon. Their common agreement became clear to the man who bore the crown— and they were not above reminding him that the crown made him first among the barons, not dictator.

Unless Richard appointed a strong leader to continue the war against the Saracen, the gravelly-voiced brother to the Earl of Chester vowed, he and all his followers —would take ship home, too. That brought a storm of clamorous shouts—and they were of agreement. In minutes, it was unanimous. The crusade was ended, here and now.

But before the king could speak into that bedlam of

lordly voices, he was assured of an additional fact: that by "a strong leader" they did *not* mean the sixty-five-year-old "King" Guy of Lusignan.

"MY NOBLE LOR-RDS!" the white-tunicked king bellowed.

They quieted, blinking, but not for him; now Stephen of Chester pointed out that the compromise of the previous year was a total failure. Lusignan could not even control a collection of Italian sailors in Acre, while Conrad, with Richard continuing his obvious favoritism to Lusignan, would not even support the crusade.

"My lords," Robert of Leicester said, and was obliged to repeat himself, with considerably more volume and force. Strangely, they became quite silent, and for a moment Richard and Stephen exchanged a look, as if wondering . . . *Leicester?*

"The foremost among us all has referred here earlier today," the Earl of Leicester said, "to petty lords with little souls. I urge that we endeavor so to behave ourselves so that none may ever so describe *us!*" He paused for a small and brief barrage of angry exclamations and faces, then added, "And what of the rumors that my lord Conrad is negotiating with the Sultan Saladin?"

It took them half a turn of the hourglass, but they made themselves clear; there were rumors that Richard had been carrying on secret negotiations, too. Besides, Conrad had been expelled from Constantinople only to *save* Tyre from the rapacious Saladin—and it was that same Conrad who had called upon all Christendom for this crusade. It was surely his *right* to treat with the Saracen commander.

Flushed, Richard demanded if this meant that he and the man whose only official title was that of Marquis of Montferrat were to be considered equals.

There was a long silence, while men looked at one another, and then Stephen of Chester rolled his bulk defiantly to his feet. *"Peers,"* he grumbled into the silence, and added, "as here are all *peers* . . . my fellow baron!"

This time the silence was of far longer duration, for it was not only the gathered barons and churchmen who were shocked, but the great-grandson of William the Conqueror himself.

At last Richard spoke, in a terribly quiet voice that was like unto that eerie stillness that preceded the cry to charge.

"The brother of my lord of Chester," he said, reminding them that Stephen was not indeed his peer, "makes it plain that I am amid a sort of trial of lords, while ye have all been at pains to demand that *I* lead you, and that if *I* leave, it is *I* who must appoint a strong leader in my place. Presumably you will follow him. Then . . . CHOOSE that man, my LORDS!"

And the King of the English threaded his way among them, to the empty place beside the arms of Ellandun whose viscount was dead at Saracen hands. There Richard sat, with the chaplet of gold in his hand.

It was a brilliant stroke, a dramatic demonstration and reminder and challenge—and surely King Richard assumed that the challenge would not be answered with *acceptance*.

It was. In less time than a stuttering priest could have said matins, Conrad, Marquis of Montferrat and Protector of Tyre had been elected King of Jerusalem and, in the event of Richard's continued intention of leaving them, war-leader of the crusade.

However staggered, Richard had left himself no choice. He heard the will of the assembled barons, and had he been on English or Norman soil he would have been hard put to do other than agree.

He was still in the place of Ellandun when the brother of the Earl of Chester approached, bent a knee, and pledged fealty to the lord of "Chester and aye, all the English: Richard of the heart of the lion!"

Thus began the parade; it was not over until full an

hour had passed. By then, every man present had re-pledged his fealty to Richard, even Henry, Count of Champagne, who surely could not have been expected to bend a knee thus to his cousin—who remained seated throughout the impromptu ceremony begun by the man who had hurt him most sorely and most seriously challenged him.

When the last man had straightened, the giant of a man in the white tunic rose, looked long about at them, and with one hand replaced his slender war-chaplet on his head.

Then from many throats roared out the century-old cry of the crusader: "DIEU LE VEULT! God wills it!" Showing them only the pale imitation of a smile, Rich-ard replied with the battle cry: "Christ and Holy Sepulchre!"

It was after that reaffirmation that the man who was still their leader asked handsome young Henry, Count of Champagne and kinsman of both himself and the King of the French, to carry word to Conrad of the will of the barons assembled. Count Henry accepted, and was most careful to include in his entourage men from many demesnes. Among them was a squire of the king, Guy Kingsaver of Messaria.

Two days later The Crusader set out on his third journey to Tyre.

TEN

My Lady Queen

In the seventh century, Chosroes of Persia captured Jerusalem from the Romans; in less than two decades he was ousted; eight years later the Romans were once again driven out by mighty Omar. It was he who built the first mosque, of wood. Others rose within the ancient city after that, for Jerusalem remained in Saracen hands from 637 to 1099. It was in that year that the men of the first crusade restored the Holy City to Christendom —by drenching the streets and even the mosques with rivers of blood. Thus was born a new Latin domain, the Kingdom of Jerusalem. It endured for nearly a hundred years, but only by dint of constant warfare against the sons of Allah, who considered it *their* holy city.

Then came the great army at the heels of a new Chosen of Allah, Salah ad-Din Yusuf, and in 1187 the City of the Sepulchre was forced to open its gates to the Saracen conqueror. Despite his lack of the advantages of Christianity, Saladin proved a far more knightly, gallant, chivalrous and "Christian" man than his enemies; Jerusalem passed into his hands without a bloodbath.

Two years later Guy of Lusignan, released from captivity by Saladin on his promise not to take action against the Saracen, promptly laid siege to Acre. He was joined later that year by the wealthy young Count of Champagne, Henry. Not until June of 1191 did King

Richard reach Acre with his Normans and Englanders; a month later, Acre fell. Now Saladin realized that it was no longer the "toothless lion" of Lusignan he had to contend with, but a younger man in the full prime of life, with a great army behind him. Had that army been such, a united force rather than the factiously divided conglomeration it was, all of the Holy Land the Turks called *Falashtim* might well have been in Christian hands once more. As it was, in the fifth year of the Third Crusade the Westerners held only a few cities along the coast.

Since he had begun the siege of Acre and had been married to the elder daughter of the last king of Jerusalem, Guy de Lusignan assumed command of the occupation—with Richard's approval. Within Acre's walls, Lusignan considered himself king and waited patiently for the taking of Jerusalem, that he might move there and assume the crown. It was unfortunate that he was old, that he was damned for having lost Jerusalem after so brief a siege—and that above all his wife and daughters had died of illness. The younger princess, Isabella, became heiress to the throne. And she was forced to divorce Humfrey of Toron and then to marry, precipitately, Conrad of Montferrat.

As husband of the only survivor of the ruling family, Conrad pressed his claim—but remained aloof from the efforts to win back the kingdom and the city for which it was named. Were the crusade to fail, Conrad had after all defended Tyre and won it for his own—and could remain safely within its walls, certain of ability to survive the longest siege Saladin might undertake. Tyre's two seaports assured her of a constant flow of supplies.

And now, though the "Kingdom of Jerusalem" was merely a *concept*, with the city itself under Saracen banners, the crusade's leader had been forced to accede to the demands of his chieftains. Just after mid-April in 1192, Henry of Champagne rode into Tyre to appraise Conrad of his undeserved honor and new title.

There was but a small celebration that night; more jubilant festivities would be announced later, though Conrad agreed that it would be restrained; they were, after all, at war.

A few brightly clad Tyrian nobles and Henry's delegation quaffed wine and talked of the new king's good fortune, while Conrad himself was absent, conferring in private with Henry. Guy Kingsaver was delighting a Syrian-attired, Arabic-speaking young noblewoman with his own knowledge of the Saracen tongue when she fell suddenly silent and touched his arm, directing his gaze to his left.

The Crusader turned to see that the young woman's claim on his attentions was being pre-empted; it was Princess—no, Queen, now—Isabella who beckoned. The youthful queen wore her red hair piled high and laced with pearls, while her slenderness was sheathed in a brocaded gown of marmoreal white whose only adornment was an appliqued border of blue—and the blue silken scarf at her throat.

Guy's stomach tightened as he walked to her, and his head churned with thoughts. They had shared bodies on two successive nights, he and this woman, and her wearing the scarf and her silent summons and inviting eyes were a clear indication that she was ready to renew that so-secret relationship.

But now she was wife of the man soon to be crowned King of Jerusalem, and The Crusader felt that a gulf had opened between them no less broad than that separating him from his native land, seabound Cyprus. Thus he had decided on his course by the time he reached her, and he made it plain when she extended her hand to him.

He took it gently in his, bowed low, and placed it against his forehead in a sign of fealty. "My lady Queen," he said quietly.

Queen Isabella gazed after him as he walked away, and she opened her eyes wide so that the tears might not spill down her cheeks.

Within the hour Guy was once again in the bedchamber of Lady Blanche, and naked with her on her soft-covered Syrian bed.

"Oh," she exclaimed suddenly, drawing back from his lips, and he feared he had hurt her. "Luisa! You were right—she is a spy!"

Instantly he went tense everywhere save in the crotch, where he began to limpen. His eyes on hers were an eloquent silent question.

Blanche smiled. *"For* Conrad," she told him, with an air of triumph.

"What?"

She nodded. Aye, Luisa de Vermandois was Conrad's agent, and she had been of value to him in his negotiations, Blanche said; by advising Conrad that Saladin much preferred Lusignan as king; Luisa had herself heard the sultan refer to Lusignan as a "toothless old jackal." That information had been of considerable value to Conrad, who had since housed and taken all good care of the still-lovely Luisa. As a matter of fact, Blanche said with a wicked smile, she was certain that Conrad and Luisa had slept together, rather more than once.

"Methinks he be with her this very night," Blanche murmured. "She is not, I know, in the palace." Her hand groped. "Mention of her name has hardly the same effect on you as on my lord Conrad—what happened to the great fleshy quarterstaff that was here but a moment ago?"

"He's not here celebrating with his queen-to-be?" Guy asked, not yet ready to return to their lovemaking. "Without Isabella, Conrad would never have had any claim to the throne at all!"

Blanche sighed and removed her hand from his loins. "Matters are . . . not well with them," she said.

113

"He . . . she . . . well, you know that she be a most passionate woman, Guy. Milord Conrad spends much time at plotting . . . and drinking. Too, 'tis *said*—and I assure you now that I have no personal knowledge of this, sweetheart—that he gains erection only by making a woman agree to be still as a corpse, whilst he doth all the . . . work."

Luisa, Guy mused, would like that; surely her dream was to have a title created for her: Empress of the World! "Um. And is Isabella alone tonight?"

The naked blonde gave him an arch look. "She wore the blue scarf tonight, and—ye be here!"

Guy said nothing, only moved his hand slightly to trace its tip over one peach-pink nipple. Its owner gasped. But he did not further the caress, and after awhile she responded to his steady gaze.

"How should *I* know, a great hulk of a Cypriot who asks more questions than my confessor? What should I know of Her Highness, first a princess, then a marchioness and wife of this city's savior and ruler—and soon to be regent of this entire land?"

Co-regent with Saladin, morelike, he thought, but he said, "Come, Blanche . . . you can't convince me you know not. Where is she?"

"Do you repent your being here, rather than with her?" she demanded, with a pout too elaborate to be genuine. Then, "Ow!" as he pinched her nipple. She shivered, though, and her eyes resumed their smoky look. "Guy . . ."

Smiling, he withdrew his hand.

"Monster! I cannot answer, she—well. I shall ask a question of my own, thou huge man who takes unfair advantage of the gentler sex. *Where is milord the handsome Count of Champagne?*" She cocked her head.

"No!"

She shrugged. "I but asked a question; I told thee nothing. But what's to be my reward, for having withstood all this questioning?"

"After I chew off both your nipples," he told her, clamping her strongly with both hands, "I shall ram that fleshy quarterstaff you mentioned up so far within you, you'll walk with bowed legs for a se'en-day!"

She shivered, squirmed, licked her lip, and her breathing quickened. "Oh Mother Mary—how hot and wet you make me!"

She thrust her wet begging mouth up for a kiss, and in seconds their tongues were curling actively around each other. She pressed her warm nudity to him and sucked at his tongue as though she were in the terminal stages of sexual starvation. Shudders took her as she felt the movement of his growing penis against her upper thigh.

Then he sent his head diving to her breast. Her mouth and squeezing, fondling hands played and cajoled and coaxed until she was making grunting sounds of uncontrollable arousal, and he was sucking delightedly away at diamond-hard nipples that seemed trying to ram themselves down his throat. Her hand snapped to him, started to claw; jerked away and tore at the silken sheet. Constant moans and twitches answered his continuing strong suction and mildly hurtful manipulation of her hard-tipped breasts.

Seizing his erect cock, she began tugging at it, sliding her hand up and down, letting him know she wanted it within her and was threatening to spill its semen if he kept it from her.

He moved quickly over her while she maintained her grip on his thick erection, ready to guide it into herself. She did; he lunged; his cock shot into her like a thunderbolt.

"Unnnnngh!" she groaned, tipping back her head and staring glassily up at the ceiling. "Ahhh God—how big it is—how good it is!"

The folds of her narrow vaginal hole, the red, fluttery lips and the oval slice between them, were marvelously dilated by hot maleness. Then it was hurling open the deepest chamber of her eager, grasping sheath. He did not pause for an instant, but began pumping hard in and out of her as if it were a new experience and he was unable to restrain himself.

His body stroked hard, ramming his meaty tool between the soft protective flaps of her vulva and far into her as he pumped with increasing strength and rapidity. He was glad to be back, glad to be in her, glad of her enthusiasm and his own potency. His every nerve was alive and churning with the feel of the moist pink flesh of her cunt clinging wetly all around his goring horn.

He could hear her rapidly gasped moans of wanton need, smell the pungent aroma of sheer lusty sexuality exuded by the vault he filled so deeply with his driving stake, hear her little cries, throaty and impassioned with lust and delight.

His pelvic bone pounded her mount's spongy, swollen plumpness, and he could hear, too, the richly titillating sound of that.

Excitement and lust overwhelmed him. The muscles of his calves straining in knots, he drilled through her soppy vaginal walls in search of her womb itself. His hand pawed her breast with a roughness she obviously liked, and she bore down, hard. Her inner walls squeezed as the entire girth and extent of him sank deep between her warm, pulsing lips and explored every pocket of her inner vagina.

The rubbing knob kindled flames of raw rapture, far inside her. She began to shake and pant violently, moaning, rolling and arching her pelvis as he rose and fell on her. The reflexive clenching of her buttocks beneath her threw her hips up to him and filled her completely with his big soothing probe.

Her eyes bulged; she cried out. Then the sweating naked lady-in-waiting was waiting no longer; her smooth, clean curves were jerked and convulsed by spasm after spasm of all-encompassing orgasm. She writhed in transports of infinite delight, consumed by sexual ecstasy. Her fisted hands pounded at his big upper arms without her knowledge, then fell weakly to the bed.

Flowing juices spilled over his deep-seated prick. In seconds the friction was gone. He lifted his left leg, swept her right inside it, then leaned the other way while he brought her quivery left leg inside the clamp of his own. She groaned and he smiled; with her legs thus pressed together from thigh to ankle and held there by his clamping thighs, she had gone virginal tight inside.

"I'm . . . not . . . getting as much . . ." she gasped, straining.

Smiling, he ground his hips to plug her the more deeply.

"Aaaahhhh! No—no matter . . . it feels . . . twice as *thick,* now!"

With such squeezing pressure all around his seething cock, he was gasping in seconds, then quivering, continuing to pump even as he began to go taut. Taut as a bowstring his back went—and then released, to send arrowing jets of his seed spurting into her.

She held him with all her might while he groaned and shuddered and creamed her insides with the warm syrup of his loins.

Long minutes later he slipped sidewise from her, so that his spent organ emerged limp and drained, leaving a sticky trail across her thigh. He drifted in and out of sleep while she played and toyed with him, kissing his chest and arm, licking and pretending to bite his nipple, then mouthing his semen and her own fluids from his limp penis. It came alive, slowly, and he came alive suddenly to lunge into her again.

This second time they fucked until they were both gasping and covered with sweat, and when they paused to rest, both of them fell asleep.

Next day he had dressed and eaten and was about to

leave Tyre's citadel to visit the city's sprawling, colorful bazaar. He was hailed at the great main door by an overweight and very dark girl with enough backside for two, and insufficient bosom for one. High-voiced, she advised that the lady Blanche had bidden her call him to the dungeon, there to witness the punishment of one woman and the reward of another.

A strangely worded message, The Crusader mused, but he was excited, instantly assuming that Luisa had been found out. In the scarlet tunic and hose of a squire of the Lion-heart, Guy accompanied the girl. They were passed through a great ironbound door by the two guards there, to descend into chilly, mouldy-smelling depths via stone steps on which flickered the yellow light of wall-mounted torches.

Guy of Messaria had never before set foot in a dungeon. The province of the nobility, they were entered by others only as guards, or torturers, or . . . prisoners, few of whom emerged unmaimed and many of whom were never again seen alive.

There were ugly devices of wood and iron and steel; there were cells from whence emerged moans and worse sounds; there were dark spots and stains of ominous origin. But he saw no one being punished, and he frowned as he followed the native of this torture-prone land from that main chamber and along an even damper, narrow tunnelway. Here there were no torches, and she paused while The Crusader took one from its cresset. He was not able to hold it on high as he followed the plump daughter of Allah; the ceiling of this subterranean passage was no more than half a foot above his head.

They reached a point at which the earth-floored tunnel swerved; beyond the turn he could see a glow of light. His guide halted, turned.

"I am forbidden to go beyond this point, Squire," she said. "Do you proceed, please." And with a shiver, she brushed past him and fled back the way they had come, despite the darkness.

Suddenly suspicious, he transferred the torch to his left hand and drew his dagger. His sword was in the castle above, in his room—the room in which he had not spent the night. With fiery brand and steely knife at the ready, he advanced.

He rounded the corner and stared.

Here the tunnel broadened again into a stone-walled chamber, lighted by four torches set in iron cressets well up the high walls. Here were wall-mounted gyves and chains, and a table on which lay pincers of dark iron, along with whips of several designs, and both chain and rope. On that table, too, lay crumpled clothing. He recognized the green and blue; this was the garb Blanche had donned but an hour ago!

The naked woman standing against the far wall, then, with her calves bulging because her chained arms were drawn up so as to force her onto the tips of her toes, was Blanche! He started forward, despite the gate separating him from her, closing off the room from the tunnel leading to it. From that new vantage point, against the grille of iron bars thick as a swordhilt, he saw that the torture chamber contained both an unlikely piece of furniture and an equally unlikely torturer.

Against the wall to his right crouched a colorfully-covered Circassian divan, with feet carved into the likeness of lions' great paws and its purple spread embroidered with the heads of cupids or angels. Beside the couch was a woman. She wore a *brasseur* of gleaming black leather on each wrist, heeled Greek sandals of black with crossed straps climbing her calves to the knees, and a torture-master's black hood. Save for the thong about her hips, she was otherwise naked, a woman of beautiful slenderness on whose chest her breasts looked out of place: They were white, unveined tits, impressive orbs of erotic shape and fullness.

"Body of Christ!" He seized the bars of the door, sure that Blanche had somehow fallen into the hands of Luisa.

Then the torture-mistress turned partially his way,

and he saw that her loins were covered by an apron of leather, supported by the black thong girding her hips. He had to assume that beneath lay the curling mahogany-colored pubic hair of Luisa de Vermandois.

There was a stripe across the naked backside of the bound Blanche. The hooded woman added another. She held a whip he had not seen, but now it darted along the floor, twitched, and jerked forward in her white arm. Out rushed the long whip of black leather. A tremor ran through the nakedly bound woman as she heard the telltale hiss of the rushing whip. Across the delicate flesh of both tight-clenched rear ovals snapped the leather lash, and Guy could well imagine the stinging that pervaded the skin and the plump flesh it so sleekly sheathed.

Blanche gasped and shuddered at the cracking cut, and he knew her bare breasts ground into the wall when she snapped forward in a futile effort to escape. Like a lazy serpent, the lash dropped from her trembling bottom, and Guy saw the new stripe it left.

His legs knotted and his arms tensed; the grille would not bulge. It was fast secured, on the other side.

"What means this?" he snarled. "In God's name, stop!"

The naked woman in the hood turned again to face him.

"It means that the door will be opened only when you are naked and unarmed and agreed to whatever I demand," a cloth-muffled voice told him, and the delicate hand made the whip twitch on the straw-strewn floor.

"Blanche!" he cried, after a moment.

The woman against the wall twitched, made a sobbing sound, and leaned her head against the gray stones. She said nothing. Her naked tormentress turned back to her again, and rustled the lash.

Guy dropped his dagger, released the bars. "Wait—lash her no more."

"You agree?"

"I agree." He was already stripping.

"To *whatever* I demand of you?"

Grinding his teeth as he undressed, The Crusader nodded. "Aye."

"Swear it. On the cross."

"I swear by the cross of Our Lord to do as you command."

"And nothing more!"

Trapped, he thought, for though peasant-born he possessed more nobility than most of those reared in castles, and could not either watch while Blanche was whipped or run for aid in breaking into the torture-room —if that were possible. And now he must pledge no attempt on the lewd figure that dominated this darkling scene.

"And nothing more," he said, and stood naked before the grilled door. That such a sight had imparted a thick length and nascent hardening to his cock shamed him; it betrayed his appreciation of the erotic aspect of a naked woman's whipping.

The torture-mistress chuckled. She came to the grille with swaying hips. Chains rattled, and clanked. Stepping back, she beckoned. The iron door swung open before Guy's push, scraping along the floor. He entered the cell, naked and having vowed himself into defenselessness.

The hooded woman pointed with her whip-stock. "Kneel."

Silently cursing himself for not having hurled his dagger, for having made such a promise to save the backside of a woman who certainly liked some roughness and might indeed enjoy a strapping, he obeyed.

Forward stepped the nearly naked commander of this strange scene, and she halted only when her leather apron was a hand's breadth from his face.

"Give me your mouth, arrogant friend of Richard!"

Guy stopped his outburst of words. He had made his

121

bargain, and may as well be done with it. His cock had gone down; he hoped the bitch noticed! Raising his hands, he lifted aside the leather veil from her loins—and stared at the coiling curling mass of dark red hair.

Surely he recognized this pubic fleece! But—*why* was she doing this? Had he angered her so?

God be thanked; her furry vulva emitted the very pleasant aroma of some eastern scent, and of woman.

He pressed a long, warm kiss into the scarlet thicket, and he heard her groan, felt her shivers. Inhaling without distaste the hot vapor rising from her cuntal cauldron, he opened the soft lips with skillful thrusts of his gentle but insistent tongue.

"Ah!" she gasped. The sound was almost a cry. The flavor of her inner fluids coated his tongue as he insinuated its wet length deep into her oozing female furrow.

"He . . . is . . . doing it, Blanche," the quivering woman gasped out.

From Blanche there came no sound; from her erstwhile tormentrix, constant sighs and little panting gasps. His loving attentions to the wet slit nestled in her crotch made her writhe in helpless paroxysms of pleasure. She trembled as every nerve in her body seemed to put forth a tendril, to center an ending in her carnal chasm. Finding the little flesh-bud at the top of her offered vulva, he began laving it with his tongue. She groaned and her pelvis contorted in an anguish of delirious pleasure.

Her entire body rocked and shivered in the prolonged orgy of a devastating orgasm, and she greeted that culmination with soul-deep cries.

Withdrawing his face from her wet crotch, the kneeling bringer of that intensity of pleasure knew that only his hands on her lower hips kept her from collapsing to the straw that covered the floor. He remained where he was, wondering, unsure whether to be furious or . . . exultant.

122

Then, in a still-weak voice, she spoke.

"How is it that one of the mightiest warriors of the host allows himself to remain on his knees before a woman, to lick her flowing slash like a dog at the dish, when the hands that hold her up could twist the head from her body?"

"First, because I made an agreement, and swore by Holy Rood. And then because it is not unbecoming to a man to kneel before royalty, and I would not lay hands on the Queen of Jerusalem in other than lust."

From Blanche came a giggle; from her torturess a gasp. Then, "Varlet! How did you know?"

"Decorating my arrow quiver," Guy Kingsaver said, "is the hair of a woman, plaited together with the tresses of another. Some strands are red, and some are blond. It was by the red that I long ago identified a woman who lay secretly with me without wishing to be known; by the same red curls, I identify my lady queen now."

This time Blanche laughed aloud.

"Oh hush, Blanche, or I'll see that you never feel a strap on your leather-loving backside again! So, Squire Kingsaver, how dared you then refuse last night's obvious invitation from a queen—and more importantly, a woman who wanted you?"

"I . . . I cannot answer," he said, kneeling at the feet of the daughter of a king, no less demeaned than would have been Richard the King on his knees before a pope.

She sighed. "You had not realized. You thought I was some silly wench you could turn down. You did not know I wanted your body on mine and your staff ensheathed in my body once more. Instead, you lay with my lady-in-waiting . . . whilst I waited, alone and in need." He felt the jerk of her body, heard the swish, and then the sound of the whip's handle, smacking the wall. The leathern lash fell to the straw well behind him. "Very well then, Guy Kingsaver. You are released of your promise. Do what you will; the whipping of Blanche was a sham, and your clothing and dagger are where you left them."

Guy rose and stood before her, towering over her. He knew that the eyes behind the hood were directed downward, to where his big, slightly curved organ came ramming out from his loins, all full of the juice her body coveted.

Then he seized her and bore her back and down. Ignoring the divan she had caused to be brought here, he stretched Isabella roughly on the floor. She grunted when his prick came tearing into her, but she was well moistened from his saliva and her spend, and it sank all the way to his scrotum in a second.

The straw cracked and swished beneath her royal arse as the Queen of Jerusalem lay on the floor of that dungeon cell and enthusiastically sought to match the hard-fucking rhythm of her peasant-born lover.

He rutted strongly into her, pushing at the floor with his toes and slapping her belly with his, listening to the sighing groans of delight that erupted from her, stoking the hot passion in her with the full broad length of his cock up her belly. And The Crusader knew that he would never again deny the sexual beckoning of a woman determined enough to gain it anyhow, and powerful enough to have punished rather than thus rewarded him!

Next day, sailing down to Jaffa, Guy shot glances constantly back in the direction of Tyre—and occasionally at Henry of Champagne. The Crusader wondered: *Had* the Count lain with Isabella, who nevertheless plotted and gained Guy's lovemaking with her strange plan? And . . . *had* Luisa become trustworthy?

ELEVEN
Guy Squiresaver

Having been placed by King Richard at Henry's disposal, Guy could only hang about in Jaffa, once again the residence of Joanna, Berengaria, and their households.

Soon after their arrival he learned that Melisende de Bois-Courtenay, seventeen and having felt anything approaching love for a man only with Guy and that within the past few months, had been married to a French knight, but ten days previous.

In a smoky-beamed inn filled with men of various lands—several of whom he knew full well to have deserted the army—Guy Kingsaver of Messaria enjoyed a mug of dark, warm wine with Count Henry's second squire, Raimond, son of a baron of Chalons. Though he had accepted the Cypriot, most likely because of the name Guy had made for himself and the fact that King Richard had been heard to call him *ami,* friend, Raimond was a snobbish fellow who groused about the smell of the place, about good prices having risen so that a man needed a yeoman's quiver full of bezants merely for a night out—and about the women's being walking cases of crotch rot.

He did not spare the other patrons of the inn, either, until at last an equally sneer-faced French squire at a nearby table wheeled about. He pointed out that Raimond talked so much he might welcome having his flapping Champagnois mouth widened with a swordpoint, so that he could talk the more.

"I do not recall having rocked your kennel, sirrah," Raimond told him rather loudly, and other voices stilled. "But as I have with me no sword, and neither have you, perhaps you were best advised merely to continue drinking your milk."

The other man blinked, looked past Raimond at Guy, and clamped his hand so tightly about his winemug that the knuckles went white.

Guy attempted to look unconcerned and as innocent as possible; he was not so taken with his pompous companion as to consider entering the fights the man might bring upon himself.

"Here," the French squire suddenly called, "a bone for this fellow to chew on, to still his yapping!"

More voices stilled; more heads turned. Thus a score and more men saw Raimond send the contents of his winemug into the other man's face. Sputtering, his dripping face working violently, the Frenchman shot out his left hand to grasp a fistful of Raimond's shoulder. But it was not there; Raimond de Chalons was on his feet with the speed and grace of a dancer. The other man blinked at him. Then he lunged.

Guy sat back comfortably, keeping his face impassive, his hand wrapped loosely around his mug, while the two men staggered into a table, each grasping the other as though they were lovers. The Cypriot was grateful for the diversion; he liked Raimond's constant griping no more than the young squire's antagonist.

The table against which they had stumbled tipped, and one of the men sitting there grunted as he was gouged with its edge. He shoved it strongly back, catching Raimond in the hip. Raimond was otherwise occupied; his opponent was making a determined effort to get a thumb into his eye. With a strong effort of his own, Raimond spun them halfway around. But he was

126

forced backward, and when his buttocks encountered the edge of the table that had been his antagonist's, the man forced him back and back until Henry's squire was nearly flat on his back. At that point one of the French squire's companions upended his winemug over Raimond's face.

"This will cool the fellow's heat, Charles!"

The Champagnois cried out as the wine stung into his eyes, and he helpless on the instant. His right hand left the body of his enemy, Charles, to flail about in search of some weapon.

Another of the three young men at the table produced a dagger, raised it, and held it poised, waiting for the blinded man's hand to come into position beneath it.

Guy had to rise, then, into the hubbub, calling, "Hold there, with the dagger—one on one seems a fair fight, but there's been interference enough!"

"Aye, that boy's blind!" an old and scarred man-at-arms growled, from another table.

The man with the dagger stared first at Guy, then twisted about to look at the man behind him. Guy was big, and wore squire's clothing; the other was older by a score of years, and was roughly dressed. The dagger-wielder started to rise, again lifting the slender flake of steel to a stabbing position.

The old man-at-arms let a foot slam out and into the other's bench. Staggered, the squire yelped, cursed, and stabbed at the swiftly retreating leg. At the same time, the blond man who had dumped his wine over Raimond's face seized Henry's squire by the hair to hold him in position while Charles pummeled him.

"Damn," Guy Kingsaver muttered, and hurried around his table.

Eyes lifted to him, apprising the dagger-wielder of his coming, and that blue-silked young man whirled to strike. Without pausing, Guy swept his left arm across the Frenchman's midsection, so that with a cry the young squire toppled backward over his own bench. In a demonstration of long experience, the man-at-arms at the next table was leaning out to relieve the squire of his dagger even before his head banged the floor.

Fair still seemed fair to Guy, and it was not the man Raimond had made his enemy he went after. Instead, he slammed one foot down on the bench, stepped across it with the other, and gave the blond the heel of his hand in the forehead. That one was propelled backward, and naturally enough he strove to maintain his place on his bench by hanging onto his grip: Raimond's hair. Raimond squealed like a dog whose tail has been stepped upon.

Guy's attempt to restore the fight to fairness was not well accepted. Raimond's opponent Charles released him to become Guy's opponent, while Raimond threw back both hands to seize the wrist of the hand dragging at his hair.

"I merely removed the distractions," Guy said quickly. "Resume your quarrel; you and I have none."

"Lowborn toad's spit," Charles snapped, and swung a wild fist at the Cypriot's face. "Bearded like a scabby Saracen, you are!"

The man on the floor kicked Guy in the leg. The man who'd been Raimond's foeman missed fisting him in the face only because the Cypriot jerked that face swiftly out of reach. And the man who had one hand in Raimond's hair now reached out to grasp Guy's belt with the other. The fourth man at that table now occupied chiefly by Raimond was rising hurriedly, with a firm grip on his glazed earthenware mug.

Raimond squealed again.

Wishing sincerely that he had gone apologetically to Leila rather than consent to go inspect the Jaffan night-life with Raimond, Guy Kingsaver stopped the next swing of Charles's fist by interposing an open hand. The Frenchman's wrist slapped into it; the hand closed. A moment later the squire's scream rose louder than Raimond's.

At that moment the blond decided to rise to the aid of his countryman, and to hell with this pig-squealing Champagnois. Aiding himself in coming to his feet by tugging hard at Guy's belt, the man let go Raimond's hair. Since Raimond had been trying with all his might to pull away, he scooted swiftly along the table and went onto the floor between it and the table he had shared with Guy. With a loud thump, Raimond's head banged the table-edge on the way down.

Guy, meanwhile, was using the first squire's hand to slap the blond man in the face. A pain-flexing finger caught an eye, and the blond staggered back with a groan, one hand coming up to his eye. Having lost interest in the Cypriot at least for the present, he released Guy's belt and reached for his dagger. The fourth Frenchman, he of the upraised winemug, was temporarily occupied in trying to get around the blond.

And the dagger-wielder was getting to his feet with no less than bloody murder in his eyes.

The Crusader's head swung left and right, conning the enemy forces arrayed against him. The one with the knife was the most serious. With a twist of his arm and a hard jerk, Guy slammed Charles into the man with the dagger. Both went down; the dagger-clutching fist struck the edge of the table of the man-at-arms; the hand opened reflexively, and the dagger slithered out. The man-at-arms snatched it up, raised his eyebrows over its jeweled hilt, and stored the nasty weapon swiftly away. He then departed the noisy inn with his booty.

Guy had released the first squire's wrist the moment he rammed his body into that of the second, and both of them were now on the floor in such a strange conformation that one of the eagerly watching noncombatants called out an extremely lewd and completely insulting comment on their activities.

While Guy wrapped both arms around both the blond man and the one with the winemug, the two on the floor disentangled themselves, staggered to their feet—

and launched themselves on the onlooker who'd called their heterosexual manhood into question. A table collapsed beneath the three of them with a terrific crash.

Guy's charge hurled both his new targets violently backward into the wall. The winemug struck and shattered; its wielder's head struck and held, though his eyes rolled up loosely. Then his head rebounded violently and with a clonk and a clack of teeth his chin slammed down into the top rear of his blond comrade's skull. Both men began sliding to the floor.

Somewhere the proprietor was screaming. The man who had first reacted to Raimond's sneering mouth, along with the erstwhile dagger-wielder, was now the proximate center of a clot of ten or more snarling, grunting, cursing, pawing and pounding men. The man-at-arms was well away with a lovely bejeweled dagger to show for his heroism. And Raimond, Guy of Messaria learned when he rounded the table again to bend over him, was asleep, with a lump on the back of his head and a thoroughly foolish look on his face.

Guy glanced leftward at the two men he had slammed into the wall. The rearmost, also, was unconscious; the blond was shaking his head groggily and trying to discover why he could not rise; the man behind him had an arm locked around him, even in sleep. Wondering only briefly if erotic dreams were possible in unconsciousness, Guy glanced the other way.

The Inn of the Green Gryphon had dissolved into a minor riot that was making sand pebbles of most of its earthenware mugs and kindling of more than one overdelicate Syrian table.

Shouldering Raimond de Chalons, squire, Guy Kingsaver, squire, departed the tavern. He made his way swiftly in the direction of the palace.

Around the corner of a darkened house came swiftly a cloak-muffled man in whose hand steel flashed in the pallid moonlight.

"Hold there, what might be the contents of your purse?"

130

"Go find your own source of wealth," Guy snarled at him, "or the guild will hear about ye!"

"Oh—uh—sorry," the footpad stammered.

He stood staring after the big man who strode on up the street as if the man he carried over his shoulder were a feather-stuffed dummy. Then, with a sigh that he had not found the unconscious squire before the big man, the footpad melted back into the darkness in search of a more cooperative victim.

A little house just beside the palace was occupied by two of Henry's squires and two pages—and, Guy discovered as he heard the noises from within, more than one female houseguest. Loath to interrupt, he unshouldered Raimond, sat him against the door, propped him there carefully, and started on his way. Then, with a grin, Guy turned back to knock loudly at the door. And he ran.

Let the arrogant idiot's comrades worry about him, Guy thought chuckling, when they opened the door and the unconscious fellow toppled in backward, reeking of the wine splashed over his face and silken tunic.

Guy went directly to the small room Leila occupied, given her for privacy by Joanna—because of the man who had saved her brother's life on Cyprus. The man now thrust open the door and stalked into the darkened room to stand over the couch.

Dropping to one knee beside it, he slid a hand gently over that marvelous curve made by the haunch of a woman lying on her side.

Her voice came softly: "My lord has returned to his woman?"

"Does Leila of Acre accept fickle and errant non-lords who come as supplicants in the night with apologies on their lips?"

She hurled the cover from her, twisted onto her backside, and sat up all in a rush. Her arms pulled his head against the warmth of her bosom. "Only one," she whispered wih a fierce fervor. His hands went onto her hips; after long silent moments she wriggled. "Your beard is . . . strange, on my titties."

"It comes off tomorrow," he said, against the swell of her inner breast.

She squeezed him the tighter. "Oh no! I *love* it!"

"Then I am sorry," he said, thinking of how different he'd look from the companion of the man who'd started all the trouble at the Green Gryphon, and grateful indeed that he had worn this silken tunic of Syrian workmanship that Blanche had given him, rather than one marked clearly with the arms of Richard the king. "For tomorrow I shave it."

"Your chin will be pale," she murmured, still squeezing his head to her.

"Nay—there's not been that much sun for long," he said, aware of the shapely, almost-hard mound against which his jaw rubbed.

She sighed. "Then I shall enjoy thy beard for the last time this night, my lover."

"One wonders if it would tickle your thighs so that you would giggle rather than sigh in pleasure."

She shuddered, but said, "I'll not have it there; it will be my face between my lord's thighs, not his parting mine, for it is not fitting in the sight of Allah."

He twisted his head to catch a nipple with his lips, and began working it into erection.

She sighed. "Ah . . . ah, thou hast been too long away, companion of kings and escort of great barons."

"Too long away from this," he muttered, aware of her nipple's firming and thickening obediently under his nuzzling lips and flicking tongue. One hand slipped into the division of her buttocks, tightened there with his thumb out on the great curve.

"What has happened in Jaffa since last I was here?"

"I have only just returned myself; only a week ago we were in Acre. There . . . there the pale-haired Frenchwoman married one of her own countrymen," she said, nervously.

132

"Good," he said, deciding against admitting he already knew of Melisende's wedded state. He teased her breast's tensing peak with his teeth. "And what else does Jaffa speak of?"

"Of the election of Conrad—but not among the Syrians," she told him, releasing him with one arm and slipping it in to toy with his own diminutive nipple through his tunic.

"Mmmm. And why not among your people, then?"

"They are not my people; you are my people. Uh—ooh, my love, a little harder . . . Thee—the Syrians of Jaffa know that the sultan has been dealing with a beauteous and wellborn woman with long, dark hair and . . . large, ah, titties, and that it is said she expects high position soon—once the lord Lusignan is King of Jerusalem."

Occupied with her perfumed breast, with his fingers working about in her rearward cleavage, and with her own erotic play with his sensitive nipple, he gave no thought to what she had said. Chuckling, he said, "She will be disappointed, then; the crown is to be placed upon Conrad's head within the month."

"Oh—ooohhh, umm my lord, my love . . . ah, that . . . hurts and . . . and it is so . . . so sweet . . ." She trembled, assailed by unappeasable sexual excitement, with her lover's teeth fastened around her nipple and his stubby index finger wiggling and worming its way into her anus.

Remembering after a time what she had said and how she loved to be told, he slid the inch or so of finger out of that soft squeezing passage and relaxed, slowly, the pressure of his teeth on her nipple. He licked it, coating it with saliva as balm, and then pushed up to his feet. She sat on the divan with one hand to her stinging breast while he undressed. Then he stood over her naked, and he planted his hands on his hips.

"On your knees, woman, and take your man in your mouth."

133

Sliding instantly down to her knees, she used her fingers to aim his semi-erect organ at her face. She slipped the softness of her lips over the pungent knob and started sucking to fill her face with beloved male meat.

It was happiness for her, and both knew it; she was trained almost from birth to accept the man as absolute lord, so that it was her source of highest pleasure, playing the part of the slave she was not. Her wide-held mouth enfolded his vibrant lovesword, and she exerted a strong suction. The dark daughter of Allah loved it. She loved sucking his cock. It was lovely.

He began to move, rocking his sweaty loins passionately against her face. Her cheeks stretched and bulged as he thrust into her sweet, enclosing mouth. The kneeling girl took more and more massively erect shaft into her angelically upturned face until she felt the hair of his ballocks against her chin. Her back arched inward in her passion. She rammed the tight-skinned, swollen mounds of her bosom against his legs.

He was mouth-fucking her, gently but deeply, filling the chamber of her face with the hardened, pulse-pounding flesh of his sex. With her nails digging in, she clutched his buttocks and seriously strove to jam her mouth and face and throat and belly full of powerful male organ.

Now and again she had to pull back, to relax her jaws and her throat. Then she returned to the feast. Her caressing, coaxing mouth slicked up and down his massive erection. He shivered and gritted his teeth under the stimulus of that sweet massage of his cock by her moist, hotly ardent mouth. Slowly, he rocked back and forth, back and forth, fucking her upturned face, burying his cock in her head, slicking it between wet, clinging lips while she gripped his butt and sucked and licked and, helplessly and of necessity, sniffed from time to time.

She felt it when his buttocks tightened and he stiffened, all over. Her hands clamped harder; she locked her mouth around his hard-throbbing organ.

Rushing hotly, almost painfully up along the canal of his urethra, semen jerked and spewed from him. She heard his groans, felt his tremors, tasted the thick fluid on her tongue. It flooded into the warm sweet cavern of her face until he could see the creamy fluid trickling over her lips.

Staggering, weak, he joined her on the divan, and they slid into sleep while fondling each other.

TWELVE

The Night-Stalker

The Crusader awoke in the middle of the night, his brain bursting with thought. He greeted the horrible thought with mixed emotions, but knew where his duty lay, whether the man was worth saving or not. Unable to return to sleep, he lay beside the softly curled form of Leila and waited, without patience, for the dawn.

He should not have waited. When, once the sky at last lightened and Guy dressed and hurried to talk with Henry of Champagne, he was told that the count was breakfasting privately with Joanna.

Hungry but knowing he could not eat, he paced and fretted. Again he approached the page; again he was told that milord count and milady queen were not finished with their repast, and were not to be interrupted. Again he paced and chewed his lip; again he asked; again he must wait. He wondered: Henry and Joanna? It was difficult for Guy to picture the handsome Henry bare-assed, white-buttocked, sprawled between the doubtless pure white thighs of Richard's slender sister while the count's rutting cock drilled in and out of an orange-filled slit that was no less juicy and dilated for its being royal.

His new thoughts roared through his mind like a storm at sea, hurling off side-gusts in a dozen directions.

He paced. He snarled at Raimond when the fellow approached, shouted his "No!" when Leila offered to bring him food, glowered at some tripping high-breasted young girl who was maid-in-waiting to the king's Navarrese wife. And the sun moved across the sky of Jaffa—and, Guy knew, the clouded sky of Tyre.

It was nearly noon before he was at last advised he could have converse with Henry of Champagne. Guy had to fight to control himself; not even a hero and friend of Richard the King could rail at a wealthy and powerful count who was more than friend to two kings: he was the cousin of each. But to be dallying about at a morning-long breakfast with a woman, while plans were doubtless moving forward for murder . . . it was monstrous, inexcusable. Guy's tight-clenched jaw worked.

The Crusader had himself in hand when he entered the room where the handsome young nobleman sat behind a marble-topped table with filigreed legs. Henry wore a rich kingly robe of gold-broidered forest green. His hair, close-cropped all around but long enough in front to form slightly undercurling bangs on his forehead, glinted in the sun from the window behind him as though he had just washed it. His expression was open, politely attentive, but unsmiling. Though he had been told that the Kingsaver had been long waiting and was anxious as a rutting stallion, there was no way for Henry II of the powerful and rich County of Champagne so much as to hint at apology.

"That growth so becomes ye I'm of half a mind to leave off shaving myself, Guy Kingsaver!"

Guy's words were ready on his lips; now, like a galloping horse thwarted by an insurmountable bulwark, he had to pause and circle despite his impatience.

"I—it was my intention to shave it off this day, my lord," he said, remembering that resolve for the first time since awakening with his terrible suspicion.

"You will break the hearts of some mooning maidens

137

I have heard of," Champagne smiled. "And some non-maidens, as well."

"My lord . . . your pardon, but I must talk on a matter of such moment that neither beard nor maiden is of any importance this day."

"Admiring members of the distaff sex of no importance?" Henry's frown was not quite genuine. "Then I shall close my lips and list to the news from yours, Squire Guy."

Swiftly Guy summed up for the young count the story of the lady Luisa de Vermandois. He related, too, what he had been told about her by Blanche—without mentioning Blanche's name. Finally, grim-faced, The Crusader came to the present, and Leila's revelation of the previous evening. It still seemed to hang together, and he outlined then his very ugly suspicion.

The Count of Champagne listened, not impassively, but without exclamations. Then came his questions, and Guy was soon aware that Henry was possessed of a keen mind, and that the nobleman was cautious, questioning, and thoughtful. It was too bad, Guy mused, in a most un-peasantlike thought, that it was Philip II and not Henry II who sat the throne of France! Surely this intelligent and reasoning man was worthy of a kingly crown.

At last Henry reached his decision: "Right or wrong —and it is a fantastic story, sure—I believe it were best then to dispatch a messenger back up to Tyre, to warn my lord Conrad."

Guy leaned forward. "My lord—I know this woman Vermandois, and I know, too, the Queen Isabella. I hope it is not unseemly of me to say that I am known in Tyre. Make me that messenger; let me take ship up to Tyre—*now.*"

The man behind the marble-topped table gazed at the earnest young Cypriot, and he tucked in his lower lip to worry it with his teeth. Then Henry nodded, once and briefly.

"Done. Get you ready. I meanwhile will write out three messages for ye to take with ye: one to a sailing master here, another to the harbor master in Tyre, and one each to the King and Queen elect. Four, then." And he called for his clerk.

Guy was ready. He was very conscious of the heel-dragging passage of time as the count prepared the four notes, the last two on fine lambskin. The sun was well past the zenith and into afternoon by the time that Guy, with Count Henry's blessing, was ready to go down to the harbor and take ship north to Tyre.

Then it was that nature or God took a hand. A stiff wind had arisen less than an hour before, and was blowing steadily south and west. There would be no northbound sailing this day.

Henry of Champagne bade his special courier wait until the morrow.

Restless, his brain still furiously assailed by many thoughts that made his armpits prickle, The Crusader wondered. Suppose . . . Isabella and *Henry* were conspiring against Conrad? Suppose Luisa was *their* tool?

Ridiculous, but he could not get the thought from him until he had gnawed at it like a mastiff with a bone. He knew that the little County of Vermandois bordered that of Champagne, up near the borders of the Holy Roman Empire—but that proximity merely heightened and made more agonizing his mental state and the feeling of helplessness, as he tarried here in Jaffa while the poison was prepared or the knives sharpened, up in Tyre . . .

Suppose . . . that Blanche, Isabella's friend and confidante, had deliberately misled him about Luisa? Suppose . . .

In a turmoil of mental anguish and bootless thinking, The Crusader learned that afternoon some idea of what it must be like to be a nobleman, with suspicions of everyone, always.

Guy of Messaria wished most sincerely that he could

gain the ear and counsel of the man he respected most. But Richard was more than a day's fast ride down the coast.

He was hardly civil, later, to the squires who wanted to take him along on another night out in Jaffa's taverns. Nor was he decent company for Leila, and he had no interest in the pleasures of the flesh with her. His brain refused to be directed elsewhere than on the matter of Tyre, and Luisa, and Conrad, and the crown of Jerusalem.

Having given up sadly and at last drifted off, Leila was sound asleep when a helplessly restless Guy Kingsaver decided to go to Henry once more. In the darkened room he shared with the dark girl who called him master, he drew on only indoor clothing, with a cloak, and felt boots.

A few minutes later he was only mildly surprised to find Henry of Champagne not in his room. That someone else appeared to have been there *was* surprising, and cause for the descent of The Crusader's brows. Frowning, nervously wondering, Guy took up the count's dagger-belt. He hesitated a moment, but then buckled it about his hips without thought of theft. Then he left the room, a tall broad figure wrapped in a cloak of wool the color of a roan horse, stalking the darkened halls of the palace of Jaffa without any thought for the fact that he resembled nothing more than an assassin.

But so did the other man he saw, as he rounded a corner in the corridor. With obvious stealth, the fellow was entering the room of Queen Joanna. The hood of the night-stalker's night-blue cloak was up, so that he resembled a monk—or an assassin.

On silent feet, the felt-shod Guy raced down the hall to the doorway through which the other man had disappeared. The Crusader slipped through that same entry, knowing that he might well be intruding on a tryst. The room he entered was darkened, and empty, and the one beyond was unlighted, too. But a bit of light, strangely broken as it filtered through the Arabically-latticed window, revealed not just redheaded Joanna but a *couple* on the broad bed, asleep.

The cloaked man was stealing upon them, and Guy saw the silvery gleam of a dagger in the moonlight. The man was no more than four feet away, intent on the couple on the bed. Swiftly and almost without sound, The Crusader moved. What sound he made availed the other nothing, for he had no time to turn.

Guy seized the cloak-draped man from behind, clamping one big forearm across his mouth at the same time as he twisted the dagger-arm up behind the hooded skulker's back. The assassin was caught, and with no sound other than a rustle of cloaks and his muffled grunt. Then he was drawn backward from the room, with his heels dragging on the thick-piled Saracen carpet.

The sated, sleeping pair on the bed did not waken.

In the hall outside, the man succeeded in wrenching away; as he did and spun about, the hood slipped down to reveal dark brown hair, wavy, a small, well trimmed mustache—and eyes that stared balefully at his attacker like glowing coals. Guy recognized the man who had sought to slay Henry of Champagne—and Joanna, of necessity: it was Sir Bertrand of Valance . . . *Melisende's bridegroom!*

"Interfering island-born scum!" the assassin muttered, and he advanced, carefully, arms well out, feet planted, dagger ready.

Just as Guy twirled his cloak about his arm, Sir Bertrand lunged with the sliver of deadly steel. Guy's cloak-swathed arm leaped out to catch the stabbing blow, so that he gained only a scratch through the woolen folds. He jerked the arm away, and for a moment Bertrand's blade remained caught in it.

Guy's right hand had already dropped to his hip, where it wrapped around the dragon-headed hilt of Champagne's poniard. It only whispered as it slid from its lined sheath and rushed upward; it made a sound like that of a dropped melon as it was sheathed again, with a jolt, just under the ribcage of Sir Bertrand.

The man stiffened, gasped, and stared at Guy with a great look of surprise on his face. He still wore that expression when he slipped to the mosaic floor of the palace hallway. Guy had released his grasp on the dagger, so that its hilt stood forth from the huddled body.

Guy looked about. There was no one, and no sound from within Joanna's chamber. He supposed she and Henry had stupidly seen to it that there was no sentry this night, that Henry might join her on her sleeping couch.

Squatting swiftly beside the other man, The Crusader was mildly surprised to find that Sir Bertrand was not breathing, and that his eyes were still wide open in that shocked expression. Withdrawing the vicious little triangular blade that must have been an invention of the count's own land, Guy wiped it carefully, then re-wiped it, on the inner lining of the dead man's cloak. He returned the dagger to its sheath, clean and shining and bearing no sign of the bloody work it had done this night—for its owner, though in the hands of another.

Within a minute more, Guy had Sir Bertrand well swathed in his own dark blue cloak and was lifting the dead man easily in his powerful arms.

Silently and grimly, The Crusade carried the corpse through the palace of Jaffa, directly to that small apartment that Joanna had kindly given over to the newly-weds. All day his thoughts had been torturous; now they were of torture, as he stalked with her dead husband to confrontation with Melisende de Bois-Courtenay de Valance.

Pushing open the door with his foot, he fully expected a familiar voice to issue from within, "Milord? Is the deed done?"

But there was no such voice. And he had wronged

Melisende, he saw at once, in his thoughts.

She was on her nuptial couch on her back, well covered. Her face had probably been covered as well. But she had managed to work the multicolored Syrian spread down, to reveal her mass of silken blond hair and the pale face it framed—a face whose mouth was invisible and soundless between a tightly knotted length of scarlet silk. Above it, her blue eyes were huge and piteous.

She writhed as, half squatting to dump his burden to the floor, The Crusader crossed the orange-carpeted room to her and drew down the coverlet.

She was naked. Her slim form was bound with rough ropes that dug in and made the skin bulge about them, even svelte as she was. Again she wriggled; a pleading humming sound emerged through her gag.

With care, Guy drew dagger, slipped it beneath the cloth just behind her ear, and sliced the silk. For a moment she licked her lips and worked her jaws, but only for a moment.

"Guy! Oh Guy—he plans to kill the Count of Champagne!"

Guy considered, studying the red lines on her cheeks, left by the tight-drawn gag. "He? Who, Melisende?"

She wriggled, sobbed. "Bertrand! He—he's a monster! He must have been hard put to be so kind and gentle—and married me only to gain easy access to the palace! Once we were wed he became another man, cruel and biting. But you must—"

"Why did you not tell someone?" he demanded. "The Lady Joanna . . . someone."

Her lip trembled and tears oozed from her eyes to sparkle on her cheeks. "Partially because I—I was afraid. But . . . because I am such a fool, and could not bear to let others know. What did I know, I who was a slave these years of my youth, and who—who thought she was loved, and . . . and . . . was left behind, like a saddlebag, while the man went to join the war without a word for the past or future, without a touch. Bertrand seemed kind . . . I—I *need* love, Guy!"

He understood, and knew it was to himself she referred, and he felt both guilt and remorse. But he had to be certain: "But how do you know he planned to slay Count Henry?"

"I learned only tonight—*after* he tied and gagged me this way, he stood over me and smiled and told me I had been most useful, that Champagne was as good as dead and soon would be in fact, and . . . and he bade me farewell."

"Where did he intend going?"

"Guy!" she cried weakly. "Please—don't stand here asking me questions—fly to the count, save him from that monster assassin!"

He noted well that she said nothing about first freeing her, but spoke once more of the danger to Champagne. Nevertheless, he said, "Answer."

Melisende stared up at him a few seconds in silence, her sea-blue eyes wide and tear-shimmering and uncomprehending. Then she said, "I don't know, Guy. He said what I told you, and then he said . . ." Her chin quivered; she gulped a sob that juddered her naked breasts. Her eyes left him to stare at the wall. "He said: 'Farewell, little stupid who thought a knight of France would want a silly child who's had up her the . . . the diseased organs of the Turk and . . . and of a peasant off some island not big enough to notice.'" A great shudder ran through her. She was taken by another gulping sob. "I shall remember those words all my life."

He heaved a sigh, relieved. "I believe you, Melisende . . . gentle Melisende."

She whipped her head back to stare up at him. "You —you thought—those questions you've asked . . . oh, *Guy!*"

He sat beside her on the bed. "I am sorry, Melisende," he said. "Let me turn you now, to get these ropes off."

"But Guy—*the count!*"

"My lord Henry is safe. And . . . so are you, Melisende," he said.

He quivered when he turned her onto her side to get at the wrists knotted with rope just above her buttocks. There were weals on her back; not old marks, from her whippings in the mountaintop aerie of Julanar the outlaw, but fresh stripes. They were high, not on her buttocks, so that they were not "love-stripes," as Leila called them, when Guy gave her the whippings she desired.

"You—you've already . . ."

"That's why I came here, Melisende. I wanted to discuss something with the count. I went to his room . . . arrived just in time to see the assassin and thwart his purpose." At the last moment he had seen there was no need to tell her *where* he and Bertrand had found Henry. "The count was not even wakened! But in the hall Bertrand wrenched free, and tried to use the blade meant for Champagne on me. It rent my cloak." As he talked, he used Henry's dagger to slice free her hands, then her thighs, and finally her ankles.

She had twisted about to gaze at him across the fine curve of her bare haunch. "And . . . Bertrand?"

Freeing her ankles, Guy resheathed the dagger and met her gaze steadily. "It would have been better had I been unarmed, Melisende. As it is—you are a widow."

For a time she stared, then she began quaking, and then the heavy, body-rocking sobs came. She collapsed on her side, faced away from him, sobbing.

"I am sorry, Melisende."

"No!" she quaked out amid her weeping. "No no—I weep because it is over—and because I feel so . . . guilty, a woman married less than a month whose first thought on hearing of her husband's death was '*Thank God!*'"

THIRTEEN

Because of Milady's Bath

The Crusader lay cloak-wrapped in a smelly stable in Caesarea and pondered the knotty question of sin.

Was it sin, what he and Melisende had done last night —or rather, early this morning?

In a stall only a few feet away, his horse made a groaning sound. Guy smiled. Deukkak was probably dreaming. He hoped the dream did not interfere with the Arabian's rest, for they must be on their way early on the morrow. As they had not been today; the contrary wind prevailed, and armed with new letters from Henry of Champagne, Guy had ridden the entire distance from Jaffa north to Caesarea this day, some twenty-three miles. Man and mount were weary. Guy had decided to sleep here, in the stable warmed by the presence of the animals, in order to be on his way the sooner came dawn.

Sin. It was hardly his business, he mused. Thinking about sin, talking about sin, warning against sin, identifying and denouncing sin, even ferreting out sin; all this was the business of the prelates. Not that he had any intention of seeking the counsel of a priest, or telling anyone at all about last night.

Had it been sinful, his lying with a woman whose husband of less than a month had been dead less than an hour, and that at his hands?

On the face of it: surely. But . . . considering that the man had tricked her into the marriage, taking advantage of a young woman who desperately needed warmth and attention and the semblance of love, because she had known none in her five years of slavery following her parents' violent deaths; taking that into consideration, along with the fact that she had said she loved Guy Kingsaver, her rescuer from slavery and from her husband . . . considering these mitigating circumstances, was not their coming together sexually more a good deed, a work of God rather than of Satan?

Guy stirred, lying on his back with his hands clasped behind his head. His eyes were closed, for there was nothing to see among the dark rafters of the stable. He felt another stirring, too, along his thigh, for as he remembered himself and Melisende, his never-tired penis began to stiffen and redden like the comb of a strutting cock.

It was right. It must have been right. It was too good, for both of them, to have been other. Melisende had *needed.*

He was not quite certain how it had come about. She had been sobbing, and he stroking her and murmuring softly, and then she had turned to press herself to his warmth, within the security of his arms, and to weep the more. She had been entirely naked . . .

He remembered her shifting, murmuring about the buckle of the dagger belt he wore, and then about the hilt of that dagger as well, for when she shifted her naked skin from the one, it was to be pressed coldly by the other. That he remembered, and her unfastening the buckle. After that . . . he was not sure. Had he undressed or had she unclad him? Had both of them divested him of the few clothes he had thrown on to go for a talk with Champagne in the night?

Probably, he thought. *Probably both of us did.*

"I love you, Guy," she had told him.

You love who shows you love, he thought; *you think*

you love the man who was your first and who won
you free from the outlaws of Egypt, and then from
Egypt itself, and still again from those raping Turks
in that nameless, unpeopled town down the coast!

He had known it even then, even last night, even at the moment when the naked blonde lay back, slim thighs askew and her parted, pale-haired lower lips so brazenly displayed. He knew, as he moved over her and then, helplessly, into her, that he would leave her again in a few hours, and that she would continue to be prey to another such as Bertrand of Valance.

Then it was too late to consider anything, to consider that she would rise in the morning to don mourning—though she mourned not—and that he must tell Henry what had happened, and then be on his way, and that she might well feel guilty about—this. About the inward plowing of his cock, swollen, stiff, and heavily veined, making her cunt stretch all around it.

She had smiled and sighed, loving that forcible stretching of her warm fleshy vault into a great O.

"Oh God . . . Holy Mother help me, for I love you, Guy Kingsaver!"

The stuffed feeling had her writhing in an ecstatic agony, practically purring in a hot heaven of sensation. Deliberately, he had heightened that stretched sensation. Deep within her body, he swung his hips. He saw the strained, concentrating expression on her face, and he felt her efforts. She was exerting the strength of her inner muscles around his fevered prick, clenching the slick membranes tenaciously all around the swollen shaft. Smiling, she bore down.

He gasped; his lips peeled back over his teeth, his brain and quivering body filled with excitement and sexual hunger. His cock responded to her squeezing efforts and the new constriction by surging so stongly inside her that she blinked, having felt the strong jerk of that broad wedge, way up her belly. A little squeal escaped her panting lips.

148

Panting, weaving and pumping her damp, shuddering thighs, she groaned aloud and her feet tried to climb the backs of his legs.

Her hands came up jerkily, fluttering, and one plucked at his nipple while the other rode and tugged at his muscular, bobbing butt. She continued to move, thoroughly enjoying the raped feeling his cock gave her, while she squeezed it with all her might in an intimately engulfed embrace.

She tossed her head to and fro. Hair like honey and sunlight flew loosely.

"Oh please! I *need* so . . . please, give it to me darling . . . *give—it—to—me!*" She accompanied each of those last words with an urgent upward surge of her hips; her feet had slid down now to plant themselves flat on the divan.

He gave it to her. He tupped her in a raging passion, with hard driving blows. His big root dipped intimately, repeatedly, authoritatively into the fleshy folds of her molten interior.

Their bodies smacked together with sharp slapping sounds and she grunted under each impact. But that did not stop her from the constant darting of her hips to impale her own oozing cunt.

"Umm," she hummed, "oh darling . . . oh Guy . . . yes, yes, more, like that!"

Their driving bodies became slick, shiny with sweat. She moaned, she grunted, she murmured her love and desire and need. Passionate gasps erupted hoarsely from both their throats. His thickly virile lance was sunk to the full length between the bright pink lips with every deep-driving stroke.

Deliberately he gathered her legs, hoisted them so that her ankles slid along his shoulders and her straining body doubled more and more upon herself as his face lowered closer and closer to hers. She gasped—and grinned lasciviously up at him, loving the new depths he explored inside her, with her vagina turned almost straight up to become a long narrow tunnel.

He crammed it in and in, trying to force its full extent through her vaginal scabbard and ram its fat, sensitive head up her cervix. The panting, sweating man rode her hard, thinking now only of dropping the full contents of his ball-pouch into her molten deeps.

She enjoyed; she loved; she did not spend. She received what she needed, and gained release of a sort, but she was too tight, emotionally, to achieve her orgasm.

Not he. He suddenly groaned and jerked, then that jerk was repeated in his prick. His semen came tearing out of him, stinging a little in the force of its expulsion from his body into hers.

It had seemed to continue a long while, his seminal pumping into her quivering body, and then they had lain there in silence, each feeling the sweat of the other, neither of them speaking, for now it was over they had to face their situation again: she was a widow who must mourn, he was her husband's slayer, and . . . the body lay nearby, all rolled and wrapped in its own cloak.

They had fallen asleep, and neither of them had spoken when he had awakened at dawn, and dressed quietly. First furtively conning the halls from her door, he had hurried away. With him he had carried the body of Bertrand, still swathed in dark blue wool.

Guy of Messaria was waiting in Henry's room, with the dagger and the corpse, when the Count of Champagne came slipping in, fresh from the bed and the redfringed cunt of Joanna, daughter of a king, sister of a king, widow of a king.

Guy spoke into Henry's embarrassment: "Both milord count and the lady Joanna are unmarried, and I make no judgments, nor am I a gossip. You have my word; I have no knighthood to swear by, milord, but I vow anyhow, for milord of Leicester would have had me wear the golden spurs long ago, in October."

"I well know," Henry had said, "and I trust you, Guy Kingsaver. But what do you here, in my room?"

Then had Guy showed him the cold corpse, and told him the story of how he and Joanna had both come within seconds of death. Both The Crusader and the shaken, grateful count were sorry only for Sir Bertrand's being dead, for now they were not likely to discover his reason—and his employer or commander.

Now, in a stable in Caesarea the night following his saving the lives of a naked sleeping count and his mistress, Guy reached out a leaden arm to touch the haft of the dagger he kept sheathed and near to hand, for one never knew. His fingers traced the outline of that poniard hilt that was now his; it was of gold, formed into the neck and head of a dragon.

Next day the determined man and his big Arabian horse covered another twenty-six miles, to reach Haifa just after dusk.

Again he was up and gone at dawn, having spent the night in an inn room with three other men . . . all of whom had snored. The coastal plain of Falashtim sped by as the leggy horse galloped when he could, cantered when he was forced by the terrain to slow, and walked impatiently when his master forced him to do, because of both terrain and the horse's heaving flanks.

"Deukkak," Guy Kingsaver whispered, and the horse's pointed ears came back, "thou art nobler than the man whose life we ride to save! Now fly, fly on, Crusher, for I must misuse thee."

As if he understood, Deukkak the Crusher strove to fly, and in truth it seemed to Guy that had he been able to watch the racing steed's passage, he might well have seen no impact of hoof with turf. Deliberately he misused the animal, so as to reach Acre just before noon.

The beast was blowing, snorting, lathered and quivering in every limb when his dusty rider dismounted.

Presenting the letter sealed with the arms of Champagne, he demanded a fresh horse. From the pouch the count had given him against his needing coin, The Crusader handed a huge-eyed boy a sum equal to two months' wages for a soldier, with the command that he care for Deukkak as he would his own brother.

The boy promised; the replacement horse was prepared while Guy wolfed down food; he was off again.

A good day's ride was perhaps twenty-five miles; that day Guy Kingsaver of Messaria covered forty, from Haifa to Tyre. Darkness had drawn its net about the land when he reached the towering walls and great gates. The helmeted sentries on the parapets behind the machicolated walls above bellowed their challenges —and assured him that no one entered great Tyre after sundown.

The big gray man who had dismounted his sagging, panting horse bawled out his name to them. He added that he was on a mission for Henry, Count of Champagne, and added still further that he had a letter for their city's lord that was of such importance they would doubtless find themselves choosing between pincers and irons, if they admitted him not, and now.

The men on the wall muttered among themselves, and asked why his horse was so blown, and laughed scornfully when he told them he'd come this day from Haifa. At last one of them threw down a pitch-smeared brand with a demand that the pilgrim hold it high, that they might see his countenance.

With misgivings about making a target of himself, Guy did so. But one of the sentries recognized him.

"I saw him the first time he came here, I tell you, him and his prodigious bow and his prowess with it. It was miraculous; of a man who can wield such a lance-sized bow and so accurately at that, I'd believe a further miracle: that he *is* come from Haifa, and all on this day!"

Holding the torch in his left hand, Guy detached his man-length bow from the saddle and waved it. A great

cloud of dust rose when its lower end struck his cloak.
No one laughed.

The Crusader was passed into Tyre, and though his
horse was surely near death, he rode straightaway to
the citadel. There he was forced to explain and threaten
and wave the letters bearing the Champagnois seal once
again, to gain admittance.

"But . . . it will do ye no good, Kingsaver," one of
the bill-armed men told him. "Our lord the Protector
be not within."

"Then where in God's name *be* he?" Guy demanded.

The man shrugged; the older one beside him grinned.
"It is this way, saver of kings. Our lady Queen Isabella
is, ah, taking one of her infamously *long* baths, y'see,
and it's angry our lord was when he departed, fully a
turn of the glass ago. Ill-humored and hungry he was,
and off to seek his dinner elsewhere!" The guard's teeth
flashed in the upward-streaming flame of the torches
set in iron cressets beside the great portal, and the
younger man covered his mouth against his snicker.

Guy slapped his leg impatiently. "And neither of ye
knows where he's gone? None knows where may be
found the man in sole control of this great city? What
if I brought news the Saracen are attacking?"

"We'd find him soon enough," the older sentry said
smugly.

"Tyre has no need to be fearful of an attack," the
other man advised, with even more smugness.

"I would speak with Lady Blanche," Guy snapped.

"She is with the queen, and I like not your tone."

Guy ground his teeth. "I represent the lord Henry,
Count of Champagne and cousin of Richard the King;
I am Guy Kingsaver, squire to Richard the King, and
—" he embroidered only a little—"friend to both your
lord and his lady. Fetch me pen and paper, and that
quickly, and see ye speak not to me in that fashion
again, knave, or I'll show ye how to bend a billhook
around a man's neck."

The two soldiers stared at him. Their grips on their

153

billhooks tightened, visibly, and Guy immediately threw back his dusty cloak in an obvious clearing of his swordhilt.

"Fetch old Petronilla," the older man said, with his eyes on Guy; he spoke from the corner of his mouth. "And paper. I saw that dragon with the emerald eyes not a se'enday ago, at the hip of Champagne when he came with word of Lord Conrad's election to the royal crown."

The younger man rolled his eyes, but did not turn his head to the other. "What dragon?"

"The one surmounting my dagger," a deathly cold voice told him, and dark eyes seemed to bore into his face like awls.

The young sentry blinked, bit his lip, glanced at his companion, then turned and hurried inside.

Guy stood there seething, thinking of the stupidity of a ruler's placing such men between others and himself. Conrad's lifeblood might dye the pavement of his own city while his underlings held life-saving news at bay, out of fear of the wrath of their commander, who doubtless feared in turn some silk-robed chamberlain. Yet The Crusader had heard that it was even worse in Byzantium, where the emperor in his robes of stiffened silk and his lordly isolation had no notion of what his underlings, men with neither spines nor balls, did in his name.

A woman came; with her was a man with gilded helm. It occurred to Guy that he had never learned the name of the fat old woman who had several times conducted him to the bed of Lady Blanche; it was Petronilla, for this was she.

"What means this—I'm told you've threatened my sentries!" the man said, with hand on hilt and chin high.

"Not your sentries," Guy said steadily, "but those of the future King of Jerusalem, worse fortune for him! Petronilla, you will recall that your mistress expects me this evening. How is it that I am treated at this gate as though I were at the head of a thousand Saracen?"

Petronilla blinked, as did the man who was presumably the commander of the citadel's guard. But she was a clever woman, else Blanche would not have entrusted her with knowledge of her liaisons and the conduct to her chamber of love. Petronilla nodded.

"Aye, and I make apology for my lady. Come with me, Guy Kingsaver."

"Hold there! No dusty-cloaked foreigner and an old woman," the man with the gilded helmet said, "are going to—"

Guy's swiftly moving hands loosened a buckle, and another, and in seconds his sword and dagger lay at the man's feet. "Move them not," he said, "I'll have need of them shortly, when I leave." And he and the old woman went inside.

"The lady," she said without glancing at him, "is with our mistress, who bathes."

"So I've been told," Guy said. "See that ye repeat my words exactly, but not within hearing of the queen. Say this to Lady Blanche: 'Guy Kingsaver has come to save the life of another king, and him yet uncrowned.'"

She froze in mid-step, thus nearly falling as she rounded on him with dilated eyes and mouth ajar. "Oh God! Is't true?"

"So we think, my lord of Champagne and I. Remember, and keep it from . . . Her Highness, and fly."

As well as she was able considering her grossness, Petronilla flew. Guy followed as far as the foot of the steps, ignoring the comings and goings of pages, squires in tabard and hose, busy richly-robed chamberlains, girls and women, and stolid sentries who looked as though they had been strung with steel wire from anus to crown. All were dressed well and colorfully enough, in ancient Tyre.

Blanche soon appeared, stumbling as she descended the steps with her train clutched up in her hand, and he saw that her face was nearly as pale as her name.

155

Swiftly, he gave her a partial explanation.

"Body of Christ!" she gasped. "He—he's gone to dine with my lord Bishop Philip of Beauvais."

"A fitting dinner partner; the hammer-wielding bald-pate's a lap dog to the King of the French! And where does he live, the bishop?"

Blanche was quivering, and her hands twisted nervously like live things she was unaware of. "Not far—wait a moment longer, and I'll be your guide. Oh, Guy!"

"Aye—but I am waiting already."

She nodded and flew with a great rustle and swirl of skirts. He fidgeted and paced the rug-strewn, parqueted floor until she came back to him at the run, the skirt and white silk lining of a long hooded cloak billowing about her. The hood was blown back; she readjusted it as they hurried back out to the gates.

"Lord Waleran," she told the thin face under the gilded helm, "this night ye've angered King Richard, Count Henry, this candidate for knighthood of the Earl of Leicester, myself, and thus my lord Conrad, who is not so inhospitable. Pray to Our Lord that ye survive!"

Guy was retrieving his weapon belts from the man's nerveless hands; without looking at him or the two gape-mouthed sentries, he strode through the gate. Blanche followed with a hiss of felt shoon and the rustling whisper of her purple-paneled blue cloak.

"This way."

"What sort of place is this," he grumbled, adjusting his baldric and belt as he walked beside her, "where a slip of an unmarried girl talks so to the commander of the citadel guard?"

"Civilization, barbarian," she snapped, then giggled. That noise she curbed swiftly. "But Guy—why ever would Lady Luisa want Conrad dead?"

"Because she's in the pay of Saladin," he told her. "And Saladin prefers Lusignan crowned."

He sighed, having decided against his wishes that the

Lion-heart was *not* infallible, and that he supported Lusignan for no reason other than that the man's family came from Richard's demesne, while Richard's rival Philip of France favored Conrad. "And because," he went on, though it hurt a bit, "with Lusignan king and my lord Richard gone, Saladin would soon have an emir in every city from Acre down to Cairo, and ye'd hear him knocking at your doors before All Saints Day —morelike by the Feast of Saint James," he added, exaggerating; surely Richard could not decamp and Saladin move so rapidly as to secure the coast and besiege Tyre by late July!

Through that ancient city they hurried, a cloaked man and equally muffled maid (or a supposed one; Blanche's hymeneal days, Guy well knew, were far in the past), unaccosted because of the size of The Crusader. To a great rich manse they came, and they found it well guarded. Here dwelt Philip of Dreux, the Bishop of Beauvais who spent his time chiefly in spreading of false tales about King Richard.

"His Grace the Bishop," a shaven-crowned prelate told them in manner austere, "dined early this night, and my lord of Montferrat went his way . . . grumbling."

"Know ye where?" Guy burst out.

The robed priest blinked and elevated his scanty eyebrows another measure. "One does not question the new king, sirrah."

Guy stared at him, and felt the juices rising and boiling about in his stomach. Somewhere in this great city of twisting streets and many houses, the barons' choice for king was dining . . . or already in the hands of the assassins Guy Kingsaver was convinced were bent on his death. This would be a perfect night; the moon was pallid in a dark-clouded sky, the coronation was imminent, and Conrad was so unwise as to leave his palace guarded by idiots whilst he went abroad by night alone, or nearly.

Abruptly The Crusader swung his pained face to the hooded young lady-in-waiting.

"Blanche," he said quietly, frowning, "you once said that . . . aye! Blanche, where dwells Luisa de Vermandois?"

FOURTEEN

Steel in the Moonlight

The house Conrad provided for his paramour Luisa de Vermandois in Tyre was a lovely little retreat, planted about with shrubs and flowers, fragrant with the delicately sweet aroma of orange trees. The lapping of the Mediterranean's gentle night waves was clearly audible as Blanche led The Crusader to that house near the sea.

All was dark within, and there was no reply to Guy's hard-fisted banging on the door—which was of wood, heavy and thick against thieves or worse.

Bidding Blanche wait where she was, off the paved street and out of the light lest there be footpads, he made his way around the house, seeking entry or signs of occupancy. There was no one—but once he had availed himself of some sort of strange, stunted tree to climb the wall in back, he had his clue. There was a gate back there, through the bushy shrubs and the orange trees, and the gate was open. Too, he heard the receding clop-clop of horses' hooves.

He *ran,* whirling his cloak up out of the way by swathing his left arm with it, scaling a broad shrub in a long bound, reaching the open gate and plunging through onto a narrow, cobbled street, dimly lit against footpads and cutpurses.

He saw them clearly: two riders pacing away from

him down the street. One wore a purple cloak that covered the croup of his mount, while the other, smaller, wore a hooded traveling-cloak of pearl gray. *Conrad and Luisa,* he thought, and again he ran, trying to be noiseless but succeeding not well. But they did not hear him; there was another distraction. Men suddenly appeared from a side street, before the two riders.

"Milord Conrad!" a voice called. "An important letter for you, O King-to-be!"

Running, Guy saw Conrad rein in and lean down as the two men approached on foot. He saw the flash of steel, heard the groan. Again bright steel flashed.

Twice stabbed, Conrad of Tyre leaned farther and farther from his horse—and fell to the street.

"NO!" The Crusader bawled, running with all his might.

The smaller rider beside Conrad's horse whirled to look back at him from within the hooded cloak. "GUY!"

It was the voice of Luisa de Vermandois.

Guy's longsword scraped from its sheath as he ran, and despite his attempt to defend himself, the first assassin followed his victim in seconds, with a great deep gash from hip to hip that spilled blood and coiling loops of pink sausage onto his thighs and then the cobbled street. Guy was forced to dodge desperately aside then—as Luisa tried to run him down. Her handsome jet-black horse plunged past within inches; the Cypriot slapped his haunch with the flat of his sword.

Then he was attacked by a curved sword, and Guy of Messaria was forced to defend himself against the second assassin, a native of this land.

"Ibn haram!" the man snarled, cutting viciously as he spewed forth the insult: "Son of adultery!"

His sword not ready, Guy danced swiftly back, half turning, so that the scymitar's point swished past his ribs. He added his own insult in the other's language, lifting his sword now and grinning wolfishly around the words: "Attempt that again, *mef'ul*," he invited, out-doing the Syrian by calling him a passive receptacle for homosexual mounting.

The man did, cutting viciously again with that thirsty blade of Damascene steel, but this time the man from Messaria interposed his own long broad blade, not merely as defense, but in a sharp muscle-backed chop that would have buried the blade in the trunk of a hardwood tree. Sparks flew amid the sound of steel on steel that set the teeth on edge—and half of a moon-curved sword went flying to clang again off the wall of a dirty white house, then still again, on the street.

Then The Crusader put the blight of death on his opponent, with a backhand return that left his head clinging to his body only by a thread of skin no thicker than Guy's little finger. The wound fountained blood as the man jerked and staggered, his body not yet aware that he was dead. At the same time Guy became aware of clamor, voices and clanking metal and running feet. Glancing back up the street, he saw bobbing torches and knew the brief engagement had attracted others. He sincerely hoped it was the City Watch.

But already Luisa's heels were jerking; her horse bolted away, down the street's long slope to the sea.

"STOP HER!" Guy bawled, but the oncoming knot of men was afoot, and they could only scatter as her black horse plunged through and past them.

The Crusader spent but a few seconds squatting to look at the sprawled man in the purple cloak. Conrad lay on his back, one blood-smeared hand at his middle, and his eyes were open and bright, staring without sight.

"Damn the bitch!" The Crusader swung to Conrad's quivering horse, which was apparently too shaken and confused to flee. "STOP THE BITCH!" Guy bawled, seizing bridle and swinging up. "SHE'S SLAIN LORD CONRAD!"

That convinced the wavering torch-bearers; babbling

161

even more excitedly, they whirled about and set off after Luisa's horse.

"WAY!" Guy bawled, booting Conrad's horse into a gallop, a dangerous proposition on paved city streets. "Way there, for Guy Kingsaver of Messaria!"

Perhaps it was his name that dissuaded them from slashing at him as he galloped past; certainly it was imminent danger of being run down by the clattering horse that made them spring aside against the walls of the buildings flanking the narrow street.

With five or six Tyrians running afoot behind him, Guy galloped down the sloping street after the fleeing black horse and its gray-cloaked rider. He saw the racing animal carrying the treacherous *kahbah* and spy for Saladin bear down on a child, who screamed at the last moment. The shriek was cut off at midpoint. The small body was slammed against a building to rebound and roll in the street.

Guy lost seconds, then, guiding his own mount around the crumpled, still child in the dark street of Tyre. His horse's foot slipped and the beast reeled; the Cypriot knew it was blood that greased the hoof.

Ahead, others abroad at night were more fortunate; they hied themselves out of the way of the plunging black horse and its heedless rider. Behind, Guy called out again and again, to make certain they stared not after Luisa and missed his precipitate following. Down and down the street dipped; closer and closer came the sound of shore-slapping waves. Luisa, Guy saw, was racing down and along the seashore. Then he was out of the street and down by the sea, too, and he saw her goal.

Riding at anchor, well off shore, bobbed a fleet carrack, its sail only partially furled. It had slipped in close, in the darkness, and aye, now he saw a little band of men ashore, just at the sea's edge. He could make out their pointed helmets: *Saracen!*

"Holy Rood! She *is* a Saracen spy—they're waiting

for her! She led Conrad into the ambush, just along the way to her waiting escape, that Turkish carrack. Rot their souls—God grant me the power to send her and her antichrist comrades to Lucifer's domain!" And bending low, his cloak over his left arm and his right swinging beside, long blade gleaming from his fist, he heeled his horse and charged along the rocky sands directly into a waiting clot of several armed Turks.

They *were* waiting; he saw the gray-cloaked arm of their Christian ally point back at him. Then he was charging into them, bent low over the neck of Conrad's fine horse with its mane whipping his face.

There was a heavy *whump* of impact as the horse slammed into one black-bearded Turk in the vicious fashion of a well trained destrier, then a cry of agony, for the warhorse's warrior-rider was busy as well: his longsword sheared away the sword-wielding hand of a second man. Then Guy was hanging on, clamping with both legs, while his mount braked his headlong rush and began to come about rightward, to charge again among the enemy. Snorting and blowing, trembling all over in high excitement, the beast was so obviously a warhorse who loved this awful work that Guy loved him and counted him comrade and friend.

Luisa was already flinging herself from her mount, in a swirl of pearl-gray woolen. A waiting Saracen caught her with uplifted hands. Even as her feet came to sandy earth she was clamoring about her saddlebag and the casket inside. Another man fetched it swiftly, grunting at its weight, but the desperate woman seized it as though it were feathers. With only a glance at the snorting horse bearing the big man back toward her cohorts, she swiftly set foot in the waiting longboat with its three dark-faced oarsmen.

Sand flew from the plunging hooves of his horse as Guy Kingsaver swung the animal seaward to intercept the boat. The remaining Turkish soldiers sprang, too, and there was a ring of steel on linked mail and a jolting pain leaped into The Crusader's right thigh; without the mailed leggings, he would have been minus a leg as swiftly as that. Down and around came his meter-long sword and a man cried out and dropped his own brand as his hands flew to his gory face.

At the water's edge a few feet from the boat, Guy kicked his right foot free. He used the other stirrup to catapult himself through the air. Hooves splashing loudly in the surf, the warhorse of a dead master swung back toward shore.

A Saracen oarsman cried out and started to stand, recklessly, in his boat. But the flying apparition of gleaming mail and long flashing sword was coming through the air like a mangonel-hurled stone, and there was no time to abandon the boat. Guy did his best to fold his legs as he came down feet-first in the boat— promptly capsizing it in four feet of water.

Oarsmen and their gray-cloaked passenger cried out and splashed and spluttered, while a heavy saddlebag dropped to the bottom like a stone. The bedraggled attacked and attacker floundered in the surf. Now Guy found his link-coat and leggings a hindrance. One oarsman Guy had sword-struck as he slammed into their boat; that man did not come up. The others sought to have their vengeance on him while Luisa, cursing, moaning, and flailing, waded to the beach.

Cutting at one of the oarsmen, Guy slammed a mailed fist into the face of the other, splintering nose and crushing mouth into a scarlet jelly through which nasal bones jutted. It was Luisa whom The Crusader wanted, and he waded after her, dragging his chainmail through the water while trying to ignore the agony in his right leg.

Far back along the beach, at the mouth of the street down which Luisa and her pursuer had flown, torches bobbed and men raised their excited shouts of discovery. They came running.

A helmeted man with flashing black eyes met the

demon-sent disrupter of their plans with flashing sword as the huge fellow waded in; Guy ducked low under the whizzing cut and destroyed the man's knee with a swing of his own long broadsword.

"GET THAT DAMNED BOAT UP!" A bedraggled Luisa screamed, waving her hands and dancing up and down.

Guy glanced at her as he splashed ashore. He should not have done; his foot came squelchingly down on damp sand, water flowed from every interstice of his mail, and he looked up—directly at a Turk with a leveled crossbow, no more than six feet away.

Desperately The Crusader hurled himself aside. He felt the sudden heavy blow in his side even as he heard the metallic *thung* of the crossbow's release. Then Guy fell into wet blackness that overwhelmed both his body and his mind.

FIFTEEN
"I Shall Live"

A strange blood-red mist swirled as The Crusader entered a weird gateway, a tall scarlet-edged oval, pointed at the top. He heard the splashing sounds and looked down to see that his mailed feet were sloshing through a thick scarlet soup with a heavy smell; the odor of a dog's breath. It was work just to walk through it; his right leg hurt fiercely. He knew that he waded ankle-deep in blood, into this strange citadel with the wavery edges and floating mist.

Then there was a corridor, dark and damp and humid, and a doorway from which burst a wild-eyed Saracen with a great curving sword. The scymitar came close, but missed, and Guy struck, slashing open the man's outer shirt and mail and the chest beneath. He watched without shock as a pair of hugely thrusting, weighty tits spewed forth both blood and, he saw with the same mild surprise, milk so warm that it smoked. The man-woman fell; Guy noticed, as he stepped past him, that the Turkish face had resolved itself into that of Luisa de Vermandois.

Good, he thought, *I've finally rid the world of that traitorous whore!*

And along the corridor of that strange dark palace The Crusader strode, his sword naked in his clenched hand, his eyes darting this way and that in search of another enemy.

And suddenly one appeared before him, as though sorcerously materialized. He was bow-armed, his left hand thrusting the curving weapon toward Guy while his right drew back the nocked arrow. The Crusader went to one knee, knowing a flash of fear, and his sword plunged upward into the man's groin. The arrow went away in wobbly flight, apparently to vanish behind him; Guy heard no clatter. The stabbed Turk before him, meanwhile, made puking sounds and fell backward so that his body slid off the deeply-piercing sword. More sorcery; his armor vanished, and the Cypriot saw that he had plunged his broad inflexible blade into an oval hole fringed with dark brown hair. Blood gushed.

He rose and followed as the Turk fell, and when Guy walked past the corpse he glanced down to see that its face was that of Luisa de Vermandois.

"Good," he snarled aloud, "I thank God for letting mine be the steely cock that slew her." But that was wrong, and he giggled aloud as he walked, all alone in the palace of sorcery. "Steely *sword,* I mean!"

He entered a room of Turkish luxury. A carpet of many colors, beautifully wrought, softly caught his descending feet, while all about him crouched low divans and low tables with filigreed legs, along with ottomans and cushions of silk and satin. Their colors rivaled those of the rainbow.

On one of the divans lay a woman, naked and with her legs spraddled in an obscene display of her genitals; it was Rosamonde, she who had first uttered to him the words "I love you." Odd; he remembered bitterly that she had died of Syrian fever one dark day before the walls of Acre. He must have been mistaken, for she smiled at him and lifted her arms.

He glanced down to see that his cock jutted forth from him like a third arm, lusting for her. Dropping his sword, The Crusader dropped to his knees on that divan between her legs. He would have spared her his armor, but she dragged him down to her and made no whimper when his steelclad arms scraped the skin of her soft bare ones.

Poising the throbbing length of his erection just at the curly little beard betwixt her thighs, he shoved it into her.

He heard himself cry out. She was *cold* inside!

"NO!" he shouted, starting to pull back and finding that her arms were holding him fast—arms that consisted of naught but dry white *bone,* for she was indeed dead as he had remembered, and her face was but a hideously grinning skull with dark pits where her sweet soft eyes had been.

Desperate, panic-stricken, Guy raised his mailed fist and struck that horrid apparition. The skull burst and shattered beneath his fist; the cold grip released his prick.

Rosamonde had loved him, and he had smashed her to bone dust.

"But why? What be the purpose of this innocent girl's death?" a voice demanded, and though Guy King-saver looked all about he saw not its source. He bit his lip, seeking the answer, aware that he was covered all over with a cold sweat. A piece of shattered bone must have cut him; his right side ached and throbbed.

"Purpose?" another voice echoed, and followed with a bubble of feminine laughter. "There is none. God does not care. That is what life means, and that's what death is. Death is something that just happens. I shall LIVE! I shall live every day, all my life, and if life be short, then . . . I shall have BEEN here!"

He rolled over in quest of the owner of that voice. And he smiled, for she was beautiful, her eyelids kohled and her hair a mass of wavy black. Her breasts were not in view, covered as they were by thrusting cups of shining gold, though she was otherwise naked. She smiled at him, though she bore a dagger in one hand and a whip in the other.

"Julanar!" he called.

"Guy, my lion!" she said, smiling, and she tossed aside whip and knife to pounce upon him as he rolled over onto his back. He felt her warm damp cunt come sliding down his prick as she knelt betwixt his legs, and he groaned at the sensation of it. God be thanked it was not cold! She began to bounce at once, plunging her vertical sheath up and down his standing staff.

"Julanar! My lioness!" He aided her self-impalement, cupping her naked buttocks in his palms and aiding her upward movements, then relaxing his arms as her hot vaginal grip ran back down his cock.

He lay there beneath the outlaw chieftain of Egypt, grinning happily, watching the muscles of her inner thighs twitch and tighten. He could see clearly her cunt sliding down his upstanding cock. The thick, hair-lined folds of moist flesh slithered greedily down to devour the hot hard tube up her belly, to the hilt. It was beautiful, exciting, delightfully lewd to watch his cunt-wet cock going up and down in her dilating pussy.

True, she was somehow wrongly seated, so that there was a throbbing pain beneath his ribs on the right, but he tried to ignore it as he watched the up-and-down flash of her gold-cupped breasts.

Then, smiling, she began leaning forward, and he too smiled. His hands started to welcome her descent upon him—until he saw that the golden breastplates were tipped with long shining blades like poniards, and knew that if he stayed with her he must die of her.

"I'll have you forever," she murmured.

Swift as thought, he hurled her from him and sat up panting and all sweaty. She slammed down to the floor, sprawled like a doll tossed aside by some fickle child, and he saw blood flowing from her mouth.

"I loved you," she said, fixing him with her accusing gaze. "I lovèd thee, and only the truth I speak. And you have slain me!"

Her face flickered; for a moment he thought she was Luisa de Vermandois, but then the flesh had vanished and again he was gazing at a fleshless skull, the skull of another of the women who had professed love for The Crusader—and who was dead, living only in the cobwebby corridors of his mind.

Trembling, Guy rolled over to leave that death couch —and cried out aloud, for a Syrian scorpion had joined him there, and its tail snapped to drive agony into his right side. Quickly he rolled the other way, to escape the deadly little sand-devil, and he heard a voice call his name.

"Guy, oh Guy, no, no! Be still my darling!"

"Another of the hot poultices," another voice said, but he knew it not.

The pain subsided in his side; Guy's panting breath slowed. And somehow he had been transported back among the crusading army where he belonged, and he and Geldemar and Wertheim, Sir Geldemar the Bastard, had just turned that desperate sally of Saladin's cavalry from—from someplace; he could not remember.

"I thought ye'd been forced off to your homeland with Leopold," Guy called to the German knight beside him.

"Nay, Guy my brother, but the tower will not fall, so come and fuck with me," Geldemar called, laughing, hurling his helm from him, and they galloped down dark streets to a house where waited two young girls of this land, both dark and firm-fleshed, with soft hips and gentle eyes.

She was very young, this Turkish girl Guy fucked, and he glanced over to see the one Geldemar's thick body surmounted was so young as to be no more bulgy of chest than a boy.

But beneath Guy's chest bulged great ballooning teats that poked him with their nipples, big as olives and nearly as dark. Her cunt as he lunged into it felt like a great coiled spring, a catapult's driving power, with youth and erotic tension and the force of her wild gyrations.

Her hands clutched at him, and her nails produced

stinging sensations in his right side. But he withstood it, knowing she clutched only in love, and he worked hard with his cock smothered in the moist heat of her.

The pain sharpened; he glanced back and down to see that it was not her nails he felt, but the slender dagger she clutched in her dark hand. He whipped his head back to look down into her treacherous face—and he cried out, for gone was the young Syriac lovely and in her place was another. Malevolent eyes stared up at him from a face of beauty in which cruelty lurked, framed all about with long brown hair.

"Luisa!" he exclaimed hoarsely, and he heard the name echoing again and again within the labyrinthine corridors of his own mind: *Luisa*, LUISA, LUISA!

"Traitorous whore!" he snapped, and with his hands fastened to her neck he slammed forward his hips. The needle-tipped sword of his loins tore viciously through her hot twitching cunt and stabbed deeply up her womb, so that he felt the bubbling, streaming, scarlet river of her blood, hot and wet on his right side and thigh.

The beauteous traitor from Vermandois gagged and gasped. Her hands jerked spasmodically, and the pain left his side, which now felt soothed by her hot gushing blood. She died beneath him and turned to corpse and then skeleton with awful, hollow skull, fucked to death as she deserved.

"But what does it matter? What's the purpose?"

Guy lay still atop the skeleton, soothing his leg and whispering. "Nothing at all," he said sadly. "God does not care. That is what life means, and that's what death is." And he began to die.

For a time he was still, but he began to feel panic, knowing he was sliding into darkness from which there was no exit.

"No!" Then he was shouting, climbing up out of that grave with the bones of Rosamonde and Julanar and Luisa. "I shall live! I SHALL LIVE!"

"He will live," a ghost voice said. *"The infection*

dies and the man lives—he is strong as a lion of the desert, my lady!"

". . . *still feverish*," he heard another voice say; it was soft and feminine, and full of concern.

Guy blinked. Walking with swaying nakedness toward him was a figure in full armor, head surmounted by a camailed helmet of Turkish manufacture, its spike seeking the heavens. About her swirled strange mists.

"You have behaved foolishly. I love you, and others love you. Think, foolish boy, and strive to be other than an ignorant peasant." Up lifted a mailed hand to doff the helmet, and a cloud of sunny hair boiled forth. Melisende's eyes of Mediterranean blue gazed at him, but she did not smile.

"Great fool! You saved the life of the noblest man in Christendom, Guy Kingsaver! And his sister, too, owes her life to you, and the Count of Champagne, forget not that noble man. My life is yours; you who gave it to me. Conrad was not worth saving—even so, you tried. Think, foolish son of a peasant. Had the wind been favorable, you'd have departed Jaffa and arrived in Tyre soon enough to save Conrad from the assassin's knife—while in Jaffa, Henry would have died, aye, and Joanna sister of Richard, too! It was the fever that slew Rosamonde, not you; you gave her happiness ere she died."

"How—how do you know of Rosamonde?"

Melisende heaved an exasperated sigh. "Think, silly peasant. Try to use that dull head of yours. How *could* I know of Rosamonde? Now of *Julanar* I know! She was doomed from the day she set herself apart and became the most unnatural of God's creatures, a woman in the role of a warrior and an outlaw—and living apart from men, leading other women in her own hate-filled war on males! You rescued her from bitterness—and it was the Turks killed her, Guy of Messaria, the Turks, not you."

"I . . . I must live . . . the Turks . . . I must live, to slay Yarok al-Jazzar!"

172

Al-Jazzar, he heard the hollow echo, *al-Jazzar al-Jazzar . . .*

"*—is he repeating that phrase again and again?*" a woman's voice asked, but it was not Melisende.

"*It means 'the Butcher,' my lady.*"

"Oh. He must be dreaming about the man who sold him as a slave."

Dreaming?

"You are dreaming, Guy," Melisende said, and he blinked, seeing that she had stripped off her armor and was naked, standing just over him.

"Oh." He thought about that. "But if I know I am dreaming, why am I unable to wake up?"

There was no answer, so she vanished. He was sorry he had asked. She was beautiful, naked, and he felt a gnawing in his loins and knew he was randy, in need of a woman.

He said so: "*Shawat daram!*"

A voice chuckled, but he did not know whose it was. The man he had heard before, talking about him as though he were not present. "*A lusty man indeed!*"

A female voice muttered something; that same voice he had heard before. White, something white . . . The man chuckled again. "*He said he wants a woman.*"

"*May I—*"

"*Only with the hand, my lady. And carefully; 'ware that wound!*"

Guy was angered that they continued to speak about him as though he were not present . . .

He was on his back amid swirling dark mists. Beside him sat Leila, dark lovely Leila with the womanly hips below a tiny waist and nakedly shorn vulva. She sighed, so that her bold, high-set, and girlishly conical breasts rose and fell, shaking their crimson tips at him. Her hand was wrapped around his prick, which was definitely up and yearning for her, a stiff column of beautifully veined pink, hard and strong and unequivocally, arrogantly male.

He pulled her down, smiling. It was strange, he

173

thought, that she asked no question concerning his wound. But she was silent, allowing herself to be manipulated by his strong, guiding hands.

"I love you, my lord," she said softly.

"Your lord desires your ass, woman!" he told her, and her hand tightened about his prick. He heard a soft giggle, too, but it didn't matter.

"White," a voice murmured, in French. *"White, white, white loves you and helps you . . ."*

But he blotted out the voice, and steadied himself, having forced her to her knees, the French traitoress with her white, white arse, its cheeks succulent-looking and smooth as milk. He heard, dimly, her soft moaning. And he bade her be still, or . . . He did not finish the threat; she was still.

He guided the distended crown of his cock between the shuddering, pillowing cheeks of her rump and set it against the tiny tight mouth of the hole there. It was all hot and trembly, a tight coil pressing back against his sensitive cock-tip.

He shoved it in.

With a little groan, she readied herself by tensing her arms. Seeming to squirm all around the red head of his organ, her elastic inner flesh yielded, stretched . . . and his prick was all the way up into the sheltered little grotto of her rectum.

A tremor ran through the firm, snowy ovals that now trembled high in the air. He knelt tall behind her, the conquering son of Peter of Messaria, reveling in the snug grip of her noblewoman's arse around the full length of his rutting horn. He slid his hands around to clamp her hips. Heat enveloped him, and he sweated.

Grunting, he tensed his arms to compress the satiny globes of her upthrust behind, and he commenced to fuck her in high delight.

He began pounding his cock in and out of her arsehole with a relentless, desire-driven fury that gave her his slippery male organ far up her hot, wet rectum.

174

She squealed, first with pain and then with pleasure as he pounded her with all his might, and she screwed her highborn butt back onto his ramming staff. It squeezed him, pumped his organ like a soft hot hand.

She writhed, rubbing her buttocks and the backs of her thighs over him and making her expanded rear-cunt slither around on his prick, moving on it, making it pulse needily inside her.

He trembled and groaned, elated. She was fucking her own ass, screwing it back onto him as if she had just learned she had ten minutes to live and wanted to enter eternity in a delirium of pleasure. And it was jerking his cock!

Warmly enclosing his throbbing pole, her anal channel slid back along it like a tightly-enveloping hand, pumping him, masturbating him with her salacious rear hole, slapping his crotch gently with the bowls of her buttocks, making him sigh and twist his face, filling him with pleasure and the tremendous desire and need to empty his aching pouch of semen into her body.

When I have done, he thought evilly and yet without rancor, *I shall carve off her tits bloodily and stuff them up her, and at last we shall be rid of the most traitorous woman in Christendom!*

He was groaning and twitching, tensing up, frowning at the slight pain brought to his side. Then his pent-up reservoir of lust burst its dam. He groaned. The marvelous, relieving sensation of it, his liquid seed leaving him in a fast-paced, angry spitting, brought sighs and little exclamations of delight from her even as it relieved his ache.

But having spent, he felt himself slipping into relaxation, utter sated lassitude, and he knew that once again she was going to escape him. He tried to be more concerned about that. Instead, he sank into a deep sleep, and this time without dreams or pain.

SIXTEEN

Saver of a King

Someone was tickling his right side. It itched. He started to scratch it. Before he felt the noose slip over his hands, he felt the pain; it hurt to scratch himself! But now his hands were drawn together, and the rope was knotted about them, and Yarok al-Jazzar grinned at him.

"Come, slave," the Butcher said, and he tugged.

Guy resisted. No, no, he would not, he would not again be forced into slavery! He would escape! Tugging violently, he fought back, and all around him the air grew turgid and dim, and al-Jazzar began fading into the the midst, and then brightness assailed his eyelids.

"NO!" he cried out, and tried to lunge.

"Guy! Be still darling—you mustn't move, that wound may re-open yet, and I want you alive, my darling."

He blinked. Her face loomed over his, her eyes sad and frightened, her blond hair carelessly filleted, stringy. There was perspiration on her forehead, and either that or a tear slid sparkling down her cheek. He gazed at her, and suddenly she smiled.

"Guy!"

He spoke her name, in the French they both understood; "Blanche"—*white,* her name meant, and for a moment there was an illusive echo in his mind, a voice he had heard, repeating her name again and again, telling him that Blanche loved him and helped him . . .

Gripping his wrists in both of hers, she clung tightly. "Oh Holy Mother, Guy . . . you're really back?"

"Back?" He tried to think. "I've . . . been . . . away?"

She nodded, and another tear spilled down her cheek; it was a cool splash on his chest.

"Oh God yes, yes, you've been away, and you've dreamed and dreamed, and muttered and called out. And just now you were trying to tear at the bandage."

"Bandage?" He gazed blankly at her. Then he remembered: he had been wounded! The crossbow! "Damn," he muttered. "She escaped!"

"Oh, *Guy!* Is that all you can think of? Why must you be so magnificently *noble?* Why couldn't you be churlish, callous—and unlovable?"

He sucked up a deep breath; winced at the stitch in his side.

"I'm through scratching; I can stand the itch. Let go my hands, Blanche."

After a moment, she did so, still bending over him, and he gave her a smile and touched the breasty bulge in the front of her garment, which was a Syriac blouse the color of a spring sky. Then, carefully, he reached across himself with his left hand. His fingers felt the bulky bandage, pressed until he felt the pain.

"Uh."

"Stop that!" she cried, tugging at his wrist.

"I had to learn what it took to make it hurt. At least that little flash of pain drove away the itch. Blanche, tell me."

"Tell you?" She was gazing down into his dark eyes as though she were a greedy woman of wealth staring into her casket of jewels.

"Aye. All of it. It is light. It was night . . . I was trying to stop her—oh. Conrad. I saw them kill him . . . last night."

She shook her head, sighing. "No, Guy. It was not

177

last night. In a few hours it will have been six nights since—aye, six nights, but be still, you *cannot* rise!"

"Six! Five days I've lain here?"

"And nights. And dreamed, and groaned, and tried to move, and muttered. Then, two days ago, you suddenly shouted: 'I shall LIVE!' and the physician and I knew that you would. You are of iron."

"I feel more like lead. I think I remember that . . . but I have been dreaming, and now I cannot remember even the dreams. I am also thirsty—"

She gave him wine and helped him to drink. Then she told him of his five days of delirious unconsciousness, and of other things . . .

She had been his nurse all the while, had remained here at night, so that when he groaned or muttered, she awoke instantly and bathed his face. He had been delirious in his unconsciousness, she told him, and he nodded, with dim half-memories of his dreams. Insanity!

The crossbow bolt had come within an inch of missing him. It tore all the way through his right side. Neither artery nor organ was hit, but he bled a great deal in the water, lying in the surf with his head only just ashore. Luisa was gone, though she had barely escaped the crowd of men who rushed down to shore. One had tried to wade out after the boat that took her out to the waiting carrack. He had stumbled over something, fallen, and returned to the beach carrying a dripping saddlebag. It contained a casket of pearls and gems; Luisa had not got away with her spoils, presents of both the sultan she had served and the would-be king she had duped.

Conrad was dead.

Some, Blanche told Guy, were saying that Saladin had ordered him slain, in hopes that Lusignan would be king. Guy nodded, but there was more. Others, she said, avowed that members of the sect of Assassins had slain Conrad, in revenge for his having seized one of their wealth-laden ships and drowned the sailors. Other

178

voices opined that Lusignan had ordered the murder.

"Ridiculous," Guy said. "The stupids—it was Saladin, with the help of Vermandois, the *bitch!*"

"Be still," Blanche ordered. "Do not excite yourself." And she told him the rest: that the Bishop of Beauvais was spreading it about—and had sent word to Europe! —that it was King Richard who ordered Conrad's death, thus to make the Lion-heart absolute ruler in the Holy Land, except for Saladin.

Guy shivered in impotent anger. The bishop knew better—why did God suffer the heads of his Church to lie? (*Because God does not care,* he thought, but he did not say that aloud. Besides . . . once again the ever-clever, ever-treacherous Luisa had altered the natural course of God's will, and thereby aided the Saracen. That, Guy felt, proved his tenet. For if God cared at all, Luisa would not succeed and escape again and again!)

Blanche was telling him, ". . . so strange. Once, on his knees, Conrad prayed that were he not worthy of the kingly crown, it should be denied him."

Guy almost smiled. "Prayers are answered in strange ways." He sighed. "All that riding, the fight, this wound . . . despite it all, I failed to save from death the man the barons chose as King of Jerusalem."

His blond nurse gave him a strange smile. *"Did* you? Listen!"

And she told him of subsequent events. First, Hugh of Burgundy had hurried up to demand, haughtily, no less than Tyre itself! But Isabella had refused, announcing that long ago her late husband commanded her to yield up this city to none save the Lion-heart or him the barons chose as King of Jerusalem.

Guy's lips twitched in a satiric little grin. "Not likely they'd offer the crown to such as Hugh of Burgundy!"

"Be still; listen. Burgundy then stalked out, and he and his men rode away. For I was present, then; the physician was with you, and the princess wanted me by her. After Burgundy had left, she sat staring before her.

179

'I am daughter of the king of all this land,' my lady Isabella said in a voice like death, 'when there *was* a kingdom. Now . . . now Tyre is all I have.' "

Guy's hand patted the hip of the blond lady-in-waiting to the saddened heiress. "Aye. But Tyre is . . . Tyre."

"Do stop straining yourself to talk! You say nothing anyhow. An infection began, and you have been drugged. Surely your brain is not itself even yet, though you may think so. It's the queen's own physician who has attended you, Guy, Ruzzik of Seleucia."

"And you," he said, stroking her hip.

She looked down into his eyes. "Aye." Then she seemed to awake, after a moment. "Ah, but there's more; now be silent and listen to what the world has done whilst Guy Kingsaver was away from it."

Burgundy had seemed to arrive almost instantly—and had departed just as swiftly, dark and stern of mien. But a day later had arrived Count Henry of Champagne—and the barons of Tyre had greeted the handsome young cousin of two kings by hailing him as King! Henry was competent, well favored and well thought of, the mightiest feudal lord of France next to Philip and Richard—and unmarried.

The Kingsaver was smiling as Blanche told him the news.

For the sake of the kingdom, Isabella had offered Henry her hand in marriage, and the young count had promptly dispatched a swift-riding deputation to King Richard, asking for the opinion and the approval or disapproval of the Lion-heart.

Guy's brows came down. "Offered her hand? For the third time, and her husband dead but a few days! How old is my lady Isabella, Blanche?"

"One-and-twenty."

"God," he muttered, "poor lady. She be only a crown —with a convenient cunt attached!"

Blanche said, very earnestly, "I thank God I was not born of royal parents."

"And I! Well, come and embrace the patient," Guy said, weakly.

She drew back. "Not now—it's food ye must have, darling, not a further draining of your pouch of seed."

"I—*further* draining?"

Blanche smiled. "Aye . . . ye were restless, and obviously having dreams of a sexual nature. I . . . helped you. A medical necessity; I considered it my duty as your nurse, of course."

"Aye," he said, after a time, narrowing his eyes in thought. "I remember . . . or think I do. And I had a *good* dream, whilst you . . . performed your nursely duties." He grinned at her—and his stomach erupted a great growl. "Hm. I count ye right, nurse, I do need food! And wine . . . wench!"

"I should greatly wish that my nephew might be king," Richard the King replied to Henry, "if it please God, when the land shall be conquered—but not that he wed the marchioness, whom the marquis took from his rightful lord and lived with in such wise that, if Count Henry trusts my counsel, he will not take her in marriage. But let him accept the crown, and I will give him in demesne Acre and its port receipts, and Tyre and Jaffa too, and jurisdiction over the conquered land. And then tell him to come back to the host and bring with him the French, quickly as he can, for I want to go and take Darum—if the Turks dare wait for me there!"

But in a very private note the Lion-heart gave Henry advice of a slightly different nature: "Better that thou takest the crown while it be offered, *then* marry her, so that your claim hinges not on her. But, as I am too well aware, there are times when one must bow to expediency and accept what terms one must."

On the fifth day of May in the year 1192, only eight days after the murder of her second husband, Isabella of Jerusalem became a bride for the third time. Thus did the ex-bachelor Henry, Count of Champagne, become King of Jerusalem, to the mutual delight of Philip of France and of Richard of England and Normandy.

And thus did old Guy of Lusignan, in Acre, find himself holding even less power.

In short order, however, Lusignan arrived at a bargain with Richard. The Templars had paid the Lionheart sixty thousand in gold for Cyprus, and owed yet another forty thousand, after nigh a year. Further, the people of The Crusader's homeland had already rebelled against the stern rule of the Knights of the Temple of the Holy Sepulchre, and news of the merciless quelling of that rebellion was already spread far and wide—and was being called the Eastertide Massacre by many. Simply put, the Templars could not govern the island birthplace of Guy of Messaria, the land that Richard had conquered so swiftly and handily, and they wanted possession of it no longer.

Lusignan assumed the debt of Richard, and shortly he set sail, the new lord of Cyprus, by the grace of God—and the Lion-heart. And thus did Cyprus lose one Guy . . . and gain another.

But a day after the wedding, the King and Queen of Jerusalem visited the palace room in which Guy of Messaria lay recuperating. His nurse had to lay forceful hands on him to keep him from attempting to rise.

"You rode north, Guy my friend, to save the life of the King of Jerusalem," Henry said quietly, "after having saved *mine*. And thus did you accomplish your mission, for it was in Jaffa that night, not here in Tyre, that you preserved the life of the *king* from an assassin's blade!"

Guy said nothing, wondering rather nervously how Isabella took such talk from her new husband.

"I stand ready to box your shoulders for you, Guy of Messaria," Henry said, white-clad, for with his bride he mourned the passing of the man first chosen king.

Guy frowned. "Sire?"

Henry smiled. "Your wits have been affected by your

wound and delirium, Squire. I refer to the fact that a slap on the shoulder and a few words from me and you will rise from that bed—Sir Guy."

The big young man with the great bandage across his middle blinked. He bowed his head.

"My lord, my upbringing has not provided me the pretty words to greet and express my thanks for what my lord says and offers. I beg the king, though, to allow me to say that I shall await the golden spurs of knighthood until they are conferred by my lord Richard."

Henry chuckled. "As I predicted, my dear," he told his red-tressed wife, and she smiled wanly. "Aye, I understand, Squire. But this ye may *not* refuse, under pain of our disfavor: A fourth part of the value of the casket you recovered from the traitor of Vermandois is yours, and you shall have, too, the finest armor and horse that Tyre has to offer."

Guy heaved a sigh, noticing that it did not hurt so much as yesterday. Both Blanche and the Seleucid physician had remarked how swiftly his wound was knitting. "I thank the gracious king," he said, "and queen."

A few minutes later the royal couple was gone, and Guy, sitting up on his sickbed, was staring morosely at the wall opposite.

"Damn," he muttered to Blanche. "DAMN Luisa—Darum is a battle I shall neither join nor even *see!*"

"Art thou so anxious to leave me, savior of two kings who so lightly turns down knighthood at the hands of a king?" She pressed against him, totally naked, for of nights Blanche warmed her patient—and oft, too, of day!

His hand tightened on her bare thigh, just below the sparse growth of filmy blond curls. "I am anxious," The Crusader said, "to ride again against Saladin, to meet again his blood-handed champion Yarok al-Jazzar, him who once sold me into slavery in Egypt."

Blanche sighed, stroking a thick, deeply-pink worm—and watching it grow.

"And then," he went on in that same tight-lipped manner, "to hunt down the world's most treacherous monster, a demon in woman's body, Luisa de Vermandois!"

"Aye," Blanche sighed, caressing, "but 'twas she, you've said, who taught you the arts of love, my love!"

Guy managed a chuckle, returning from reverie to awareness of her and her scent and her soft hand that was hardening his organ. "Arts I dare not practice, with this great bandage on my side and the flesh not yet healed, woman!"

Blanche chuckled, moving down in the bed with nakedly jouncing breasts. "Ah, but your wound will not prevent your being an *object* of love," she murmured, and then she bent to stopper her loving mouth with his growing erection.

A shiver went through him when her pale hair brushed his lower belly and groin, and he felt her breath on the tip of his penis. He gazed down the length of his body at her crown as she bent over his loins. Again he shivered, for after blowing her breath over the fat dark head of his cock, she slid her tongue with loving tenderness over its liquoring tip. Deliberately titillating him, she made a little slurping noise as she sipped that male nectar.

She sucked and tongued and blew gently, making it swell up in the luscious recess of her mouth, until she had created a stiff column of beautifully veined pink, so hard and strong and intensely masculine. She smiled at his groan, and at the series of long, rippling shudders that ran through him.

"Be still," she whispered, and slid her mouth down and down over that tall spike, seeking to envelop its entire length in her face—which was not possible.

She knelt before him, between his legs, like a harem slave adoring her master, like a naked princess of some pagan faith devoted to phallic worship, on her knees before her carnal god. The warm clasping flesh of her lovely cocksucking mouth sweetly ensheathed the big, swollen length, and the wet carpet of her wriggly tongue slid and slavered all over it.

Half sitting in the silk-covered Syrian bed, he closed his eyes in pleasure, slid his hand over her soft hair, and opened his eyes again to watch the bobbing of her head.

Her downflowing curtain of blond hair framed her cock-filled face, shimmered on her soft shoulders, curled on his thigh. Her naked breasts, lusciously thick fruits heavy with passion, swung before her, beneath her, dangling against his legs, surging their engorged and firming peaks. Her face was beautiful with swollen-looking pink lips impaled on the thick shaft of male meat she seemed determined to swallow.

Suddenly straightening, she smiled lasciviously at him as, with both hands, she swept up and somehow knotted her hair so that it was out of her way and could no longer block his view. And she returned her mouth to his twitching cock.

He was filled with an indescribable elation and a tremendous desire to flood simmering spurts of hot sperm into her darling face until his seed slithered down her throat to form a sloshing lake of semen in the very depths of her belly. It would look beautiful, he thought, his milky liquor overflowing her sultry mouth to splash onto the thrusting firm struts of her naked tits!

Visualizing that intoxicating sight, he was taken by surprise with her next action.

She tightened her teeth in a menacing ring around his shaft, low down where it was less sensitive, and she sucked hard, bringing in no air at all so that he felt the tremendous suction and saw her face cave in to tighten the skin over the cheekbones. Her fingers, meanwhile, fondled his balls with more firmness.

He groaned. His hand tightened in her hair.

Releasing the toothy grip and relaxing her fingers, she slid her mouth up his cock and met his gaze with her desire-glazed eyes.

"Do I make you want me?" she whispered.

"Dear God!" He shivered. "Don't tease me, woman, or I'll assfuck you until my wound opens and only loss of blood stops me!"

"I will remember that promise," she said softly, "and remind you of it—after your wound has healed. In the meantime, I ask you again: Do you want me?"

"I want you. I want to plug up your throat with cock and fill your belly with its seed!"

She smiled. "Then we want the same thing," she whispered, and while he watched, her mouth opened and rounded and cruised slowly down the thick, blood-darkened staff of his loins again.

The sweet, exciting sensation of that big sexual organ throbbing away in her mouth made her sigh around it. She sucked with all her might, but slowly, treating him to the almost unbearable sensation of a thrillingly slow suctioning and blowing.

He saw that her face was as flushed with excitement as he felt. His eyes feasted on the sight of his lust-thick organ slithering wetly in and out of her face, the torrid and yearning clutch of her loving and thoroughly delightful mouth. Mother of Jesus, what a nurse! She tended him, fed him—and now happily pleasured him—and herself—nursing at the hard, veined flesh of his sexual shaft like a babe at the teat!

Tremors began to rock his body while that beautiful mouth assailed his pounding maleness like a mobile cunt. His blood pounded fiercely in his temples as, contracting her sweet lips on the stalk just behind the glans, she tugged. And her tongue writhed lewdly, a titillant serpent over the sensitive corona of his tool.

Heedless of the twinges of pain in his side, he began moving, tightening first one buttock under him and then the other, rocking his hips and fucking her face. His great source of strain, now, was in holding back as a knot seemed to build in his stomach and extend down into his balls, a knot that could never be untied, but must be broken violently.

She slurped now with obscene carnality, realizing his almost painful urgency and coating his long hard shaft with her abundant saliva. Her fingers kneaded and pressed the sperm-laden rounds of his balls, stroking, rolling, milking them.

With a loud groan, he quivered, stiffened—and began flooding into her mouth.

"Oh—Blanche—ahhh!"

She began gasping and swallowing as he pumped semen into her face, coating her mouth with the thick life-carrying syrup. It splashed off the back of her throat, whirled down and down to warm her belly, filled her tongue with its taste, near to that of thick salt-water.

When she was sure that she had it all and he was sinking weakly in the bed, she licked and licked, and then moved up beside him into the circle of his arm.

"Ummmm," she hummed into his ear, and licked her lips. "That was so delicious, my love!"

He trembled; his hand crossed his bandaged lower body to begin gentle attentions to the softly firm flesh of her mount of love. Shivers ran through her as he held her against him with one hand and with the other traced his fingers up and down the moist warm rift of her vulva. The pulpy lobes relaxed and parted to sag wetly aside in a mute invitation to invasion.

When the fingertips slid within, she hunched, moaning, beginning the slow movements of gentle fuckery on his thick finger.

Soon she was sighing and groaning, gasping and hunching, for The Crusader, more a man than most men, more noble than those counted as nobler than he, used his hand in giving her the liquid quenching of lustful flames that she had given him.

She spent in short seconds, convulsing in the paroxysms of her powerful crescendo, and then lay sighing and moaning, pressing herself close to him. . . .

And a week later he was practicing those arts he and

she had talked of, riding her exhausted, supine body with his own mending one, deliberately prolonging this first honest tupping in over two weeks by letting his mind wander: What, The Crusader wondered, might his next adventure be, in this land of fierce men and fiercely loving women?

Selected Grove Press Paperbacks

E380	DURRENMATT, FRIEDRICH / The Physicists / $2.95
B342	FANON, FRANTZ / The Wretched of the Earth / $3.95
B389	GENET, JEAN / Our Lady of the Flowers / $2.45
E760	GERVASI, TOM / Arsenal of Democracy II / $10.95
E792	GETTLEMAN, MARVIN, et. al., eds. / El Salvador: Central America in the New Cold War / $7.95
E830	GIBBS, LOIS MARIE / Love Canal: My Story / $5.95
B437	GIRODIAS, MAURICE, ed. / The Olympia Reader / $3.95
E720	GOMBROWICZ, WITOLD / Three Novels: Ferdydurke, Pornografia and Cosmos / $9.95
B448	GOVER, ROBERT / One Hundred Dollar Misunderstanding / $2.95
B152	HARRIS, FRANK / My Life and Loves / $4.95
E769	HARWOOD, RONALD / The Dresser / $5.95
E446	HAVEL, VACLAV / The Memorandum / $5.95
B436	HODEIR, ANDRE / Jazz: Its Evolution and Essence / $3.95
B417	INGE, WILLIAM / Four Plays (Come Back, Little Sheba; Picnic; Bus Stop; The Dark at the Top of the Stairs) / $5.95
E259	IONESCO, EUGENE / Rhinoceros & Other Plays / $4.95
E552	KEROUAC, JACK / Mexico City Blues / $4.95
B394	KEROUAC, JACK / Dr. Sax / $3.95
B454	KEROUAC, JACK / The Subterraneans / $3.50
B479	LAWRENCE, D.H. / Lady Chattlerley's Lover / $3.50
B262	LESTER, JULIUS / Black Folktales / $3.95
B351	MALCOLM X (Breitman, ed.) / Malcolm X Speaks / $3.95
E697	MAMET, DAVID / American Buffalo / $3.95
E801	MARIANI, PAUL / Crossing Cocytus / $5.95
B325	MILLER, HENRY / Sexus / $4.95
B10	MILLER, HENRY / Tropic of Cancer / $3.95
B59	MILLER, HENRY / Tropic of Capricorn / $3.50
E789	MROZEK, SLAWOMIR / Striptease, Tango, Vatzlav: Three Plays / $12.50
E636	NERUDA, PABLO / Five Decades Poems 1925–1970. Bilingual ed. / $5.95
E364	NERUDA, PABLO / Selected Poems. Bilingual ed. / $6.95
B429	ODETS, CLIFFORD / Six Plays (Waiting for Lefty; Awake and Sing; Golden Boy; Rocket to the Moon; Till the Day I Die; Paradise Lost) / $7.95
E807	OE, KENZABURO / A Personal Matter / $6.95

GROVE PRESS, INC., 196 WEst Houston St., New York, N.Y. 10014

Also Published by Grove Press

☐ *The Amorous Memoirs of Capt. Charles De Vane* / B478 / $3.95
☐ *Beatrice* / B472 / $3.50
☐ *Birch in the Boudoir* / B483 / $3.95
☐ *The Boudoir: A Journal of Voluptuous Victorian Reading* / B445 / $3.50
☐ *Crimson Hairs* / B487 / $3.25
☐ *The Crusader: Books I and II* / B440 / $4.95
☐ *The Crusader: Books III and IV* / B441 / $4.95
☐ *Emmanuelle* / B439 / $3.50
☐ *Emmanuelle II* / B453 / $3.50
☐ *Eveline: The Amorous Adventures of a Victorian Lady* / B451 / $3.95
☐ *Eveline II: The Continuing Amorous Adventures of a Victorian Lady* / B473 / $3.95
☐ *"Frank" and I* / B444 / $3.50
☐ *Illustrated Emmanuelle* / E765 / $9.95
☐ *Love Victorian Style: Boxed Set (Romance of Lust, Suburban Souls, My Life and Loves, A Man with a Maid)* / B465 / $15.35
☐ *Love Victorian Style II: Boxed Set (The Boudoir, Eveline, A Man with a Maid: Book Two, My Secret Life)* / B480 / $15.00
☐ *A Man with a Maid* / B181 / $3.95
☐ *A Man with a Maid: Book Two* / B434 / $2.95
☐ *A Man with a Maid: Book Three* / B476 / $3.95
☐ *My Life and Loves* / B151 / $4.95
☐ *My Secret Life* / B334 / $4.95
☐ *Oh Wicked Country!* / B485 / $3.25
☐ *The Olympia Reader* / B437 / $3.50
☐ *Pleasure Bound: Three Erotic Novels* / B470 / $3.95
☐ *Romance of Lust* / B424 / $3.95
☐ *The Sign of the Scorpion* / B450 / $2.95
☐ *Story of O: Part II* / B438 / $2.25
☐ *Suburban Souls* / B435 / $4.95
☐ *Venus in the Country* / B477 / $3.95

At your bookstore, or order below.

Grove Press, Inc. 196 West Houston St., New York, N.Y. 10014.

Please mail me the books checked above. I am enclosing $_____
(No COD. Add $1.00 per book for postage and handling.)

Name _____

Address _____

City_____State_____Zip_____